A Sheaf of Bluebells

Baroness Emmuska Orczy

A Sheaf of Bluebells

The present edition is a reproduction of previous publication of this classic work. Minor typographical errors may have been corrected without note, however, for an authentic reading experience the spelling, punctuation, and capitalization have been retained from the original text.

ISBN: 978-1-64799-103-6

CONTENTS

CHAPTER I THE MASTERS OF FRANCE

I

Among the many petitions presented that year by émigrés desirous of returning to France under the conditional amnesty granted to them by the newly-crowned Emperor, was one signed by Mme. la Marquise de Mortain and by her son Laurent, then aged twenty-one years, and one signed by M. le Comte de Courson for himself and his daughter Fernande. Gaillard says in his memoirs of Fouché that the latter was greatly averse to the petition being granted; but that Napoleon, then on the point of starting for his campaign in Prussia, was inclined to leniency in this matter—leniency which roused the ire and contempt of the Minister of Police—the man who, of a truth, and above the Emperor himself, was virtual dictator of France these days.

"A brood of plotters and intriguers," he said scornfully. "I should have thought your Majesty had had enough of those soi-disant great ladies and gentlemen of Normandy and Brittany. I wouldn't have them inside these dominions if I had my way."

It seems that this phrase: "If I had my way," highly amused the Emperor. Was it not a well-known fact that in all matters pertaining to the internal organization of the new Empire of France, Fouché ruled far more absolutely than did Napoleon? He knew more. He suspected more. Minister of Police and Minister of the Interior at this time, Fouché had made himself feared even—so it was said—by his imperial and capricious master.

And so—the obscure secretary who was present at this interview tells us—the Emperor laughed, and for once Fouché did not have his way. On the eve of the campaign which was to culminate in the humiliation of Prussia and the Peace of Tilsit, the soldier-Emperor had a throe of compassion, of mercy, a shrugging of the shoulders which meant immunity from exile for hundreds of men and women—a home for countless wanderers in foreign lands.

Fouché argued. "The Fouvielles I don't mind, nor yet Joubert, nor those Fumels. They won't do much harm. We might allow the Liancourts to return, though their property has been sold by the State, which always leads to trouble. But the Mortains!!! and the Coursons!!... Why! I would as lief grant the shades of Fox and Pitt a free permit to wander through France at will."

But we may take it that for once his arguments were of no avail. Napoleon's clemency was extended to the Mortains, as it was to the Coursons—this we know, seeing that both the young Marquis and the Comte de Courson, his maternal uncle, figured so prominently in the events which this true chronicle sets forth to record. As to the cause of

1

this clemency, or, rather, as to the cause of Fouché not getting his way this once ... well, 'tis our turn to shrug our shoulders.

Had Fouché really desired to keep the Mortains and the Coursons out of France, Fouché would have had his way. Of this there can be no doubt, seeing that Napoleon left the country at the head of his army soon after the day when he had that interview with his Minister of Police, leaving the latter more absolutely master of France than he had ever been before; so why should Fouché not have had his way with the Mortains and with Baudouin de Courson and his daughter Fernande?

Have we not cause for shrugging our shoulders? and for giving credence to the rumours which were current throughout France at this time—namely, that the dreaded Minister of Police had at this time begun to coquet with the Royalist party, as well as with the Jacobins and the English agents, with Talleyrand and with the Comte d'Artois—with any and every party in fact, who plotted against the master whom in his heart he had already betrayed.

II

The aforesaid obscure secretary who hath so aptly described the interview between the Emperor and Fouché, tells us that the latter, after he had bowed himself out of the Presence, returned to his private chamber in the ministry, and promptly sent for M. Dubois—then Chief Préfet of Police.

"M. Dubois," he commanded, "I want the dossier of the Mortains and also of the de Coursons now at once. The Emperor is inclined to grant them leave to return ... but I don't know ... I must consider...."

"I can tell you all about the Mortains and the Coursons without referring to their dossier," retorted Dubois gruffly.

"Well?"

"The ci-devant Marquise de Mortain...."

"Not ci-devant any longer, M. Dubois," broke in Fouché with a suave smile. "The lady is Mme. la Marquise now ... you yourself are 'Monsieur,' are you not? We have left the 'citizen' and 'citizeness' of our revolutionary era well behind us, remember, since our illustrious Master placed the crown of Imperial France upon his own head. France is an Empire now, Monsieur Dubois. There are no ci-devants any more, and quite a number of aristocrats."

Dubois gave a growl of understanding. It was not easy for his rough, uncultured mind to grasp all the various subtleties of Fouché's irony. He hated Napoleon's all-powerful Minister, hated him all the more that Fouché's astute and tortuous mentality was beyond his

2

comprehension and that he never knew whether the great man was laughing at him or not.

"Well," he said finally, with a shrug of his wide shoulders, "Marquise or ci-devant I care not; but, anyhow, she is not a woman I would care to trust, and the Emperor is very ill-advised...."

"The Emperor, my dear M. Dubois," once more broke in the Minister urbanely, "takes advice from no one. He starts next week for Prussia at the head of his army; he will return anon, having won fresh laurels for France and further undying glory for himself ... to-day he is inclined to clemency. Mme. la Marquise de Mortain and her son will be allowed to return to France, so will M. le Comte de Courson and his daughter Fernande; they will be allowed to retake possession of their château and of such of their lands as have not been sold by the State...."

"The lands have all been sold," rejoined the préfet curtly, "to worthy farmers whom it were a scandal to dispossess...."

"Are we dispossessing any one, my dear M. Dubois?" queried Fouché, with an indulgent smile directed at the other's Republican ardour—"any one, I mean, who happens to have bought confiscated land?"

"Not yet," muttered the other under his breath; "but...."

"As you were saying, M. le Préfet?..." here interposed the Minister more haughtily, "Mme. la Marquise de Mortain is a widow, I think."

"Yes. For the second time."

"She was first the wife of Bertrand de Maurel...."

"Who would have been a good patriot had he lived."

"We must imagine so," said Fouché, with a smile.

"He died in '82—separated from his wife whom he hated."

"But there was a child of that marriage."

"Yes, Ronnay de Maurel, a loyal patriot ... a fine Republican...."

"Shall we say a fine Bonapartist, my good M. Dubois?" said the Minister of Police significantly. "I like and trust Ronnay de Maurel. I would not like to see him tarred with the worn-out brush of the past decade."

"Well ... Republican or Bonapartist—'tis all the same—what? I was one of those who voted for the proclamation and Ronnay de Maurel was another. First Consul for life, with all the splendours of past monarchies, or frankly Emperor of the French, there was not much to choose. You were an ardent Republican, too, at one time—eh, M. le Ministre?"

"Quite so—quite so. But we were not speaking of mine unworthy self, but of Mme. la Marquise de Mortain and of her son Ronnay de Maurel."

"Son, indeed!" retorted Dubois, with a gruff laugh. "M. de Maurel has been taught to execrate his mother. He was only four years old when his father died, but an uncle brought him up—old Gaston de

Maurel—a magnificent patriot if ever there was one. Nothing of the whilom aristo about him ... eats peas with his knife and wears sabots and a blouse ... he voted for the death of the King ... just as you did—eh, M. le Ministre?"

"Just as I did, my dear friend—and I am proud of it. Gaston de Maurel and I sat in the Assembly of the Convention as representatives of the people of France, and in the name of the people we decreed that the tyrant Louis Capet, known to the world as Louis XVI., King of France, should die upon the scaffold as a traitor to the nation which he had set out to govern. Gaston de Maurel may eat peas with a knife, but he rendered the Republic and the Directorate infinite services in quelling the so-called Royalist risings in his own province of Normandy."

"Now he is old. Some say that he has not many months to live. Ronnay de Maurel dwells with him in his Château de la Vieuville, near Villemor. They both live like peasants in a couple of rooms in the sumptuous château. The old man is a miser: he has accumulated immense wealth in these past twenty years. Ronnay de Maurel, on the other hand, owns the sumptuous demesnes of La Frontenay, which he inherited from his father, together with the foundries, where he employs five thousand men and manufactures war material for the Grand Army. He is already one of the richest men in France—and he is his uncle's sole heir; when old Gaston dies the de Maurel riches will be uncountable...."

"And he, too, eats peas with his knife," concluded Fouché, with a sardonic smile.

"And hardly knows how to read and write," assented the préfet of police. "A succession of tutors at La Vieuville testify to the rough temper and the obstinate savagery of this descendant of aristos."

"Yes, so I have been told," mused Fouché. "I understand that a de Maurel fought in the First Crusade, that another was Captain of Musketeers under Louis XIII.; but the present holder of the historic name is an ardent Bonapartist, as you say. He fought like a lion against the Royalists in Vendée; he crossed the Alps with Napoleon, and was wounded at Marengo and at Ḥohenlinden. At Austerlitz, where he accomplished prodigies of valour, an Austrian bullet lamed him for life. He is a Grand Eagle of the Legion of Honour. His religion is Bonaparte ... he knows no science save that of arms—reads no books and does not know the Carmagnole from the Marseillaise—he is illiterate, uncultured, almost a savage.... These are all facts, are they not, M. Dubois?"

"Aye! Ronnay de Maurel is all that and more. He lives at La Vieuville, not ten kilomètres from Courson, where Mme. la Marquise, his mother, will now be taking up her abode. Oh!" added the préfet of police with a malevolent grin, "how those two will execrate one another!"

"And watch over one another," commented Fouché with his enigmatic smile. "Ronnay de Maurel will act as a check on the intrigues which might be hatching presently in Mme. de Mortain's fertile brain."

"Nothing—and no one can act as a check on that woman's love of intrigue," growled Dubois surlily. "She and her son Laurent will give us all plenty to do until...."

He made a significant gesture with his hand against his neck. Fouché smiled. "We can always give them plenty of rope," he said. "How old is Laurent de Mortain?"

"Twenty-one or two ... but he has fought against his own country since he was sixteen. Mme. de Mortain favours a marriage for him with Fernande de Courson, his cousin."

"The daughter of Baudouin de Courson?"

"Yes. His only daughter. He is Mme. de Mortain's only brother. Their properties adjoin."

"I know. He, too, has been granted leave by the Emperor to return to France."

"A whole pack of those confounded émigrés," once more growled the préfet of police—this time with a savage oath, "settled down in the most disaffected province of France. Joseph de Puisaye still at large ... the department seething with discontent ... everything ready for rebellion ... the Emperor away.... Ah! we shall have a fine time down there, I reckon."

"Bah!" quoth Fouché lightly, "they are not very dangerous now. For one thing, the Mortains, the Coursons and the whole pack of them are as poor as church mice. Their lands and farms have all been sold; the Mortains have not even a château in which to live."

"The Château of Courson stands."

"A dilapidated barrack."

"Quite so—but large enough to harbour every rebel who chooses to hatch a plot against the safety of the Empire. The Mortains and Coursons will herd together there: Joseph de Puisaye, François Prigent and D'Aché will use it as their headquarters. From there their bands of brigands will be let loose upon both departments—highway robbery, intimidation, pillage and arson—those Chouans stick at nothing nowadays. England no longer supplies them with money for their so-called Royalist cause, and they must get money somehow. You remember their criminal outrage upon old M. de Ris, and their theft in his château of money, valuables and jewellery. You remember the murder of Andrein, the Constitutional Bishop of Quimper, and the abduction of the Bishop of Vannes—all for purposes of robbery.... Well, in my opinion, those exploits will sink into insignificance beside the ones which will be invented and organized in Courson under the presidency of Mme. la Marquise and her precious son and brother."

M. Dubois, préfet of police, had, while he spoke, worked himself up into a passion of fury. He gesticulated wildly with both arms, shrugged his wide shoulders, and banged his fist from time to time upon the desk in front of him, so that the inkstand and the papers rattled unceasingly and M. le Ministre's nerves were irritated beyond endurance. Now M. Dubois had perforce to pause for want of breath. He drew his large coloured handkerchief from his pocket and mopped his forehead, which was streaming.

"You exaggerate, my good M. Dubois," said Fouché soothingly. "You have an excellent colleague at Caen in the person of M. Vincent...."

"Bah!" ejaculated Dubois contemptuously. "He is hand in glove with the Royalists."

"And there's M. Caffarello, the préfet...."

Again an expressive shrug of the shoulders from M. Dubois, who apparently had not much faith in the capabilities of his subordinates.

"And in Ronnay de Maurel you will have a valuable adjunct," added the Minister, "unless...."

He paused, then continued with seeming irrelevance:

"Is Fernande de Courson pretty?"

"She has a reputation for beauty," replied Dubois. "Why do you ask?"

"Nothing ... nothing ... a passing thought ... a dart shot at random.... You will have to keep your eyes very wide open, my good M. Dubois."

"You may trust me to do that, M. le Ministre," rejoined Dubois, with a leer of comprehension; there was no subtlety about the suggestion, and he had understood it well enough this time.

"There's not much of the lady-killer about Ronnay de Maurel," he added, laughing.

"Perhaps not," rejoined Fouché dryly.

"And he may rejoin the army, after all."

"No. He cannot do that. The Emperor won't let him. He is far too useful in Normandy just now to be mere food for Prussian cannon."

There was a pause. The préfet of police was tacitly dismissed. M. le Ministre drew some papers close to him, and his delicate, blue-veined hand toyed with the pen.

"You don't want me any more?" queried Dubois abruptly. He was always thankful to shake the dust of the ministerial chamber from his feet.

"Well ... unless you have anything else to report, my good M. Dubois," rejoined Fouché pleasantly, "or any further information to impart to me about those Mortains—or the Coursons."

"There's nothing else. But I wish to God that the Emperor would reconsider his decision."

"The Emperor seldom reconsiders any decision, my dear Dubois

... once it is a decision. The Mortains and the Coursons have probably landed in France by now."

"May they break their necks on the gangway," growled Dubois.

"Amen to that," quoth Fouché lightly. "In the meanwhile, will you see M. de Réal on that subject and send special recommendations to the préfet and the commissary of police at Caen?..."

"And to Ronnay de Maurel, I should say."

"No," interposed the Minister peremptorily, "leave de Maurel alone. I will write to him myself."

Such in substance was the interview between the Minister of Police and the chief préfet. The secretary, among whose papers was found the above account, goes on to say that M. Dubois, having taken his leave, the great man was busy for the next half-hour writing a letter with his own hand. With his own hand also he folded it, sealed it and addressed it. Then he handed it to his secretary with the express order that it should be sent to its destination by the next ministerial courier.

The letter was addressed to M. le Comte Ronnay de Maurel, at his Château de la Vieuville, near Villemor, Département de l'Orne.

CHAPTER II THE RETURN OF THE NATIVES

I

"What devastation! What wanton devastation! Oh, those fiends! those cruel, callous fiends!"

Mme. la Marquise de Mortain, for once in her life, was thoroughly unnerved. She was ready to cry ... but tears had not come to her eyes for the past twenty years; their well-spring had run dry under the influence of an unconquerable energy and of a glowing enthusiasm for a cause which, at any rate, for the moment was doomed. Mme. la Marquise did not shed tears when she first arrived on a cold, showery night early in May to what had been the luxurious home of her childhood. She did not cry when she wandered half aimlessly through the salons and apartments of the Château de Courson—all that was left to her brother of his once splendid patrimony—a mere barrack now where most windows were cracked, where the paper hung in strips from the walls and the ceilings painted by Boucher were stained with smoke and damp.

7

It was just fourteen years now that the château had been standing empty and desolate—fourteen years during which snow, rain and tempest had worked their cruel way with shutters and window frames, with stucco, plaster and roofs. It was only the fabric itself—the fine solid stone walls of sixteenth century architecture which had remained intact—the monumental staircase, with its marble balustrade, the terraces and façades. True, the stone was stained by damp and mildew, and the ivy, which fourteen years ago had been a pretty and romantic feature of the copings, was now a danger to them through the vigour and rankness of its growth; but these were matters which could easily be remedied, and which in themselves enhanced rather than detracted from the picturesqueness of the stately pile.

It was the aspect of the interior of the château which had wrung from Mme. la Marquise de Mortain that cry of bitter sorrow. Fourteen years!!! She herself had been staying at Courson when her brother was at last compelled to dismiss all his servants, and to flee from the country, as many an aristocrat had done already in order to save not so much himself as his family—his young children—from the terrible doom which daily appeared more inevitable. Baudouin de Courson was then a widower, his daughter Fernande was a mere baby. He himself intended and did join the army of the Princes at Coblentz, together with Arnould de Mortain, his brother-in-law; Mme. la Marquise, with her son Laurent and with little Fernande de Courson, found refuge and hospitality in England, as many fugitive Royalists had already done; and the Château de Courson remained for a while under the care of old Matthieu Renard and of his wife Annette—faithful servants of the family.

M. de Courson had left some money with them to cover the strictly necessary expenses of upkeep, and he promised to send them more from time to time. He was so sure that this abominable Revolution would not last. God and the Allied Powers would soon avenge the murder of King Louis, and sweep the country clean from all these assassins and cut-throats. He would restore the Dauphin to the throne of his fathers and the loyal adherents of their King to their lands!

Fourteen years had gone by since then. Military autocracy had succeeded the excesses of tyrannical democracy; the Directorate had supplanted the Republic; the Consulate had followed, and now Napoleon Bonaparte, the son of an obscure Corsican citizen, was Emperor of the French—conqueror of half Europe, master of the world—and the cause of the Bourbons appeared more hopeless than it had ever been before. Even the truculent Vendeans—the Royalists of Brittany and Normandy—had been pacified. It was no use fighting any longer. Cadoudal, the invincible champion of a lost cause, had perished on the scaffold, and his scattered followers were having recourse to robbery, arson and pillage, in order to collect funds for their needs, since England had ceased to pour money and treasure into their bottomless coffers.

Matthieu Renard and Annette, his wife, had long since been forced to abandon the château. No money was forthcoming from Coblentz or from England. Food was dear and Matthieu still vigorous. He took up work with the farmers and cultivators who had supplanted his aristocratic masters on the domain of Courson. The decree of the National Convention of the 1st of February, '92, had finally dispossessed of their lands those émigrés who did not choose to return to France; the land and farms were sold for the benefit of the State. Worthy bourgeois and peasants settled down on them and planted their cabbages in the former well-preserved enclosures of M. le Comte's pleasure grounds. Alone, the vast château, with its reception-rooms in enfilade, its numerous state-bedrooms, elaborate servants' quarters, stablings and coach-houses, proved unsaleable. It remained the property of the nation until the day when the soldier-Emperor with a stroke of his pen restored it to its original owners.

It was little more now than an empty husk—swept clean by ruthless, thieving hands of every relic from the past—stripped of every object of value. When M. le Comte arrived, the tricolour flag was still waving on its staff up aloft, and across the stone façade was writ in large letters the great Republican device: "Liberté, Egalité, Fraternité!"

Mme. la Marquise de Mortain, who accompanied her brother on his return to his home, as she had done in exile, had the flag torn down and the device erased; but it would take months of labour and a mint of money to restore the château to its former splendour; and labour was scarce these days when the Grand Army, fighting half Europe risen in coalition against the Corsican usurper, was taking heavy toll of the manhood of the country and winning undying laurels at Marengo and Austerlitz, in Italy and in Prussia. And even labour was less scarce than money.

Mme. la Marquise, wandering through the dismantled salons and through the dank apartments eaten into by rust and damp, did not cry, nor did she wring her hands, but the hatred which had burned in her heart for fourteen years against the persecutors of her caste and the murderers of her King stirred within her with renewed violence, and she registered an oath that all the energy, the strength and the cunning which she possessed would more than ever be devoted to the undoing of the usurper and the triumph of the cause of her King.

"And for this," she said to M. le Comte de Courson, who had viewed his devastated patrimony in moodiness and silence, "for this the château is admirably situated. The country round seems more lonely than it ever was before, the woods are more dense, the moors more inaccessible. The spies of that infamous Bonaparte can never penetrate to our villages. We are within easy reach of Brest and of the English agents, and the whole country is seething with revolt against the tyranny of militarism, the dearness of food, the excessive taxation. We have not come here, Baudouin," she continued vehemently, "in order to lament and to sit still under crying injustice and the rule of a base-born usurper. We have come in order to do and to fight. It is going to be war to the knife in Normandy once again, and let the Corsican and his crowd look to themselves. Cadoudal's bomb failed—daggers, poisons have failed.... Bonaparte is surrounded and guarded by the most astute and the most unscrupulous police the world has ever known. Well, we'll bribe his guard and outwit his police. Never for one single hour of the day or night shall the usurper feel that his life is safe from lurking executioners! Daggers? poisons? We'll try them all again in turn. He has stuck at nothing—we'll stick at nothing; an eye for an eye and a tooth for a tooth; we'll meet murder with murder and pillage with pillage. And, in the meanwhile, we'll fight—fight to the last man—fight with every resource at our command. Money we must have ... we'll loot and we'll rob and we'll burn.... They are all bandits, those revolutionary cut-throats; well, we'll be bandits, too, and cut-throats and assassins if need be, and we'll not cry 'peace' or 'halt' until Louis XVIII., by the grace of God, has come into his own again."

Later in the day, fired by her own enthusiasm, lashed into fury by the sight of her ruined childhood's home, Mme. la Marquise was still making wild plans for the coming guerrilla campaign against the Corsican and his army. M. de Courson tried to pacify her with a few counsels of prudence.

"At any rate, for the moment, my dear Denise," he said, "we must not brusque matters. We must let Joseph de Puisaye and Prigent make their plans quietly. Enough that for the moment they know that this house is at their disposal...."

"Enough?" retorted Madame vehemently. "Nothing will be enough, save the death of that abominable Bonaparte. Oh!" she added, with a sigh of desperate impatience as she stretched out her arms in longing, "how I long to be even with that usurper and his crowd of vulgar sycophants! How I long to see him fawn for mercy and cringe at Versailles at the foot of King Louis' throne, whilst...."

"We are not there yet, my dear Denise," quoth the Comte gently, "and you must remember that our party has become very scattered and very weak. Bonaparte has an enormous following at this moment. His victories have caused this blind and stupid nation to deify him. Indeed, the people of France look on him as nothing less than a god. His popularity is immense, his power unlimited. The loyal adherents of our rightful King are a mere handful now—a few of us of the old régime have remained true—a few unruly peasants have rallied to the fleur-de-lys. What can a few hundred of our men do against some thousands of Bonaparte's trained troops? And he has threatened to send a hundred thousand against our Chouans, if they should ever rise in a mass again."

"Bah!" exclaimed Madame exultantly. "We'll oppose him with ten thousand whose ardour will outweigh his numbers."

"He has threatened to burn down our cities."

"We'll take refuge in our villages."

"He'll burn our villages."

"We'll seek shelter in the woods. Nay, my good Baudouin," added Mme. la Marquise firmly, "counsels of prudence come ill from you. You and Laurent will lead our brave peasants to victory—of this I am as convinced as that I am alive. And if we cannot fight in the open we'll fight in the dark; we'll oppose force with ruse and power with cunning. The brutal Corsican may, in the meanwhile, destroy the homes of peaceable citizens, or ruin the properties of worthy bourgeois who have nothing to do with this war; but as for us, he shall only find us when our brave little army is ready for him—and not before; and then we'll destroy him and his battalions one by one."

It was impossible to resist for long the power and influence of Madame's wonderful enthusiasm. For her there was no lost cause—no hopelessness. Louis, the eighteenth of his name, was effectively King of France in her sight, whether the Corsican usurper chose to place an imperial crown on his own head or not; and God was bound by the decrees of His own laws to see that King Louis—King by divine right— did eventually sit upon the throne of his forbears after this unexplainable period of exile and of stress.

II

In the evening when, in the small boudoir which had been made habitable, the lamps were lit and a fire burned in the tall hearth, when the shutters were closed and chairs drawn nearer to one another, the place looked a trifle less desolate. Matthieu Renard and his wife Annette had thrown up their work under the farmers and cultivators whom they despised, and returned to serve the masters, whom even in their poverty they recognized as alone worthy of their services. Annette had cooked a good dinner, Matthieu had unearthed a bottle of wine from a disused cellar, which had almost miraculously escaped perquisition. The world did not appear so callous or so inimical as it had done earlier in the day.

"What about Ronnay?" M. de Courson had asked as soon as Matthieu and Annette had gone and the doors were closed on the intimate family circle.

"What about him?" retorted Mme. la Marquise. The sound of her eldest son's name grated unpleasantly on her ear.

"Does he know you have arrived?"

"Yes. I have written to him."

11

"So soon?"

"There was no object in wasting time. He and I will have to meet within the next few days. I want to get that first meeting over."

"You have asked him to come here?"

"Of course."

"Do you think that he will come?"

"He cannot refuse to pay his respects to his mother."

M. de Courson shrugged his shoulders and stared moodily into the fire.

"Have you heard anything fresh about Ronnay de Maurel, Baudouin?" queried Mme. la Marquise sharply. "Anything that I ought to know?"

"Only what is common talk round the neighbourhood, my dear," he replied.

"And that is?..."

"That Gaston de Maurel has brought up his nephew—your son, my dear Denise—as little better than the workmen in his factories. Ronnay, it seems, is quite illiterate, and his manners are those of a peasant. The most violent democratic principles have been inculcated into him from childhood...."

"Ever since the law freed me from his father's brutalities ..." broke in Madame coldly.

"Exactly," assented M. de Courson, in an obviously conciliatory spirit, "when your husband died, my dear, his brother Gaston took up his work with the boy. You know the type of man Gaston de Maurel always was—the Revolution suited his temperament exactly. Cruel, vindictive, jealous, violent, he voted for the September massacres and for the execution of the King. Had Ronnay been old enough he, too, would have been a regicide."

Mme. la Marquise shuddered.

"And even you, Baudouin," she said, "have oft rebuked me for my hatred to the boy."

"Your son, Denise, your own flesh and blood. Aye!" he added more emphatically, "so much your own flesh and blood; that he has your character in a great measure—your energy, your enthusiasm.... Unfortunately he misapplies both...."

"To crime and disloyalty."

"Yes; there is the pity of it. He is a dangerous man, Denise," continued M. de Courson earnestly. "It were best to keep him at arm's-length."

"At arm's length," retorted Madame hotly. "My dear Baudouin, are you serious?"

"I have never been so serious in my life. I think that it is a boundless pity that you have already made overtures in the direction of the de Maurels. I would have left the whole pack of those revolutionary brigands severely alone."

12

He spoke with unwonted energy, for in all matters of argument M. de Courson invariably gave in to his more energetic sister. But he felt strongly on the subject, and looked as if he were determined to assert his will this time, at any rate. But Mme. la Marquise was not prepared to give in, and she broke in once more, in her authoritative way:

"I shall not leave the revolutionary brigands alone, my good Baudouin," she said. "I mean to try and win my son Ronnay over to our cause...."

"You are mad, Denise!" exclaimed M. le Comte.

"Will you deny that he would be invaluable to us if he were on our side?" she argued.

Then as M. le Comte remained silent, with frowning eyes fixed in deep puzzlement before him, she added with ever-growing energy:

"Remember that Ronnay is passing rich, and that old Gaston cannot last long, so they say. I hear that he is dying. When he dies all his accumulated wealth, which is immense, will also go to Ronnay, who will certainly then be one of the richest men in France. Moreover, he already disposes of five thousand skilled men, and of the means of making engines and munitions of war. The men, so I am told, are devoted to him—except for a few malcontents. They look upon him as one of themselves; they would as soon follow him on our side as on that of Bonaparte. Think what that means, my dear Baudouin! Men and money to our cause! and we need both sadly. It means conciliating an ogre who no doubt is too stupid, too illiterate to have any rooted convictions of his own. Tell me!" she concluded, with a note of triumph at her own unanswerable argument, "were it not passing wise to make friends with such a man?"

"Ah! if you could do that, Denise...!" quoth M. de Courson, with an impatient sigh and a dubious shrug of the shoulders. "But if your son Ronnay hath aught of the de Maurels in him, you will fail. Bertrand de Maurel was not amenable, remember, and you tried hard in those days to win him over to our side."

Mme. la Marquise was silent for a moment or two. It was her turn now to stare moodily into the fire. Memory had carried her back to those early years of her marriage, when Bertrand de Maurel's dictatorial ways and crude love-making had caused her ever-rebellious spirit to chafe under his tyranny. Brought up under the strict régime of the time which made of the jeune fille little more than a puppet to dance to the piping of her parents, Denise de Courson had hoped to find emancipation in marriage. Bertrand de Maurel, however, soon taught her that a husband's yoke can be more irksome than a father's. Where Denise hoped to find independence of thought and of action she found a tyrant whose democratic ideals amounted to bigotry; where she hoped to lead a free and intellectual life of her own, she found herself a slave to a system of philanthropy which was repugnant alike to her

13

aristocratic sense and to her love of her own comforts. Bertrand de Maurel had mapped out for his young wife a life of usefulness and of sound influence among his dependents, and Denise loathed the very propinquity of those whom she was wont to call "the great unwashed." Bertrand had schemes for improving the conditions of labour, the housing of his peasantry, the production of the land. They were crude, embryotic ideas, perhaps, but they sprang from a mind attuned to the growing discontent of one class against the glaring injustice imposed upon it by the other; they sprang from a heart that was warm and sympathetic, if not always logical. He was at first only feeling his way toward a better understanding with his dependents, scenting the approaching danger of those horrible reprisals which were destined to remain a perpetual stain upon the history of the nation, and which a little conciliation, a little goodwill, a few more men like Bertrand and Gaston de Maurel might perhaps have averted.

But with none of her husband's aims or his ideals had Denise the slightest sympathy. It was a case of hopeless incompatibility of tempers, further aggravated by irascible and imperious characters on both sides. Bertrand de Maurel had no more understanding of his wife's nature than she had of his; no more sympathy with her ideals and her train of thought. Perpetual bickering led to outbursts of passionate recrimination; an impassable abyss of divergent political views did the rest. Revolutionary and democratic ideals had already eaten into the soul of Bertrand de Maurel and of his brother Gaston; and with Denise, belief in the divine right of kings was an integral part of her religion. After five years of miserable and acrimonious conflicts separation appeared the only solution of an impossible situation. Denise shook the dust of La Frontenay from her aristocratic feet, leaving all her illusions behind her, together with the child born of this unfortunate marriage—a boy not yet three years old, whom she had already learned to hate.

Ronnay had never been her child. As a tiny baby he was already the image of his father—with the same wilful and tyrannical temper, the same outbursts of passionate wrath, the same characteristic toss of the head that shook recalcitrant curls from the low, square forehead. Ronnay had his father's auburn hair, his father's deep-set eyes, which at times were almost black, at others of a deep violet-blue; he had his father's massive limbs and square-set jaw. Oh, yes! Ronnay was a true de Maurel. Not all the upbringing in the world, not all a mother's influence, would have trained the lad to walk in the footsteps of his aristocratic forbears. The word "democrat" was already writ plainly upon the sturdy form of the tiny child, as he toddled, unaided, through the sheds of his father's foundries, scorning the delicate feminine hands of nurse or governess, who would have guided his footsteps, clinging to the overseers and the roughly-clad workmen, who placed their tools in his little hands and showed him the way to use them. The spirit of democracy shone out of the lad's blue eyes when, standing between his Uncle Gaston's knees, he listened spellbound to marvellous tales of the tyranny of kings and of the heroic stand which was even then being made in the New World over the ocean far away by a nation which was resolved to be free.

Yes, Ronnay de Maurel was, indeed, a true son of his father—a worthy nephew of Gaston de Maurel and the godson of La Fayette; he had nothing of the de Coursons in him. And in the years that ensued, when Gaston had voted for the death of his King and Ronnay had won his first laurels under the base-born Corsican adventurer fighting against his own kith and kin and against the King's most holy Majesty, Denise de Mortain—as she now was—often wished that some beneficent Fate had smothered her first-born at birth.

III

Mme. la Marquise roused herself from her meditations. There had been silence between her and her brother for some time, while her mind took this sudden incursion into the past; but at the further end of the room Fernande de Courson and Laurent de Mortain were whispering and laughing together. Madame turned and looked over her shoulder at the two young people; then she said abruptly and with seeming irrelevance to her brother:

"Fernande is getting too old for all that childishness."

"Childishness, my dear," said the Comte, somewhat bewildered at this sudden change in his sister's train of thought. "I don't understand...."

"You can't wish her to become the butt of all the gossips in the village ... which she will do if you allow this childish philandering to go on."

"You mean Laurent?" he queried blankly.

"Why—of course. Fernande is seventeen—Laurent has not a sou to bless himself with...."

"For the moment," interposed the Comte. "When King Louis comes into his own again, Laurent will retake possession of his heritage...."

Madame la Marquise shook her head impatiently.

"Confiscated lands will never be restored," she said firmly, "not even by King Louis. The process would be too dangerous; it would kindle a fresh revolution. Those of us whose lands have been sold by that execrable Revolutionary government will remain poor and dispossessed to the end of our days."

15

Baudouin de Courson looked keenly at his sister, still not understanding her sudden new mood.

"Does that mean," he asked, "does that mean that the project of marriage between our children is not to come to pass?"

"No, no," Madame broke in hurriedly; "I did not mean that, of course. You know, dear, that I could not have meant that.... You misunderstood me ... or I, mayhap, expressed myself clumsily. Pessimism led me too far ... no wonder—eh, my dear Baudouin? The spectacle of our ruined home has grated harshly on my nerves. No, no! I did not mean that. King Louis,—may God guard him!—will richly reward those of us who have given up everything for his sake. There will be money compensation for you and money compensation for Laurent ... and, please God, the past splendours of Mortain will one day be revived ... but it will all take time ... years perhaps ... and, in the meanwhile, I think you should talk seriously to Fernande. She ought to be a little more circumspect, and not proclaim her affection for Laurent quite so openly as she has done hitherto."

"Would it not be best, in that case," rejoined M. de Courson coldly, "if Fernande and I took up our abode elsewhere and left you in possession of Courson? We might go to Caen, perhaps, or to Brest.... We should still be in touch with you...."

"Impossible, my good Baudouin," interposed Madame decisively. "You must remain here while our army is being organized; this place is most central—it shall be our headquarters. Already we have arranged that it shall be the meeting-place whenever any of our leaders wish to communicate with us. No, no, there can be no question of your going! Moreover...."

"Yes?" he queried, seeing that she had paused, obviously hesitating whether to go on or not.

"I don't see why I should not tell you of my project, my dear Baudouin," she said quietly. "I propose to take up my abode at La Frontenay."

"La Frontenay? I don't understand...."

"There is no doubt that old Gaston de Maurel is dying. Ronnay is his heir. La Vieuville will then become his home.... Why should not La Frontenay become mine? It was my husband's."

"But ..." stammered the Comte, reluctant to put into words the thought that was uppermost in his mind.

"You mean," broke in the Marquise coldly, "you mean that Ronnay de Maurel has been taught to hate me as bitterly as did his father to the day of his death, as bitterly as does old Gaston de Maurel to this day. I know that; but, remember, my dear Baudouin, that there is nothing in the world which I would not do for the sake of our cause, and that, as I told you just now, it would be of immense help to us if Ronnay and I became good friends and I could take up my abode at La Frontenay. I should get the control of his house ... of his money, too, to

16

a great extent. The château is vast ... three times the size of Courson; it has extensive cellars, which would be immeasurably useful for the storing of arms. Even if Ronnay desired to live there after Gaston's death rather than at La Vieuville, he still would probably be absent from time to time, and then the château would be entirely at our disposal.... Oh!" she added more warmly, "the advantages of my residing at La Frontenay are too numerous to name."

"I don't deny it, but I fear me that you will find it difficult to get over your son's dislike ... and over his mistrust."

"Difficult, I know. But not impossible. I must play my cards well ... that is all."

"You must also remember, my dear Denise, that—even if you succeed in your designs, which I take leave to doubt—you will, first of all, have to make sure that Ronnay de Maurel has no thought of marriage. If you take up your residence at La Frontenay—if we are to make use of the château for our campaign—we ought to be certain that a young bride won't turn us out within the first few months if she found La Vieuville not sufficiently to her liking."

Madame mused for a second or two in silence, then she said quietly:

"I had thought of marriage in connection with Ronnay.... I must confess, in fact, that such an eventuality has very much entered into my calculations, but...."

"But what?"

"I'll tell you my project later on, my good Baudouin—not just now. But be assured that if my son Ronnay marries, it will be a wife of my choice. For the moment there is no danger of his turning his thoughts to courtship. If rumour has spoken correctly, he is little better than a savage, and if he has turned his sentimental thoughts to some village wench—as illiterate and rough-mannered as himself—why, she must be got out of the way, that is all."

Baudouin de Courson said nothing more. He stared back into the fire, and to his mind also there came back some memories of the past. While his sister spoke with that air of authority which became her proud beauty and majestic figure so well, his thoughts had flown back to the dead husband—to Bertrand de Maurel, dictatorial and authoritative, too, the martinet who tried to drill this imperious woman into submission. No wonder that husband and wife had quarrelled! No wonder that the passion of a brief and romantic courtship had so soon changed to invincible hate!

M. de Courson sighed. He loved and admired his sister, whose aims and ideals were akin to his own, whose stern virtues guided her every action; but all that he had heard about Ronnay de Maurel did not lead him to think for a moment that he would be amenable to his mother's tyranny. Rumour had described him as rude of manner, abrupt of speech and turbulent in his ways; nor had this description of his nephew altogether displeased M. de Courson. A wild creature is more easily tamed than one which is crafty and subtle, and where passions are most tumultuous there gentleness and love have easier access. But gentleness and love only—not tyranny. Ronnay de Maurel as an enemy might prove as dangerous as he was undoubtedly powerful. His active sympathy or even passive indifference would be of inestimable value to the Royalist cause; this M. de Courson was bound to admit. But he was equally convinced that it would require all a woman's tenderness and tact to win Ronnay over, and, even so, success was more than doubtful and the task a risky one at best. A spark of motherly love, a touch of womanly sympathy might succeed; peremptory ways, a harsh, authoritative manner was inevitably doomed to failure.

What his sister's plans were with regard to this delicate matter Baudouin de Courson did not attempt to guess. Like all men of action, he was wholly unversed in that subtle knowledge of the feminine heart which no man has ever completely fathomed. Perhaps if at this moment he could have read what was going on in Denise's fertile brain, he might have been spared all the heartburnings which lay in wait for him in the near future; he and those he cared for might have been spared the coming bitter conflict 'twixt warring ideals; they might have been spared more than one abiding sorrow.

But Mme. la Marquise did not choose to take her brother into her confidence then, and he did not try to penetrate her secrets. And thus were the Fates left to weave unmolested the threads of five people's destinies.

CHAPTER III THE HERMITS OF LA VIEUVILLE

I

At the self-same hour, whilst Denise de Mortain and her brother, the Comte de Courson, were discussing their future plans for rousing the country-side once more into open revolt, Gaston de Maurel and his nephew Ronnay were poring over a letter which was written in a bold and firm hand, and which a village courier had brought over from Courson an hour ago.

The letter by now was little more than a rag, stained with finger marks, with corners torn off and contents blurred by constant crushing of the paper in hot, impatient hands.

Gaston de Maurel sat in a huge arm-chair, his head leaning against a number of pillows which had been piled up behind his back; his eyes—the deep-set eyes of the Maurels—were fixed inquiringly, almost appealingly, upon the bowed head of his nephew, who, with elbows resting upon the table, was effectually shielding his face from the searching gaze of the invalid.

The room in which the two men sat was one of the kitchens of the small old-fashioned Château of La Vieuville—the appanage of the younger sons of the house—granted to them in perpetual fief by the head of the family in the days when the de Maurels were Dukes of Montauban and held their lands direct from the King. Bertrand de Maurel, the last holder of the title, fired by democratic ideals, had cast aside what he termed an empty bauble, long before the wave of social equality had swept over the land. His younger brother Gaston had followed in his footsteps. A passionate and uncompromising Republican, he had voted for the death of the King—dispassionately and from a firm conviction that such a course was vital for the welfare of the nation; and thenceforward he divested himself voluntarily of every appurtenance and privilege of rank. He lived up to his convictions from the first day that he gave expression to them in the National Assembly; and from that time forth not one single contradiction, not one single concession to past traditions or past love of ease and luxury, marred the Spartan-like purity of his life. He mixed with the proletariat, lived with the proletariat; and the boy Ronnay, whom his dead brother Bertrand had committed to his care and wholly to his discretion, he brought up in the same thoughts, the same feelings, the same ideals as his own.

Bertrand de Maurel had left his boy an immense fortune; Gaston administered it by turning the celebrated iron foundries of La Frontenay into a gigantic factory for the manufacture of munitions of war. That was the time when the people of France were called to arms by the Revolutionary Government against the whole of Europe. France demanded of all her children that they should give the best of what they had in order to help her to fight all the foreign nations who had banded themselves in coalition against her. Gaston de Maurel was in the forefront of those who gave their all. An incurable affection of the heart prevented his taking up arms for the Republic which he had helped to create; but he had talent, brains, money, influence, a genius for organizing and an inexhaustible fund of patriotism and self-sacrifice. At once he marshalled up for the benefit of the State all the vast industrial forces over which his brother's will had given him absolute control, until the day when Ronnay chose to take up the reins of government himself.

He toiled side by side with the workmen in the factory. To each

19

man he assigned his part, so that each man was able to do his best. He sorted, sifted, arrayed the manpower at his disposal, so that every individual in his turn was able to give of his best. And his own eye was everywhere. He methodized everything; he supervised everything.

And—almost despite himself—he accumulated immense wealth, not only for his nephew, but also for himself. He, too, had inherited quite a substantial fortune from his mother, who was the sister and co-heiress of the Marquis de Rouverdain. His capital he lent to the State at interest, and he kept up the fabric of his Château of La Vieuville; but beyond that he spent nothing on himself. He only looked upon himself as the administrator of his nephew's patrimony—as the chief overseer of the Maurel foundries. People called him a miser, and he was that in a sense, for money in his hands perpetually begat money.

The gossip of the village had it that Ronnay de Maurel hardly knew how to read and write. That, of course, was mischievous. The days of the Terror and the Revolution did not allow of grand tours abroad, of courses at the Sorbonne, or of dancing and deportment classes; but old Gaston taught Ronnay all that he knew himself, even though he brought him up as a peasant. The lad wore a peasant's blouse and sabots on his feet; he was ten years old before he tasted any meat, twelve before he opened a book. But when, at fifteen years of age, he joined the army of the Republic, he fought like a hero until that Austrian bullet disabled him; then he retired—a Grand-Eagle of the Legion of Honour, one of the twenty men in the whole of France whom the newly-crowned Emperor thus honoured and trusted most.

It was at Austerlitz that Ronnay de Maurel got the wound which had lamed him for life. Napoleon sent him home to look after the de Maurel munitions factory, and, incidentally, to keep an eye on the hot-headed Royalists of Normandy, who were still brewing mischief against the new Empire and trafficking with the foreigners against their own country. Ronnay de Maurel returned to La Frontenay covered with honours, but eleven years' campaigning in Italy and on the Danube, under General Bonaparte, did not tend to the softening of manners or the acquisition of social graces. In the early days of the Republic and the Directorate—and even of the Consulate—campaigning meant fighting often on an empty stomach, nearly always with insufficient clothing; it meant tramping shoeless through the snows of the Alps or sleeping shelterless on the sodden bog-lands of Belgium. It meant living in comradeship with all the scum of humanity which the Republican Government had scraped together, in order to compose an army numerous enough to stand up against the overwhelmingly superior forces arraigned against France. It meant all that and more for many years; and when de Maurel obtained at twenty-six the grade of general of division—for promotion was over-quick then under the eye of the greatest war-lord the world has ever known—and donned the gorgeous uniform of an officer of high rank in the Imperial army, he knew neither how to enter a drawing-room, nor how to kiss a lady's hand. He knew less than did the sons of the more prominent overseers of his own factory; his manners were more uncouth—his speech more rude.

Having laid aside his fine uniform as general of division, he once more took up the peasant's blouse and the sabots which his Uncle Gaston—on his part—had never laid aside.

The days of democracy were at an end; the Imperial Court vied in brilliancy with the royal courts of long ago, but Ronnay de Maurel saw nothing of it. He had never been to Paris, and when he had stood face to face with his Emperor, both were covered with the grime and smoke of battle, both had their clothes half torn off their backs, both had muddy boots and unwashed hands.

"You fight our enemies with both hands, General," Napoleon had said to de Maurel on that occasion; "with one you wield a sword, with the other you make our cannon balls. In you France has two citizens— our beloved country two sons."

Yes! the days of democracy were at an end, nor had old Gaston de Maurel ever aught to do with the new days of splendour. He had continued to live in two rooms of his beautiful château, both on the ground-floor and away from the main façade; to these rooms one of the small back doors gave access; he lived like a workman, he fed and dressed and toiled like a workman.

One evening there was a knock at the back door. Gaston went to open it, for he only had an old woman from the village to cook his dinner for him and to make his bed, and she had gone back home an hour ago. On the threshold stood a man in a tattered uniform covered with tarnished gold lace; on his breast was the highest insignia of the newly-created order. Uncle and nephew shook one another silently by the hand. No warmer greeting passed between them. That evening Ronnay de Maurel shared his uncle's frugal supper, and the next morning saw him at the factory, having already taken over the command of the gigantic undertaking of which henceforth he became sole master.

And from that same day onwards a tall, massive figure, with head erect and deep-set, violet eyes fixed upon the horizon far away, could be seen every morning at break of day wending its way across the fields from the château to the factory, a matter of three kilometres, in all weathers—wet or fine, snow or rain, in the teeth of a gale or of blinding sleet—a woollen cap upon his head, his bare feet thrust into sabots. The country-folk, as he passed them by, would nudge one another and murmur "The General!" and would point to his left leg, which he dragged slightly as he trudged across a newly-ploughed field.

"If you go, my lad, mark my words, you'll rue it to your dying day. That woman is dangerous, I tell you."

The sick man spoke as forcibly, as emphatically as his growing weakness would allow; he brought his emaciated hand down upon the table with extraordinary vigour; his eyes, hollow and circled, were fixed upon his nephew, who still held his head persistently buried in his hands.

"I am not one to turn my back on danger," said de Maurel after a while, "and I must obey the Minister's orders."

"The Minister of Police does not know your mother, Ronnay," rejoined the invalid insistently.

"It is because he does know her—or, at any rate, because he suspects her—that he wants me to keep an eye on her and her doings. I cannot do that very well if we are to persist in this open enmity."

"Aye! in open enmity!" exclaimed the old man, whilst a look of bitter rancour crept into his hollow eyes. "Open enmity," he reiterated firmly, "that is the only correlation possible between us and a de Courson."

"The Minister thinks otherwise," responded Ronnay dryly. "And from what he says, so did the Emperor. My mother apparently thinks otherwise, too, else she had not sent for me so soon. She says that she desires speech with me. I'd better, in any case, hear what she hath to say."

"Oh, I can tell you that, my boy, without your troubling to go all the way to Courson to hear it. Your mother, my good Ronnay, has realized that you are passing rich; she has heard that I am dying, and that after my death your wealth and influence will vie with that of any man in France. She wants to see if she can cozen you into placing it at her service."

"I am not easily cozened," muttered de Maurel stubbornly, "and fear of her wiles is not like to make me disobey the Minister's orders."

"You will do as you like, my lad," rejoined the invalid dryly; "you are as self-willed and as obstinate as your father was before you. And I can do nothing save to warn you."

"Warn me of what?" queried Ronnay impatiently. "Am I a child that I cannot be trusted to look after myself?"

"You are a child in many ways, my dear General. A child in this, that you are no match for the pin-pricks which your lady-mother knows so well how to deal."

"I care nothing for women's pin-pricks. My hide is tough and smooth-tongued stabs will glide off me like water off a duck's back. If my lady-mother is disagreeable, I can be disagreeable, too. If she refuses to be friends, I need never set foot inside her doors again."

"Oh, she will not refuse to be friends with you, my lad! Have I not said that Mme. la Marquise de Mortain knows her eldest son to be wealthy and influential? She will not refuse to be friends with a man who might prove useful to her in her many and varied intrigues. Your lady-mother, my good Ronnay, will pour honey and sugar on you, I have no doubt of that. 'Twas not against an open enmity on her part that I desired to warn you."

"Against what, then?"

"Against her protestations of goodwill and of love."

"Love?" commented de Maurel, with a shrug of his broad shoulders. "I am not like to listen to protestations of love. But what use is there to argue the matter at such length, Uncle Gaston?" he added, with obvious exasperation. "Have I not read you the Minister's letter and told you that my mind was made up? How could I act otherwise when—as the Minister tells me—the Emperor himself, ere he left for Prussia, desired me to try and make friends with the de Coursons?"

"Friends!" ejaculated the invalid, and a sardonic grin almost distorted for the moment his thin, pale face. "Friends!"

Then he continued more calmly: "There is no friendship possible, my lad, between us and the de Coursons. I know that I may as well be talking to that bedstead over there as to you. You say your mind is made up, and you have all your father's obstinacy and more. You will go to Courson, in spite of what I say. You'll go and you'll weep bitter tears of repentance for the rest of your life; of that I am as convinced as that I have one foot in the grave and am dragging the other one in as fast as may be. I am sick and weak; some will tell you that old Gaston de Maurel is already in his dotage; but you are the one being in the world whom I care for now, and I am not going to let my weakness get the better of me, and allow you to run your stupid head against a stone wall which will bruise, if it will not crush you, without raising my feeble voice in protest."

"You but waste your precious breath, Uncle Gaston," rejoined de Maurel more gently. "I am nothing if not a soldier, and I'd as soon think of cutting off my right hand as to ignore my Emperor's wishes. When he pinned the Grand-Eagle of the Legion of Honour upon my breast, he gave me the highest proof possible of his belief and trust in me. I cannot fight for him for the present, with this accursed maimed leg of mine; but I should be a coward and a cur were I to disobey his responsible Minister in so small a matter. Be assured, Uncle Gaston, that no harm will come to me. No harm can come to any man through friendship with his mother, even if she be a de Courson."

"Oho! you think so, my lad, do you?" retorted the invalid, with a cynical laugh. "All the harm in the world, which not an ocean of tears could ever wash away, came to your father, because he fell in love with Denise de Courson. My brother Bertrand worshipped that woman!" continued old Gaston, and from his enfeebled frame he seemed to gather force as he spoke, with white, marble-like finger uplifted, and eyes which already had looked closely on death fixed upon the bronzed face of his nephew. "He poured out the full measure of his lavish heart at her feet, the full measure of his keen intellect. His dream—God forgive him for a blundering fool—his dream was to associate her in all the schemes which he had devised for the welfare of his dependents. She scorned his ideals, she ran counter to his aims. She was an aristocrat—in the worst acceptance of the word—to her finger-tips. She hated—yes, hated—everything that was poor and dependent and ignorant. She hated the people for whom your father schemed and toiled; she poured ridicule on all his efforts; with a flick of her be-ringed fingers she would have destroyed the whole edifice of his often misguided but always generous philanthropy. Whatever he did, she immediately opposed—on principle—her principle—the principle that humanity began with the chevaliers, with the privileged few who had a handle to their name. For her the proletariat, the bourgeoisie, the toilers and the workers were all so much scum, whose very touch would pollute the hem of her gown. The life and welfare of one of her husband's peasantry was of less account to her than the health of her pet dog. Oh, there were women like that in the old régime—and men, too, my boy! Else, think you that so bloody a revolution as the one which the people of France have made would ever have swept an entire caste off the face of the land? There were women and men in those days—before the Revolution—who would see, and did see, their fellow-creatures starving at their doors, who saw them half naked with hardly a roof above their heads, and would not raise a finger to help them. There were men and women like that—'tis no use denying it. And they made the Revolution—not we. The death of their King upon the scaffold, the outrage to their Queen, was their making—not ours. The Bourbons stood for all that was callous and purse-proud and disdainful. They had to go, so had those on whom a people bubbling over with wrath and thirsting for revenge succeeded in laying a hand. Your mother was one of those who escaped. She has since married another aristocrat—de Mortain—a fool and a fop, and has brought up a son who no doubt would like to carry on her principles through another generation. But that woman broke your father's heart as surely as the guillotine ought to have broken her aristocratic neck. True, Bertrand was obstinate and self-willed and passionate. Would he have loved his wife as he did had he not been passionate? Would he have toiled for the welfare of his dependents through scorn, opposition and ridicule had he not been self-willed? True, that one day, exasperated beyond his powers of self-control, he struck that cruel, callous creature who deserved neither his consideration nor his chivalry. True, he did that, and earned for ever after the contumely of his aristocratic connections; but he also earned his freedom, for Denise left him after that, and thereby rendered him the one service she ever did in her life. Now that

24

woman has returned to France—returned in order to work mischief in this peaceful corner of Normandy. On this I would stake my life. And she wants to get you into her toils—you and your influence and your wealth. She will smile on you, my boy, as she once smiled on your father; but in her heart she will hate you because you are his son; she will despise you for your rough ways and inelegant speech; she will laugh at you behind your back, she will vilify you and cover you with ridicule. And in the end, she will either break your heart if you remain strong, or tarnish your honour if you show the least sign of weakness. Avoid her, my lad, as you would the plague. There is no peace, no happiness where Denise de Courson holds sway...."

III

The invalid fell back against the pillows. The long, sustained effort had well-nigh snapped the last feeble thread of life on which he hung. Ronnay had not interrupted him. He knew that the old man was passing weak—that he was well-nigh spent, yet he let him talk on. Old Gaston had spoken in short, jerky sentences, interrupted by the indrawing of his breath or short attacks of coughing. He had never before this spoken to Ronnay about his mother—never before had he allowed himself to be carried away by the flood of his own rhetoric. But he looked upon the threatened reconciliation as a calamity for the nephew, whom in his own rough way he loved better than anything else on earth; and out of that love—which had always remained unspoken— he had drawn the strength which had enabled him to speak this last forceful and deliberate warning.

But Ronnay had often been proclaimed before now the true son of his father, and old Gaston, in the course of his panegyric upon his dead brother, had owned that Bertrand de Maurel had been obstinate and self-willed. Perhaps the invalid had spoken so passionately and lengthily because he knew—with that keen knowledge which so often comes to the sick—that he was making no impression upon Ronnay's fixed determination, and while he spoke there had crept into his dim eyes a look that was almost one of appeal. Ronnay had listened in silence; it would have been cruel to have refused to listen to a sick man's impassioned entreaty. But the obstinacy which had helped to wreck his father's life had been transmitted in a full measure to himself; and Fouché—clever, astute Fouché—had used the one argument which was unanswerable, when he appealed to de Maurel's loyalty.

"Go to Courson, my dear General," the Minister had writ with his own hand, "go as soon as your mother bids you come. You would be

25

rendering the State an inestimable service if you would keep an eye on the doings of all these repatriated émigrés in your department. That they are up to some mischief I need not perhaps impress upon you. They have been raising money in their own lawless fashion in that part of Normandy for some time now. Pillage, highway robbery, arson and intimidation are rife. I believe that the Royalists are trying to raise another army which might give us an infinity of trouble—and, in any case, will cause the shedding of a deal of innocent blood. The Château de Courson is so admirably situated and adapted for the headquarters of those sort of intrigues. I entreat you, therefore, during the absence of our Imperial Master in Prussia and at his own earnest desire, which I herewith transmit to you, to keep in touch with your relatives there, so that you may, by your influence and presence, avert the mischief which I feel to be brewing in those quarters. I know that by asking you to do this, I am imposing an uncongenial task upon so gallant a soldier as yourself, and demanding of you a heavy sacrifice; but I understand from His Majesty that you require some rest for another six months at least, after the serious wound which that Austrian bullet dealt you at Austerlitz; but that after those six months you will be able to resume your command and to join him in Poland in the winter. Until then, my dear General, may I claim your priceless services against a foe no less insidious and hardly less powerful than the one you so gallantly helped our Imperial Master to subjugate."

That was the letter which had taken the Minister of Police over half an hour to prepare. Oh, clever and astute Fouché! How thoroughly you understood the science of making men the engines of your will! Here was Ronnay de Maurel, who had earned for himself undying laurels on fields where every man was brave and worthy of distinction, ready—at your bidding—to throw himself into a maze of intrigue where his uncultured mind was bound to be at once at a hopeless disadvantage. But Fouché had made appeal in the name of France, and the democrats of this age, who had emerged chastened and purified from out the withering fire of a sanguinary Revolution, had in their hearts a boundless store of love for their country who had suffered so much.

Gaston de Maurel had spent much of his reserve of strength in trying to counteract the effect of Fouché's letter in his nephew's mind. Long before he had said all that he meant, he knew that he had failed. When—some time after he had finished speaking—Ronnay still remained silent, the invalid, half prostrate after the exertion, threw back his head and broke into a strident laugh.

"I might have saved my wind—eh, Ronnay?" he asked, panting.

Ronnay made no reply.

"I suppose you'll go to-morrow?" continued old Gaston.

"Yes," replied the younger man curtly, "I'll go to-morrow."

"As you are now?"

26

"As I am now."

Again the invalid laughed, but the laughter was choked in a spasm of coughing. Without another word Ronnay de Maurel rose and readjusted the pillows behind the sick man's head. Gaston was still chuckling inwardly to himself; his dim eyes, feebly glittering now with a glance of mockery, wandered restlessly over the massive and uncouth figure of this soldier of Napoleon. Ronnay de Maurel—General of Division in the most marvellous army the world has ever known—looked at this moment very like an overgrown, over-developed product of industrial Normandy. Ungainly in his movements, with that dragging gait which always appeared more accentuated whenever he laboured under fatigue or excitement, untutored of speech, unversed in every one of the gentle arts which mark the preux chevalier, or the squire of dames, Ronnay was not like to find favour in his mother's eyes. His linen blouse was stained with the grime and smoke of his foundries, his hair was wont to rebel against the conventional tie at the nape of the neck, his hands were rough, his nails unpolished. How the fine, if impecunious, entourage of Mme. la Marquise de Mortain would sneer at this handiwork of democratic France!

Ronnay felt the invalid's mocking glance, but he was far too indifferent to all that it implied even to wince under it.

"I may put on a clean blouse," he said, with a smile which suddenly lit up his face like sunshine after a storm.

Gaston de Maurel gave a curious little sigh, and—if the whole countryside had not known him for a hard, unemotional man—one might almost have said that a look of tenderness had suddenly crept into his sunken eyes as their glance embraced the ungainly figure of his nephew. Ronnay was so singularly unfitted to cope with the difficulties which were about to beset him. He was so little versed in the arts and graces wherewith his mother of a certainty had already set out to cajole him. His untrained mind was not up to the intrigues which were as the breath of life to these aristocratic ladies, who had thrown themselves into the whirlpool of their tottering cause. Ronnay was just a soldier—untaught, unenlightened. Since the age of fifteen he had known no life save that of camps, learned no lessons save those taught on battlefields and in the face of the enemy. He had learned neither self-control nor dissimulation. His untamed spirit would rebel against all the pin-pricks which his mother and her associates would know so well how to deal him.

Poor Ronnay! The invalid sighed again, this time somewhat less bitterly. The smile which still lingered round his nephew's rugged face had told him much. It told him that out of the maelstrom of a checkered and turbulent life Ronnay had rescued one priceless gift which had remained his own—a subtle sense of humour, which mayhap would cause him to suffer many things less acutely than he otherwise would have done.

There was silence after that between the two men. Each was busy with his own thoughts, and when anon they talked together again, the subject uppermost in both their minds was not broached by either of them again. Matters of business, of the factory, of the new dwellings on the estate, absorbed the conversation, and half an hour later the invalid was ready for bed. And, more tenderly than any mother could have gathered her baby to her breast, Ronnay de Maurel picked up the invalid out of his chair and carried him in his powerful arms gently into the next room, where he laid him on his bed, undressed him and washed him—an office of mercy which he had performed for the old man every evening since he came home from Austria and laid aside his fine uniform for the peasant's blouse.

CHAPTER IV KINDRED

I

The very atmosphere of the old Château de Courson had become electrical—excitement was in the air. Even Mme. la Marquise, that perfect pattern of aristocratic sang-froid, had been unable to sit still all morning.

She wandered restlessly from room to room; she held long conversations with her son, with her brother, with Fernande—even with old Matthieu Renard and with Annette.

"I expect my son, M. de Maurel," she said to the worthy couple, who, of a truth, could not understand why it was not the most natural thing in the world for a mother to receive her son. "He may come over at about noon and may stay to have dinner with us. Watch over your cooking, my good Annette—see that everything is very plain but thoroughly good."

"Bien, bien, Mme. la Marquise," nodded Annette, who, womanlike, was more ready to become impregnated with that fever of excitement which pervaded the château than was sober old Matthieu. "You may be sure that I will do my best. I saw the General when first he came home from the war...."

"Not General, my good woman," interposed Madame la Marquise haughtily; "my son is no General in the army of a parvenu. He is Comte de Maurel, Duc de Montauban, and bears no other grade or title; and all the democratic governments in the world cannot strip him of his rank."

Now that Ronnay had so quickly—if somewhat coldly—acceded to her request for an interview, Mme. la Marquise's imagination went galloping on the wings of fancy.

"We'll convert him yet," she said to her brother. "You'll see, my dear Baudouin! I'll make that unrelenting democrat dance to my piping before long. Once I have succeeded in drawing him away from that old fiend Gaston's influence, I'll twirl him round my little finger."

M. de Courson gave a slight shrug. He was doubtful as to that. Madame promptly turned to her son.

"Laurent, you are prepared to make friends with your brother, are you not?" she said, in a tone almost of entreaty.

"If he will meet me half-way," retorted Laurent, not too genially. He had been taught from his babyhood to hate his elder brother, not only for the latter's political convictions, but because of the wealth which an indiscriminating Fate had chosen to pour down at his feet. It was difficult for a young and impetuous creature like Laurent de Mortain to adapt himself quite so readily to his mother's new mood.

"At any rate, promise me that you will not quarrel!" added Mme. la Marquise with unwonted earnestness.

At ten o'clock in the forenoon Madame decided that she would receive her son in the noble—if somewhat dilapidated—reception-room where a few gilt-legged fauteuils and the satin-wood parquet floor bore mute testimony to past dignity and grandeur. Half an hour later she wandered out upon the terrace, from whence, she thought, the aspect of the neglected and overgrown garden would of a certainty touch the heart of the visitor and incline him to generosity.

At eleven o'clock she thought that the small boudoir—the only living room which she and her family had in use at the present moment—would shame the wealthy son by its air of poverty and of simplicity. At half-past, she was once more inclined to favour the reception-room, and at noon she was back in the boudoir, discussing the question with her brother and with her son, when a heavy and halting footstep was heard in the corridor outside, and the next moment the door was thrown open and Ronnay de Maurel appeared upon the threshold.

II

He had certainly put on a clean linen blouse, but a blouse it was—just the same as those which his own employés wore at their work—of a faded shade of blue, with wide sleeves and low, turned-down collar, out of which rose his straight, firm neck, strong as a bull's, and crowned by the square, massive head, which he threw up as he

29

entered, with a gesture that implied defiance. He certainly had discarded sabots; a pair of heavy jack-boots reached just below his knees, and dark cloth breeches encased his powerful thighs. His thick brown hair was held in at the nape of the neck with a black ribbon, hastily tied. And—pinned to his blouse—he wore the ribbon of Grand-Eagle of the Legion of Honour, the highest distinction the new Empire could confer.

Madame's first sensation on seeing her son was one of horror. She had heard tales of Ronnay de Maurel's uncouthness, of his rough clothes and his bad manners, but in her mind she had—almost involuntarily—associated all these rumoured rude ways of his with a certain picturesqueness, a rough grandeur which she thought would appeal to her.

But there was nothing either picturesque or grand about this ugly apparition which had so summarily thrust itself into her presence. With a genuine sinking of the heart Mme. la Marquise took in at a glance Ronnay's uncomely appearance, the well-nigh repellent scowl which disfigured his face, the heavy frown across his brow, his hands discoloured by toil and by inclement weather—in fact, the whole of the inelegant, not to say forbidding, aspect of this man whom a while ago she had hoped to win over to her side.

And that this coarse, boorish creature was her son she could, alas! not doubt for a moment. He appeared before her as the living image of the man whom she had hated so bitterly throughout his life, and whom she had never wholly succeeded in eradicating from her memory. In Ronnay she saw the Bertrand of long ago, the heavy figure, the leonine head, the firm neck, and obstinate jaw; she saw the unruly hair which rebelled against comb or tie, she saw the eyes beneath the square, straight brow, which appeared of a violet-blue in repose and flashed dark, almost black, in anger. And in Ronnay de Maurel, too, she saw at this moment the man who in the past had tyrannized over her, had contradicted her at every turn, had struck her ... that once ... on that unforgettable day, when at last she was able to regain her freedom.

And all the hatred which she had felt for Bertrand throughout all these years, and which for a few brief hours she had tried to forget, was suddenly reawakened at sight of the man whose whole demeanour as he faced her at this moment seemed to proclaim the triumph of the proletariat which she had never ceased to despise.

She made no sign to welcome him. Her eyes scanned him from top to toe with what she intended to be a withering glance—a mute reproach at his total lack of respect towards her, which his rough clothes and neglected hands implied. But Ronnay de Maurel seemed quite unconscious both of his own appearance and of the effect it had upon his lady mother. He advanced further into the room and quite unceremoniously slammed the door to behind him.

"You sent for me, Mme. la Marquise," he said quietly and

30

unconcernedly, "and I have come at your bidding. Will you tell me as briefly as you can what it is you desire to say to me?"

The man's indifference, his callous attitude, put the final touch to Madame's exasperation. The look in her eyes became more trenchant, more withering than before. She drew herself up to her full height, which was considerable, and folded her arms over her breast.

"When M. le Comte de Maurel, Duc de Montauban," she said, "has learned how to present himself before his mother, I will speak to him and not before. Baudouin," she added loftily, turning to her brother, "I think that I may rely on you to teach this ... to teach my son the first lesson of respect which he owes to me. Laurent, the door!"

Laurent hastened to obey. He held open the door, through which Mme. la Marquise de Mortain now passed out, holding herself very erect—the personification of outraged dignity.

III

De Maurel had taken refuge in a distant corner of the room. He was gazing in utter bewilderment at the retreating figure of his mother. Her tirade had evidently puzzled rather than angered him, for his deep-set eyes were full of vague questionings as they wandered from the face of his uncle to that of his young step-brother.

"Our lady-mother," he said at last, when Laurent had once more closed the door, and the frou-frou of Madame's skirts no longer could be heard swishing softly down the corridor, "our lady-mother seems somewhat wayward in her moods. Yesterday she sent for me post-haste—to-day she turns her back on me."

"Can you wonder?" broke in Laurent hotly. "Your conduct is outrageous...."

"My conduct?" rejoined de Maurel. "Why? What have I done? I scarce opened my mouth...."

An exclamation of wrath and of contempt escaped Laurent's quivering lips ... a hot retort was obviously on the tip of his tongue. M. de Courson was only just in time to avert an avalanche of wrathful words which may have led to a sudden, irretrievable quarrel. He interposed between the two men with the perfect courtesy and tact of a high-born gentleman receiving an honoured guest.

"My good de Maurel," he said, holding out his slender, aristocratic hand to his nephew, "it is close on a quarter of a century since we have met, and it is a pleasure to me to welcome you at Courson. Do you know that I am your godfather, an honour which I share, if I remember rightly, with M. le Marquis de la Fayette? I hope that you will always think of me in that capacity and accept my help

31

and counsel in all matters where the experience of a man of the world may be useful to you."

Somewhat tentatively—more like a naughty child who is being coaxed into good humour—Ronnay de Maurel took that thin, white hand which was being held out to him. He could have crushed it in his own toil-worn one.

"I thank you," he said curtly, "I am too old now for help or counsel, and my life has been spent in fighting for my country. I have no use for the experiences of a man of the world, by which, I suppose, you mean a dandy of drawing-rooms, a courtier or a sycophant."

"No, no, I did not mean that," rejoined M. de Courson conciliatingly. "It is not necessary to be a dandy, nor yet a sycophant, in order to win the regard of one's own kindred—those of one's own caste. Unfortunately, it had not occurred to me to give you a word of warning ere you came to meet your mother ... in this guise."

"In this guise!" echoed de Maurel roughly. "What hath my guise to do with my coming here? My mother sent for me. Surely she did not do that in order to look at my clothes."

"Good God, man!" here interposed Laurent sharply, "is this bland simplicity of yours a pose or what? Do you really pretend not to know that a workman's attire is not a suitable one wherein to present yourself in the salons of the Marquise de Mortain?"

"The Marquise de Mortain was once Mme. de Maurel. I did not come here in order to present myself in her salon, but to speak with my mother and at her wish."

"You might have washed your hands and slipped on a decent coat in order to do that," rejoined Laurent, who, forgetting his mother's entreaties of a while ago, was letting his ebullient temper gradually overmaster his prudence.

But de Maurel, too, seemed to have come to the end of his small stock of patience.

"Have done, boy, with that nonsense," he retorted roughly, "I am not a man of patience. I owe nothing to the lady, remember, who has long since forfeited the name of 'mother' as far as I am concerned. I came at her bidding, and against my better judgment—the son of my father can have nothing in common with the Marquise de Mortain."

"An you turn to insult ..." exclaimed Laurent hotly.

"There is no insult in an unvarnished fact. Mme. la Marquise de Mortain cares less about me than I do about an ill-conditioned cur. And if she desires to see my clothes, I can send her a suit fashioned by a tailor and stay at home myself the while."

"Pardieu, de Maurel," quoth M. de Courson with a laugh, "I had heard tales of your tenacity and of your self-will, but none of a certainty that do justice to the truth. Come, man! you surely will not allow petty obstinacy in so trifling a matter to interfere with the amity which should exist between your mother and yourself and towards which she hath, you must admit, met you already more than half way."

"But, nom de Dieu!" rejoined de Maurel gruffly, "what do want me to do enfin?"

"Let me take a message to Mme. la Marquise from you," replied M. le Comte, "craving her pardon for your want of respect to her this forenoon.... There is no shame in humbling one's pride before a woman and...."

Then, as de Maurel, moody and wrathful, made no immediate rejoinder to the proposal, M. de Courson added more lightly: "Well, what say you?"

"That I've neither mind nor leisure to lend myself to Mme. la Marquise's whims and fancies," retorted de Maurel, whose obstinacy was growing in proportion with the impatience and arrogance of his kinsmen.

"Nor decent clothes to wear, I warrant," broke in Laurent, as he felt his temper flaring up into fury against this ill-bred creature, who seemed wholly unconscious of his enormities. "Uncle Baudouin," he added, with a sneer, "do not, I pray you, waste your time in trying to instil some semblance of good manners into this oaf. One would think he had sprung out of the gutter...."

"Hold on, boy!" interposed de Maurel, with a sudden hoarseness in his voice, and a clenching of his mighty fist till the knuckles shone like ivory through the flesh. "Have I not said that I am not a man of patience...?"

"'Tis I who am not a man of patience," retorted Laurent. "Think you I can bear much longer the studied insult to us all which your attitude implies? Think you that because we are poor you can treat us as you would hesitate to treat the meanest peasant on your land? Is your apparel a pose or what? You cannot be as ignorant of the usages of good society as you pretend to be. After all, we have all been in exile— we have lived apart from those of our own breeding, of our own caste, but, in spite of our misfortunes we have kept up in our hearts the traditions of courtesy and gentle manners which were handed down to us all by our fathers—aye, to us all!" he added vehemently, "to you as well as to us. You bear one of the noblest names in France, and you pretend to have forgotten the most ordinary elements of respect due to the sex which hath every claim on our chivalry. Where, in Heaven's name have you been, man? Where have you spent your life that you could so far forget the traditions of your race?"

De Maurel had proclaimed himself to be a man devoid of patience. Yet he had listened attentively to every word that his young brother said. He had acquired throughout a hard, self-denying life the supreme virtue of silence; he knew—no one better—how to listen. Therefore he did not break in on Laurent's tirade. He listened to it to the end, and did not even wince at the sneers which his younger brother hurled very freely at him. But now that the latter had finished speaking, Ronnay came a step or two nearer to him, and drawing himself to his full height, he said, with perfect, outward calm:

"Where I spent my life, brother mine? Will you let me tell you, since you do not know? My childhood I spent in the old Château of La Vieuville, where my uncle Gaston took care of me since my father died and my mother had abandoned me in order to pursue her own aims in life, which were not those of the man to whom she had sworn fealty at the altar...."

"Silence, man!" interposed Laurent excitedly. "I'll not have you vilify my mother, whom...."

"I vilify no one," riposted de Maurel quietly. "You have taunted me with the query as to how I have spent my life, and you must listen to my explanation. My uncle Gaston brought me up as best he could. His life was spent in the service of his country; he had but little time to devote to my education. Our country then, my good brother, required the services of all her children, since those of our kindred and of our caste were inciting half Europe to take up arms against her. My boyhood I spent helping with my feeble might in the work of defending France against the invasion of alien enemies who were bent on destroying her, because forsooth they disagreed with her political ideals, and had no sympathy with the aims of an entire people, goaded into rebellion by centuries of tyranny. I was twelve years old when my uncle Gaston de Maurel converted my father's iron foundries into huge factories for the manufacture of steel and of gunpowder, wherewith to fight the foreign foe abroad and the traitor at home ... aye! twelve years old, my dear brother, when my hands ceased to be white and slender and aristocratic in shape and colour, and became stained and rough ... unwashed you called them just now. At the age when boys of my caste learn how to dance and to strum on a spinet, to point their toes and kiss the ladies' hands, I learned how to fashion saltpetre out of grit and how to transmute church bells into cannon balls. At fifteen I knew how to wield a sword and how to handle a gun. My manhood has been spent in camps, in the armies of the finest military leader that hath ever led men to glory and to victory. When France was attacked from the north and the south, from the east and from the west by Austria and Prussia, by Italy and England and Russia and Spain, a young general of artillery, not yet twenty-three years of age, led her triumphantly from victory to victory till the sacred soil of our beautiful country was swept clean of every foe. I followed that young leader wherever he went. I fought under him at Toulon, I followed him to Austria. I crossed the Alps in his train. I fought and bled under his eye for the honour of France and the glory of her flag. I starved with him in Egypt; I froze with him in Poland; I stood by his side at Austerlitz when the Austrian sued for peace. At first we marched and fought in wooden shoes, or with hay-ropes tied round our feet; at dead of winter we fought half naked with bast-mats slung round our shoulders. But we fought like men and kept whole Europe at bay. No, my good Laurent, I did not learn how to enter a salon, or how to turn a pretty compliment before ladies, but I know how to dispose an army corps when the enemy is in sight. I do not know how to wave a scented handkerchief in the air, but I do know how to meet a resolute foe in a hand-to-hand combat. My life has been spent in ridding France of foreigners, and of traitors, of idlers and slackers and useless good-for-nothing sybarites, and in the process my hands have remained rough and stained. I am a cripple now—not for always, I hope—and I wear a workman's blouse, because I have become a workman since I no longer can be a soldier. As soon as I can walk straight again I'll be back to fight under the Tricolour flag of France—to fight against the foreign enemy—to fight against treachery at home—to fight for the rights of manhood and citizenship, with unquenchable spirit and dogged determination, and continue to spend my life, as I have done up to now, until, please God, mine will be the glory to shed my last drop of blood for France!"

He paused—for want of breath mayhap—for, indeed, his rugged eloquence was carrying him away on the wings of his fervour and his burning patriotism. M. de Courson and Laurent de Mortain had listened to him in sullen silence. Once or twice Laurent had made an effort to interrupt, but de Maurel spoke very loudly and forcibly, and the other perforce had to remain silent. Once or twice he affected to smother a yawn, and he would have given much to be able to turn his back on this ranting demagogue—as he inwardly termed him—and to leave him to continue his ravings in solitude. But, in spite of himself, something held him back. There was a certain forcefulness, a certain directness as well as pride in Ronnay de Maurel's impassioned harangue which compelled attention, even if it did not call for respect. Laurent de Mortain—and M. le Comte de Courson also, for that matter—were soldiers and patriots, too. There was much in them which was every whit as fine and brave as the soul of de Maurel which was finding expression in his eloquent words. It was only the divergence of ideals which stood between these Royalists and the man who they considered had been a traitor to his caste.

There was the pity of it! The miserable, irretrievable pity! The children of France were at deadly enmity with one another; their different political aims had caused an abyss to form between them, which nothing now could bridge over. There was a total lack of understanding, and, alas! the many outrages perpetrated on both sides had rendered the breach for ever impassable. M. de Courson and Laurent de Mortain saw in de Maurel the product of the spirit of regicide, of the sanguinary revolution which had committed the most brutal excesses the civilized world had ever seen; and Ronnay de Maurel saw in his kinsmen only the incarnation of that spirit which had not been content to fight for the cause of its traditions, but had

35

treacherously sold the country to the foreign foe, had brought foreign armies within the sacred boundaries of France, had sought the aid of foreigners to gain victory for its arms.

And these three men, in whom flowed the same blood of kinship, stood now confronting one another with something like deadly hatred flashing in their eyes. The two brothers, indeed, presented a strange contrast: Laurent, slender and graceful, with smoothly-dressed dark hair crowning a face full of charm and delicacy, with hands white and soft, with clothes that fitted his elegant young figure to perfection; and Ronnay de Maurel, tall and ungainly, in rough blouse and heavy boots, with rugged face bronzed by campaigning in all weathers and furrowed long before its time, with eyes of a deep blue, that appeared almost black beneath the straight, square brow and firm mouth set in hard, obstinate lines. Indeed, it was not six years that lay between them in age, but a whole century—a century of thoughtlessness, of easy-going tyranny, of selfishness on the one hand, and one of rebellion and self-will on the other, and there was a century of suffering and of wrongs to be avenged on either side.

IV

It seemed, indeed, as if nothing now could avert an immediate quarrel between the two brothers. The breach between them had been widened by bitter words on both sides, and if at this juncture it came to open enmity between them, that breach mayhap would never be patched up again. M. de Courson, as usual, tried to play his part of peace-maker. In his heart of hearts he could not help but give a certain measure of admiration to de Maurel's fearless exposé of the situation. He himself being innately loyal, recognized and appreciated loyalty in others. He did not want to see a quarrel between the brothers now. His sober judgment still clung to the desire for conciliation, and he still clung to the hope that this semi-educated boor could be tamed into something that was not only presentable, but also useful to the cause which he and his kindred had so much at heart.

Therefore he made one more effort to interpose in a conciliatory spirit between these two smouldering tempers.

"It was not your brother's intention, my good de Maurel," he said, "nor, I vow, was it mine to cast aspersions upon your manhood or your valour. Your tirade—an you will permit me to say so without offence—was, therefore, quite superfluous, since it had no bearing upon the subject which we were discussing...."

"Namely, your want of respect to our mother," concluded Laurent wrathfully.

36

"Nay!" retorted de Maurel curtly. "Methought that we were chiefly engaged in discussing my clothes."

"Until you chose to cast aspersions on Mme. la Marquise de Mortain, which I for one will not tolerate."

"If I have said aught to offend Mme. la Marquise," said Ronnay curtly, "I'll crave her pardon.... I had no intention to offend."

"Yet you do, man, you do," riposted Laurent hotly; "not only with your words, not only with your clothes, but by flaunting before her eyes that badge of infamy which you wear upon your breast."

"Laurent!" interposed M. de Courson quickly, for unobservant and obtuse though he was, he had not failed to note that de Maurel's face had suddenly become extraordinarily livid in hue, and that the breath came and went through his tightly clenched teeth with a curious, hissing sound.

"Nay, M. le Comte," he broke in slowly after a while, "I pray you do not try and stem the flow of my brother's eloquence. Meseems that the next few moments will clear the somewhat close atmosphere of Courson from a veritable fog of misunderstandings. I was under the impression that my linen blouse and muddy boots had alone offended Mme. la Marquise's aristocratic glance; it seems that there's something more about my person which hath not found favour in her sight."

Laurent, at these words, uttered in a husky voice as if the man were choking, broke into a strident laugh, and with uplifted hand he pointed to the crimson ribbon on Ronnay's blouse.

"Eminently suitable in colour," he said with a sneer, which suddenly sent the hot blood rushing back to the other's pale cheeks, "and well chosen by a baseborn adventurer to commemorate all the innocent blood which his treachery and vanity have helped to shed."

There came a quick flash in de Maurel's eyes, which the younger man would have been wise to heed. "Hold on, man! hold on!" he said, still speaking slowly and with seeming calm, "ere your profane mouth utter a sacrilege! This ribbon was pinned upon my breast on the glorious field of Austerlitz by the man whose valour and glory have won undying laurels for France—by the patriot who swept the soil of our beautiful country clean from foreign foes ... and whom an adoring nation hath proclaimed its Lord and Emperor."

Laurent threw back his head, whilst a glance of withering scorn shot from his fine eyes and swept the uncouth figure of his soldier brother.

"Lord and Emperor!" he exclaimed. "Hark at the miserable besotted fool! at the traitor! the regicide! Lord and Emperor forsooth! the base-born son of a vulgar father—a Corsican adventurer and knight of industry, who is clever enough to gull a wretched nation into kissing the rod which God hath devised for its punishment...."

"Silence!" thundered de Maurel, and with a quick movement forward he gripped Laurent by the wrist. "Silence, you dolt! you fool!

37

Another word and I force you down on your knees to crave pardon in your stupid heart for the impious nonsense which your insentient tongue hath uttered. Silence, I say!"

"Silence!" retorted Laurent, who by now had lost complete control over his nerves and whose voice sounded shrill and cracked. "Nay! why should I be silent, when the whole of Europe cries anathema against the usurper? Shame on you, my brother, shame! for parading your own dishonour upon your breast."

"Dishonour?"

"Aye, dishonour! What else is it, I pray, but the livery of traitors, of regicides and of murderers? Legion of Honour the Corsican has dared to call it—and you, it seems, are one of his Grand-Eagles ... but we who are loyal to France and to our King, we proclaim it the Legion of Dishonour, and you and such as you a herd of devouring vultures. Shed your livery of shame, my brother, ere I smite you with it in the face."

De Maurel up to now had been perhaps more bewildered than infuriated by the ravings of this young madman; but now, ere he had time to realize what Laurent was doing, and before M. de Courson could interfere, the young Marquis had, with a quick and almost savage gesture, gripped the crimson ribbon on his brother's breast and torn it violently from the blouse. The next moment he threw it with an exclamation of loathing upon the floor. A cry as of an enraged bull came from de Maurel's throat, and his two hands—the hard, strong hands of the toiler—fastened themselves like clamps of steel upon the young man's shoulders.

"On your knees, on your knees, you blasphemous malapert," he said, as with well-nigh brutal strength he gradually forced Laurent down. "On your knees! You shall lick the dust for this monstrous sacrilege.... Your unhallowed hands shall not touch that sacred badge ... with your lips you shall pick it out of the dust ... you...."

"Let me go!" cried Laurent hoarsely. "Uncle Baudouin, à moi!"

"On your knees!" reiterated de Maurel fiercely.

He was possessed of immense strength. Laurent, despite his every effort to free himself and to remain defiant, felt his knees giving way under him. The pain in his shoulders and his back, caused by that iron grip, turned him sick and faint, whilst M. le Comte's attempts at interference were obviously of no avail. Insults and protests died upon his lips; he saw the stern, dark face which was bending over him as through a veil of mist ... that mist soon became of a crimson hue ... like blood. Laurent felt all the tumultuous blood of his race rushing through his veins; his head was swimming, his ears buzzing, and he saw red ... a sea of red in front of his eyes. His hand with a last convulsive gesture wandered to his hip, and was buried for a moment under his coat. The next moment it reappeared with a hunting-knife in its grasp.

"Laurent, in the name of Heaven, think of what you are doing!"

The call, soft as that of a frightened bird, came from the door immediately behind Laurent. He was down on one knee at that moment, with one hand he was steadying himself against the floor, the other, holding the large hunting-knife, was raised ready to strike. For one second only; the next the grip on his shoulders was relaxed, the dark face, distorted with wrath and contempt, seemed to fade away into the dim distance, and he fell back half swooning against a heavy chair close by.

At the sound of that agonized woman's cry de Maurel's grip on his brother's shoulders had suddenly relaxed. He looked up, and for a moment it seemed to him as if he were gazing on something unreal; there was a veil in front of his eyes, and he could see nothing clearly, not even the apparition in the doorway ... a slender apparition clad all in white ... the exquisite form of a woman—a mere child—dressed in a white gown cut low round the shoulders, in accordance with the prevailing mode; her neck, shoulders and arms were bare; her tiny head was crowned with a wealth of fair hair, which clustered in unruly curls round the perfect oval of her face; her eyes, with large pupils dilated now with fear and horror, were of an unfathomable blue. She had been carrying a sheaf of bluebells in her arm, the spoils of the woodland round Courson; but at the awful sight which greeted her as she pushed open the door of the boudoir, the flowers fell from her hands and now lay scattered in a delicious tangled mass of blue—like the colour of her eyes—at her feet.

As Ronnay de Maurel slowly straightened out his herculean figure, the details of the exquisite picture before him reached his perceptions one by one. He saw the delicate hands stretched out toward him with a feminine gesture of protection; he saw the dainty feet encased in sandals, which looked as if they scarce would touch the ground; he saw the full, red lips still parted with that cry of horror which she had uttered, and the eyes of that unfathomable blue like the sea in the Bay of Genoa, fixed upon him with puzzlement not unmixed with awe.

The vision cleared and he became conscious that it was reality. He heard M. de Courson saying with a sigh of relief: "Fernande, thank God! you came just in time." He saw the exquisite apparition hurrying to Laurent and helping him to rise. Never in all his life had he seen anything so ethereal and so pure—and suddenly he became conscious of himself—of his rough clothes and his stained hands; he could have called to the inanimate objects in the room to close in upon him and to bury him out of sight. Like a wild animal at bay, he gave a rapid furtive glance around; his eye alighted on the bit of red ribbon which a boy's impious hand had torn from his breast. This he picked up, swiftly, stealthily; then holding it tightly in his clenched hand, he turned without another word, without another look, and fled precipitately from the room.

CHAPTER V THE SPRINGTIME OF THE YEAR

I

An hour later Mme. la Marquise de Mortain had been put in possession of all the facts which related to Ronnay de Maurel's quarrel with his brother and of his hasty exit from the château. Laurent had recovered from his sudden access of madness, and was not a little ashamed that Fernande had seen him at the very height of his outburst of fury against his brother, when fratricide was in his eye and in his uplifted hand. M. de Courson preserved a non-committal attitude. He was bound to maintain that de Maurel had been unduly provoked, yet owned that he was guilty of a grave social solecism in wearing the badge of the usurper in the house of his kinsfolk who were loyal adherents of the King. He thought the whole episode a grave pity, since it had undoubtedly jeopardized, if not entirely upset, every plan for ultimate conciliation.

"You promised me, Laurent," said Madame, with a frown of impatience, "that you would not quarrel with your brother."

"He exasperated me beyond endurance," retorted Laurent moodily, "and I consider that the manner in which he appeared here in Courson was an insult to us all."

It became very noticeable after a while that Fernande offered no opinion upon the brooding catastrophe which her timely interference alone had averted. At the midday meal, whilst every phase of the momentous interview with de Maurel was being discussed by the others, she remained strangely self-absorbed and silent. She was eating her dinner with a childish and hearty appetite, but whenever she sipped her wine, she looked over her glass and through the window opposite with eyes that seemed to dance with inward merriment and with elfish mischief, and whilst her father and her aunt talked and argued and conjectured, a whimsical smile played round the corners of her full, red lips.

40

"Something seems to have tickled your fancy, Fernande," said Laurent at last with some irritation, when on two separate occasions the young girl failed to reply to a direct question addressed to her by him.

"Something has," Fernande replied demurely.

"May we know what it is?" queried Mme. la Marquise. "The situation," she added tartly, "has become so grave for us all that, personally, I fail to detect any humour in it."

"That's just it, ma tante," rejoined Fernande gaily. "You fail to detect any humour in to-day's occurrence, so does father—so does Laurent. That is just what seems to me so ludicrous. The situation may be grave, but it is also very funny, and whilst you were all lamenting over it I was turning it over in my mind how best we can utilize it to our advantage."

"You are far too young, Fernande," interposed M. le Comte dryly, "to turn over any grave situation in your mind."

"Let us allow, then, that I have said nothing," retorted Fernande, with the same demure casting down of her eyes, which implied that a fund of worldly knowledge was concealed behind her smooth, white brow.

"Nay, my dear Baudouin," rejoined Mme. la Marquise sharply, "'tis like a father to belittle his own child's wisdom. I for one am over-ready to listen to advice wherever it may come from. I feel so guilty about the whole affair, for I fear me that we have gravely compromised the interests of His Majesty by quarrelling hopelessly with my son.

"I had made such firm resolutions," she added with a sigh, "to conciliate him, to make friends with him if possible. His help—or, failing that, his neutrality—would have been of such immense value to our cause. I had dreams of establishing myself at La Frontenay, of using the place as an arsenal—as headquarters for our leaders ... of suborning or winning over the workmen at the factory.... I am heart-broken at the thought that my own foolishness hath all in a moment destroyed my best laid schemes."

"Nay, ma tante," here broke in the young girl, with an elfish toss of her dainty head, "your schemes have not yet gone agley, that I can see. My cousin Ronnay—he is my cousin, is he not?—has of a truth departed hence in high dudgeon—but surely he can be brought back?"

"Never!" asserted M. de Courson emphatically.

And Mme. la Marquise shook her head. "No one can gauge the obstinate temper of a de Maurel—and Ronnay is the living image of his father. It was a delicate business to get him to come here at all. I declare that I am at my wits' ends how to bring him back."

For a moment or two Fernande de Courson was silent; a gentle glow suffused her cheeks, her eyes danced with mischief, her whole face was lit up with inward merriment.

"Will you let me try?" she asked suddenly.

"You, Fernande?" exclaimed Mme. la Marquise. "What in the world can you do in the matter?"

"Quite a great deal, ma tante," replied Fernande with that demure little air, which sat so quaintly upon her laughter-loving face.

"Ronnay de Maurel," here interposed M. de Courson, "is not bait for a feminine fisher. If you have thoughts of casting your nets in that direction, my child...."

"I for one would protest," broke in Laurent hotly.

"Protest against what?" queried the girl, and she turned wide, inquiring eyes on the young man, eyes in which injured innocence, unfettered mischief and provoking coquetry were alike expressed.

"Against your sowing seeds of hope of ... of ..." stammered Laurent with a scowl; "against your exercising your arts on that lout, who no doubt is filled with self-conceit, and might imagine things which...."

Fernande leaned back in her chair, and her rippling childlike laugh roused the echoes of the ancient walls around.

"Oh, you funny, jealous old Laurent!" she said breathlessly. Then seeing that the young man still looked morose and wrathful, she went on, with a quick turn to seriousness: "You are childish, my dear cousin. Let me begin by reminding you that your jealousy is not only unjustifiable but singularly out of place. The interests of His Majesty being at stake, it behoves us all to sharpen our wits by mature reflection, rather than to dull them by senseless outbursts of temper. Ma tante declared just now that M. de Maurel's wealth and influence would be of inestimable value to His Majesty, and yet owned that she was at her wits' ends how to bring him back repentant or reconciled to Courson. Well, where ma tante owns to having failed, I still believe in success; and though father says that I am too young to turn a grave situation over in my mind, I am convinced that I can turn the present one to our advantage."

"But how, my dear child?" sighed Madame dejectedly, "how?"

"I don't know yet," rejoined Fernande, "but I would dearly love to try."

"To try and do what?" queried Laurent, who was by no means mollified.

"To make the bear dance to my piping," replied Fernande archly.

"That is what I could never allow."

"If ma tante grant me leave," quoth Fernande dryly, "you, my dear cousin, will not be asked to give your consent."

"Fernande!" exclaimed the young man, in a tone of passionate reproach.

"There! there!" she said gently, "do not look so glum. It was you, remember, who talked of sowing seeds of hope in the impressionable field of M. de Maurel's fancy.... Father and tante Denise spoke of the necessity of making friends with that untamed bear, and I...."

"Yes? You, Fernande?" queried Laurent, his glowering eyes fixed moodily upon the exquisite face that smiled so tantalizingly upon him.

"I," she said lightly, "have no other wish save to bring back that same untamed bear to heel, and to make him pay his respects to ma tante; to bring him back to Courson, not once but often and willingly, until we are all the best of friends."

Then as her sally was greeted by a shrug of the shoulders from her father, a sigh of despondency from her aunt and a further scowl from Laurent, she continued more earnestly:

"Surely, if M. de Maurel's friendship is so important to the interests of His Majesty as ma tante and father think, it is worth while making an effort to gain it. No harm can come in trying. If I fail we shall be no worse off than we are now."

"You will fail, my dear," concluded Mme. la Marquise, with her usual authoritative decision. "You will fail. No de Maurel has yet succumbed to a woman's charm unless interest or obstinacy prepared him for the fall."

"Well, in this case obstinacy mayhap will prepare M. de Maurel for the fall. Laurent," added the young girl, turning once more to her cousin with merry, glowing blue eyes, "will you take me in a level bet that this day month Ronnay de Maurel will dance to my piping like a tamed bear? He will at my suggestion ask you and ma tante to take up your quarters at La Frontenay, he will close his eyes to everything that we don't wish him to see. His money and his influence will be at our disposal. With his help we'll dethrone that impudent Bonaparte whom at present he worships and who has dared to seat himself upon the throne of France, and we'll bring His Majesty King Louis XVIII. back to his own heritage again."

She rose to her feet, and with mock solemnity she held up her glass. "Long live Ronnay de Maurel!" she said, "by the grace of God and the machinations of Fernande de Courson the most loyal adherent His Majesty has ever had."

Then she placed her small white hand on Laurent's shoulder.

"I entreat you not to look so glum, dear cousin," she said, with that tender earnestness which at times lent to her dainty face an additional and contrasting charm. "Your own courage and loyalty will have their due; the courage and loyalty of all those who have sacrificed everything for King and country will have their just reward. But, remember, that the prospects of the cause which we all have so much at heart are none too rosy just now. We may despise Bonaparte for an usurper and impudent knight of industry, but we must grant that he is passing clever, and that he holds the allegiance of the nation at this moment in the hollow of his hand. We cannot go with flying banners

43

through the villages and towns of Normandy and rally enthusiastic recruits to our armies; we shall have to go very warily to work and meet cunning with cunning ere we succeed. We want M. de Maurel's wealth, we want his influence. You knew that this morning, dear Laurent; ma tante knew it and desired it passionately. Yet you both quarrelled with him within half an hour of his arrival here."

"He insulted my mother," broke in Laurent hotly. "He...."

"I know he did," she rejoined quietly. "He is a bear—one with a sore head and an ill temper. But even flies must needs be caught with honey. You all think me very babyish and stupid, I know! Father says that I am too young even to weigh a serious situation in my mind. Well, that may be so, I don't know. But childish instinct hath oft been a guiding star, where hoary-headed wisdom has groped in the dark, and in any case, there is no one in the whole of France who has the cause of our King more at heart than I have."

"We all know that, my child," said the Comte gravely; "it was far from me to impugn your loyalty."

"Only my wisdom—eh, father mine? But 'tis not wisdom that is required now. Wisdom has quarrelled with Ronnay de Maurel—guilelessness shall bring about the reconciliation. M. de Maurel's wealth shall be placed at the service of the King on the faith of Fernande de Courson!"

"God hear you, my child!" concluded Mme. la Marquise fervently.

II

After that the conversation drifted to other subjects. Laurent remained morose until the end of dinner and Fernande made no effort to cheer him up. In the late afternoon she wandered out into the open. The garden was a mere tangle of weeds and overgrown shrubs; there were neither lawns nor parterres, but it smelled good of fresh earth and spring rains, of wet young leaves and opening blossom.

Fernande had slipped a coarse gardening apron over her white gown and, gardening tools in hand, she set to work to disentangle a fragrant hedge of hawthorn and lilac from a mass of encroaching weeds. Despite the sorrowful outlook in her young life, despite the cares and heavy thoughts which weighed upon her father and her friends and kindred—almost despite herself—she felt singularly gay and elated. It was not the fashion to be merry in the circles of these émigrés who had just returned to their devastated homes, through the clemency of the Corsican usurper; tempers had to be sober and looks demure. The cause of the King had to be fought again; thoughts of danger, of conspiracy and self-sacrifice—aye! even of crime—all in a just cause—were in the air. Women, men, young girls and boys were prepared to shed the last drop of their blood in order to restore the Bourbons to their heritage, even though the nation had ceased to want them, and to oust from his self-constituted throne the soldier of fortune—the Emperor, who to many was still the little corporal, and who was the idol of France.

These aims were so high and so serious, that levity appeared out of place. Mme. la Marquise never smiled, M. de Courson was a pattern of seriousness, Laurent was ofttimes self-absorbed and always thoughtful, and Fernande—when her natural gaiety, her youth and healthful spirits caused inward laughter to bubble up and a song to rise to her throat—would take refuge in the tangled garden and share her joy in life with the birds.

She was fond of the solitude, the quietude of those avenues of limes, wherein the call of mating birds alone disturbed the silence that reigned around. Fernande was very young still—little more than a child, scarce out of the school-room, wherein the only lesson of life which she had learned was that of loyalty to a degenerate cause, of sacrifice to ideals and political aims which she really was far too inexperienced thoroughly to understand. Her heart was full of the aspirations of a healthy young being who sees life lying a rose-coloured dream stretched out before her, of a desire for a happiness at which she could only vaguely guess, for joy and gaiety, for poetry and for beauty. And it was full, too, of that vague longing for love which stirs the sensibilities of every woman the moment she steps across the threshold of childhood. But of this Fernande de Courson was no more conscious than is the rose-bud when it opens its sweet-scented corolla to the kiss of the sun. Ever since her fair curls had been dressed to the top of her head she had looked on Laurent de Mortain as her future husband. Never in so many words had she plighted her troth to him, but she knew that she loved him with a tenderness that no other emotion in her could surpass. He was so handsome, and his voice had a delicious tremor in it when he spoke her name. No other man had touched her heart as he did, no words of love spoken by other lips—and she had heard many—had caused the same delicious blush to rise to her cheeks. She was never so gay as when, hand in hand, with Laurent, she could wander through the peaceful lanes of Devonshire in far-off England, even though the shadow of poverty and of exile had already darkened her young life. She was never so happy as when Laurent sat or knelt beside her, and in impassioned tones spoke to her of the future, when the sombre cloud of anarchy and rebellion would be lifted from fair France, and he and she together would enjoy the delights of repatriation, of home and comfort and peace.

Yet in spite of all this, in spite of her deep love for Laurent and her delight in his company, Fernande on this late afternoon of early May was conscious of a slight feeling of impatience when she suddenly spied him coming towards her from the terrace. Her head was so full of exciting and riotous thoughts that she longed for solitude so that she might co-ordinate them. The project which she had so boldly formulated a while ago of bringing Ronnay de Maurel back to heel like a repentant cur, had of a certainty been the result of impulse, but not of a thoughtless one. It had its origin in the flash from his dark eyes as they met hers for one second across the uplifted arm of a would-be fratricide. During that one second Fernande, with that swift intuition which some women possess, had read each varying emotion as it became reflected in their depths: wrath, puzzlement, bewilderment— then that gradual softening of the sinister scowl, the changing hue of the orb from black to a deep violet, the look of self-consciousness and of shame. Fernande had seen the pathetic and furtive glance cast on the stained blouse and the toil-worn hands; she had seen the stealthy grasp of that bit of crimson ribbon, the one brief flash of pride wherewith the outraged soldier clasped the insignia of glory to his breast.

And from out that one peep into a man's troubled soul Fernande had woven her project of winning him to the cause which was so dear to her heart.

III

The project being still immature, Fernande had wandered out into the garden with the intention of thinking out its preliminary details; she was not attuned to Laurent's society just then. In her heart she knew that he disapproved of her plan; that his jealousy—which at all times was on the qui-vive—would flare up at the first bond of harmony which she would succeed in effecting with Ronnay de Maurel. Indeed, she would have need of all her sharp wits and her feminine wiles to bring the two brothers together again and yet to avert a quarrel more deadly than the first.

For the moment she was intent on her work, and not prepared to listen to Laurent's tender reproaches. The weeds were many, and despite the earliness of the year had already become rank. She had been humming a little ditty quietly to herself: "Et ron et ron! petit Pataplon! Il était une bergère!" But now, when she heard Laurent's footsteps on the path behind her, the song died upon her lips. She made pretence not to hear his coming, nor did she turn her head in his direction until he called her name:

46

"Fernande!"

Even then she appeared too busy to do more than respond quite calmly: "Yes, Laurent. Is that you?"

Then, as he remained silent, and seemed to have come to a halt immediately beside her, she continued serenely:

"I am sorry if you want me to come for a walk just now. I must finish clearing this piece of hedge. Will you go and get a hoe and lend me a helping hand?"

"I will in a moment," he replied, "but not just yet. I must speak to you, Fernande—just for a few minutes.... Will you turn to me and put down those tools a while? Upon my soul, it is passing serious ... Fernande!" he reiterated more earnestly, seeing that with strange obstinacy the young girl still kept her head resolutely bent to her work.

But at his insistence she threw down her tools and straightened her young figure. "What is it?" she queried as she faced him, with a mocking glance in her blue eyes.

He took her hand, which for just the space of a second she tried to free from his grasp.

"Fernande," he said in a tender tone of appeal, "you are not angry with me, are you?"

"Angry? You foolish Laurent!" she retorted gently. "Why should I be angry?"

"You did not mean all that you said at table?" he insisted.

"What did I say?"

"You implied by your words that ... that it was not within my rights to control your actions."

"Well," she asked, holding her tiny head a little to one side, and giving him an arch look of coquetry from beneath her long lashes, "is it?"

"Fernande," he entreated.

"Well, what is it?"

"You don't know how you hurt me, when you speak so flippantly. If you only knew how every word from your dear lips sinks into my heart! The cruel words make it ache so that I could cry out with the pain ... and one sweet word from you makes me so happy that I would not exchange this earth for the most glorious corner of paradise."

"Dear, foolish Laurent!" she sighed. Indeed, her heart was, as usual, inexpressibly touched by his ardour. She could see that his eyes were moist with unshed tears. She allowed him to take both her hands and to draw her nearer to him; she did not protest when anon his arm stole round her waist, and he buried his face against her shoulder. Indeed, she felt a wonderful fondness at this moment for the companion of her youth, the playmate of her childhood in the far-off days in England, when they were all poor and wretched together and had only each other to cling to, to trust, to look to for solace and for

47

sympathy. She felt his burning kiss upon her neck, and with her small hand she stroked his hair and patted his cheek with a tender, almost maternal gesture.

The day was fast drawing in. The softness of the night—of a spring night laden with the fragrance of opening buds and ripening blossom—wrapped the sweet tangle of young growth in its embrace. The lilac and the hawthorn were weighted with April rain, overhead the branches of a young lime quivered in the evening breeze ere it sent down a shower of scented drops upon the two young people who were clinging to one another in the pure embrace of budding love. The mating birds in the branches of the old elms had already gone to rest; from far away came the monotonous croaking of frogs and the soft call of the wood-pigeons from the tangled woodland close by.

"Fernande," reiterated Laurent with growing intensity, "you do love me, do you not?"

And nothing could have been more tender, nothing more serene than her reply, and the kiss wherewith she just touched his hair:

"Of course I love you, dear Laurent. You have so often asked me that. Why do you ask again?"

"Because I want to make sure of you, Fernande," he retorted vehemently, as both his arms closed round her now. "I want to make sure," he reiterated passionately. "I would give my soul to know what goes on behind that exquisite, white forehead of yours. Oh, of course you are a child: you don't understand—you cannot—the torture which the serenity of your blue eyes inflicts on me at moments like this, when I long to kiss you and yet feel that your sweet lips will not answer to mine with the same thrill of passion which has gone nigh to searing my soul."

"Dear Laurent," murmured Fernande with tender indulgence. She disengaged herself quite gently from his arms, and then coolly divested herself of her gardening apron.

"There," she said gaily, "it is too dark to go on weeding. We'll go for a walk, dear cousin, an you have a mind. Dear, foolish Laurent! I believe you are ready to cry! Why, on such a lovely spring evening as this I feel as if I could run singing and shouting through the woods! Come with me to the lake. I feel sure the fairy pigeons will be cooing to-night, and the white dove rise from its watery prison, never to be captured again. You know the legend, dear cousin, do you not? Old Matthieu told it me in his quaint, halting way. Come to the lake and I'll tell it you. Perhaps we'll see the white pigeon. If we do, it means that we have found lasting happiness...."

"More like we'll only hear the grey ones," he rejoined with a sigh. "Yes, I know the legend of the fairy pigeons—but they are not like to foretell happiness for any of us just now."

48

"Father is very anxious," she mused.

"So are we all. We are arming the countryside as fast as we can, but we have so little money ... so few opportunities for drilling the raw village lads in the use of arms, so little place wherein to keep our stores. Fouché's spies are everywhere. One does not know whom one can trust. Oh, if we had La Frontenay and Ronnay de Maurel's wealth at our disposal, King Louis would be back in France ere the leaves which are now unfolding have fallen from the trees."

"You shall have both. That is to be my affair."

"But...."

"Nay!" she broke in a little impatiently; "but methought you had the cause of our King at heart. Are you going to allow petty jealousy to stand in the way of success?"

"I would give my life for our cause, Fernande," he retorted firmly. "You know that. But," he added, with one of those sudden waves of passion which had the power through their very might to raise a responsive thrill in the young girl's heart, "God help me! I do believe that if I had to choose 'twixt my duty to my King and my love for you, I would forget everything for the sake of my love."

Darkness was closing in around them, and they wandered together through the broken-down monumental gates of the park, in the stone ornaments of which thrushes and finches had built their nests. An intoxicating scent of lilac was in the air; Laurent's arm was round his beloved, and she leaned against his shoulder. The gathering gloom lent him courage; he poured into Fernande's shell-like ear the full phial of his impassioned eloquence, and for once it seemed to him as if she responded with all the fervour of her young soul. The danger which encompassed him, the duty which he set out to fulfil, the spirit of self-sacrifice which caused him to give up a life of ease and of pleasure for stern adherence to his ideals—all helped to render him dear to Fernande; and when, leaving the park behind them, they wandered in the woods, where at their feet the dead leaves of yester year made a soft carpet whereon they walked, and where overhead soft, almost imperceptible twitter of birds proclaimed the spring of the year, Laurent suddenly raised her face to his and mutely asked for that first kiss which would transform a girl's tenderness into a woman's love.

She looked up into his eyes and thought him handsome and brave, and when his lips at last sought hers, she gave caress for caress with all the selflessness born of springtime, of youth, of a passionate yearning for happiness.

CHAPTER VI

THE LEGEND OF ST. FRONT

It all occurred when the world was very young indeed, and when knowledge and civilization had not yet penetrated to this far-off corner of romantic Normandy. In those days—oh, it was long before the house of Capet had ceased to reign in France—long before St. Louis had taught his subjects that spiritual power came from God alone—it was long before the noble lord Archbishop of Caen preached the First Crusade against the Turks—in those days then, there lived in what was then the hamlet of Villemor a man who was deeply versed in the sculptor's art. The tales of the country-side have it that he could fashion men and beasts out of stone with such marvellous skill, that none could distinguish God's own living work from that accomplished by this, one of His most humble creatures.

So clever, indeed, did he become in his art, that the priests and monks of the district became alarmed, fearing that this man's skill was instigated by the devil, and that unless something was done to exorcise Satan, that Spirit of Evil might take up his permanent abode in the hamlet of Villemor. One day the good Jean Front—such was the sculptor's name—carved from out a block of stone a group of pigeons; the birds were grouped around a fountain, and on the ground below could be seen the grains of maize wherewith an unseen hand had apparently been feeding them. So exquisite was this work, that those who were privileged to see it could almost have sworn that the birds moved along on their tiny feet, that they arched their graceful necks, pecked at the grains of maize and drank at the water of the fountain. Indeed, the pigeons appeared so alive, that many declared that they could hear them coo, and all vowed that they were ready to fly away.

Now the goodly Abbot of Villemor had no liking for such devilish arts; but he also was troubled by the sin of curiosity. Assembling the most learned monks of his order around him, he declared his intention of going forth into the hamlet, and of seeking out that mysterious artificer, whose fame was spreading beyond the confines of the fief. In state then, his gold-broidered mitre on his head, his staff in his hand, my lord Abbot sallied forth on a fine June morning to betake himself to the hamlet of Villemor. Behind him walked the Prior and other dignitaries of the Abbey, singing canticles and swinging censers, for, of a truth, the devils hate the smell of incense, which is the emblem of prayer when it rises straight up to God.

The legend goes on to say that my lord the Abbot was greatly shocked at sight of the sculptor's handiwork. There were the pigeons of a truth—feathers, feet, beaks, eyes and all—just the same as the Creator Himself would have fashioned them.

"So! Ho! Thou impious malapert!" or words to that effect, we are told, did the holy man hurl at the unfortunate craftsman. "Darest thou to fancy thyself the equal of thy Maker?"

Whereupon poor Jean Front seems vigorously to have protested that such sacrilegious thoughts had never entered his head, and that, on the contrary, his only desire was to dedicate his skill to the service of God.

But this humility wholly failed to satisfy the learned Abbot.

"Such skill as thou hast," he thundered in his holy wrath, "thou couldst not of thyself acquire. 'Tis the devil hath taught thee ... 'tis the devil hath given thee the strength to defy God by arrogating unto thyself the power to multiply the creatures of His hand!"

There appears to have ensued a somewhat lengthy argument between the noble Abbot and the humble artificer as to the provenance of that power which of a certainty passed comprehension. The Abbot maintained that such power could only come from the devil, seeing that it was, as it were, in direct competition with God, whilst the unfortunate sculptor maintained that God Himself had blessed his work and given him the skill to accomplish it. I imagine from the ancient story—which is far too long to set down here in its entirety—that the learned Abbot was distinctly getting the worst of the argument, when a brilliant idea occurred to him, wherewith he hoped, once for all, to confute the vainglory of this skilful braggart and save himself from the humiliation of being worsted in the wordy warfare.

"Prove to me," he said firmly, "that the devil hath had no hand in thy work. If God is on thy side, He will surely stand by thee in thy need, for, of a truth, if thou hast consorted with the devil, it will be my duty to see thy body burned at the stake in order that thy immortal soul may be saved from the fires of Hell!"

This was obviously a quandary for the poor village sculptor. But, according to the old legend, he seems to have been possessed of that faith which moveth mountains—or, rather, pigeons; for he then and there dropped on his knees and prayed fervently to God to give some sign that these stone pigeons had been fashioned for His glory. Whereupon we are told that the air, which up to now had been still, became stirred with a breath which was as the most balmy, most sweet-scented breeze from Heaven, and for miles around, though even the leaves of the aspen did not quiver, there was a sound as of myriads of wings, and all of a sudden the stone-pigeons fashioned by Jean Front the artificer spread out their wings and flew upwards from their stone pedestal. For a moment they circled round and round the head of their maker, then they rose up to the blue ether above, and took flight in the direction of the woods beyond La Frontenay.

The air became still once more. But the holy Abbot and all his monks had been vastly frightened by this manifestation. They declared more emphatically than ever before that this was devil's work, and then and there they seized upon the unfortunate sculptor, and having anathematized him and exorcised the devil out of him, they built up a stake in the market square and burned him to death.

But it is a recorded fact—one vouched for by many eye-witnesses, and who, indeed, would care to doubt it?—that at the very moment that poor Jean Front was put to torment, the pigeons, which up to now had been seen hovering above the trees, gliding through the summer air, their wings outspread, their feathers gleaming in the sunshine— suddenly fell, as if turned back to stone, with vertiginous rapidity into the silent pool which lies hidden in the woods of La Frontenay. And it is equally a fact, vouched for by equally reliable witnesses, that at the precise moment when poor Jean Front's soul fled from his martyred body, a snow-white pigeon flew out of his mouth, and spreading its wings, it, too, flew above the woods of La Frontenay and then fell straight into the pool.

So true is this, that the great Abbot and his monks returned to their monastery greatly perturbed, and that within the year the Abbot lay dying, his soul tortured with remorse at the wrong which he had done. So true is it, that ere he died that same holy man made a pilgrimage to Rome, and laid before His Holiness the Pope his testimony of the miracle performed by Jean Front, the sculptor of Villemor; so true, in fact, that the humble artificer became a canonized saint and performed many miracles every whit as marvellous as that of making pigeons which took unto themselves wings on that memorable day in June.

But ever after it was averred that all those who were threatened by some dire calamity, by grief or by death, would hear beside the silent pool of La Frontenay the pigeons of St. Front cooing softly from out the depths. It is also averred that if God, in His goodness, purposed to send lasting happiness to tread on the heels of sorrow, the white pigeon would rise from out the pool; it would spread its wings until they gleamed in the sunshine ere it took flight to the empyrean above.

CHAPTER VII THE SILENT POOL

I

The woods were unusually still. Not a sound broke the delicious hush which lay over this summer's morning, when Fernande de Courson made her way stealthily through the tangled undergrowth, avoiding the trodden paths and the clearings, flitting in and out among the trees like some young elf at play. The mischievous light which was scarcely ever wholly absent from her eyes was more apparent to-day than it had ever been before. She was wearing a white dress; her arms and shoulders were bare, and on her way she had gathered an armful of bluebells, there where they grew thickest with long stalks and giant bells, on the fringe of the wood.

It was still very early in the morning, so early that the bluebells were dripping with dew, and the sun came slanting in through the trees, making the vivid green of tiny elm and birch leaves gleam like emeralds and suffusing the gummy tips of the young chestnut with a vivid crimson glow. The carpet of last year's leaves made a soft swishing sound under the girl's feet; from the branches overhead the birds peeped down on the intruder with quaint inquisitiveness in their tiny, beady eyes, and now and then there would come a louder rustle, a murmur through the trees as a frightened squirrel hopped from bough to bough, fleeing at the approach of the human foe. But the human foe, clad all in white, and with the morning sun touching her fair curls with living gold, did not pause in order to gaze up at white-throat or finch; she did not hearken to the call of the mating linnet, nor did she watch the squirrels in their flight. She had heard something last night which had caused her to rise very early this morning and to start out for a walk in the woods, armed with a sheaf of bluebells and a very arsenal of feminine wiles.

A week had gone by since she had pledged her faith that she would make the untamed bear of La Vieuville dance to her piping. Since then she had quietly but with marvellous perseverance studied the ground whereon she desired to lay her trap for the catching of the unwary beast. During that week she had had to endure some ridicule from her father, a few gibes from her aunt, and renewed scowls from Laurent. But she was not to be deterred, and none of her kinsfolk—not even Laurent—had the least idea what was going on in that young head, nor what mischief was brewing behind the mocking glance of her blue eyes.

Fernande de Courson had spent that week trying to find out something definite about "the General's" habits and movements during the day. That had been an easy task. Anyone in the district could have told her that the hero of Austerlitz and Hohenlinden, and of a hundred other fights, toiled down from the Château of La Vieuville up on the height to his foundries in the valley below, every morning at seven o'clock, and returned home again every evening at nine. That he took a short cut across the fields between the edge of the wood and the foundry, walking rather slowly across the rough ground, and dragging his wounded leg slightly toward the end of his journey.

Any one could have told Fernande de Courson that Ronnay de Maurel could be found every day and all day, either in one of the workshops or else in the small office which he had fitted out for himself, and from whence he supervised the administration of his huge estate and of the works which supplied the Emperor's army with the material wherewith to conquer the world and subjugate the enemies of France. Any one, too, could have added that when "the General" was not at the foundry, he was sitting in the back kitchen of the Château of La Vieuville, trying to cheer in his rough way the monotonous hours of a confirmed invalid.

All these facts Fernande had learned in four-and-twenty hours. It took her a week to find out something more. That something was the fact that "the General" was mightily fond of shooting, and that during the winter he had often been seen with a gun on his shoulder and a dog at his heels, at break of day, roaming through the moors and forests of La Frontenay, dragging his wounded leg at the close of two or three hours' hard tramping, and often returning with a young deer slung across his shoulders, or a few snipe, or pheasant, or golden plover swinging round his belt. But in the springtime of the year, when the close season set in and the gun had to be laid aside, M. de Maurel did not discontinue his wanderings, and there were many who averred that at break of day "the General" could still be seen wending his way towards the woods, his dog at his heels, his breakfast in his wallet. People said that he was overfond of pushing as far as the silent pool, which was close to the boundary that separated the domain of La Frontenay from that of Courson.

"They say that his heart is always with the army," so Fernande's informer told her, "and that he goes daily to the silent pool, in order to listen if the pigeons of St. Front are cooing—for, indeed, 'tis a sure sign, Mademoiselle, that if the pigeons coo, great sorrow or disaster, or even death, awaits the one who hears them; and to the General sorrow and disaster to himself only means sorrow and disaster to the Emperor. They say that he sits for hours beside the pool, and if he does not hear the pigeons, he goes away satisfied."

It was in Villemor itself that Fernande had gleaned this information. She had driven in one day in Père Lebrun's carriole, sitting upon the pile of vegetables which he was taking into the town. Père Lebrun was a cultivator who owned a bit of land of his own whereon he grew cabbages which he sold when and how he could; he also owned an old nag and a broken-down carriole, and once a week— when the weather was propitious—he drove into Villemor—a matter of eight kilomètres—and combined pleasure with business, by going to see his sister, who lived in the village of La Vieuville, on the way to Villemor. This Fernande learned while she sat on the pile of Père Lebrun's cabbages. She had desired to be driven into the town for the sake of a few commissions which she had to do there; but thoughts of Ronnay de Maurel were never absent from her mind now, and as soon as the pointed roofs of La Vieuville came in sight, she led Père Lebrun to talk of the inmates of the old château. And Père Lebrun was as ready for gossip as is a peach to fall from the tree when it is ripe. One word set him going, and he had a great deal to tell of old M. Gaston's eccentricities and miserliness, as well as of "the General" and his queer, rough ways. But though he spoke much, he could only quote hearsay, and Fernande was waxing impatient, when Lebrun suddenly told her that his sister Adèle Lapin did the ménage daily at the château, and that all his information about the two eccentric dwellers thereof came from her.

Whereupon Fernande discovered that her commissions in the town would easily keep for another day, and, moreover, that riding in a carriole on the top of a pile of cabbages made her sick. She demanded to be put down at the door of Mme. Adèle Lapin, declaring that she would wait there until Père Lebrun had finished his business in Villemor and came to pick her up at his sister's house before driving back to Courson.

The result of this change of plans was a wealth of information gleaned from Mme. Adèle's voluble talk. She knew all about old M. Gaston, who, indeed, was very ill, and all about "the General," who was as savage, as morose and as shy as a bear. But Lapin, her husband, worked at a farm the other side of the La Frontenay woods, and when he went to his work at break of day, he nearly always met M. Ronnay tramping through the thickets, and once or twice he had seen him sitting beside the silent pool. Other people had seen him, too, and they said that he sat so still that undoubtedly he was listening for the cooing of the pigeons of St. Front.

And Fernande de Courson drove home that afternoon in Père Lebrun's carriole feeling like a soldier on the eve of battle. She hardly spoke to anyone the whole of that evening, and Laurent had serious cause to complain of her lack of responsiveness. She pleaded fatigue from her expedition and went early to bed. But the next morning she was up betimes and tramping soon after sunrise in the direction of the woods of La Frontenay.

II

Women have often, as a sex, been comprehensively accused of not being truthful—of being full of deceit or at best of guile. It is averred that women will stoop to ways and means for gaining their own ends which men will disdain to utilize for theirs. Be that as it may, this chronicle, not being a dissertation, nor yet an argument one way or the other, but a faithful transcription of events, it behoves us to say that Fernande de Courson did sprain her ankle just as she was skirting the silent pool and treading through the tangle of wild iris and budding

55

meadowsweet; also, that the sprain caused her acute agony; that the water of the pool looked deliciously cool and healing, and that she had no other thought at the back of her mind but the desire to alleviate the pain, when she took off her shoe and her stocking, soaked her handkerchief in the cold water and then laid it as a compress round her ankle.

To say that Ronnay de Maurel was at the time very far from her thoughts would perhaps be putting it a little too strongly; but he was far enough—shall we say?—from her immediate mental vision to cause her considerable surprise by his sudden appearance through the thicket, right in front of her, whilst she was reclining full length on a carpet of moss with the sheaf of bluebells held to her face and an impish glint of sunlight playing with the tendrils of her fair hair and with the tips of her bare toes.

Now de Maurel, had he seen her before she caught sight of him, would undoubtedly have beaten a precipitate retreat. But he was apt to walk along buried in his own thoughts—thoughts of Prussian or Italian campaigns for the most part—and seeing little but the dome of leaves above him, or the squirrels that ran away at his approach; nor did he expect to see anyone beside the pool. At times, certainly, a labourer or a charcoal burner, or a couple of children violet-poaching, would cross the small clearing at the far end of the water; but, as a rule, he had the place to himself, and loved it for its loneliness and its solitude.

Whilst Fernande not only did expect to see someone here, but after the pain in her foot had become easier, every one of her senses became on the alert to catch the sound of a footfall that might be drawing nigh. She heard the approach of a heavy footstep from quite a considerable distance; it was unmistakable, because of the slight dragging sound caused by one leg being weaker than the other.

She had only just the time to arrange her gown in its most becoming folds, to decide on the exact position of the sheaf of bluebells and of her outstretched arm, and to assure herself that the sunlight was, indeed, playing with her hair and with her toes in just the manner she desired.

Then she closed her eyes and waited.

There is nothing on earth more difficult or more tantalizing to do than to wait with eyes closed while something is going on around which one would give the world to see. Twenty times and more in the space of a few minutes did Fernande positively ache with the longing to open her eyes. She heard the heavy, unequal step approaching, she heard the smothered exclamation which proclaimed impatience at seeing someone in possession of the lonely spot ... she heard the stealthy approach of her quarry—the pause not a step or two away from her, and almost felt the hot breath which came and went from his nostrils as he stooped in order to look at her.

But she had the strength of mind to wait until she was quite sure

56

that dark, scowling, inquiring eyes were close to her face; then she opened her own.

At once the man drew himself up and retreated as if the glance from those blue eyes had struck him in the face. Yet there was nothing very formidable in the pathetic, white-clad figure reclining there upon the moss, and with its poor injured foot swathed in a half-dried bit of gossamer rag. Fernande watched the retreating ogre until he had fairly turned to go; then she said in a quaking voice, and with a sigh that would have rent a heart of stone:

"Oh, I'm in such pain!"

Then she closed her eyes again.

There was a pause, during which even birds and squirrels seemed to have passed the word "Silence!" round. Only a slight flutter among the young leaves overhead disturbed the perfect stillness of this fateful moment. Fernande's entire hope of success rested on the efficacy of her last heartrending appeal.

For a second or two the ogre appeared to hesitate. Then a halting voice broke the spell of expectancy which had fallen over the woods.

"Can I be of any help?"

And the dragging, heavy footstep was once more audible as it approached quite close to her. Again Fernande sighed, more woefully than before.

"Alas!" she moaned, "I am utterly helpless. But...."

She raised herself upon her elbow, looked round her in perfect bewilderment, passed her hand once or twice over her forehead, and finally made up her mind to allow her blue eyes to rest on de Maurel.

"M. de Maurel!" she murmured, with the most profound astonishment that human voice can possibly express.

"Mademoiselle," he responded with obvious embarrassment, "I chanced to be passing by.... You seem to be in pain.... Is there aught that I can do?"

"There is, Monsieur," she replied unblushingly. "I fear that I have broken my ankle. I am in great pain, and very far from home. My name is Fernande de Courson...."

"I know that, Mademoiselle," he broke in simply.

"We are cousins," she suggested demurely.

"At your service."

"Then I pray you help me to get up."

Had Ronnay de Maurel been asked to hoist up on his shoulder a cannon which weighed a couple of tons, he would have felt less puzzled how to proceed than he did now, when an exquisite thing which looked as if it might break at the slightest touch asked him to help her to raise herself from the ground.

He was, as usual, dressed in blouse and rough breeches. He had no cap on his head, and his feet were encased in heavy riding-boots. For a second or two he looked round him with pathetic helplessness, as if he expected the dwellers of the forest to come to his aid in this awful dilemma. But no one came, and the lovely creature, whose tiny bare foot looked like an exquisite flower, was appealing—oh, so piteously, for help!

"Alas, Monsieur!" she said, "an you'll not come to my assistance, I shall have to wait till some chance passer-by prove more full of pity than you. It is six kilomètres from here to the Château of Courson and I am breakfastless."

Her voice—the tone of which appeared to Ronnay de Maurel like the singing of a nightingale—broke in her plucky effort to keep back the tears of mortification and of pain. He suddenly felt like a brute to stand by and see her suffer so.

"I wish I could help you, Mademoiselle," he said tentatively, "but I am so clumsy, so rough. I should spoil your gown and...."

"Eh, mon cousin," she retorted, "I would sooner have a spoiled gown than remain here till noonday. Give me the support of your arm and I will try to raise myself. Perhaps, with the aid of your stick, I might then be able to hobble home."

Thus admonished, Ronnay de Maurel, stooping low, held out his arm, and the exquisite creature placed one tiny hand upon it, then coolly bade him hold the other. Mechanically he obeyed, thinking all the while that the lovely fingers—slender and velvety like the petals of a lily—would be crushed to pieces in his grasp.

But they remained unscathed, and every succeeding moment he felt her hold tightening upon his arm, whilst a delicious fragrance as of spring air laden with blossom seemed to come from her entire person, and the soft tendrils of her fair hair brushed against his cheek like a fairy's kiss.

"I don't think that I shall be able to walk," said Fernande ruefully, as she clung more firmly with both her hands to his arm.

"Will you try?" he suggested. "Lean on me and let me support you. Don't be afraid. Perhaps if you held the stick with one hand and...."

"And," she interposed decisively, in perfectly matter-of-fact tone, "if you will put your arm round my waist, I think that perhaps...."

He did as he was told, and felt the whole weight of her lissom body against his arm.

"There, now," she said, "if I can put my foot to the ground...."

She tried. But the movement wrung a cry of pain from her lips. She fell back against the broad shoulder which was so conveniently held for her support and leaned her head against it. She closed her eyes as if ready to swoon. De Maurel was ready to anathematize Heaven for perpetrating such wanton cruelty against a being so perfect and so frail.

A pair of blue eyes that were swimming in tears were turned dolefully up to him.

"I fear me that I shall have to remain breakfastless, after all," murmured Fernande, with lips that quivered like those of a child about to cry. "I pray you leave me, dear cousin. You cannot afford to waste your time over the ailments of an insignificant person like me. Perhaps you may find some one in the village good enough to take a message over to my father by and by, asking him to send Père Lebrun's carriole hither. But oh! I pray you haste! I shall be so desperately hungry ere the carriole come."

"Mademoiselle Fernande," rejoined de Maurel earnestly, "you have, I've no doubt, every excuse for looking upon me as an ill-mannered cur, but none, I think, for imagining that I am an inhuman wretch. Nothing would induce me to leave you here ... in this lonely spot ... alone and in pain...."

"But how am I to get home, dear cousin?" she queried, darting a glance on him from under the fringe of her dark lashes that would have tantalized a saint.

"An you will grant me leave," he said simply, "I will carry you."

"Carry me?" she exclaimed. "Why, it is six kilomètres to the château!"

"If it were twenty I could carry you thither," he interposed with that quaint smile which was wont to lighten his stern face like sunshine on a troubled sea.

Strangely enough and quite unaccountably, Fernande felt a quick blush rising to her cheeks under the look which accompanied that smile.

"Why," he added simply, "you weigh less than a bird."

"Less than one of the pigeons of St. Front, perhaps," she retorted gaily.

"They were of stone," quoth he dryly.

"Ah! you know the legend, too?"

"Of course," he said. "I was born at La Frontenay."

"Have you ever heard the pigeons cooing, then?"

"Yes," he replied curtly. "Once."

"When was that?"

"The day," he said, "before an infernal bomb was hurled by an assassin at Napoleon Bonaparte, the idol of France, and his precious life was only saved by a miracle."

Fernande had been leaning with both hands upon de Maurel's arm all this while; but at these words, which he spoke with renewed roughness, she drew back quickly as if she had been stung. Strangely enough, she appeared quite able to stand on her injured foot now, and equally strangely he failed to notice this. For a second or two a look that was nothing short of hate crept into her eyes, and the flush which rose to her cheeks was one of hot anger and of defiance.

He did not flinch under her gaze, even though he would gladly have recalled the foolish speech which had escaped his lips and which obviously had wounded her. Indeed, he could not help but see that the allusion to the aborted conspiracy against the life of Bonaparte planned by the Royalists of Normandy had stung her pride to the quick, and already he was cursing himself for a clumsy lout, and trying to find in his limited vocabulary words wherewith to win her pardon.

But for the space of a few seconds, at any rate, he knew that she stood before him in avowed enmity, and Fernande had to close her eyes lest he should read in them that hatred and contempt which she felt and which she knew that she would always feel for this traitor to his King and to his caste. She had to force herself to remember the rôle which she had set herself to play, to force herself to think of this abominable regicide as a tool for furthering the very cause which he was now helping to crush; and there was a marvellous fund of energy and of enthusiasm lurking in the heart of this child—a marvellous power of duplicity and of self-control, there where her patriotism and her ideals guided her.

As she closed her eyes the hot flush fled from her cheeks, leaving them pale and transparent, and with a pearly shadow cast over them by the drooping fringe of her lashes.

"Mademoiselle Fernande," exclaimed de Maurel, overwhelmed with shame and contrition at his own brutality.

But already Fernande had recovered her self-possession; and even before the first words of abject self-abasement had passed his lips, she uttered a low moan of pain and tottered as if about to fall. She would have fallen—no doubt most gracefully—had not his arm proved to be once more so conveniently near.

"'Twas cruel, mon cousin," she murmured feebly, "to speak such words, whilst I am too weak to raise my voice in defence of those I love."

"Mademoiselle Fernande," he said appealingly, "I said just now that I had never given you cause to call me an inhuman wretch. Until a while ago I could have asserted on my soul that I had never been cruel to a woman in my life. Now you see me shamed beyond endurance. Will you believe me when I say that I would give twenty years of my life to unsay the thoughtless words I spoke just now? Mademoiselle Fernande, will you deign to forgive a poor wretch who hath never had a knowledge of soft words, but who would sooner have bitten out his tongue ere he uttered the senseless ones which have so justly angered you?"

Ronnay de Maurel's head was bent, in utter humility and remorse, while he spoke, or he could not have failed to note the look of triumph which shot out of the girl's eyes from beneath her half-closed lids, or the swift sigh of satisfaction which escaped her parted lips.

"We'll call those words unsaid, dear cousin," she said softly. "I know, alas! that between your political aims and our own there is an abyss of divergent ideals! You and your party have the power now—we are humbled and helpless—and must, therefore, rely on your generosity not to embitter the joy which we felt when we trod once again the soil of our beloved country, after years of poverty and of exile."

"Protestations would come ill from me," he murmured. "You would scorn them—and justly, too—after my unwarrantable transgression."

"You will have to be patient with us, mon cousin. We may have erred in the past, we may be foolish and misguided now, but you must try and remember always that every one of our actions is guided solely by our love of France—by the burning patriotism which helped us to endure exile and untold misery for the sake of our beliefs and of our aspirations. Mistaken we may be; but until you have heard the advocacy of our cause, I pray you do not judge us as harshly as you have obviously been led to do."

"Mademoiselle Fernande...."

"Nay, dear cousin, let us not dwell on that sad subject any longer. See! the sun is high in the heavens—the birds are singing a deafening anthem of joy ... and," she added archly, "I am still breakfastless."

Again de Maurel had to chide himself for a clumsy and selfish lout. For himself he would gladly have continued to dwell on the sad subject, seeing that it was being argued by an exquisite creature with the rosiest of lips and the most enthralling voice he had ever heard, even whilst she leaned her ethereal form against his arm, and cast an occasional look on him from out a pair of eyes as limpid and as blue as the sky. But the word "breakfastless" once more struck him with remorse. To think that this beautiful and diaphanous being could suffer hunger, discomfort, even pain, seemed to him the most monstrous outrage in the whole scheme of creation.

"God forgive me," he said, "for a thoughtless dolt. I was forgetting the flight of time. Now, Mademoiselle Fernande, if you will trust yourself to me...."

"Do you really mean," she queried, "that you will carry me all the way to Courson?"

"If you will let me."

She threw him a mute glance of gratitude, which somehow seemed to addle his brain in a manner which he thought strangely unaccountable, but not altogether unpleasant.

"Oh, my flowers!" she suddenly exclaimed ruefully. "I had taken such trouble to pick them!"

The sheaf of wild hyacinth was lying in a disordered mass of blue at her feet.

"Mon cousin, I pray you pick them up for me!" she added with a pretty tone of appeal.

At once he was down on his knees; it seemed practically impossible that he should disobey the slightest of her commands, and, mechanically, he gathered together the bunch of bluebells and handed it up to her. He was strangely awkward in the accomplishment of this

61

task, and when he looked up to her again, a mischievous light was dancing in her eyes.

"You think me a clumsy oaf, I'll warrant," he said, while that ghost of a smile which became him so well lit up his face in response. "'Tis the first time in my life I've waited on a lady, and...."

As she took the flowers from him her fingers closed for a moment over his hand.

"'Tis most gallantly you do it, Sir Knight," she said graciously.

She held the sheaf of flowers in both her arms and buried her face in the tangle of blue. It was amazing how little pain the sprained ankle was causing her at this moment; nothing more perfect or more graceful could be imagined than the picture which she presented, standing thus in her white gown beside the silent pool, with the spikes of the wild iris framing her knees, behind her a background of tender green and russet branches. Her broad-brimmed hat hung against her shoulder, and its black velvet ribbon, tied round her neck, enhanced still further the perfect whiteness of her throat.

"God's masterpiece, indeed!" thought Ronnay de Maurel, as, despite himself, his eyes would feast themselves on the exquisite apparition, wandering in rapt admiration from the golden crown of her fair hair to that tiny bare foot which stood half buried in a bed of moss.

Suddenly he perceived that her white dress was soiled, there where it had come in contact with the sleeve of his blouse. He could have cursed loudly in an agony of contrition, and in a moment a hot flush of intense mortification spread over his forehead. He would have given worlds to be able to strip off that horrible blouse before he ventured once more to touch that fragrant and delicate creature, whose airy white robe his work-stained hands had sullied. Unfortunately he was not certain whether his shirt was not in holes. Never in his life had Ronnay de Maurel felt so deeply shamed.

"I am afraid ... I ... I fear," he stammered, and looked down ruefully on his hands and blouse.

"That you have dirtied my frock," she broke in with a laugh. "Well, you know, dear cousin, that our meeting was impromptu, else, I am sure, you would have donned more suitable attire. Believe me, that in moments of pain an invalid takes no heed of a kind healer's clothes. Allons!" she added gaily, "will you carry me pick-a-back, or...."

"In my arms, if you will permit."

Indeed, he lifted her from the ground as if she were a weightless fairy or a bird.

"Will you deign to put one arm round my shoulder?" he said. "There! Is that comfortable?"

"Quite," she murmured, as she snuggled like a white kitten against him.

"You are not afraid?"

"Afraid?" she exclaimed. "Of what?"

To this query he made no reply, but started on his way. It was six kilomètres to Courson, through the woods first, and then across the fields. To Ronnay de Maurel ever afterwards it seemed as if the distance had been less than one. Leaving the pool on his right, he struck the footpath among the trees, treading softly and warily on the carpet of leaves and moss, lest his clumsy, dragging gait should cause her pain. She lay quite quiescent in his arms, holding the sheaf of bluebells so that it lay between her face and his. The dewy petals brushed against his cheek and mouth, and he was conscious of the delicious fragrance which filled his nostrils and of the cool dewdrops which moistened his lips. Her face he could not see, only the pellucid tendrils of her hair, as the soft breeze that murmured through the woods made them flutter in the sunshine. And he could see the little foot, half swathed in its gossamer bandage, each delicate toe so like the petal of a rose. He felt neither weight nor fatigue; he would have walked thus through life, thinking that it had suddenly become marvellously fair. Once or twice he asked her if she was comfortable, and she always answered: "Very comfortable, I thank you!" But she never asked him if he were fatigued. She knew that he was not. Once, when he put the question, he was not far from Courson, and the wood was already far behind, and through the veil of bluebells he could just see that her eyes were closed. He thought that she slept. From the earth close to his feet a lark rose, singing its joyous anthem, and fluttered upwards into the heavenly blue above.

III

It took Ronnay de Maurel two hours to reach the village of Courson. The château was half a kilomètre further on. Never had he cursed its circular, pointed roofs as heartily as he did to-day. He would have liked to push them to the outermost confines of the earth.

"Where are we now?" Fernande asked softly.

"Very near home," he replied.

"I must have been asleep."

"I hope you have."

"And you are not tired?"

"No, I am not tired," he said curtly.

All the while that he had tramped with his burden through the woods and across the fields, he had felt contented with only the squirrels and the birds around him to mock him for his heavy gait, his stained blouse and muddy boots. The sight of the first cottage of Courson suddenly took all the zest out of his spirit. Self-consciousness returned, and with it his full measure of wrath against his kinsfolk, whom of a truth he had no mind to meet again—not while his fatigue, of which he suddenly became conscious, and the additional mudstains on his clothes after the long tramp, placed him at such obvious disadvantage. Their presence, he felt, would jar upon his mood to a degree which he felt he could not endure.

Fernande, who had been silently watching him from behind the bunch of bluebells, saw the scowl which gradually gathered on his brow and chased away that strange rapt look and the sunny smile, which she had noted with such satisfaction every time that she contrived to catch a glimpse of his face. Her womanly instinct had been so unerring up to now, the success of her undertaking so assured, that she had no mind to mar it by a false move in the end.

"Mon cousin," she said suddenly, just as de Maurel, avoiding the main village street, had struck through an orchard and along a by-path, which led to a postern gate in the boundary wall of the château, "mon cousin, by your leave, an you'll take me as far as the Lodge, I could try and walk up the avenue to the château—alone."

"But there's no one at the Lodge," he said, "and the avenue is over long."

"Annette will be at the Lodge," she argued; "she goes thither every morning to air the rooms. The door will be open. I could slip in.... No one would see us...."

Now that she suggested just what he would have liked to do, he was ready with opposition.

"I should not like to leave you. You might be in pain again," he said.

"Oh, my ankle is much better! It has had two hours' rest. I can wait at the Lodge till Annette comes."

Mechanically he had obeyed, and turned back in the direction of the main gates of the park. The Lodge—a small stone pavilion—was just inside the gates.

"We don't want to be spied from the château, do we, mon cousin?" added the young girl, whilst a ripple of laughter, musical as the song of a lark, helped to chase away the last lingering remnant of de Maurel's moodiness. "Ma tante would be vastly shocked, for my hair is dishevelled, and my gown wet and stained. Laurent would be angry and father would scold...."

She paused and suddenly uttered an exclamation of dismay.

"Holy Virgin! what have I done?"

"What is it?" he asked. "Mademoiselle Fernande, what is it? Are you in pain?"

"No. No, it is not that. My foot is so much better ... but ... but...."

She seemed ready to cry, and just now he felt that he would curse loudly and long if he saw her in distress.

"In Heaven's name, Mademoiselle Fernande," he implored, "I entreat you to tell me what troubles you."

"My shoe and my stocking," she murmured in a weak, trembling voice. "I left them beside the pool."

Ronnay de Maurel literally gave a gasp of horror. A calamity such as this seemed to him to be beyond the confines of possibility.

"Beside the pool!" he exclaimed aghast. "Impossible!"

"How impossible?" she retorted impatiently. "I haven't my shoe and stocking on, have I?"

He took a peep at the bare, rosy toes, which vied in delicacy with the apple-blossom overhead.

"You certainly have not!" he replied.

"Well? And have you got them in your pocket, mon cousin?"

Sighing with regret, he vowed that he had not.

"Then I must have left them by the pool," she concluded.

"I'll go and fetch them," he said at once.

"And walk another dozen kilomètres to-day?"

"When shall I bring them?" was all that he said by way of rejoinder.

"Well, it will have to be soon ... that is if you really think that you wouldn't be too tired to go and fetch them.... But, you know, Mme. la Marquise is so rigid in the matter of decorum ... she will be so angry when she hears that I have lost my shoe ... and she will scold me ... and...."

We may take it that de Maurel was far too unversed in the usages of feminine amenities to notice how hopelessly the lovely creature in his arms was floundering in the mazes of her own rhetoric; he was obviously far too unsophisticated to suggest that if Mme. la Marquise was, indeed, so rigid in the matter of decorum, she would hardly approve of his walking in at Courson one day with her niece's shoe in one pocket and her stocking in the other. Just for a moment Fernande had a slight qualm of anxiety. She had engineered this final move in her campaign on the spur of the moment, and she had not had the time to think it out in detail. But, indeed, her fears were futile. De Maurel did not even notice the glaring discrepancy in the tale of Mme. la Marquise's supposed attitude towards the proprieties. As a matter of fact, the thought that Fernande should be scolded for having lost her stocking was so horrible, that his one idea now was a longing to get to the Lodge, to deposit his fair burden—if possible in Annette's charge—and then to start running at once, as fast as his wounded leg would allow—in search of the two precious articles.

The calamities which might overtake Fernande in the interval—her father's wrath, her aunt's reproaches—were so awful to contemplate, that poor Ronnay felt a cold sweat breaking out upon his forehead. Fortunately the incident did not weaken the power of his arms. He reached the Lodge without untoward accident; the gates, luckily, were open and there was no one about. Fernande declared that she was now not only able to stand, but also to hobble as far as the

Lodge parlour, and to sit quietly there until Annette arrived, when she would forthwith proceed to the château, where, no doubt, every one was devoured with anxiety about her.

How thankful was de Maurel that the park of Courson was so lonely and deserted. He would have hated it if prying eyes had been nigh when, with infinite precaution, he lowered his precious burden to the ground. It was terrible to see how he had crushed her gown, and, alas! the bluebells hung their tiny heads in a very drooping fashion.

"I thank you, mon cousin," she said, as leaning against the stone pillar of the porch she held out her hand to him. He knew quite well that he ought then to have taken that little hand, which was as white and delicate as a snowflake, and that he ought to have kissed the tips of those flower-like fingers. But had he not boasted a brief while ago that he did not know the art of kissing a lady's hand? This was so true, that at this moment, when he would have bartered his life for the pleasure of pressing his lips against that hand, he could only murmur a few meaningless and clumsy words. His whole bearing became awkward and ungainly; he was self-conscious, furious with himself, angered against that world which had shut him out from its reserved precincts.

He threw one quick look of appeal to the young girl, encountered her glance of indulgent mockery, muttered a hasty farewell, and then turned abruptly on his heel.

Fernande remained standing in the porch until the tall, massive figure with the curious, dragging gait had disappeared beyond the gates of the park; then—oh, shame! unblushing shame!—she executed a pirouette upon that sadly injured foot. She stretched out her arms with a gesture of triumph, and threw back her head, filling her lungs with the intoxicating air of this glorious spring morning. Her eyes were dancing with glee, the quick breath came and went through her full, parted lips, and there was a glow of excitement upon her cheeks.

IV

The paths were too rough for Fernande to attempt to go back shoeless to the château, so she waited in the porch, leaning against the pillar, in the same attitude wherein she had received de Maurel's final clumsy farewell; she waited with her own triumphal thoughts for company, for close on half an hour, when she suddenly spied Laurent walking briskly down the drive toward the Lodge.

She called to him and he uttered a cry of obvious relief.

"We were all getting so anxious," he shouted breathlessly, as soon as he was near enough to make himself heard. "It is nearly eleven o'clock. Matthieu said that he saw you walking through the orchard soon after daybreak. Where have you been, Fernande?"

"I went for a walk in the woods," she replied simply; "incidentally I sprained my ankle. Look!" she added, holding up her skirt and pointing her bare foot at him.

"Ye gods!"

"You are quite right there, Laurent," she said earnestly, "the gods had much to do with my sprained ankle. In fact, they have been busy with me all the morning."

"What do you mean?"

"I will tell you what I mean, as soon as I have a stocking and a shoe upon this foot—and not before. So if you are devoured with curiosity, my dear cousin, I pray you find Annette and tell her to bring me the wherewithal to clothe my injured foot with decency. It is getting blue with cold."

"Yes, yes!" he retorted. "I'll go immediately; but do tell me first, I entreat...."

"I'll tell you nothing till my foot is clad," she responded firmly.

Now Laurent de Mortain was pastmaster in the knowledge of feminine moods and caprices, wherein his elder brother was so woefully ignorant. He did not stop to argue the point. That something unusual had happened, besides the sprained ankle, was, of course, plainly writ on Fernande's glowing cheeks and in her glittering eyes; but that she did not mean to tell him anything about it for the present was equally plainly marked round the lines of her obstinate little mouth. Therefore, Laurent, with a shrug of his shoulders and a muttered: "As you will!" at once turned on his heel and walked rapidly back towards the château in obedience to his lady's commands.

And Fernande was once more left alone in the porch of the Lodge, gazing after the retreating figure of a man. In this instance she could watch an elegant and graceful retreat—a springy gait, the knightly bearing of a well-groomed head. She could not help but compare the two brothers, greatly to the advantage of Laurent—vastly to the detriment of the uncouth creature whose stained and shabby blouse had soiled her white gown.

"I said that the bear would soon be dancing to my piping," she mused, "and he is standing on his hind legs now, ready to begin...."

"But," she added, and here her thoughts became confused and unruly, "the bear would not have gone to fetch Annette; he would have put his great strong arms round me and carried me to the château. And oh! how I should have hated him for it!" she concluded, with a little shudder as she smoothed out the creases in her muslin gown.

All that Fernande vouchsafed to say, once she was duly shod, was that the Château of Courson might expect the visit of M. le Comte de Maurel that self-same afternoon. Mme. la Marquise was incredulous and M. dc Courson angry. Laurent looked very glum and remained silent and morose all through dinner.

"Mais enfin, Fernande," he had asked a score of times, "what actually did happen?" And a score of times he had received the same answer: "Nothing has happened to anger you, dear cousin. I met M. de Maurel in the woods and suggested to him that he should renew his visit to us. To this suggestion meseemed that he agreed. He may come this afternoon ... but he is rude and obstinate ... so who can tell?"

When he pressed her for fuller explanations, she gave him a curt answer and a haughty little look, two things which poor Laurent never could bear patiently.

Mme. la Marquise thought that Fernande was over-confident. "Your wish is father to your thought, my child," she said. "Why should Ronnay come at your simple bidding?"

"I don't know why he should, ma tante," rejoined the young girl imperturbably, "but somehow I think that he will."

And in order to proclaim her faith in her own prophecy, she went and changed her soiled gown after dinner for an entirely fresh and very dainty one.

CHAPTER VIII

THE GENERAL

I

Mme. la Marquise's incredulity with regard to her niece's assertion lasted well into the afternoon. She could not bring herself to believe that de Maurel's hostile attitude towards all the inmates of Courson, which he had so steadily maintained since his first unfortunate visit, could have undergone such a material change in so short a time.

She had looked on Fernande's childish boasting as mere

nonsense, and during the past week had been eating out her heart in vain regret and remorse at her own folly, her own insentient pride, which had undoubtedly precipitated the catastrophe, and turned into an open feud what had, after all, only been a kind of skulking neutrality before. Mme. la Marquise was quite sure in her own mind that if she had been present throughout the interview between the two brothers, she would have known how to avert the quarrel. Once it had occurred, she felt that nothing would ever bridge it over. The short glimpse which she had that day of Ronnay de Maurel had told her plainly that he was, indeed, the son of his father—endowed with the same passionate and violent temperament and the same obstinacy. Some latent impulse—or perhaps mere idle curiosity, she thought—had prompted him to come the once. But unfortunately he had been made unwelcome, and Madame la Marquise knew that he would resent this most bitterly, and that he would prove as irreconcilable as her husband had been, as old Gaston de Maurel still was.

Was it likely, therefore, that he would surrender at a word from a mere girl, and come and eat that humble pie at Courson which was bound to be very distasteful to him? Madame thought not; and in this she proved herself as ignorant of male temperament as her son was of feminine wiles. But Fernande was so positive that M. de Maurel would come, that something of her confidence communicated itself to the others. Her appearance in a new frock of delicate muslin, with tiny puffed sleeves and the shortest of waists, the folds of her long skirt clinging very closely to her girlish figure, finally brought Madame's incredulity to an end, and though nothing was done this time in preparation of M. de Maurel's coming, the excitement which pervaded the château was none the less acute.

The weather continued to smile the whole afternoon. It had been the warmest day of the young year, and Madame—still pretending that she was not expecting her son—ordered Annette to bring some semblance of order in the vast circular veranda that overlooked the park. In olden days this veranda had been a favourite spot on warm afternoons; the view between the stone pillars right over the ornamental water and the English garden beyond was magnificent. In those days the flagged floor was covered with soft carpets, chairs and lounges stood around, with one or two card-tables and stands for wines or coffee. Now there were neither carpets nor lounges; a few garden seats of stout wood had alone survived the years of disrepair. But after Annette had scrubbed the floor and the chairs, after Madame had ordered a table or two to be brought out and light refreshments to be disposed on them, after she had spread a couple of gaily-coloured Paisley shawls—remnants of her own depleted wardrobe—over the seats, the place looked inviting enough, and nothing could spoil the view across the park, right over an apple orchard aglow with blossom to the distant wooded heights beyond.

Madame took her seat beside the coffee-urn, her knitting in her hand. M. de Courson, feeling unaccountably restless, joined her after a while, making pretence to read the Moniteur—a week old—which a courier from Paris had brought that morning. Soon afterwards Laurent and Fernande were seen coming round the ornamental water. They came up the stone steps to the veranda, Fernande's unconcerned prattle and her merry laugh raising the echoes of the old walls.

Laurent was moody, as he always was when his brother's name was so much as mentioned; but Fernande was in the highest possible spirits, even though she masked her gaiety behind a look of sober demureness.

Everyone's nerves were on the jar. The paper rattled in M. de Courson's hands; Madame's knitting needles clicked jerkily.

Laurent sat with his two hands tightly clasped between his knees, staring down most of the time at Fernande's little feet, which were stretched out before her. They were encased in a delicious pair of heelless black alpaca sandals, with satin ribbons criss-crossing over the instep and tied in a bow just above the ankle. Her fingers were busy with a delicate piece of embroidery, and she was expounding her views to Laurent on the subject of the rearing of chickens.

II

At half-past three Annette came rushing from the house on to the veranda.

"The General!" she cried excitedly. "He is just coming up the avenue. Matthieu sent me to ask if Mme. la Marquise will receive him."

Madame looked up from her work and turned cold, reproving eyes on worthy, perspiring Annette.

"The General?" she queried calmly. "I know no General in the King's army who is like to pay me a visit to-day."

Whereupon Annette, thus rebuked, was covered with confusion, from which it took her some time to recover.

"I beg a thousand pardons, Mme. la Marquise," she stammered ruefully, as she wiped her hot, red hands on her apron. "I have known the Gen—I mean M. de Maurel all these years, and ... I ... I was meaning that...."

"That what, my good woman?" asked Madame tartly.

She appeared very detached and haughty, but Fernande, who shot one of her keen, mischievous glances at her aunt from beneath her long lashes, noted with vast amusement that though Madame was not working for the moment, the knitting needles in her hands were clicking audibly one against the other.

70

"I mean, Madame la Marquise, that M. le Comte de Maurel is coming down the avenue," Annette was at last able to blurt out. "Will Mme. la Marquise receive him?"

"Of course I will receive M. le Comte," replied Madame with perfect dignity. "Tell Matthieu to show M. le Comte up here."

"Yes, Madame la Marquise," murmured Annette, who felt a little awed by the atmosphere of pomp which had so unaccountably descended on the old veranda and its inmates, and to which she—poor soul!—was wholly unaccustomed. "And Matthieu says, Madame la Marquise, what is he to do about the horse?"

"The horse?"

"The Gen ... I ... I mean M. le Comte is on horseback and the stable roof fell in six years ago."

"My good Annette," here interposed M. de Courson with marked irritability, "do not worry Madame la Marquise with such trifles. Surely Matthieu can look after a horse for an hour or so while a visitor pays his respects up here!"

"Well ... Matthieu says," muttered Annette, whose temper was none too equable at any time, "that he cannot come up and announce a visitor and look after a horse at one and the same time."

An exclamation of impatience came from Laurent as he rose from his seat.

"Why all this pother, I wonder?" he said. "I'll go and see after the man's horse. One of his own vanners, I suppose. He must look funny on horseback with that linen blouse of his flopping round him in the wind."

He crossed the veranda, ready to follow Annette. The worthy woman, having shrugged her fat shoulders and thrown up her hands with an expressive gesture of complete detachment from the doings of her betters, started to shuffle back the way she came. But before either she or Laurent had reached the wide glass portières which gave on the principal State apartments of the château, a firm tread, with a curious drag in it and accompanied by the click of spurs, was heard to cross the hall and then to resound on the parquet floor of the vast reception-room which led directly to the veranda.

"Too late, mon cousin," said Fernande in her tantalizingly demure way. "M. de Maurel has apparently been too impatient to await your welcome. He...."

She paused—the next words dying upon her lips—her hands poised in mid-air holding her work and the embroidery thread. Even she could not repress a slight gasp of astonishment as Ronnay de Maurel's tall figure appeared under the lintel of the door.

III

He wore the uniform of a General of Division in the army of the Emperor—the uniform which he had last worn at Austerlitz, and which he had since laid aside for the blue linen blouse. He carried his chapeau-bras under his arm, and there was, indeed, nothing visible now of the slouchy attire which had so offended against Madame la Marquise de Mortain's ideas of what was picturesque. The gorgeous uniform, though worn and patched, became the tall, massive figure admirably, and though the gold of collar and epaulettes was so tarnished that it looked almost black, and the cloth of tunic and breeches so faded that their original dark green colour was almost unrecognizable, they lent a certain barbaric splendour to this last descendant of an ancient lineage turned democrat from conviction and temperament. From out the tall, stiff collar, covered with tarnished gold, the neck rose erect and firm, and the shoulders were squared as on parade. Ronnay de Maurel had halted on the threshold, and with a rigid military salute had greeted the assembled company. Instinctively, and on the spur of the moment, M. de Courson had risen in order to greet the new-comer; he now advanced with hand extended. Madame la Marquise could scarce believe her eyes; a change had, indeed, come over the uncouth figure of a week ago. Her cold and quizzical eyes took in at a glance all that was fine and picturesque in her eldest son's demeanour. The gold-embroidered tunic pleased her, despite the stains on it caused by the grime and smoke of powder, and a quick look of compassion, which was almost furtive, so unwonted was it, crept into her grey eyes when they caught sight of the large stain and the obvious patch in the left leg of his breeches—there where the cloth had been torn away, when a bullet from the Austrian gun had laid this splendid soldier low.

As Ronnay came forward Madame rose slightly from her seat.

"It is a pleasure to see you, my son," she said graciously.

She gave him her hand, which he did not take. Obviously he did not see it, nor yet M. de Courson's kindly gesture. But he took Laurent's hand. The awkwardness which he felt was manifested in all his movements and in the few vague words of thanks which he uttered. Then suddenly Fernande's clear, young voice rang out merrily through the constrained atmosphere which de Maurel's appearance had produced on everyone present.

"Eh, mon cousin," she said gaily, "am I then so small or so insignificant that I alone am not worthy of your regard?"

She did not move from her seat, but this time de Maurel was not slow either in coming to her side or in taking the tiny hand which she held out to him. With a clumsy gesture, though without the slightest hesitation, he raised it to his lips. Laurent smothered an exclamation of

72

wrath; but into Madame la Marquise's cold, grey eyes there came a sudden light of satisfaction.

"Will you not sit down, my son?" she said, with a well-bred air of condescension. "I trust that you have come to pay us a nice long visit. My brother-in-law is no worse, I hope?"

She pointed to a chair which, though at some distance from Fernande, would afford the sitter a clear view of the charming picture which the girl presented. That something more than a mere casual rencontre had taken place between her eldest son and her niece she no longer doubted; the child went up in her estimation at once, for obviously she had played her cards well. Nothing would suit Madame la Marquise's plans better than that de Maurel should evince an ardent admiration for Fernande de Courson; and if that admiration warmed into love—well, so much the better for the cause of the King. The bear was certainly beginning to dance, thought Madame, whilst the smile of satisfaction lingered round her lips and her thoughts went off roaming in the realms of fancy. Laurent would have to console himself with a rich heiress for the loss of his charming fiancée. At best, Madame herself did not greatly favour the match. M. de Courson had not a sou wherewith to endow his daughter, and Madame la Marquise had oft expressed her doubts as to His Majesty—even when he came to his throne again—being ever rich enough to compensate all his loyal adherents for the losses which they had sustained. Laurent was so handsome, that any rich girl would only be too proud to regild his escutcheon for him in exchange for all the advantages which his gallant bearing and his sixteen quarterings would bestow upon her. Indeed, everything was shaping out for the best. Madame, while talking platitudes to de Maurel to which he only listened with half an ear, was able to note with practised eye every symptom of profound attention which he bestowed on the slightest word or movement from Fernande.

In her mind she had already appraised the enormous advantages that would accrue to the King's cause if a marriage between a de Courson and this wealthy adherent of Bonaparte could be effected. Madame la Marquise de Mortain belonged to a generation which had often seen petticoat government ruling the destinies of nations. And though—Ronnay being what he was, the true son of his father, and having perhaps inherited his father's temperament as well as his democratic ideals—she could not fail to appreciate the possibility of a de Courson once again reducing a de Maurel to complete, if short-lived, slavery.

IV

"You have not suffered from the result of your accident, Mademoiselle Fernande?"

"Not at all, mon cousin, I thank you."

A pause. Then a pair of blue eyes were once more raised from what seemed very absorbing work.

"The woods round La Frontenay are very beautiful, mon cousin."

"Very beautiful, Mademoiselle."

"I had never visited the silent pool in the early morning before."

Another pause, necessitated by an intricate stitch in the embroidery.

"The silent pool is a very romantic spot, do you not think so, mon cousin?"

"I know so little about romance, Mademoiselle."

"The woods will teach you, mon cousin."

"I would be grateful."

"Laurent and I often wander in the woods—don't we, Laurent?"

Laurent, sitting on the edge of the stone balustrade, with his arms folded over his chest and a sinister scowl upon his face, did not vouchsafe an answer to the direct query.

"We have been as far as the silent pool," continued Fernande unconcernedly.

"It is a short walk from Courson," rejoined de Maurel.

"A very long one, I think ... over six kilomètres."

"Over six kilomètres.... Yes."

"Therefore, we have never been further than the pool."

Yet another pause. Madame la Marquise had resumed her knitting. M. de Courson tried not to appear ill at ease, and Laurent, whose exasperation became more and more obvious every moment, jumped down from the balustrade and began pacing up and down the veranda, hoping thereby to keep his nerves under control.

"But from the distance I have seen the smoke of your foundries, mon cousin," again resumed Fernande, wholly unperturbed.

"!!"

"I have never seen the interior of a foundry in my life."

"It is not a romantic sight, Mademoiselle."

"Oh, que si, mon cousin!" she retorted with sudden seriousness. "There is nothing more romantic than to see a man toiling with his body and with his brain, using his intelligence and the power which his mind has given him, in order to overcome the many difficulties which God has laid in his path, in face of the great natural advantages which He has assigned to His brute creation. And then to see hundreds of men all working together in the same way and for the same end—working in order to wrest from Nature her manifold secrets and enchain them in the service of Man. Oh, it must, indeed, be a very inspiring sight, and one I would dearly love to see!"

She had spoken with an air of quaint earnestness which became the spiritual aspect of her personality to perfection. De Maurel had listened to her with grave intentness, his brows knit together as if he was afraid to miss some hidden meaning in her words. Laurent, on the other hand, had found it difficult to contain himself while she delivered herself of her somewhat pompous little speech. Now before his brother could reply he broke in with a harsh laugh:

"An inspiring sight, mayhap, but also a mightily unpleasant smell. Smoke, grime, dirt," he added tartly, "mingled with perspiring humanity, make up a sum total of unpleasant odours which you, Fernande, would be the first to resent if my brother Ronnay were so foolish as to accede to your whim."

"You must leave me to judge, my dear Laurent," retorted Fernande, with one of her demure little pouts, "as to what I would resent and what not. Well, mon cousin," she added once more, turning to de Maurel, "you hear what Laurent says. Are you going to be sufficiently foolish to gratify my curiosity?"

"Nay, do not appeal to Ronnay, dear cousin," rejoined the young man testily. "He hath no liking for women's company. Rumour hath it that the foundries are encircled by a wall beyond which no feminine foot hath ever trod, and anxious wives are not even allowed to bring hard-working husbands their dinner. 'Tis said that all the jail-birds in France are employed in forging cannon and manufacturing gunpowder, and that the overseers have to stand over them with flails and loaded muskets, for fear that the spirit of insubordination which is always rampant should break into open riot, and the foundries of La Frontenay be blown up sky-high by rebellious hands."

De Maurel had waited with outward patience and in his own calm somewhat sullen way until his young brother had come to an end with his tirade; then he interposed curtly:

"Rumour hath lied as usual."

"You cannot deny, anyhow," retorted Laurent, "that all the deserters out of the army are made to slave in your factories."

"There are not enough deserters in the armies of France to keep a single foundry going," rejoined de Maurel simply. "But these days, when foreign enemies threaten the country on every side, we cannot afford to keep even jail-birds idle. So we employ them in the powder factory, where the work is hard and full of danger, and where accidents, alas! are frequent. But the pay is good, and men who have a crime upon their conscience can redeem their past by toiling for their country, who hath need of their brain and of their muscle. Many pass out of the workshops into the army, and the Emperor had no finer soldiers than a company of our jail-birds, as you call them, who fought under my command at Austerlitz."

75

He paused, for, as usual, every reference to the army and to his Emperor, whom he worshipped, was apt to stir his blood, so that his words became less sober and less measured. And he had come here this afternoon with the firm determination not to lose control over himself as he had done the other day.

"If Mademoiselle Fernande desires to see the foundry," he said quite quietly after a while, "I will accompany her and show her all that there is to see."

"If accidents in your works are frequent, my good Ronnay," rejoined Laurent, who was vainly trying to conceal the irritability of his nerves, "'tis obviously not fit that our cousin should visit them."

"I would not take her there where there is any danger," retorted de Maurel curtly.

"There is always danger for a refined woman in the propinquity of men who have been nurtured in class-hatred. The sight of a delicate and aristocratic girl is like to rouse the same resentment in your jail-birds that led to the atrocities of the Revolution. Fernande would certainly run the risk of insults, if not worse. I for one marvel at you, my dear brother, that you should think of exposing our cousin to the danger of hearing the blasphemous and obscene language which I am told is the only one spoken inside the foundries of La Frontenay."

"There is neither blasphemous nor obscene language spoken inside my workshops when I am present. If Mademoiselle Fernande deigns to entrust herself to my guidance, I'll pledge mine honour that she shall neither hear nor see a single thing that may offend her eyes or her ears."

"But, indeed, mon cousin, I am over-ready ..." began Fernande, when Madame la Marquise interposed in her wonted decisive way:

"Hoity-toity!" she said. "Here are you young people discussing projects which obviously cannot be put into execution without the consent of your elders. 'Tis I and my brother who alone can decide whether Fernande might go to visit the foundry or not. Nor hath M. le Comte Gaston been consulted as to his wishes in the matter."

"My uncle would raise no objections," said Ronnay moodily. "The inspection of the foundry is open to the public...."

"'Tis not a case of objections, my son," rejoined Madame with quiet condescension; "nor is your cousin Fernande to be classed among the public to whom casual permission might thus be given."

De Maurel frowned and that old look of churlish obstinacy once more crept into his face.

"I don't understand what you mean," he said.

"Yet 'tis simple enough, my good de Maurel," interposed M. de Courson in his turn. "There are certain usages of good society which forbid a young girl to go about alone in the company of a man other than her father or her brother."

"Surely you knew that?" queried Laurent ironically.

"No, I did not," replied de Maurel curtly. "Why should not Mademoiselle Fernande come with me to visit my foundries, if she desires to see them?"

"Because ... because ..." said Madame somewhat haltingly, obviously at a loss how to explain to this unsophisticated rustic the manners and usages of good society.

"I would see that she came to no harm."

"I am sure of that, mon cousin," quoth Fernande with a little sigh and a glance of complete understanding directed at de Maurel. "I should feel perfectly safe in your company."

"Fernande!" exclaimed Laurent hotly.

"There, you see?" she said, with a shrug of her pretty shoulders. "La jeune fille is a regular slave to a multiplicity of senseless conventions. Do not argue about it, mon cousin, it is quite useless. Ma tante will hurl the proprieties at your head till she has made you feel that you are a dangerous Don Juan, and unfit to be left alone in the company of an innocent young girl like me."

"Fernande!" This time the exclamation came from Madame la Marquise, and it was uttered in a tone of stern reproach.

"A thousand pardons, ma tante! please call my words unsaid. And you, mon cousin, I entreat take no heed of the sighings of a young captive chafing against her fetters. Indeed, I am a very happy slave and only resent my chain on rare occasions, when it is pulled more tightly than suits my fancy. Otherwise my gaolers are passing lenient, and I am given plenty of liberty, so long as I indulge in it alone; and when in the early morning I take my favourite walks in the woods, I am even allowed to wander as far as the silent pool and listen to the pigeons of St. Front, unattended by a chaperone."

Fernande, while she spoke, appeared deeply engrossed in disentangling a knot in her embroidery silk; this, no doubt, accounted for the fact that her words came somewhat jerkily, and with what seemed like deliberate slowness and emphasis. Laurent, lost in the whirl of his own jealousy, watched her less keenly than he was wont to do. Certainly he did not notice the glance which accompanied those words—a glance which de Maurel, on the other hand, did not fail to catch. It was directed at him, and was accompanied by an enigmatical little smile which he was not slow to interpret—so much guile had a pair of blue eyes already poured into the soul of this unsophisticated barbarian! Twenty-four hours ago he would have been intolerant of a young woman's diatribe on the subject of conventions, with which he had neither sympathy nor patience; to-day he heard in it certain tones which for him were full of meaning and of a vague promise.

The feeling, too, that this exquisite creature took him, as it were, into her confidence, that she implied—by that one glance of her blue eyes—that a secret understanding existed between her and him, was one that filled him with an extraordinary sense of happiness—of detachment from everything else around him—of walking on air, and of seeing the blue ether above him, open to show him a vision of intoxicating bliss.

V

The minutes after that went by leaden-footed. Ronnay de Maurel was longing to take his leave, to ride home as fast as he could, and in the privacy of his bare, uncomfortable room to think over every minute of this eventful day, and to anticipate as patiently as possible the hour when it might reasonably be supposed that an angel would take its morning walk abroad. Madame la Marquise made great efforts to keep the ball of conversation rolling pleasantly; but she found it difficult owing to the fact that de Maurel scarcely opened his lips again. Fernande, too, had become silent and tantalizingly demure. Her aunt thought that she was sulking owing to the veto put upon the proposed visit to the foundries. Madame would have wished to reopen that subject, for, of a truth, she would not have been altogether averse to going over to La Frontenay or La Vieuville, or even to bearding old Gaston de Maurel in his own lair; but Ronnay, after his one suggestion that he would take Fernande over the works, did not again renew his offer. Laurent, too, had become indescribably morose, and for once in her life Madame found it in her heart to be actually angry with her beloved son. Obviously the rapprochement with the de Maurels would be impossible if Laurent remained so persistently on the brink of a quarrel with his brother.

Though after a while Annette brought wine and biscuits on a tray, and M. de Courson and Madame la Marquise performed miracles of patience in trying to remain genial, the atmosphere became more and more constrained every moment.

Fortunately, after a while de Maurel appeared quite as eager to go as was his mother to be rid of him. He rose to take his leave, and beyond making a clumsy bow in the direction where Fernande was sitting, silent and industrious, he took no more intimate farewell of her than he did of the others. This had the effect of allaying in a slight measure Laurent's irritation. He even unbent to the extent of accompanying his brother to the gates of the château, an act of courtesy in which M. de Courson also joined.

But the moment that de Maurel's back was turned, and the steps of the three men had ceased to echo through the house, Fernande threw down her work and ran over to her aunt. She stood before the older woman, holding herself very erect, her little head held up with a remarkable air of dignity, her hands clasped behind her back.

"Ma tante, tell me," she said abruptly, "for, of a truth, I have become confused—which of the two things in life do you prize the most—the cause of our King or the fetish of social conventions?"

"Fernande," retorted Madame sternly, "meseems that for the past day or two you have taken leave of your senses. I will not be questioned in this fashion by a childlike you...."

"Ma tante," broke in the young girl solemnly, "I entreat you to believe that I am asking no idle question. I beg of you most earnestly to answer the question which I have put to you."

"The question hath no need of answer. It is answered already. And you, Fernande, are impertinent to put the question to me."

"Nevertheless, ma tante, I ask it in all seriousness, and I beg for an answer in the name of the cause which we all hold dear."

"If you put it that way, child," rejoined Madame coldly, "I cannot help but reply: you are foolish and impertinent, and I almost feel bemeaned by pandering to your foolishness."

"Ma tante," pleaded Fernande insistently.

"What is it you want me to say, enfin?"

"Tell me plainly and simply, ma tante, which you prize most: a few hollow conventions or the success of our arms in the cause of our King."

"Tush, child! of course you know that I prize the cause of our King above all else on earth."

"And you are ready to make any sacrifice for its success?"

"Of course I am! What nonsense has got into that childish head of yours, I wonder?"

"One moment, ma tante. Tell me one thing more."

"Well?"

"In your opinion, do you think that every one of us should be ready for any sacrifice that might help to further the cause of our King?"

"Of course, child. I trust you are prepared to make whatever sacrifice the cause of the King may demand from you. I know that your father is more than prepared, and so is Laurent."

"And so am I, ma tante," said Fernande firmly. "Therefore, one day soon I'll go to meet M. de Maurel in the woods of La Frontenay, and together we'll visit the Maurel foundries—all in the name of the King, ma tante."

CHAPTER IX

THE COOING OF THE PIGEONS

I

But it was close on a fortnight before Ronnay de Maurel saw Fernande again. He went every morning to the silent pool, soon after break of day, and every morning he waited for her until the sun was high in the heavens, and he was obliged to go back to his work. He spent his time in gazing into the pool or listening to the murmur of the woods. He knew the note of every bird, he knew where each tiny couple had built its nest; he watched the crimson tips of the young chestnut unfold and turn to bronze and then to green; he read every morning in the book which God hath laid out in springtime for every one of His creatures to read. He also spent a considerable amount of time in gazing at a silk stocking and a tiny sandal shoe, which happily he thought Fernande had forgotten to claim. He would draw these treasures from out the breast pocket of his blouse and hold them in his hands and toy with them, and gaze till a mist would come to his eyes and a curious, impatient sigh would come through his parted lips.

But he never tired while he lay in wait for the beautiful fairy-like creature who had so graciously intimated to him that one day she would come. It never occurred to him to give up waiting for her; that was not his nature. The same dogged obstinacy of the de Maurels, which had driven Denise de Courson well-nigh distraught, brought Ronnay daily to the spot where he knew that he must one day meet Fernande.

Often he would wax impatient and at times anxious, but never weary; nor did he ever lose hope. He would grow anxious when two days went by and he could glean no news of her; then perhaps that self-same afternoon he would tramp over after work as far as Courson and hear from one or other of the villagers that they had seen Mademoiselle walking to church or in the orchard, or else, mayhap, he himself would catch a glimpse of her through the gates of the park or in the carriole of Père Lebrun, and he would go home satisfied.

And he would wax impatient when the sun was specially bright overhead and glinted through the trees till every tender fibre of moss looked like a tiny emerald, and the wings of the dragon-flies glistened with myriads of iridescent colours as they skimmed the surface of the pool. Then he would long for Fernande with a longing which was akin to physical pain; he longed to point out to her the play of the sun upon the tender leaves of the alder, and show her just where the white-throats had built their nest.

Then one day the sun rose behind a veil of rain-clouds, and all morning the sky was overcast. It had rained heavily during the night, and a boisterous wind stirred the branches of the trees and shook down from them the cold showers of raindrops that had lingered on the leaves. De Maurel had started out later than usual. He had no hope of meeting Fernande on such a grey day, when the clouds overhead still threatened and no gleam of sunshine came to cheer.

Yet this was the very day which she had selected for her walk in the wood. He saw her the moment he reached the clearing. She was moving slowly between the trees towards the pool. She had thrown a shawl over her shoulders and a hood over her hair; from between its folds her fair young face peeped out somewhat sober and demure.

Directly she saw him she gave a little cry of surprise and held out her hand to him.

"'Tis strange to meet again, mon cousin," she said lightly, "and on such a day as this. Brr!" she added, with a little shiver as with the other hand she drew the shawl more closely round her shoulders, "I am perished with cold. It seems more like December than May."

She noticed, with a little smile of satisfaction, that he was not slow this time in taking her hand, or clumsy in raising it to his lips.

"From what you said, Mademoiselle Fernande," he said in his abrupt way, "I knew that you would come one morning. Was I like to stay away?"

"From what I said?" she retorted with perfect surprise. "Why! What did I say, mon cousin?"

His direct and searching look brought a hot flush to her cheeks. Yet she did not know why she should blush, and was greatly angered with herself for letting him see that she was, of a truth, covered with confusion.

"Ma tante gave me leave to visit the foundries of La Frontenay," she said, with a quaint assumption of dignity, "so I came this morning, thinking, mayhap, that you would remember your promise to conduct me round the workshops ... and that perchance I might meet you here."

"I came here every morning for the past fortnight," he rejoined simply. "I hoped that you would come."

"I had to wait," she said unblushingly, "till ma tante gave me leave."

"I am sorry," he said curtly.

"Sorry? Why?"

"I loved the idea of meeting you here ... in secret ... unknown to any one...."

For some reason which she could not have accounted for, this—his first really bold speech—angered her, and she retorted coldly:

"I would not have come at all, if Laurent had not approved."

"Ah! It was Laurent then who gave you leave?"

"Yes," she replied, "it was Laurent."

Somehow she felt strangely out of tune this morning, and wished heartily that she had not come. For one thing, she hated to see him in that odious blouse which he wore; it seemed to have the effect of making him, not only clumsy and loutish, but dictatorial and arrogant. The other afternoon, when he came to Courson, she had thought him passable—in a rough and picturesque way. The faded and tarnished uniform had lent, she grudgingly admitted, a certain look of grandeur to his fine physique. To-day he looked positively ugly—one of "the great unwashed," she thought, and despised him for a demagogue—he who bore one of the finest names in France.

"Are you prepared to come to the foundry this morning?" he asked abruptly.

For the moment she had a mind to say "No!" then remembered her folk at home and the boast she had made about taming this bear. It would have been passing foolish to give up the enterprise at the first check.

"Yes, I'll come," she said, as graciously as she felt able.

He, too, felt the constraint which seemed to stand like a solid wall between her and him, and in his rough, untutored way he was seized with a sudden, wild desire to pick her up again, as he had done that other morning a fortnight ago, and to carry her through the woods which were dripping wet with the rain. He wanted to carry her through the tangled undergrowth, so that her little feet brushed against the low branches of the trees, and caused them to send down a shower of cool drops over his head, which felt hot and aching all of a sudden, as if some unseen and heavy hand had dealt him a blow between the eyes.

The exquisite fairy of two sennights ago looked like a haughty and unapproachable woman to-day, sedate and grave, with that dark shawl folded primly round her shoulders, and the folds of her hood hiding her golden hair and casting a shadow over her limpid blue eyes.

"Will you not give me your arm, mon cousin?" she asked after a while, just as he was beginning to wonder whether he would not turn on his heel and run away as the simplest way out of his present misery. He looked at her—puzzled at the sudden graciousness of her mood, and then he encountered her blue eyes, from whence all sternness had vanished as swiftly as does a snowflake under the warm kiss of the sun. He held out his arm and she placed her hand on it.

For a brief moment their eyes met, with strange, inward questioning on both sides. Even she—Fernande—with all her hatred, all her contempt for this traitor to his King, this enemy to his kindred and his caste, could not help but feel that here was no ordinary man with whose passions and whose feelings she could toy with impunity. That subtle intuition which comes to every woman even before she has stepped over the threshold of childhood, had told her before now that Ronnay de Maurel's rough and unbridled nature had already been stirred to its depths by her beauty, and that he loved her at this moment with a love all the more ardent that he himself was as yet scarce conscious of its glow.

A sense of triumph chased all other thoughts from her mind. She had it in her power—she, Fernande de Courson, who had seen kindred, friends, her own father, driven to poverty and exile by the brutal excesses of these democrats—she had it in her power to bring this protagonist of those revolutionary ideals to humiliation and suffering. Not one spark of pity did she feel for the man who was doomed to suffer for her sake. That he would suffer—keenly, grievously—was plainly writ in those deep-set eyes of his which, she now noticed for the first time, were of that mysterious violet colour which reveals a passionate soul. It was writ, too, on that sensitive mouth round which the lines of pleasure and of pain were wont to chase one another so swiftly. Yes, he would suffer and at her hands—suffer quite as much, mayhap, as her father had suffered when he had to flee from his home at dead of night, leaving his one motherless baby to the care of a sister as helpless, as homeless as himself. He would suffer less, at any rate, than did the martyred Queen, when her royal husband was torn brutally from her arms by that revolutionary mob whose ideals Ronnay de Maurel would uphold.

It was, indeed, the law of reprisals which was pursuing its course with ruthless impartiality, and Fernande, with the fire of an ardent patriotism filling her entire soul, could not find a spark of pity for the enemy of her cause. She hated him as she never thought that she had it in her to hate any man; she longed for that freedom of thought and of action when she need no longer dissemble, when she need not endure the look of boundless admiration wherewith he dared to envelop her as with a caress, and when she could tell him to his face, the utter contempt, the hopeless loathing wherewith he inspired her.

The intensity of her feelings at the moment literally swept her off her feet. Her heart was so full that tears of self-pity welled up to her eyes; and he, seeing her tears, was clumsy enough to misinterpret them.

"Mademoiselle Fernande," he said, with a soft tone of entreaty in his rugged voice, "meseems that you are sad to-day. Will you not tell me if aught hath angered you, or caused you distress?"

Then, as she made no reply—for, of a truth, she felt that the next words which she uttered would choke her—he added more gruffly: "Will you believe me, I wonder, when I say that I would give my life to save you a moment's pain?"

She would have liked to withdraw her hand from his arm, for she was afraid that he would perceive how it trembled. But he held her close, and she felt too numbed to struggle. But he—poor wretch!—once again felt that wild, mad longing to pick her off the ground, and to carry her away—away out of this world of sordid quarrels and of strife, away to a land of which his ignorant, uneducated soul had only vaguely dreamed—a land where the trees were always of a tender green, wherein the mating birds sang a never-ending anthem—a land where there were no tears, no clouds, and wherein the sunlight danced for ever on the golden tendrils of her hair and the flower-like tips of her toes ... away to a lonely spot where only fairies and angels dwelt, and where he could lay her down on a bed of dewy moss and kiss away the tears that hung upon her lashes ... one by one.

And as with a sigh that came from the depths of his overfull heart, he made a motion to lead her away from this enchanted spot, wherein he had tasted the first bitter-sweet fruit of unending love, it seemed to him that from out the limpid mirror of the silent pool there came a call as of many living, breathing creatures in pain. The call rose and fell as if on the unseen bosom of gently lapping water, and overhead the tender branches of birch and chestnut whispered softly to one another, stirred by a newly-awakened breeze. Fernande, too, had paused—she, too, evidently had heard, for she turned inquiring, almost frightened eyes up at de Maurel. The call was so like the cooing of innumerable wood-pigeons—mournful, soul-stirring, and with a tender wail in it that spoke of sorrow, of heart-ache and of farewells.

"The pigeons of St. Front!" she murmured under her breath.

For a moment both stood still, until the melancholy plaint was wafted away on the wings of the wind. A strange feeling of awe had descended upon them. It seemed as if the Fates sitting in their eyrie far away had taken up the threads of their destiny, and were weaving and weaving, until their spindles came into a tangle which nothing but godlike hands could ever straighten out again.

"It was fancy, of course," said de Maurel after a while, seeing that Fernande had turned very white and that she clung with a pathetic unspoken appeal for support to his arm. "I have often heard this melancholy call when the wind stirred among the trees. 'Tis no wonder the poor folk of the country-side fly from this place in terror! There is something spectral in the sound."

"You don't believe," murmured Fernande, "you don't believe in the pigeons of St. Front?"

"What is there to believe in such an ancient legend?"

"That the cooing of the pigeons foretells disaster to those that hear it?"

"No," he replied decisively. "I do not believe it in this case, Mademoiselle Fernande. The world would be topsy-turvy, indeed, and God asleep in the heavens, if disaster were to overtake so perfect a creature as you."

She broke into a low, little laugh, which to a more sophisticated ear would have sounded mirthless and forced.

"Eh, mon cousin," she said, "you attribute to the world certain desires for my welfare which, of a truth, scarcely concern it, and God, I imagine, when He endowed us with free-will, left us to be the architects of our own destiny."

"With an overseer, mayhap," he added with earnest significance, "to watch over the safety of the building."

She chose to misinterpret his meaning and not to see the look which accompanied his words.

"Is it not time we went to the foundry?" she asked.

The spell was broken. Fernande de Courson became the self-possessed young woman of the world once more, and Ronnay de Maurel the clumsy rustic, who is greatly honoured by the condescension of a great lady infinitely above him in station. They turned away from the pool, which seemed more absolutely silent now that the cooing of the pigeons had been merged in the ceaseless murmurings of the woods. Fernande leaned on Ronnay's arm, and he guided her along the paths and through the clearings, walking silently by her side.

When they reached the open, he pointed to the left where the main country road wound its smooth ribbon at the foot of the distant hills. Here a small one-horsed vehicle was standing, some few metres away from the edge of the wood.

"It is another five or six kilomètres to the foundries from here, Mademoiselle," he said, "so every morning, always hoping that you would come, I ventured to order a carriole to await you here; one of our men will drive you by the road."

Fernande was conscious of a slight feeling of vexation. "But you, mon cousin?" she asked.

"I walk across the fields," he replied curtly, "they are ploughed and ankle-deep in mud; but I will be at the foundry in time to await your coming."

She had it on the tip of her tongue to demand that he should sit beside her in the carriole, or to insist on walking across the ploughed fields with him, but her pride would not permit her to do either. Perhaps, also, she thought that having been intermittently out of tune in the woods, an hour's jolting in a rickety carriole would shake away the cobwebs that clung persistently round her mood. The carriole proved to be of very modern build, high and comfortable; a perfect English cob—priceless in value these days—was in the shafts, looking a picture of gloss and experienced grooming. A young man in sombre livery coat sat with the reins in his hand.

De Maurel lifted Fernande into the vehicle, then stood by, giving a comprehensive glance to the turn-out with an obviously experienced and critical eye. Then, as the driver gave a click of the tongue and the cob started off at a smart trot, he turned brusquely on his heel, and Fernande for a long time could see his tall figure making its way, with its peculiar, halting gait, across the ploughed fields, till a group of trees that marked a homestead hid him from her view.

CHAPTER X

THE FOUNDRIES OF LA FRONTENAY

I

It was a strange experience for Fernande to see Ronnay de Maurel in the midst of the men who worked under his orders. Outwardly—by dress and appearance—one of themselves, there was obviously an inward force and authority in him which the workers readily recognized. Somehow her visit to the foundries discouraged and disappointed her. Not that Ronnay was in any way less under her sway than he had been in the romantic atmosphere of the woods. On the contrary, every time that her eyes met his, she read in them more and more clearly the progress which his passion for her was making in the subjugation of his will-power and of his senses; and every time that in the course of his demonstrations to her, of the various processes which went to the making of the "mouths of fire," his hand came in contact with hers, she could feel the tremor which went through him at her touch.

No, indeed! she had no cause to think that the untamed bear would not be ready to dance the moment she began to pipe; but here, in the foundries where he ruled as lord and master, where thousands of men obeyed at a word or sign from him, she first realized that between enslaving a man like de Maurel, through his passions or his sensibilities, to the chariot wheel of her beauty, and gaining a real mastery over his thoughts and actions, there was the immeasurable gulf of ingrained convictions and of the fetish of intellectual freedom.

That de Maurel was the real master in the foundries of La Frontenay Fernande could not doubt for a moment.

"Keep your eyes and ears open, child," Madame la Marquise had said to her, when she at last expressed reluctant approval of her niece's plan to visit the ogre in his lair. "We hear many rumours of discontent at the works—of insubordination—of open revolt. It would serve an abominable democrat like my son Ronnay right, if the proletariat which he upholds against his own traditions and his own caste were to turn against him now as they turned against us in '89. Keep your eyes and ears open, Fernande; the discontent of which we hear may prove a splendid card in our hands."

Fernande had not altogether understood what Madame la Marquise was driving at.

"Of what use can discontent among M. de Maurel's workmen be to us?" she had asked, wondering.

"If they were to turn against their master, my dear," quoth Madame dryly.

"Oh!"

"And rally round to us...."

"Do you think it likely, ma tante?"

"More than likely. Laurent and your father and I have a plan ..." said Madame with some hesitation; "we have put it before de Puisaye and our other leaders.... I can't speak of it just yet, child," she added somewhat impatiently, "but it is most important that you should keep your eyes and ears open to-day. We must reckon, remember, that King Mob, in whose name these execrable revolutionists have murdered their King and hundreds of innocent men, women and children, has felt the power of his own will. He has tasted the sweets of open revolt against constituted authority, and he has been given a free hand to murder, to pillage and to outrage. He is not likely to be so easily curbed again; he will rebel as he has rebelled before. His so-called Emperor has placed an iron heel upon his neck ... and Ronnay de Maurel and his like think that they can quench the flame of lawlessness which they themselves have kindled. Bah! methinks that it is King Mob who will avenge us all one day, by turning against the hands that first led him to strike against imaginary tyrants, and then forged the chains that made a slave of him."

And Fernande de Courson, as she wandered through the workshops of La Frontenay, thought of Madame la Marquise's impassioned tirade. How little revolt was there in these ordered places wherein men toiled and sweated in order that the Emperor might have all the cannons and powder he wanted wherewith to conquer the enemies of France! Here were no murmurings, no rebellion over authority; every man knew, as de Maurel passed him by and gave a look to the work in hand, that here was the master whose word and will must be law if all the toil, the patriotism, the enthusiasm which went to the making of these "mouths of fire" were to prove useful to the State.

The place was not picturesque. It was not inviting. The men, stripped to the waist, were covered with grime. But on their bearded faces they wore the same look of energy and of determination which glowed in the eyes of the soldiers who followed the young General Bonaparte over the Alps and across the Danube, through the snows of Poland and the sands of the desert from victory to victory. There was the same spirit—of that there could be no doubt—which had roused the whole nation to defend itself against the foreigners—the same spirit that made every man, woman and child, who could not fight the foe, toil in order to help subjugate him.

That de Maurel understood how to deal with the men was equally obvious. They evidently looked up to and trusted him, and Madame la Marquise's dream of seeing the proletariat turn against the hands that fed it would certainly not come true at La Frontenay.

Not that every cog-wheel of the gigantic machinery worked with equal smoothness. Though, for the most part, de Maurel's progress through his workshops was accompanied by looks of deference and at times of genuine affection and gratitude, there were murmurings, too. More than once Fernande caught the drift of a muttered complaint: "The heaviness of the toil, the unhealthy conditions, the dearness of food at home." De Maurel, however, had only one answer for all and sundry: "France," he said, and his ringing voice sounded above the din of hammers and heavy tools, above the roar of furnaces and bellows, "France has her back up against the wall, my men! the whole of Europe is up in arms against her! every one of her sons must either fight or toil till victory is assured. After that ... well ... toil will be less hard ... life more healthy ... food less dear!"

"My wife and children have not tasted meat for a month," retorted one man moodily.

"I have not tasted any for half a year," was de Maurel's cheerful reply. "My uncle and I up at La Vieuville live as you do down here; we toil as you do, suffer as much as you. When the Emperor hath brought the Prussian to his knees and compelled Austria to sue for peace, we'll all feast together ... and not before."

"'Tis dog's work sweating in front of these furnaces all the day ..." growled another man.

"Try sweating in front of the Prussian cannon, mon ami," retorted "the General," with a careless shrug of his broad shoulders.

He passed on and in his wake the murmurings somehow died down. He had a way with him, and he was so full of energy and breathed vitality from every pore to such a degree, that instinctively toil appeared lighter, and it seemed a humiliation to grumble.

It was only in the powder factory that the tempers of the men appeared of a different mettle.

II

The factory stood some little way from the smelting works. It was surrounded by a high wall, and its numerous sheds and imposing magazine, surmounted by a clock-tower, nestled at the foot of the hills some distance back from the road.

Mathurin, the chief overseer—a burly giant, who followed de Maurel's every movement with the look of a faithful watchdog—ventured to lay a restraining hand on his master's arm when he was told to lead the way to that more risky and dangerous portion of the great armament works.

"Leroux," he said, and there was a tone of anxiety in his gruff voice, "is in one of his most surly moods. He has given a deal of trouble lately."

"All the more reason why I should speak with him," retorted de Maurel.

"But the lady, mon général," rejoined Mathurin, as he indicated Fernande.

De Maurel turned to the young girl. "Would you care to wait, Mademoiselle Fernande," he asked, "till I have spoken to the recalcitrants? Mathurin will make you comfortable in his office...."

"Eh, mon cousin," she said boldly, with a toss of her pretty head, "are you thinking that I am afraid?"

"Indeed not, Mademoiselle," he rejoined; "nor would I allow you to enter the factory if there was the slightest cause for anxiety. But the men in there are rough; they are," he added with a harsh laugh, "the jail-birds for whom my brother Laurent hath such great contempt. They rebel against their work—and it is hard and dangerous work, I own—but the State hath need of it, and ... well, someone has to do it. But, of course, some of them hate their taskmaster, and I for one cannot altogether blame them."

"And," queried Fernande, "do they hate you, mon cousin?"

"Of course," he replied with a smile; "I am the taskmaster."

"But ... in that case ..." she hazarded, somewhat timidly this time, "are you not exposing yourself to unnecessary danger by...."

She hesitated, then paused abruptly, as he broke in with a loud laugh. "Danger!" he exclaimed. "I? In my own workshops? Why, I fought at Austerlitz, Mademoiselle."

She said nothing more, for already she was ashamed of her

89

sudden access of sensibility. Mathurin, once more ordered to lead the way to the factory, obeyed in silence.

No doubt that here the men wore a sullen and glowering aspect which had been wholly absent in the foundries. The risky nature of the work, when the slightest inattention or carelessness might cause the most terrible accident, the rank smell of the black carbon, of the saltpetre and sulphur, together with the dirt and the mud and the weight of the mortars, all seemed to produce an ill-effect upon the tempers of the men, and as de Maurel entered the first and most important workshed, the looks which greeted him and which swept over Fernande were furtive, if not openly hostile.

It was clear that muttered discontent was in the air, and as de Maurel went from one group to another of the workers, and either praised or criticized what was done, murmurings were only suppressed by the awe which his personality obviously inspired. Mathurin stuck close to his heels, and the look of faithful watch-dog became more marked on his large, ruddy face.

A word of severe blame from the master for grave contravention of rules set the spark to the smouldering fire of discontent. A short, thick-set man, with tousled red hair and tawny beard, on whom the blame had fallen, threw down his tool at de Maurel's feet.

"Blame? Blame?" he snarled, showing his yellow teeth like an ill-conditioned cur, "nothing but blame in this place of malediction. Are we beasts that we should be made to work and risk our lives for a tyranny that would make a slave of every free citizen?"

"You'll soon become a beast, mon ami," retorted de Maurel coolly, "if you refuse to work; a useless beast and a burden to the State, fit only to be cast into a ditch, or thrown as food for foreign cannon. Pick up your tool and show that you are a man and a free citizen by doing your duty for France."

"Not another stroke will I do," growled Leroux sullenly, "till I've eaten and drunk my fill, which I've not done these past twenty days. Not another stroke, do you hear? And if I lift that accursed tool again it will be to crack your skull with it! Do you hear, mon Général? I am under one sentence for murder already—another cannot do me much more harm. So look to yourself—what? for not another stroke of work will I do ... Foi de Paul Leroux."

"Then by all means go and eat and drink your fill, friend Leroux," rejoined de Maurel imperturbably; "go, and wait as leisurely as you please for the hour when the Emperor's orders send you to join your battalion in Poland. Never another stroke of work will you do in this factory, mon ami, but 'tis the Russian cannons who will eat their fill of you."

Then he turned to the overseer.

"Mathurin!" he called peremptorily.

"Yes, mon Général!"

"Give Leroux the money that is due to him. He is no longer in my employ."

"Name of a dog ..." came with an ominous imprecation from Leroux, "is this the way to treat an honest citizen?..."

"There is no honest citizen, my man," spoke de Maurel firmly, "save he who toils for France. Get you gone! Get you gone, I say! France has no use for slackers."

"You'll rue that, General, on my faith," here interposed one of Leroux' mates in tones that held an overt threat. "No one can finish this crushing save Leroux. If you dismiss him now, some of us go with him ... and the twelve hundred cannon-balls of this high calibre which the Emperor hath ordered will not be completed for want of a few skilled men."

"Those of you who wish to go," retorted de Maurel loudly, "can go hence at once, and to hell with the lot of you," he added, with a sudden outburst of contemptuous anger. "Have I not said that France hath no use for slackers? You grumblers! you miserable, dissatisfied curs! Go an you wish! The workshop stinks of your treachery!"

Then as some of the men, somewhat awed by his aspect and by the flame of unbridled wrath which shot from his glowing eyes, congregated in a little group of malcontents, egging one another on to more open revolt, he went close up to them, forcing the group to scatter before him, till he stood right in the midst of them, looking down from his great height on the skulking heads which were obstinately turned away from him and on the furtive glances which equally stubbornly avoided his own.

"You miserable cowards!" he exclaimed. "Have you no entrails, no hearts, no mind? When the sons of France—her true sons—bleed and die on the fields of Prussia and in the mountains of Italy—sometimes unfed, always ill-clothed, under a grilling sun or in snowstorms and blizzards—dragging half-shattered limbs up the precipitous heights of the Alps, or falling uncared for, unattended and unshriven, into the nearest ditch—when your brothers and your sons die for France with a 'Vive l'Empereur' upon their lips, with the unsullied flag held victorious in their dying hands, you murmur here because food is dear and work heavy! To hell, I say! to hell! Give me that, tool, Mathurin. The Emperor shall not lack for gunpowder because a few traitors refuse to toil for France!"

To Fernande, who watched this scene from a remote and dark angle of the workshop, to which she had crept on tiptoe, terrified lest her presence be noticed and considered an outrage in the midst of these turbulent quarrels—to Fernande, it seemed as if the whole personality of de Maurel had undergone an awesome change. There was something almost supernatural in that huge, massive figure with the proud head thrown back, the face lit up by the grey light which came through the skylight above.

Then suddenly, with a quick, impatient gesture, he cast off his blouse and shirt and stood there in the midst of the sullen and threatening crowd—a workman among his kindred—a man amongst men; stripped to the waist as they were, with huge, powerful torso bare, and massive arms whereon the muscles stood out as if carved in stone, as he lifted from the floor the enormous iron pestle which Leroux had flung down, and wielded it as if it were a stick. And Fernande bethought herself of all the mythological heroes of old of which she had read as a child in her story-books; of men who were as strong and mighty as the gods; of those who defied Jupiter and Mars and dared to look into the sun, or to enslave the hidden forces of the earth to their will.

For a while Leroux and the others looked on "the General" with shifty eyes wherein hatred and murder had kindled an ill-omened light. But in the mighty figure which towered above them there was not the slightest tremor of fear; in the commanding glance that met their own there was not a quiver and not the remotest sign of submission. The intrepid soldier, who at Austerlitz, bleeding, muddy, with leg shattered by a bullet, a sabre-slash across his forehead, a broken sword in his hand, had with two thousand men—some of them ex-jail-birds, as he said—held ten thousand Russians and their young Czar at bay, until the arrival of Rapp and his reinforcements, and then fell with shattered leg almost beneath the hoofs of the victorious cavalry still shouting: "Vive la France!"—he was not like to give in or to retreat before a few murderous threats from a sulky crowd of dissatisfied workmen. No, not though he knew that in the hip-pocket of more than one pair of breeches there was—always ready—the clasp-knife of the ex-jail-bird made to toil in the defence of the country which his crimes had outraged, and still at war with the authority which he had once defied. Rumour in this had not lied; it was with flails that some of these men were kept to their work—the flails of the mighty will-power of one man, of his burning patriotism and of his boundless energy. Even now his look of withering contempt, his open scorn of their threats, his appropriation of Leroux' tool and the skill and strength wherewith he wielded it, whipped them like a lash. In a moment Leroux, the leader of the malcontents, found himself alone, a hang-dog expression in his face, hatred still lurking in his narrow eyes, but subdued and held in submission by a power which he could not attack save by the united will of his mates.

"I'll finish my work," he muttered after a while.

"You'll do double shift at half-pay for ten days," said de Maurel, ere he handed him back his tool, "and one month in the black carbon factory for insubordination."

For a moment it looked as if the men would rebel again. A murmur went round the workshop.

"Another sound," said the General loudly and firmly, "and I send the lot of you back to rot in jail."

He threw Leroux' tool down and quietly struggled back into his shirt and blouse. The incident was obviously closed. A minute or two later the men were back at their work, with renewed energy, perhaps, certainly in perfect silence and discipline. Mathurin, the overseer, shrugged his shoulders as he conducted Fernande and "the General" out of the workshop.

"That means peace and quiet for a few weeks," he said gruffly, "but Leroux is a real malcontent, and gives me any amount of trouble. He was condemned to deportation for murder and arson—one of the worst characters we have in the place. I wouldn't trust that man, General...."

"He is a good workman," was de Maurel's only comment.

"A good workman? Yes," Mathurin admitted, "but he is always ready with his knife. We have had two or three affrays with him. He gave me a nasty cut on the forearm less than a week ago."

"You did not tell me."

"Why should I? The cut will heal all right."

"And I would have had the fellow thrashed like the cur he is," came with a harsh oath from de Maurel. "So no doubt you were wise not to tell me—good old Mathurin," he added, and placed his hand affectionately on the workman's shoulder.

"It would be better to have him sent elsewhere," suggested the overseer.

"No one would have him."

"Let him join the army. He is good fodder for Prussian cannon."

"A mischief-maker in the army is more dangerous than here at home. And if he is a skilled workman, the Emperor hath more need of him just now at La Frontenay than in Poland."

Mathurin was silent for a moment or two, then he muttered between his teeth:

"We ought to have a couple of military overseers here, as they have at Nevers and at Ruelle. The Minister of War is ready to send us help whenever we want it."

"Are we puling infants," rejoined de Maurel lightly, "that we want nurses to look after us? You must have a poor opinion of your employer, my good Mathurin, if you think he cannot keep a few recalcitrant workmen in order."

"No one can guard against a madman striking in the dark."

"If a madman chooses to strike at me in the dark," rejoined de Maurel coolly, "all the military representatives in the world could not ward off the blow."

"But...."

"Enough, my good friend," broke in the other, with a slight tone of impatience. "You know my feelings in the matter well enough. I do

93

not intend to have military overseers in my works, whilst I have the strength to look after them myself. When the Emperor allows me to rejoin the army I'll write to the Minister of War, for a couple of representatives to take my place during my absence ... but not before."

III

Then at last he turned to Fernande.

She had been terribly frightened at first, but the same magnetic power which had quelled the turbulent spirit of a pack of jail-birds had also acted on Fernande's overstrung nerves. Her fright had soon given way before the power and confidence which de Maurel's attitude inspired. In the same way as she had marvelled at his dealings with the workmen who were loyal, so did she render unwilling homage in her thoughts to his unflinching courage in the face of treachery. Perhaps she realized more completely than she had ever done before that here was a man whom it was easy enough to hate, but not one whom it was possible to despise. That she—Fernande—still hated him, she felt more than sure ... hated him for his rough ways, which had perhaps never been so apparent as now, when he tried to reassure her. His blouse was more stained and crumpled than ever. It had lain in the mud of the workshop, when he flung it away from him in a fit of passionate wrath. As for his hands, they were smeared with grime, and she could see that the sweat was pouring down from his forehead when with an impatient movement he brushed his thick, brown hair with his hand away from his brow.

"I am deeply grieved, Mademoiselle Fernande," he said in his unapt and halting way, "that your ears should have been offended and your eyes outraged by the sayings and doings of a pack of traitors. Meseems you will be able to regale your kinsfolk up at Courson with tales of the mutinous spirit of these unworthy soldiers of the Empire. I can hear my brother Laurent laughing his fill at your tale. Indeed, I know that I am to blame. I ought not to have brought you here. But Mathurin and I are passing proud of the work done by these men, and I wanted to show you what the spirit of patriotism will often do with fellows, whom my brother Laurent hath so scornfully dubbed my jail-birds. 'Twas unfortunate," he added with quaint shamefacedness, "that the rascals just chose to-day for breaking out in such senseless and childish revolt."

"Childish and senseless," Fernande said, with a contemptuous smile round her pretty lips; "you take things easily, by my faith!" Then she added earnestly: "Take care, mon cousin! one of them will kill you one day."

He turned brusquely to face her, and for a moment looked at her with a dark, puzzled frown between his eyes; then he asked abruptly: "Would you care if they did?"

She drew back suddenly, as if his strange and earnest query had hit her in the face. He did not withdraw his gaze from her, however—a curious, searching, intense gaze—which sent the blood coursing hotly through her veins in unbounded pride and anger. Indeed, for the moment she forget her rôle, forgot her foolish boast, her childish wager that she would bring this untamed ogre to his knees. For the first time now she felt appalled at the magnitude of a passion which she had wantonly kindled, and with the marvellous prodigality of youth—she would at this moment have bartered twenty years of her life to undo the mischief which she had already done. She felt like a sleep-walker who—suddenly awakened—sees a yawning abyss at his feet, and with a strange instinct of self-protection she put up her hands as if to ward off a threatened blow.

The gesture, and a vague look of fear in her eyes, sobered him quickly enough, and after a while he reiterated quite gently:

"Would you care, Mademoiselle Fernande?"

Fernande de Courson, young as she was, had a great fund of self-control and self-confidence, and already she had recovered from that sense of fear which had paralysed her for a moment and of which she was already heartily ashamed.

"Of course I would care, mon cousin," she replied coolly and with a forced little laugh. "Did you not care when our kinsfolk were murdered on the guillotine by a lot of insensate brutes? You are my kinsman, too! Surely you do not credit me with less sensibility than you or M. Gaston de Maurel possess?"

She had hit back boldly this time, and he was not quite so unsophisticated as not to know that she was punishing him for all the bitter words which he had spoken so freely—even in the woods, when her beauty and her helplessness ought to have put a curb upon his tongue. A hot flush rose to his brow, and a look of remorse, which seemed intensely pathetic and appealing, crept into his eyes. But Fernande, after her fright of a while ago, was in no mood for gentleness, and she responded to his mute prayer for forgiveness by a light, ironical laugh and a careless shrug of the shoulders.

Before she had time to speak again, however, good old Mathurin had intervened in a blundering fashion, which had the effect of adding more fuel to the smouldering flames of Fernande's wrath.

"Ah, Mademoiselle," he said, his voice quivering with emotion, "I would to God you could persuade the General not to expose himself alone in the midst of those hellhounds in there. As you say, one of them will be sticking a knife into him one day ... and...."

"Mathurin!" came in stern reproof from de Maurel.

But Mathurin had ventured too far now to draw back. He gave a shrug of his broad shoulders, as if to show that he was prepared to take all the consequences of his boldness. Worthy old Mathurin—who was wholly unversed in the ways of women—had an idea that in Fernande he had found an ally who would second him in his anxiety for his master.

"Mademoiselle," he went on, imperturbed by de Maurel's glowering look, "the General's life is too precious to be thrown to those dogs.... Mademoiselle ... if you love him...."

"Silence, Mathurin!" thundered de Maurel roughly, and this time he succeeded in stopping the flow of the worthy man's eloquence. Mathurin hung his head, looking shamed and sheepish.

"What have I said?" he queried ruefully.

"Nothing that you need be ashamed of, my good friend," said Fernande de Courson with gentle earnestness, "and I honour you for your devotion to your master. Indeed, he were well advised—I feel sure—to listen to your counsels." Then she turned to de Maurel and said coolly:

"Shall we go, mon cousin? My father and ma tante, not to speak of Laurent, will be desperately anxious if I do not return."

Once more it seemed as if between her and him some subtle sortilege had suddenly been broken. De Maurel felt as if he had been roughly wakened from a dream, wherein angels and demons had alternately soothed and teased him. His brother's name acted as a counter-charm upon his mood. In a moment he became constrained, halting in his speech, clumsy in his manner. His self-consciousness returned, and at the same time his delight in Fernande's company vanished. He thought that in the blue eyes which met his now so unconcernedly, he read mockery and contempt, as well as the indifference which had stung him a while ago, but which he had schooled himself in a measure to endure. Once again he felt hot shame of his ignorance, of his soiled blouse and grimy hands; and his shame and irritation were aggravated by the sting of suddenly awakened jealousy against the young and handsome brother, who even in absence appeared to exercise a sort of acknowledged mentorship over Fernande. He lost control over his temper and retorted with unwarrantable gruffness and worse discourtesy:

"Do not let me detain you, Mademoiselle," he said. "Mathurin will see you safely into the carriole, and the man will drive you to Courson as fast as the horse can trot. I would not like to be the innocent cause of my brother's anxiety. But I fear me," he added, "that you will carry away a very unpleasant impression of La Frontenay—the jail-birds have pecked at their keeper, eh? Well, if I have to dismiss some of them, they'll be available for the campaign of highway robbery and pillage which I hear the adherents of the dispossessed King have set on foot, in order to fill his coffers; and my brother Laurent will be satisfied, I hope."

Strangely enough, Fernande—proud, imperious, high-handed Fernande—felt all her anger against de Maurel suddenly melt away at his scornful tirade. Indeed, had he been less blind and more sophisticated, he could not have failed to notice the little smile of triumph which lit up her entire face as she listened to words which of a surety ought to have filled the measure of her wrath. There could be no doubt now that the bear was over-ready to dance whithersoever he was led, seeing that the mere mention of his brother's name had caused him to forget himself completely in this new feeling of jealousy, and to hit out senselessly in every direction. Well, thought Mademoiselle Fernande—and she drew a contented little sigh—he should suffer punishment for this outburst of temper—punishment far more severe than he had endured a while ago, for it would be accompanied by stinging remorse and a gnawing fear that forgiveness would never be granted to him again. With this thought of retributive justice in her mind, she allowed becoming tears to gather in her eyes and a slight tremor to veil her voice, as she drew herself up to her full height with stately dignity and said coldly:

"My cousin Laurent would, indeed, be satisfied if he saw me once more safely at Courson, where, though we are poor, and still, in a measure, strangers in our native land, we are at least not subjected to insult. My good Mathurin," she added, placing her small white hand on the grimy sleeve of the overseer, "I pray you escort me to the carriole. The heat and noise of the workshops have made me faint. I should be grateful for the support of your arm. Au revoir, mon cousin!" she said in conclusion, with a slight nod of her dainty head toward de Maurel, accompanied by a look of cold reproach. "Let us go, my good Mathurin!"

And before de Maurel had time to throw himself at her feet, as he, indeed, was longing to do, and to sue for pardon on his knees, weeping tears of blood for his brutality, she had sailed out of the workshop, with small head erect, her final glance turned deliberately away from him. And he remained there as if rooted to the spot, his heart aching with the bitterness of his remorse, gazing on the marks which her tiny heelless shoe had made upon the mud floor of the workshop, and longing with a mad and senseless aching of his whole heart to grovel on that floor and kiss each small footprint which was all that was left to him of her fragrant presence and the magic of her person.

CHAPTER XI

THE FIRST TRICK

I

It was over a week before Ronnay de Maurel dared venture as far as Courson in order to sue for pardon; and then mayhap he would not have gone, only that Madame la Marquise sent over repeatedly to La Vieuville, complaining of his want of attention to her and desiring his presence as soon as may be.

"'Tis hard, indeed," she said in one of her letters, "that when I thought I had found my son again, I should so soon lose him through no fault of mine own."

And at the end of another epistle she had added:

"I know everything, and pledge you my word that you need have no fear. Forgiveness is assured you."

It was a strange fact, and one of which de Maurel was in his heart mightily ashamed, that he did not speak to his uncle Gaston of his mother's letters, or of his own desire to go to Courson and obtain his pardon from the girl, the thought of whom now filled his entire soul. Of course, the invalid knew of Fernande's visit to the foundries; he knew of the incident that had occurred during the visit, and felt just strong enough to resent bitterly the fact that his workmen had shown their disloyalty in the presence of one of these "cursed Royalists."

But after that one serious attempt which he had made to keep Ronnay away from Courson, old Gaston de Maurel had not said another word on the subject; nevertheless, the keen insight which his fondness for his nephew gave him soon showed him the clue of what was in the wind.

"One of those satané de Coursons has got hold of the boy," he muttered to himself, "and God help him; for she'll make him suffer, as my dead brother suffered. God grant he does not break his heart over the wench."

He sent for Mathurin and questioned him. But Mathurin was not reassuring. He thought that the General did not seem to pay much court to the lady, but, on the other hand, he declared that the lady was very beautiful, and had tantalizing, blue eyes. Old Gaston was nearer scenting the trap that was being set for Ronnay than the latter was himself. But it is passing likely that even if Ronnay had been warned he would still have deliberately courted his destiny.

II

The last message which his mother sent him set his pulses on fire. He could not have kept away from Courson after that. Some strange instinct for which he despised himself, caused him to avoid the invalid's room after he had donned his uniform and made ready to start for Courson. He feared his uncle's gibes and his counsels of prudence, even though in his heart he knew that his uncle was right.

When he reached Courson he found his mother in a soft and tender mood; she and Fernande were sitting together under the trees in the garden. M. de Courson and Laurent had gone fishing, he was told, and the ladies professed themselves delighted at his company. Fernande said little, but her smile was kind, and she gave de Maurel her hand to kiss. She was sitting on a low stool beside her aunt, and now and then she shot a glance from her blue eyes at him—a glance which set him galloping once more to the land of dreams. But Madame la Marquise talked a great deal and with marked affection to her son, telling him something of her troubles, something of her anxieties about Laurent. She had no home, she said, for, of a truth, she could no longer live on the bounty of her brother. Laurent chafed at the thought of owing bread and board to his uncle.

De Maurel listened in silence to everything she said. Indeed, he was glad that his mother talked at such lengths. He would have sat here and listened for hours, all the while that he could watch Fernande, as she put in a word here and there, or made a movement to show her love and sympathy with her aunt. The sun came slanting in between the branches of the trees, and there was nothing in the world that Ronnay loved more than to watch the play of light upon Fernande's fair hair, or to see it creeping round the contour of her exquisite neck and shoulders, outlining their pearly hue with gold. When he went, he promised to come again the next day.

III

For the next fortnight he came nearly every day. Sometimes M. de Courson would be at home; sometimes—more seldom—Laurent would be there; but nearly always the two ladies would be alone, and Madame would talk about her troubles, and Ronnay de Maurel listened with half an ear, while his eyes followed Fernande's every movement.

Within a week he had offered to his mother and to Laurent his own Château of La Frontenay as a residence, and Madame la Marquise had graciously accepted the offer. It had been made because at the precise moment when de Maurel had his eyes fixed on Fernande, she had looked up at him, and Madame had said quite casually: "Fernande will make her home with me for the next few months while my brother and Laurent are away," and Fernande had added with a pathetic little sigh: "Is it not pitiable that ma tante has no home of her own, whilst you are so rich, mon cousin, and your château stands empty?"

By this time every counsel of wisdom and prudence spoken by Gaston de Maurel had long since been forgotten. Ronnay saw things through a pair of blue eyes, his thoughts only mirrored those which had their birth behind a smooth, white forehead and beneath a crown of golden hair.

To Laurent, however, his brother's daily visits at Courson were nothing short of martyrdom, and it took Madame la Marquise all her time and all her powers of persuasive eloquence to keep her younger son out of the way when de Maurel called. If by some mischance the brothers met, a quarrel was only averted by Madame's untiring tact and—it must be admitted—by Ronnay's own determination to avoid another scene which might hopelessly imperil the friendly footing which he had earned for himself in the house where dwelt his divinity.

That Ronnay de Maurel was by this time deeply in love with Fernande no one could fail to see. Madame la Marquise chose to pooh-pooh the idea only because she was afraid of Laurent's outbursts of jealousy, which would thwart all her carefully laid plans before she had put them into execution. Laurent, of a truth, was almost beside himself during these days; even though Fernande soothed his jealous temper with more soft words and more endearing ways than she had been wont to bestow on him in the past. Though the young man suffered acutely all the while that he knew de Maurel to be in Fernande's company, she very quickly sent him into paradise the moment the ogre was out of the way.

"I am working for King and country," the young girl would say, with a kind of dreamy exultation, whenever—after the departure of de Maurel—she had to endure one of Laurent's outbursts of insensate rage. "Think you that it is a pleasure to me to be in daily contact with such an odious creature? Bah! meseems when I speak with him that I can see the spectre of our martyred King and Queen calling to me to avenge them! Surely," she added reproachfully, "if I can endure the looks, the touch, the propinquity of the traitor, if I can bear the thought that he actually dares to sully me with his love, you, Laurent, might for the sake of our cause try to keep your unwarrantable jealousy in check."

"How can I?" exclaimed Laurent vehemently, "when I know that the man has dared to make love to you...."

"Nay, he has not yet done that, dear Laurent," broke in Fernande thoughtfully.

"But you mean to allow him to make love to you when the fancy seizes him!" he retorted angrily.

"Indeed I do. I have a wager on it with you. Have I not said that the bear would dance to my piping?"

"He doth that quite enough already. And I'll release you of that wager, Fernande."

Flushed with wrath, wretched with maddening jealousy, he drew nearer to the girl, and with a brusque movement seized her in his arms.

"Fernande," he cried, "you torture me...."

She looked up at him—there certainly was a look of acute suffering in his young face. She disengaged herself from his arms and said gently:

"Poor Laurent! If it were not that we have need of the man and that ma tante sets such great store by La Frontenay, I would turn my back on him for ever to-morrow."

But he was not satisfied, even though she had spoken with singular vehemence, and his misery wrung from him a last passionate appeal:

"You do not love him, Fernande?"

For a moment or two she stood quite still, her eyes fixed on the distance, far away where lay the woods of La Frontenay—a dark green patch on the lower slope of the hills; then she turned slowly and looked calmly into Laurent de Mortain's glowering eyes.

"I hate him," she replied.

IV

Madame la Marquise, on the other hand, encouraged Fernande with all her might. She was one of those fanatics in the Royalist cause who would stick at nothing in order to gain influence, men, money that would help toward ultimate success. In fact, she dreaded that Fernande was really only playing with de Maurel's love, and that she really meant to throw him over. In her heart she was hoping that the child could be persuaded to accept his attentions. As the wife of Ronnay de Maurel, the master of the foundries of La Frontenay, she could render incalculable services to the King. What was a girl's happiness worth, when weighed in the balance with the triumph of a sacred cause? But Madame was too shrewd a campaigner to show her hand to the enemy—the enemy in this case being both Laurent and M. de Courson.

The latter, of a truth, saw little of what went on, even though Laurent boldly tackled him one day on the subject.

"Fernande sees too much of Ronnay de Maurel, mon oncle," he said, when as usual he and M. de Courson were out of the way at the hour when de Maurel paid his visit to the ladies. "He pesters her with his attentions...."

M. de Courson shrugged his shoulders at the idea. "You are dreaming, my good Laurent," he said. "My sister would never allow Fernande to accept the attentions of one of that pestiferous crowd."

And when Laurent hotly pressed his point, M. de Courson had an indulgent smile for his vehemence.

"Your jealousy blinds you, my good Laurent," he said. "Fernande loves you and she is not a girl to change her feelings lightly. Just now she is coquetting with de Maurel because it is in all our interests to keep on friendly terms with him. We are beginning to organize our army; we shall be wanting money, arms, munitions, suitable headquarters. All these de Maurel can supply us with—if he remain friendly. Fernande has gained influence over him. Already he is less bitter when he speaks of the King. Let the child be, my good Laurent. There is no more enthusiastic patriot than our little Fernande. She vowed that she would make the Maurel bear dance to her piping. Let us not place any obstacles in the way of success."

"But, mon oncle," protested Laurent hotly, "our future happiness is at stake ... both Fernande's and mine ... and if my brother...."

"Ah, çà," broke in M. le Comte tartly, "are you insinuating, Monsieur my nephew, that my daughter is like to be untrue to her promise to you?"

"God forbid!"

"Then why all this pother, I pray you? Fernande knows just as well—and better than both of us—how far she can go with de Maurel. Her coquetry—I'll stake my oath on it—is harmless enough, nor would my sister countenance de Maurel's visits here if they erred against the proprieties."

But though M. de Courson refused to admit before Laurent that there was anything but the most harmless coquetry between his daughter and de Maurel, he, nevertheless, made up his mind then and there that he would talk seriously on the subject with Madame la Marquise.

This he did, and she soon succeeded in reassuring him. A little patience, she argued, and Ronnay would be definitely pledged to place La Frontenay at her disposal; after which Fernande need never see him again.

"I am going over there within the next few days in order to select the rooms which are to be got ready for me. I shall arrange it so that Vardenne, the chief bailiff, shall see me there, and hear Ronnay speak definitely of my future residence in the place. Once he has done that in front of Vardenne, it will be impossible for him to go back on his word. Moreover, Fernande will be with me, and Ronnay will say anything, promise anything, while I let him think that she will take up her abode at La Frontenay with me."

M. de Courson frowned. There is always a certain esprit de corps in the male sex, which is up in arms the moment one man sees that a feminine trap is being set for another.

"You are not playing a very dignified game there, Denise," he said.

"Bah!" she retorted. "Did those infamous revolutionists play a dignified game, I wonder? Is not everything fair in war—such war as we must wage—we who are poor and feeble, against the whole might of this mushroom Empire? Fernande is a true patriot. She is willing to be a pawn in the great game which we are about to play, and the stakes of which are the immortal crown and sceptre of St. Louis."

Then as she saw that M. de Courson still remained moody and silent, she said reassuringly:

"You must not fear for Fernande, my brother. If I have no fear for Laurent—and, believe me, I have none—then surely you may rest satisfied that the happiness of our children is not at stake."

V

That same afternoon de Maurel spoke of the woods and of the silent pool before Fernande. The warm summer mornings were exquisite there just now, he said; the water-lilies on the pool were in bud, and the sun glittered with myriads of colours on the iridescent wings of the dragon-flies. The mountain-ash was in full blossom and the white acacia filled the air with its fragrance. Fernande seemed to be listening with half an ear, but anon she said: "I will have to resume my early morning walks again some day. I have been lazy of late."

He took this to mean that she would come, and seemed quite unconscious of the fact that while Fernande spoke, Laurent had stood by with an unusually dark scowl upon his face.

But a whole month went by ere she came—a month during which Ronnay walked every morning in the woods, going as far as the silent pool, and there waiting on the chance of seeing her. It was a weary month for him, because matters at the armament works were going from bad to worse with the discontented workmen. Leroux, smarting under the punishment imposed upon him, worked hard to rally his

103

more unruly comrades around him. Exactly what it was the men wanted, even they would have found it difficult to say. They had been called to the colours and allowed to take on work in the powder factories, but they were amenable to military discipline. The fact that most of them had been let out of prison, in order to help supply the Emperor and his armies with their needs, should have made them more contented with their lot, even though that lot was not an easy one.

'Tis true that the hardest and most dangerous tasks were put upon them; hours of idleness were few, and they were not free to come and go, as were the other workmen in the foundry. They dwelt in compounds, always under supervision; those who had families were not allowed to live with them—the boys belonged to the State and were drilled for soldiers as soon as they were old enough; the girls were set to make clothes and shirts for the army as soon as they could handle a needle.

Leroux took for his main grievance this segregation of the men away from their families, choosing to remain oblivious of the fact that had he and his mates been serving their full term of imprisonment or been deported to New Caledonia, they would have been still more effectually separated from their wives and children. But he was able to talk impassioned rhetoric on the subject, and men are easily enough won over by the bait of a real or supposed grievance.

It took all de Maurel's energy to cope with the trouble, and it was only in the early morning, before work in the powder factory had properly begun, that he was able to absent himself from the works. He had to discontinue his afternoon visits to Courson, and in the hope of seeing Fernande again he could only rely on the vague words which she spoke the last time he saw her: "I will have to resume my early morning walks again some day."

While the trouble with his men filled his thoughts, he did not become a prey to that melancholy which was gnawing at his heart, when day after day went by and Fernande did not come. To a man of de Maurel's wilful and dictatorial temperament, the delay was positive torture, and it is quite likely that this constant jarring of his nerves, this aching desire for a sight of the woman whom he loved so passionately, tended to make him less lenient with Leroux and the malcontents.

He who throughout his administration of the great factory had always been in complete sympathy with every one of his workmen, found himself often now in complete disharmony with them— impatient of their complaints, severe in punishment, bitingly scornful in the face of threats. These had become more numerous and more violent of late. Mathurin and the other overseers, who were loyal to a man, went in fear and trembling for their master's life. And all the while old Gaston de Maurel was sinking. His life at times seemed literally to be hanging by a thread; at others he would rally, and with marvellous tenacity would refuse all medicaments and declare that he had still many years before him wherein to defeat the machinations of those Coursons whom he abhorred.

He knew quite well all that was going on; he knew that his nephew had started on that pilgrimage of suffering, wherein a de Courson led the way, and which could but end in a broken heart at the journey's end; but he said nothing more on the subject. He was a de Maurel, too, and knew well enough that against the wilfulness of one of that race, all the warnings and all the tears of a faithful mentor would be in vain.

VI

Toward the end of June Ronnay de Maurel sent a courier over to his mother, asking her to come over to La Frontenay and select the rooms which she would like to be made habitable for her use.

Madame handed the letter over to her brother with a triumphant smile.

"The first battle has been won," she said firmly. Then she turned to her niece and placed her hand affectionately on the young girl's shoulder. "Thanks to Fernande," she added. "And in years to come, my dear, think how proud you will be that you have rendered such a signal service to His Majesty—God guard him!"

"It has not been easy, ma tante," rejoined Fernande with a whimsical smile. "Laurent has been a perfect ogre; lately he has taken to dogging my footsteps. He lies in wait for me at every turn. I dared not meet M. de Maurel outside the château, lest Laurent pounced upon us and provoked a scene. I was beginning to fear that my bear would escape me, after all."

"No fear of that, child. My son Ronnay is deeply enamoured of you. His absence from you these last few weeks has provoked him into capitulating sooner than I thought. To-morrow will clinch the pledge which Ronnay has already given me, and by autumn we shall be settled at La Frontenay."

"And Fernande, I trust," here interposed M. de Courson with stern decision, "need never meet that abominable democrat again."

As usual, when the subject was alluded to, Madame held her peace. She was in no hurry to settle anything with regard to Fernande. Everything would depend on Ronnay's attitude toward herself and toward her political schemes. If he remained impassive and indifferent, or if he could be kept in ignorance of the Royalist plans till these were sufficiently mature to ensure success, things between him and Fernande might very well be left as they were. He was far too shy and inexperienced to brusque a crisis with any woman, and Fernande might easily be trusted to keep him at arm's length, whilst allowing him to hope, until such time as he was no longer in the way of the Royalist schemes.

On the other hand, if he proved openly hostile, then Fernande must still be the bait whereby so dangerous a fish would have to be caught; she would have to be sacrificed in order to win him over completely. Once Ronnay de Maurel had a de Courson for wife, it would be her business to see that he closed his eyes to the Royalist intrigues which had the armament works of La Frontenay for their chief objective.

Madame la Marquise knew well enough that discontent and disloyalty were rife in the powder factories of La Frontenay. Her task would be to see that the disaffection spread to the foundries. The dearness of food, the oft times' irksome military regulations for the defence of the realm, were always safe cards to play when men were to be won over from constituted authority to a cause wherein promises were cheap and plentiful. Rumours of disturbances at the factory had become more insistent of late, and they were an augury of further disturbances to come. And, after all, thought Madame, even jail-birds were not to be disdained as allies in a cause which was both sacred and just.

VII

Laurent, backed by M. de Courson, raised so many objections to Fernande going over to La Frontenay again, that Madame la Marquise was for once obliged to yield. Nor did she regret Fernande's absence when she realized that Ronnay was all the more determined to push her own installation at the château forward as a means of his seeing the young girl again.

"Fernande will settle down here with me," Madame said very judicially at the most critical moment of the interview; "she will help me to put things in order, and bear me company in my loneliness, as my brother and Laurent will be going away very soon."

Vardenne, the head-bailiff, had much ado to keep his master's impatience in check after that. He was to see at once that the rooms which Madame la Marquise had selected were put ready for her occupation. If men were not available capable women and girls would have to be brought up from the village; in any case, Madame la Marquise should be installed here within the week, and suitable servants engaged for her. He himself was so absolutely ignorant of what ladies required in order to be comfortable in a château, that he then and there placed the bailiff entirely at Madame's disposal for any orders she might deign to give.

Nothing could have pleased Madame better. She was quite ready to take up her abode at La Frontenay, where already she had arranged to meet M. de Puisaye and the other Royalist leaders, and where every kind of plan and scheme could be discussed and prepared at leisure. Madame had plans of her own to think of as well—plans intimately connected with the armament works of La Frontenay and its disaffected workmen, and which she felt sure would commend themselves at once to Joseph de Puisaye. So she returned to Courson in a high state of exultation. The rapidity wherewith happy events had moved along surpassed her wildest expectations. That same evening M. de Courson decided that he and Laurent had best join de Puisaye, their chief, immediately. The whole aspect of the proposed rising was wearing a different aspect now that such perfect headquarters were at the disposal of its leaders.

"Directly you are settled at La Frontenay," M. de Courson said, "I'll communicate with Prigent and d'Aché, and they can come over with de Puisaye as soon as you are ready to receive them. The park is so marvellously secluded and so extensive, that there is practically no fear of Bonaparte's spies being about, and I feel confident that our chiefs can come and go when they like, and as often as they like, without fear of discovery...."

"Till we are ready for our big coup," asserted Madame eagerly.

"Yes," mused M. le Comte; "it begins to look feasible now."

"Feasible?" exclaimed Madame, whose optimism and enthusiasm nothing would ever damp. "Feasible? I look upon it as done. Give Fernande and me three months, and we'll have won over two-thirds of the workmen at La Frontenay. When our recruits march upon the foundry and demand its surrender in the name of the King, they will be received with acclamations of loyalty, and within the hour the foundries of La Frontenay will be manufacturing munitions of war for the triumph of the King's cause and the overthrow of that execrable Bonaparte."

"God grant that your hopes may be realized, my dear Denise," rejoined M. de Courson; and Laurent added fervently:

"What a triumph that will be for us! The mouths of fire and engines of war fashioned by regicides and traitors for the exaltation of the baseborn Corsican, suddenly turned against that very idol whom they have dared to set up against their lawful King!"

CHAPTER XII
A FOOL AND HIS FOLLY

I

At last there came a morning when Fernande felt free from Laurent's untiring vigilance. Since the day when she had thrown out the vague hint to de Maurel that she would resume her walks in the wood, Laurent had never wearied of keeping an eye on every one of her movements.

Morning after morning, when the sun irradiated the distant slopes with gold, she had started out at an hour when even old Matthieu was not yet about; she had tiptoed out of the house, certain that she would not wake anyone; she had stolen out into the garden by way of the veranda, her soft, heelless shoes gliding noiselessly along the parquet floors as well as upon the flagged stones. She had then skirted the château, in order to reach the park gates, only to find Laurent pacing up and down the avenue of limes, ostensibly engaged in reading a book, quite self-possessed and unconcerned, and exhibiting only the very slightest show of surprise at seeing her abroad so early in the day. He then suggested a walk round the park, or even at times a stroll as far as the woods, and she, inwardly exasperated at her own discomfiture, had perforce to appear gay and unconcerned too.

Once she thought that she would try to cross the park as far as the postern gate and to slip out into the orchard that way and thence to the woods; but she had not yet reached the park wall before she heard Laurent's voice calling her by name. The avenue of limes commanded an extensive view of the gardens, and he had caught sight of her white dress flitting in among the trees.

She did not wish to be caught stealing out of the precincts of the château like some country wench tripping to a rendezvous, so she had perforce to give up her matutinal excursions for a while, and to be content with an inward vision of poor Laurent getting up at break of day and cooling his heels morning after morning under the lime-trees while she lay snugly in bed, breaking her little head in order to devise some means of eluding his watchfulness.

Why she should have wished to meet de Maurel again—alone in the woods—she herself could not have said. Encouraged by Madame la Marquise, she had certainly come to look upon her final subjugation of the Maurel bear as a work of selfless patriotism, and even an actual duty to her King and his cause. At the same time, the subjugation was already so complete, that it lay well within her power—this she knew—

to precipitate the crisis at any moment when she felt so inclined. At a word, a look now, she could bring de Maurel to his knees and force from his untutored lips the avowal of his love which he himself was at no pains to conceal. One word from her—a message sent by courier to the foundries—would bring him to her side, even though the factories were on fire or the workmen in open revolt. She knew all that, and felt at the same time that she would sooner cut off her right hand or cut out her tongue than pen the message or speak the word. And yet she could not conquer the desire to meet him once again—alone—there where the romance of the pool, the song of birds, the murmur of the trees would all help to bring about that very avowal which she dreaded.

Of Madame la Marquise's more serious intentions with regard to herself and Ronnay de Maurel she knew nothing as yet. Had she known of them, she would have fought against them with her whole might. She had far too much ardent hatred for the man to think of him as anything but a mere tool for the success of her own cause—a tool to be speedily cast aside once it had served its purpose.

That her coquetry with the man was not only capricious and thoughtless, but also wantonly cruel, she did not realize for a moment. Just now she felt more amused than thrilled by the thought that she had aroused tender feelings in the heart of a man of de Maurel's calibre; and she was only eighteen, and had no one to guide her in the somewhat tortuous path in which she had embarked. Madame la Marquise encouraged her openly. Her father was indulgently detached, and Laurent somewhat ridiculously jealous, whilst all the while she never brought herself to believe that de Maurel had it in him to love— sincerely, tenderly, unendingly. To her he was—he still remained—the enemy and the traitor; the man who perhaps had had no actual hand in the atrocities and the murders of the Revolution, but who had, nevertheless, countenanced them by openly professing democratic principles. Such a man was, therefore, fair prey for any loyal subject of His Majesty the King who had it in her power to make him suffer—as those of his kind had made the innocent suffer—and to make him weep tears of longing or of shame, that those very principles which he professed had shut him out for ever from the heart of his kindred, from their family circle, from home life and from happiness.

Yet, hating the man as she did, detesting all that he loved and despising all that he worshipped, Fernande—such are the contradictions of a woman's heart—manœuvred day after day, at great risk to her own comfort and to her reputation, for the chance of meeting that same man alone and on the self-same spot where in his deep and ardent eyes she had already more than once read the secret of a passion which he himself had not yet probed to its depths.

109

Fernande was not at all surprised when she saw de Maurel sitting beside the silent pool—obviously waiting for her.

Laurent and M. de Courson had gone to Avranches the previous day in answer to a summons from their chief; they were not expected home till the late afternoon. And that morning Fernande was free—free to steal out of the park gates while the morning sun tipped the distant hills with rose and made each dewdrop upon the leaves of beech and alder glisten like a diamond. She was free to wander through the orchards, where the apples were beginning to ripen, and where the cherry-trees were already stripped of their rich spoil; she was free to plunge into the cool and shady wood, to flit between the larches and the pines, feeling the cones crackling under her feet and the exhalation of warm earth rising to her nostrils and sending a delicious intoxication through her veins.

The moment she saw de Maurel she was ready to run away. But it was already too late. He had spied her white dress, and in a moment he was on his feet, and a look of strange, exultant happiness lit up his entire face. Before she could move he had reached her side and taken her hand.

"I knew that you would come, my beloved," he said simply.

She tried to be flippant, or else wrathful, but somehow the words died on her lips. Such an extraordinary change had come over him, that she caught herself looking intently into his face—studying wherein lay that subtle transformation of his whole personality which made him seem like a triumphant lover. Indeed, the manner in which he had greeted her had taken her breath completely away, and it was quite mechanically that she allowed him to lead her to her favourite bank of moss, there where the broken stump of a tree trunk made a comfortable seat whereon to rest, and where the wild iris grew thickest and the meadowsweet in full flower sent its delicious fragrance through the air.

She sat down on the tree trunk and arranged the folds of her gown primly round her feet, and he half sat, half lay, on the moss beside her, and all the while that she fumbled with her gown he sat quite still, with his elbow resting on the stump of the tree, his head leaning upon his hand. She felt restless and not a little nervy, and was vastly vexed with herself because—strive how she may—she could not steady the slight tremor of her fingers, and she could see that he was watching them.

"I did not think of meeting you here, mon cousin," she contrived to say after a while.

"Ah! but I think you did," he rejoined quietly. "How could you think not to meet me once you gave me hope that you would come?

Every morning I have lain in wait for you until the hour when I knew that it would be too late for you to venture out so far without being seen. Then I have gone back to my work. If I had not seen you to-day, I would have come again to-morrow, and the day after, and the day after that—for a month or for a year—or for ten years—until you came."

"You talk at random, mon cousin," she said coldly, choosing to ignore the intense passion which vibrated in his voice, and the ardent look wherewith he seemed to hold her, just as he had held her once in his strong arms. "You talk at random," she reiterated. "Your words seem to imply that my desire was to meet you here, without being seen by others, whereas it is my custom to walk here often, sometimes alone, but more often with Laurent."

"Ah! that was a long while ago," he said, with that same smile which was wont to light up his bronzed face with a strange air of youth and of joy. "You used to walk in the woods with Laurent in the olden days, but not of late. Of late you sometimes started in the early morning, hoping to steal from out the park unperceived. But Laurent has always been on the watch, and you could not come. To-day he is absent...."

"Indeed, mon cousin," broke in Fernande vehemently, "your imagination carries you far. I do not know whence you have gleaned this fantastic information, but...."

The smile still lingered round his firm lips as he rejoined quietly:

"Every morning at break of day I have prowled around the park of Courson. Every morning, until a week ago, I saw your white dress gleaming amongst the trees. I also saw Laurent wandering, disconsolate, under the lime-trees until he caught sight of you and turned you from your purpose."

"You have, indeed, a vivid imagination, mon cousin," she retorted, somewhat abashed, "if you connect my early morning walks in the park of Courson in the company of Laurent with any desire on my part to meet you here."

"For the past week," he went on, wholly unperturbed, "I have only seen Laurent, still walking dolefully under the limes. You did not come. But yesterday Laurent went to Avranches and this morning I saw you from afar. I saw your white dress, which looked like an exquisite white cloud on which the sun had imprinted a kiss and covered it with a rosy glow. I saw your hair like a golden aureole and the outline of your shoulders and your arms as you flitted like a sprite in and out amongst the trees. Then I knew that you were on your way hither; I soon outdistanced you. How I walked I cannot tell. Meseems that fairies must have carried me."

"Meseems that your work cannot of late have been very absorbing, mon cousin," she rejoined with well-assumed flippancy, "if you have spent every morning spying on my movements ten kilomètres away from your home."

111

"I would walk fifty on the chance of catching sight of you for five minutes in the distance," he said, "but not because I am idle. Work at the foundries and in the factory has been arduous and heavy. Rumour will have told you that some of our men have been troublesome...."

She looked straight down into his eyes and said earnestly:

"Those for whose sake you and yours became false to your King and to your caste are turning against you now, mon cousin. Yes! Rumour hath told me that."

"And you have rejoiced?"

"And I have rejoiced."

"Because in your thoughts you still hate me?"

"Because in my thoughts I condemn you as false to your country and false to your King."

"But in your heart, Fernande," he said slowly, "in your heart you no longer hate me."

"Mon cousin," she protested.

"Do you hate me, Fernande?" he insisted.

She would have given worlds for the power to jump up then and there and to run away. But some invisible bond kept her chained to the spot. She could not move. There was a clump of meadowsweet close to her feet, all interwoven with marguerites, and overhead a mountain-ash was in full bloom and the pungent scent went to her head like wine. Her cheeks felt glowing with heat, and there were tiny beads of perspiration at the roots of her hair, but her hands felt cold and her feet numb, and her throat was dry and parched.

She had just enough strength left to try and hide her confusion from him. She stooped and picked a marguerite, and thoughtfully, mechanically, her delicate fingers began to pull the white petals off one by one.

"An that flower does not lie," he said, with the same quiet earnestness, "it will tell you that I love you ... passionately...."

The word, the look which accompanied it—above all, his hand which had without any warning seized her own—suddenly dispelled the witchery which up to now had so unaccountably held her will and her spirit in bondage. With a brusque movement she jumped to her feet and wrenched her hand out of his grasp, and now stood before him, tall, stately, with flaming cheeks and wrath-filled eyes, whilst a laugh of infinite scorn broke from her lips.

"Ah çà!" she exclaimed, "you have methinks taken leave of your senses, Monsieur mon cousin. Or hath rumour lied again, when it averred that you led an abstemious life? The cellars of La Vieuville are well stocked with wine apparently, and its fumes have overclouded your brain, or you had not dared to insult me with such folly."

He, too, had risen and stood facing her, his cheeks pale beneath their bronze, his hands tightly clenched.

"There is no insult," he said quietly, as soon as she had finished speaking, "in the offer of an honest man's love."

"An honest man's love?" she retorted. "The love of a man whose hands are stained with the blood of all those I care for!"

"A truce on this childishness, Fernande," he rejoined almost roughly. "Are we puppets, you and I, to dance to the piping of political wirepullers? I say, that when a man and a woman love one another, political aims and ideals soon sink into insignificance. What matters it if you desire to see this nation governed by a descendant of the Bourbons, or I by a newly-risen military genius? What matters it, dear heart, if one loves?..."

"Aye! if one loves!" she exclaimed, with a derisive laugh. "But you see, I do not love you, mon cousin."

"That is where you are wrong, Fernande," he riposted, still speaking calmly, even though his voice had now become quite hoarse and choked. "You do not know your own heart, my dear ... you are too young to know it. But I knew that you loved me the day that first you came to meet me here! You remember? It was a lovely day in May; the sun shone golden between the branches of the trees, the mating birds were building their nests, the woods were fragrant with the scent of violets and lilies of the valley. You had gathered a bunch of wild hyacinths and they lay scattered at your feet, and I knelt down and picked them up for you, and for one instant your hand came in contact with mine. You loved me then, Fernande! you loved me when you nestled in my arms, and I carried you through the woods and out in the fields beneath the clear blue sky, less blue than your eyes. And from below a skylark rose heavenwards and sang a hosanna in the empyrean above. Your eyes were closed, but you did not sleep. You loved me then, Fernande! I felt it in every fibre of my heart, in every aspiration of my soul. My entire being thrilled with the knowledge that you loved me. You love me now, my dear," he added with ineffable tenderness, "else you were not here to-day."

"M. de Maurel!" cried Fernande, "this is an outrage!" Her voice was choked with tears—tears of shame and of remorse for the past, tears of wrath and of misery at her own helplessness. She buried her face in her hands, lest he should see her tears; her feet were rooted to the ground; she dared not move, she dared not fly! she was only conscious of an awful, an overwhelming sense of fear.

"It is the truth, Fernande," he rejoined calmly. "Ah! you may scorn me, your beautiful eyes may flash hatred upon me. No doubt that I deserve both your scorn and your hate. I am rough, uneducated, illiterate, common, vulgar—what you will; but I am a man, a creature of flesh and blood, with a mind and a soul and a heart. That soul and that heart are yours—yours because you filched them from me with your blue eyes and your enchanting smile. You may turn away from me now—and we may part to-day never perhaps to meet again! We may each go our ways—you to sacrifice your youth, your beauty, your life to a degenerate cause; I, to eat my heart out in mad longing for you; but what has passed between us will never be forgotten. My words will ring in your ears long after an assassin's hand, which your kinsfolk have armed against me, has done its work and sent me to fall obscurely in a ditch with a Royalist bullet between my shoulders...."

Her hands dropped away from her face. She drew herself up and looked at him with large, puzzled, inquiring eyes.

"What do you mean?" she asked slowly.

With a careless laugh and a shrug of the shoulders, he pointed to the thicket immediately behind her.

"I mean that day after day an assassin lurks in the undergrowth, dogging my footsteps, watching his opportunity. I mean that three times in the past week I have caught a man in there with a musket in his hand—a musket which was aimed at me. Three times I dragged a man out into the light of day, and the terror of being handed to the hangman forced an avowal from his lips. An avowal! always the same! He had been paid by an agent of Joseph de Puisaye to put a bullet into my back."

"It is false!" she cried.

"It is true!" he retorted. "Why should the hands that pillaged the home of M. de Ris, that murdered the Bishop of Quimper and outraged the Bishop of Cannes—why should they hesitate to strike a de Maurel who happens to be an inconvenient foe?"

"It is false!" she reiterated vehemently.

"False, think you? Then I pray you listen."

He put up his hand, and instinctively she obeyed. The wood lay quite still under the heat of this July forenoon. There was not a rustle among the trees; the birds were silent, and from the mysterious pool there only came the gentle lapping of lazy waters against the mossy bank.

Fernande strained her ears to listen, and soon she heard a stealthy, furtive movement in the undergrowth close by, and she was conscious of that curious, unerring sense which in the midst of Nature's silence proclaims the presence of a hidden human being. She felt more than she heard that somewhere amidst the tangled chestnut a creature was lurking, who was neither bird nor beast—a creature who might, indeed, be hiding there with sinister intent, his hand upon a musket which he had been paid to wield.

A shudder of horror went right through her. She knew well enough that the Chouan leaders nowadays openly boasted of the reprisals which they meant to take; she had often heard fanatics, like Madame la Marquise, declare that in this coming war they would stick neither at murder, nor pillage, nor outrage, and an icy terror overcame her lest, indeed, some malcontent had been bribed to strike at this dangerous opponent from behind and in the dark.

De Maurel moved toward the thicket, and she, with an impulse that was almost crazy, caught at his arm and clung to it, carried away by that same agonizing and nameless terror which in a swift vision had shown her the lurking assassin, and this splendid soldier of France lying murdered in a ditch.

"Where are you going?" she cried wildly.

"To find the assassin," he replied with a loud laugh. "Those Normandy peasants are vastly unapt with their muskets. God forgive him, but in aiming at me he might succeed in hitting you."

"You must not go. It is madness to go."

"It were madness not to go, Fernande. I entreat you take your dear hand from off my arm...."

"You shall not go," she reiterated half deliriously.

He could not have wrenched himself free from her grasp without hurting her delicate hands. "Dear heart," he said more gently, "I'll return in a trice."

"You shall not go."

"Fernande!"

"You shall not go."

Then suddenly he yielded. With a quick movement he turned and caught her in his arms.

"Ah, Fernande!" he said exultantly, "can you tell me now that you do not love me?" And as she, suddenly brought back to her senses, tried to drag herself away from him, he seized both her wrists and held her there one moment firmly, almost brutally, so that she was forced to look him straight in the eyes—his deep-set, passionate eyes, wherein love, triumph, joy, a mad jubilation had kindled a glowing light.

"It was all a ruse, Fernande," he said, and the words came with vast rapidity, tumbling through his lips, "a ruse to catch you unawares. Do you think that I care if an assassin doth lurk behind a thicket? Our fate is in God's hands, and I have affronted Prussian or Austrian cannon too often to think twice of a peasant's musket. But I wanted you to know, to realize what love means. And just now, when you thought my life in danger, there came a call from your heart, Fernande, the hearing of which I would not barter for the highest place in paradise."

"It is false," she cried. "Let me go!"

"You love me, Fernande."

"I hate you. Let me go!"

"Not until you understand. Ah, my dear, my dear, if you only realized what it means, you would not fight—like the shy young bird that you are—against the most glorious, the most magnificent, the most overpowering joy that God can grant to his miserable creatures. You would understand, Fernande, how paltry a thing are country, kindred, friends, King or Emperor, life or death? You love me, Fernande, and in love you would forget aught but love. Together we would forget, together we would live, my arms around you, your sweet head upon my breast. Look up to Heaven now, my dear, there where through the branches of that delicate birch you can see glints of blue and of gold, and swear now before God that you still hate me ... swear it, Fernande, if you can."

She remained silent, numbed, bewildered, her very senses aching with the intensity of her emotion, her gaze held by the fascination of that transcendental passion which glowed from out his eyes. Just for a moment they remained thus, hand in hand, whilst the murmurings of the woods were hushed, and a soft breeze stirred the delicate tendrils of her golden hair—just for one moment—that supreme second which in the life of God's elect spells immortality!

III

Then, as when in the midst of a master's touch upon a perfectly tuned violin, a string suddenly snaps with a harsh and grating sound, so did a strident laugh break upon the exquisite silence of the woods.

"Well done, Fernande! well done!" came in ringing accents from out the thicket. "You have, indeed, won your wager. The bear is dancing to your piping, and I am just in time to see that he doth not commence to growl."

At the first sound of that laugh and of those words de Maurel had suddenly dropped Fernande's hands; he drew away from her and staggered almost as if that shot from the assassin's musket had struck him in the back. He put his hand up to his forehead and gazed out into the depths of the undergrowth close by, where Laurent de Mortain's slim form could be seen with outstretched arms pushing aside the thick branches of the young chestnut, his face—set and pale with passion—peering out from amongst the leaves.

Fernande had not moved; only the tender glow of a while ago had suddenly fled from her cheeks and left them pale as ashes, and her eyes—which looked preternaturally large and dark with their dilated pupils—were fixed upon the approaching figure of Laurent. And de Maurel gazed from one to the other, from Laurent to Fernande, in a dazed, uncomprehending manner. He could not speak, he could not confront his young brother with the taunt that he was lying. He had looked on Fernande, and, God help him! he could not understand.

But already Laurent had extricated himself out of the tangled coppice, and was striding rapidly toward them both.

"It was very well done," he said as he approached. "Many a time these past two months we all thought that you would fail. But you were so sure, were you not? Ah!" he added, as with a nervy gesture he flicked his boot with the riding whip which he carried, "how well I remember your boast, after that day when de Maurel and I quarrelled so hotly that we all feared he never would come nigh us again. 'The Maurel bear,' you said, 'will dance to my piping on the faith of Fernande de Courson!' No offence, dear brother," continued the young man with well-affected unconcern; "our fair cousin's innocent coquetry must have vastly pleased your vanity. But there's no harm done, is there? We all have to go through the mill of women's wiles, and are none the worse for it in after life. You'll learn that, too, my good de Maurel, when you become better acquainted with the world. Shall we go now, Fernande?"

With an air of proprietorship as well as of perfect courtesy he bowed before his young cousin and held out his arm to her. She appeared to be in a dream, all the life seemed to have gone out of her, and she stood there like a wooden doll, motionless and with wide-open eyes still fixed upon Laurent. Now, when he seemed to expect her to place her hand on his arm, she obeyed with a mechanical, automatic gesture.

That half-crazy vacancy which had descended on de Maurel's mind when first Laurent's derisive words had hit him as with a blow, was gradually lifted from him. Sober common-sense, of which he had an abundant fund, had soon begun to whisper insidiously that here was no misunderstanding, no arrogance or perversion on the part of Laurent, since Fernande had not by word or gesture attempted to deny the truth of what he said. She had been ready enough to cry out: "It is false!" when those whom she loved were being indirectly attacked. That cry had come from her heart, whereas now she did not deny. She gave no word, no look. She allowed Laurent to lead her away. She had had her fun—her game with the besotted rustic, who had dared to raise his eyes to her unapproachable beauty—she had had her fun with him; now she was in a hurry to get home, in order to laugh at her ease.

But to see her go away like that was something past the endurance of any man. De Maurel felt that even a word of torturing cruelty from her would be more bearable than this icy silence. And, after all—who knows?—the magic of her voice might dispel even this horrible dream. And so just as she was about to move away, he spoke to her, slowly, deliberately, forcing his rough voice to tones of courtesy.

"One moment, I pray you, Mademoiselle Fernande," he said. "Surely, ere you go, you will at least deign to confirm the truth of what my brother hath said?"

"You need no confirmation from Mademoiselle Fernande," broke in Laurent harshly. "I am not in the habit of lying."

"'Tis to Mademoiselle Fernande I was speaking," rejoined de Maurel quietly. "I would humbly beg her to answer for herself."

Then only did she turn and look at him, and at sight of the hopeless shame and misery which were imprinted on his face, she felt the hot tears welling up from her heart, and she had to close her eyes, lest he should read in them all the agonizing remorse which she felt.

But she could not speak; every word she uttered would have choked her. And he, seeing her coldness, that proud aloofness which seemed to have descended upon her like a mantle the moment Laurent de Mortain appeared upon the scene, could have cried out in his humiliation and his wretchedness like some poor animal that has been wounded unto death. Not to these two proud aristocrats, however, would he show how terribly he was suffering. She—Fernande—held him in ridicule, it seemed—in contempt and derision. With cruel scorn she had toyed with his tenderest heart-strings, and laughed at his coming misery with those who would gladly sweep him off this earth. How she must have hated him, he thought, to have planned his abasement so thoughtfully, so deliberately.

That first day in the woods, the sheaf of bluebells, her exquisite bare toes ... all a trick! a trick! and he stood before her now—before Laurent his brother—shamed to the innermost depths of his being— openly denounced as a self-deluded fool—an unpardonably vain, besotted, unjustifiable fool!!

For the moment he could do nothing, save to try and rescue a few tattered shreds of his own self-respect; so now, when after a second or two of silence, Laurent made as if he would speak again, Ronnay interposed firmly:

"I have had my answer," he said, as calmly as the hoarseness of his voice would allow, "and there is nothing left for me to do, meseems, save to tender to Mademoiselle Fernande de Courson my humble apologies for the annoyance which this present scene must have caused her. I may be a rustic—and I know that I am a fool—still, I am not quite such an one as not to realize how very unpleasant even a chance meeting with me in the future would be to her. I should like to assure her, therefore, as well as Madame la Marquise, my mother, that I shall be leaving for Poland soon to join the Emperor, and that the sight of my soiled blouse and unkempt hair will not offend their eyes for many months to come."

Laurent, vaguely stirred by shame at his own attitude at this moment, felt that he ought to say something amicable or conciliatory, but with a decided gesture of the hand, de Maurel repelled any further argument. He remained undoubtedly the master of the situation, a curiously dignified figure despite his rough clothes and the humiliation which had been put upon him. He remained standing close by the mossy bank whereon he had first dreamed—a foolish fond dream of happiness. The exquisite vision of loveliness and of grace who, with small, cruel hands had oped for him the secret door and shown him a glimpse of paradise, was even now turning away from him, without a word, without a look, arm in arm with the man for whom she had reserved her kisses, her fond embrace, the mere thought of which had sent fire through his own veins.

She went right round the lake, her hand resting on Laurent's arm; then they struck the woodland path which led straight to Courson. For a while de Maurel could see her white dress gleaming amongst the trees, and once a ray of sunshine caught the top of her tiny head and made her hair shine like living gold. Then the thicket gradually enveloped them, and in the next few minutes they were hidden from his view.

The breeze of a while ago had begun to rustle more insistently through the trees; the birds flew back to their nests. Overhead a squirrel looked down with beady, inquisitive eyes on that motionless figure of a human foe. And wafted upon the breeze, there came from out the depths of the silent pool the sustained, dulcet cooing of wood-pigeons. The soft and melancholy sound rose up like the wail of a broken heart; it floated through the leaves of the wild iris and the clumps of meadowsweet, until it soared up finally among the quivering leaves of birch and mountain-ash, and then was still.

And with a cry like that of a dumb animal in pain, de Maurel fell upon his knees, and burying his face in the dewy moss, he sobbed his poor, overburdened heart out in desolation and utter loneliness.

CHAPTER XIII

AFTER A YEAR

I

"Then," said Madame la Marquise, "you mean to be childish and obstinate about this, Fernande?"

"You may call it childish and obstinate, ma tante, if you wish," replied the young girl quietly.

"Meseems that you evince a singular want of loyalty in the matter. To leave La Frontenay—now—when the work of the past year is on the point of bearing fruit, when our chiefs are here every day, planning, concerting, arranging everything for our great coup. I, for one, would not be absent at such a time for the world."

"If I thought that my presence at La Frontenay would be of the slightest use to M. de Puisaye or to our cause, I would not hesitate, ma tante. But obviously women are de trop in war councils. What can I do save listen in silence? We must all accept blindly whatever our chiefs decide. I am quite prepared to do that; on the other hand, I see no object in my being present at their deliberations."

"But why?" ejaculated Madame, with a sigh of impatience. "In heaven's name, why?"

"I think that I could be of some use at Courson," replied Fernande firmly. "Sister Mary Ignatius, from the Visitation at Mortain, has promised to come and stay with me for a while. She is wonderfully clever at healing the wounded ... and meseems that we shall have need of her skill."

"You could make yourself more useful by organizing your base hospital here."

"Courson is more central and...."

"And what?"

"I could not bear to tend our wounded under the hospitality of M. de Maurel," concluded Fernande very quietly, with an intensity of feeling which caused Madame to exclaim angrily:

"You are stupid and childish, Fernande. Your father and I and Laurent have each told you that we look on your present attitude as nothing more than a silly whim. Last year's nonsense is a thing of the past. Ronnay, no doubt, has long forgotten all about it. In any case, it did not influence him in any way, and before he went he ordered Vardenne to attend to my installation at La Frontenay just as if nothing had happened. So why you should harbour so much foolishness in your head I cannot imagine."

Fernande made no reply. She turned away with a slightly impatient sigh, but a strange look of tenacity round her delicate mouth made her young face suddenly seem old and set.

Laurent de Mortain was sitting in a corner of the room, seemingly absorbed in turning over the pages of a book, and taking no part in the discussion, but now—at Fernande's obvious distress—he threw his book down; then he rose and came up to her.

"Do not let my mother worry you, Fernande," he said, as he took her inert hand in his and fondled it timidly. "There is—as you say—no special reason why you should remain at La Frontenay after to-day, and every reason why you should not. It will be almost impossible, I imagine, to avoid unpleasant rencontres in the future."

Quite gently but coolly, and with a detached little air, Fernande withdrew her hand, but she threw him a grateful look.

"I suppose that there is no doubt that de Maurel has come back?" interposed Madame coldly.

"No doubt whatever," replied Laurent. "He arrived at La Vieuville three days ago. The military overseers left La Frontenay yesterday."

"Oh, I knew those brutes had gone! The very sight of them in and about La Frontenay made me sick with hatred these past twelve months."

"I am not sure that you will find my worthy brother more pleasant to look on."

"Perhaps not," rejoined Madame, with a careless shrug of the shoulders. "Our bear is no doubt still suffering from a sore head, after the correction you administered to him last year. What a million pities that was!" she added with a sigh. "If you only had kept your temper then, Laurent!"

"Kept my temper?" he retorted hotly. "At sight of that lout forcing his attentions on my future wife?... I had been less than a man!"

"Fernande was not your future wife, then, Laurent."

"She was that in her heart already. Were you not, Fernande?" he added, as once again he drew near to the young girl and took hold of her hand. "Thank God she is that now!" he added, as he raised the little hand to his lips.

Madame la Marquise frowned. With all her love for her youngest son she yet was wroth with him for having so clumsily upset all her plans. She had but little patience with sentimental dalliance, and would have parted Laurent from the object of his heart's desire even now if it suited her purpose, and without the slightest compunction.

II

"In any case, mother," rejoined the young man, after a while, "you have had no cause to quarrel with Ronnay's burst of ill-temper, which took him off to Poland for close upon a year. Had he been at home, I doubt if you could have trafficked so easily with Leroux."

Before Madame la Marquise had time to reply the door was thrown open, and M. le Comte entered in the company of three other men, every one of whom Madame greeted most effusively:

"M. de Puisaye!" she exclaimed. "It is really an honour for this house to harbour our valiant chief! And you too, my dear Monsieur Prigent, and M. d'Aché!" she continued, as the three men in turn kissed her slender, finely-chiselled hand, then bowed to Mademoiselle Fernande and shook Laurent de Mortain by the hand.

"What a presage of greater things to come," she added excitedly, "that you should be able to enter the grounds and the Château of La Frontenay like this, in open daylight ... without fear of spies!"

The shorter of the three men—he whom Madame had addressed as de Puisaye—rubbed his hands gleefully together. He was a small man, dressed in worn and shabby clothes, who might have been termed good-looking but for the air of recklessness and dissipation which had already furrowed his face and dimmed the brightness of his eyes.

"A presage, indeed, Madame la Marquise," he said. "M. de Courson tells me that you have everything ready for our big coup, and that all we need decide now is the day on which it were best to carry it through."

"Optimistic as ever," broke in François Prigent, a tall, lean man, whose threadbare coat was a miracle of neatness, his down-at-heel boots polished till they shone, and whose nails were carefully manicured. "Our friend Joseph already sees himself the master of the Maurel foundries."

"And so he will be, by the grace of God," broke in Laurent confidently. "Personally, I do not see how we can fail. We were just speaking of our chances when you arrived, and as far as it is humanly possible to foresee events, the foundries will be turning out arms and munitions for the King's Majesty within the week."

"I should just like to hear exactly how we stand," here interposed the Vicomte d'Aché—a stout, florid man, with full lips and protruding eyes, which he kept fixed on Mademoiselle de Courson with undisguised admiration. "De Puisaye has told me nothing definite; in fact, he has been talking somewhat at random. I never saw a man quite so confident of success."

"And no wonder," quoth M. de Courson, whose sober manner contrasted vividly with the feverish excitement of all his friends. "No wonder that de Puisaye is confident of success. The situation in this little corner of Normandy is more favourable to the King's cause than any that hath ever gone before anywhere. Of course, we all know the importance and the value of the La Frontenay foundries."

"We do," assented d'Aché solemnly.

"They belong to my nephew, Ronnay de Maurel. He inherited them from his father—who was my sister Denise's first husband—when he was a mere baby. Old Gaston de Maurel administered his fortune and the foundries for him for many years, as Ronnay joined the Republican army when he was little more than sixteen, and was away from home for over twelve years."

"Old Gaston de Maurel is dead, is he not?" queried one of the men.

"No, he is not, worse luck!" commented Laurent, "though he was said to be dying a year and more ago."

"Anyhow," rejoined M. de Courson, "he has ceased to count for some time—in fact, ever since Ronnay came home wounded after Austerlitz and took over the management of his works himself."

"There are rumours all over the country of the eccentricity of the two de Maurels," interposed Prigent; "they are said to be hopeless rustics and quite illiterate. I trust," he added, with old-fashioned gallantry, "that Madame la Marquise will pardon this uncomplimentary remark about her eldest son."

"I pray you, do not spare me," said Madame, with a forced little laugh. "My son and I have nothing in common. As a matter of fact, people have talked a great deal of nonsense. Ronnay de Maurel may be a rustic, but he is not illiterate, and I looked upon him from the first as a dangerous enemy."

"He has influence with his men?" asked de Puisaye.

"He had," she assented, "a great deal."

"But what about now?"

"Well," resumed M. de Courson in his slow and deliberate way, "as to that we are somewhat in the dark. Ronnay de Maurel, after spending several months at La Vieuville, managing and reorganizing his factories, went away again about a year ago, to rejoin the army—so 'twas said—though I personally would have thought that his wounded leg unfitted him for the hard campaigning to which Bonaparte subjects his troops. Be that as it may, however, Ronnay de Maurel has been away from home for over a year now. He only returned a few days ago—much aged and still more severely crippled, so I am told. I have not seen him. While he was away old Gaston de Maurel took up the reins of government at the foundries in his own feeble hands. He seems to have rallied somewhat unexpectedly after Ronnay's departure, and though he really is sinking fast now—so they say—he certainly kept an eye on his nephew's interests, with the help of a military commission whom the War Office sent down here at Ronnay's desire to supervise the armament works."

"A military commission!" exclaimed d'Aché, with a contemptuous shrug of his wide shoulders. "The War Office! Hark at the insolence of that Corsican upstart!"

The others laughed, too. The Empire of France and its vast military and civil organization were mere objects of derision to these irrefragable Royalists.

"What was this military commission?" queried de Puisaye after a while.

"Ah, my good de Puisaye," exclaimed M. de Courson with a sigh, "you have lived so completely out of the world these past six or seven years, that I suppose you have no notion how absolutely this unfortunate country has come under the sway of military dictatorship. Everything, my good friend, is under military control—the police, of course; the municipality, the hospitals, the schools, the Church—let alone factories and munition foundries. Every man who owns and controls any kind of armament works and who finds it difficult to cope with his men has, it seems, the right to apply to the War Office to send him as many representatives as he may deem expedient to help him keep his workers in order. These representatives are really overseers with military rank and military authority; very convenient for the masters, but none too pleasant for the men!"

"Military tyranny invariably treads on the heels of democratic revolt," said Prigent sententiously. "The English have had their Cromwell, the unfortunate French nation is groaning under its Bonaparte."

"It does very little groaning just now," quoth M. de Courson dryly. "Bonaparte is amazingly popular. The army worships him—cela

123

va sans dire—but so does the populace. We have had great difficulty in rallying the proletariat round here to their allegiance."

"Well," interjected d'Aché somewhat impatiently, "what did this military commission do enfin? What did it consist of?"

"It consisted of four or five exceedingly vulgar men in uniform, who ruled the Maurel foundries with a rod of iron. Punishments for slackness and disobedience were doled out with a free hand, and the slightest attempt at concerted grumbling was instantly met with handcuffs, arrest, bread and water and other unpleasant manifestations of military discipline. The men openly sighed for the return of 'the General,' as they call Ronnay de Maurel, though he was none too pleasant a taskmaster either, so I've been told."

"And I suppose that while that military commission sat at La Frontenay, you were able to do very little in the way of recruiting for the King?"

"Very little indeed. You see, most of the able-bodied men in the neighbourhood are employed in the foundries, and it is only here and there that we have found a malcontent who was willing to come over to us. But we have got the two hundred men from the powder factory; they are ready to join us the moment your men march on La Frontenay."

"Ah!" exclaimed de Puisaye, as he once more rubbed his wrinkled hands together with an excited gesture which seemed habitual to him. "Ah! there you have it at last, my good d'Aché. Our friend de Courson has explained the situation to you as it has been this past year; now let me tell you how we stand at this present, and what causes me to be so certain for the future. The two hundred men of whom de Courson speaks are convicts employed solely in the more dangerous processes of the manufacture of gunpowder. They are a rough, surly, discontented lot, who live segregated from their fellow-workmen in compounds, which are under special supervision, and they are subject to special discipline. Personally, I should say that even so with these restrictions it was pleasanter to manufacture gunpowder in the factories of La Frontenay than in the jails of Caen or the galleys of Brest. But apparently Paul Leroux, who is in some sort of way the acknowledged leader of the gang, and his mates do not think so. They hate old Gaston de Maurel, they hate Ronnay, they execrated the military commission. They only work under strict compulsion—some say under the lash; in any case, they only work under the terror of punishment, and they are ready at any moment to rebel, to murder, to blow up the factory or to come in on our side—to do anything, in fact, for a change from their present condition, and, above all, for a bribe in the form of a promise of liberty and of money."

While de Puisaye spoke all the men had sat down and drawn their chairs together round a table which stood by the window in a corner of the room. Madame la Marquise, too, had joined the conclave, her enthusiasm and her energy were at least equal to that of any man. Only Fernande sat a little outside the circle, at the end of a sofa, near her father and close beside the window, from whence she could see right over the park to the distant wooded hills, thick and heavy with foliage now, and with the brilliant June sun picking out the clumps of wild roses round the edge of the wood, and the little stream in the valley which wound its turbulent course to the silent pool far away.

"Of course," resumed Joseph de Puisaye, after a while, "we all know that a set of jail-birds are not to be trusted in the long run, and it is not my intention that we should rely on them. But our friends here, Madame la Marquise de Mortain, M. de Courson and our ever loyal Laurent, have had certain access to these men for the past year, and they seem to have made marvellous use of their opportunities."

"I marvel that they were allowed to visit the foundries at all," commented François Prigent.

"We were only allowed the one visit," said Madame dryly. "Vardenne, my son's chief bailiff, engineered that for me. It seems that when Ronnay went away last year he never revoked the orders whereby he placed Vardenne entirely at my disposal; and though old Gaston de Maurel tried to interfere once or twice, Vardenne looked upon me as his mistress, and his attitude towards me influenced a good many others. I have been treated with marked respect by all and sundry in and around the property. It was only in the factories that Gaston and the military representatives held masterful sway, and there, after that one visit, not one of us was ever allowed to set foot."

"That being so, Madame la Marquise," continued de Puisaye with flattering earnestness, "I can only say that what you have accomplished is nothing short of miraculous."

"Oh!" rejoined Madame unblushingly, "my son Ronnay left a large sum of money behind for my use."

It was only Laurent, whose eyes never wandered away for long from the contemplation of Fernande, who noticed the quick, hot flush which at Madame's words had suffused the young girl's cheeks.

"I know, I know," interposed de Puisaye; "and, indeed, His Majesty owes you a deep debt of gratitude, Madame, for the privations which you endured so nobly, in order to place the bulk of that money at our disposal."

"I had to use some," rejoined the Marquise, "for bribing Leroux, and also our go-betweens. Unfortunately, those men to whom I had free access—the workmen in the foundries and armament works who live in the villages round—were not at all tractable. They are disloyal almost to a man. For them Bonaparte is a god and Ronnay de Maurel his prophet; we had to fall back on the convicts in the powder factory."

"With that man Paul Leroux as the chief asset," added M. de Courson.

"Beggars must not be choosers," commented de Puisaye with a

sigh. "Two hundred jail-birds in the King's cause," he added naïvely, "are better than five hundred on the other side."

"Well, and what about Leroux and his gang, then?" queried d'Aché.

"On the occasion of our only visit to the foundries," replied Madame, "my brother, Laurent and I had agreed that one of us must have conversation with the man Leroux, with the help and connivance of the other two. Rumour had already told us that Leroux was the chief malcontent, who had given even the military representatives plenty of anxiety. We knew that we must get hold of him before we could approach any of the others. Fortunately luck was on our side. Something—I forget what—engaged the attention of one of the military representatives who were escorting us round the powder factory, my brother was able to engage the others in conversation, whilst Laurent drew the overseer Mathurin's attention to himself. This gave me just two minutes' talk with Leroux."

"Not very much," put in Prigent dryly. The others were listening in eager silence to Madame's narrative.

"Enough for my purpose," she continued. "Leroux was in a surly mood, smarting under some punishment which I've no doubt he deserved. A curse and a snarl from him directed at the overseer gave me my opening. In two minutes I managed to promise him freedom from his present position and money wherewith to create for himself a new one. He sucked in my suggestion greedily, and I asked him how we could communicate with one another in future. 'The boundary wall,' he muttered, 'where it was repaired recently—the stones are new-looking. I will throw a message over at that point when I can—during exercise hours—eight o'clock and two o'clock—you can be on the watch.' There was no time to say more. But I was satisfied. We had made a beginning. For over a week one of us was on the watch twice every day outside the boundary wall at the spot which Leroux had indicated. It was easily recognizable because of the new-looking stones. The spot is a lonely one. There is a footpath which follows the boundary wall at this point; the other side of the footpath is bordered by a bit of coppice wood. Either my brother, or Laurent, or I remained in observation, hidden in the coppice, while we heard the tramp of the men exercising inside the boundary wall. After a week, a piece of dirty paper, weighted by a stone, was flung over the wall. It had been my turn to watch. I picked up the paper and managed to decipher the scrawl upon it. Leroux explained that on this self-same spot in the wall—but on the inner side—he had succeeded in loosening a stone, immediately below the coping; he suggested that messages to him should be slipped behind the stone exactly five minutes before exercising time, and the stone replaced. The yard, he said, was always deserted then. Needless to say that we acted upon his suggestion, and the very next morning Laurent succeeded in clambering over the wall—though it is a high one—at exactly five minutes before eight o'clock, and managed to slip a message for Leroux into the hiding-place behind the stone."

"It all sounds like a fairy tale!" broke in d'Aché enthusiastically.

"Of course," here interposed M. de Courson, taking up the interrupted narrative, "after that, matters became comparatively simple. Leroux was more than ready to do all that we asked of him, and he kept us posted up with everything that went on inside the factory. Thus we enjoined him, for the sake of his own future and for the success of our undertaking, to drop his rebellious attitude—to become industrious, willing, a pattern amongst the workmen. We told him to gain the confidence of the War Office representatives by every means in his power and so to ingratiate himself with them that he might obtain the post of chief overseer of the powder factory, which would confer upon him privileges that he then could utilize for our service."

"Well, and did he succeed?"

"Indeed, he did," assented Madame la Marquise. "We have offered him a bribe of ten thousand francs if he served us in the way we required: the first step towards this service was to be his good conduct—the second his appointment as overseer."

"And what happened?"

"Paul Leroux is now overseer of the powder factory at La Frontenay. He was appointed by old Gaston de Maurel, who has been completely taken in by the man's change of front. Leroux is quoted throughout the district as a marvellous example of how a man can rise from his dead self, through patriotism and discipline, to a new life of industry and consideration. The epic of Leroux," added Madame with a laugh, "forms the comedy side of the palpitating drama which we have been enacting at La Frontenay these past twelve months."

"Splendid! Marvellous!" acclaimed the men in chorus, and d'Aché, less well informed than the others of what had been going on, added eagerly: "So much for the present; now what about the future?"

III

"The future," resumed M. de Courson quietly after a while, "is, in fact, rosier than any of us had ever dared to hope."

"Leroux will prove useful, you think?" queried Prigent.

"Leroux, my dear friends," broke in Madame triumphantly, "is prepared to hand over the entire factory to us, lock, stock and barrel. He has both the power and the means to do it. With the factory in our hands, the foundries and armament works will fall to us automatically."

"But how?" exclaimed d'Aché impassionedly, "in Heaven's name how? Believe me, the whole thing still seems to me like a fairy-tale."

"I am sure it does," she retorted gaily, "and yet it is all real ... so real ... Laurent!" she continued suddenly, turning to the young man, "I pray you go and see if Leroux hath come."

Laurent obeyed readily and de Puisaye said approvingly:

"Ah! you have the man here; that is good!"

"He can come and go at will now, out of his working hours," said M. de Courson, "and for the past two weeks has been up to the château every day to make report to us, as to what is going on inside the factories. Comparative freedom is one of the privileges which have been granted him now that he is chief overseer."

"You have, indeed, accomplished miracles, Madame," said de Puisaye, gallantly kissing Madame la Marquise de Mortain's well-shaped hand.

"Wait till you have spoken with Leroux," retorted Madame with a triumphant smile.

For the next moment or two no one spoke; obviously the nerves of every one in the room were strained to breaking point. Madame la Marquise leaned back in her chair. She was flushed with satisfaction and triumph; she kept her glowing eyes fixed upon Fernande as if she desired to challenge the young girl now to persist in her obstinacy of a while ago. "How can you think of abandoning this scene of coming triumphs?" she seemed to say. But Fernande kept her eyes resolutely averted from her aunt as well as from the three men, who seemed willing enough to while away these few minutes' suspense by casting admiring looks on the beautiful and silent girl by the window.

"Mademoiselle de Courson," said d'Aché, who had always been known for his gallantry, "has not honoured us by an expression of opinion on any point as yet."

"My father would tell you, sir, and justly, too, no doubt," said Fernande coldly, "that I am over-young to have an opinion on any point, and men have oft averred that danger looms largely on ahead whenever women meddle with politics."

"Then will Madame's diplomacy prove them wrong this time," cried de Puisaye gaily. "And I'll warrant that you, Mademoiselle, have borne no small share in the noble work that has been going on at La Frontenay for the behalf of His Majesty the King."

"There you do me too much honour, sir," rejoined Fernande. "I have been a passive witness here, seeing that I was—unwillingly enough, God knows!—a guest beneath M. de Maurel's roof."

Then, as Madame la Marquise uttered an exclamation of reproof and M. de Puisaye one of astonishment, M. de Courson broke in quietly:

"My daughter," he said, not without a stern look directed on Fernande, "hath meseems proved the truth of her assertion to your satisfaction, my friends. She is obviously too young to understand the grave issues which are at stake and wherein overstrung sensibilities must not be allowed to play a part."

Madame was frowning, and Fernande turned her little head once again obstinately away. And the three guests, scenting a family jar, promptly fell to talking of something else.

CHAPTER XIV

THE TOOL

I

A moment or two later Laurent returned closely followed by Leroux. Fernande instinctively turned to look at the man whom she had last seen in the factory, covered with grime and smoke and sweat, threatening by foul words and furtive gestures the master who had controlled and punished him.

Of a truth, she scarcely recognized him. Paul Leroux, actuated both by greed and by the desire to free himself from present constituted authority, had played his part over well. From the surly, ill-conditioned jail-bird of twelve months ago, he had succeeded in eliminating every unpleasant aspect, save that of the eyes, which had remained shifty and glowering as before. But he wore the cloth coat and corduroy breeches of a well-to-do artisan now; his hair was combed and oiled and held back in the nape of the neck with a tidy piece of ribbon. He wore neckcloth, stockings and shoes with buckles. His hands were almost clean.

De Puisaye and the others surveyed this new recruit to the Royalist cause with genuine satisfaction. Except for that shifty look in the eyes, which perhaps these men, unaccustomed to psychological analysis, failed to note, Paul Leroux looked a well-conditioned, reliable, well-fashioned tool, ready for any guiding hand.

"Well now, Leroux," began Joseph de Puisaye, with a sort of condescending gruffness which he thought suitable for the occasion, "Madame la Marquise de Mortain has been telling me that you have resolved to become once more a loyal and independent subject of His Majesty King Louis the Eighteenth by the grace of God, and that you are ready to throw off your allegiance to the adventurer who has dared to set himself upon the throne of France. That is so—is it not?"

"If by all that talk," retorted the man surlily, "you mean that I and my mates are heartily sick of de Maurel and of the tyranny of his minions, and that we don't mind throwing in our lot with you for a consideration ... then you are right. I am your man."

De Puisaye threw his head back and laughed, and even solemn Prigent could not suppress a smile.

"Well said, my good Leroux," riposted de Puisaye unconcernedly. "You put things bluntly, but that certainly is the proposition. Let me put it quite as bluntly to you. We have eight hundred men between this and Avranches, ready to march on La Frontenay on a given night. We want to obtain possession of the factories, the foundries and the armament works. Can you help us to them?"

"I can and I will," replied the man gruffly, "if you'll give me ten thousand francs for my pains, and a hundred francs apiece for my mates."

"We have already agreed to that," rejoined de Puisaye, "and I pledge you my word of honour that you shall have the money on the day when I myself walk into the foundries of La Frontenay as their master. Now how do you propose to do what we want?"

For one instant Leroux' shifty eyes had flared up beneath their flaccid lids, as the Comte Joseph de Puisaye pledged himself to pay that ten thousand francs for which Leroux would readily have sold his soul to the devil.

"Will you explain to these seigneurs, Leroux," commanded M. de Courson, "the plan which we have agreed on? They would prefer to hear it from your own lips, so that we can all be assured that you thoroughly understand all that you will have to do."

"Am I not to sit down?" queried Leroux roughly.

The gentlemen looked at one another in some consternation. Here was a problem which, simple as it seemed, nevertheless embodied a good many of the puzzles which would inevitably confront the old régime when it did succeed in re-establishing itself above the ruins and the ashes of Equality and of Fraternity. For a man in Leroux' position to dare think of sitting down in the presence of his seigneurs was, indeed, an unheard-of possibility in the days before the proletariat had ventured to assert its rights to live like human beings rather than like beasts of burden. Now, of course, things were very different; the theory of social levelling—which had found expression in the title of "citizen" applied equally to the whilom aristocrat and to the vagrant in the street—made even de Puisaye marvel if he dared impose upon a man like Leroux those conventions which in the past would have been as natural to him as the indrawing and exhaling of his breath, but which now might arouse his resentment and turn him, headstrong and wrathful, against the project wherein his co-operation was of such vital importance.

Compromise that did not grate upon the susceptibilities on either side was obviously the only wise course to adopt under the circumstances, and de Puisaye, keeping an air of haughty condescension that satisfied himself, said in a pleasant tone intended to conciliate Leroux: "If the ladies have no objection, my man, you certainly may sit."

Madame la Marquise nodded approval, and Leroux, muttering something which fortunately remained inaudible, sat down.

II

"Well, now," resumed de Puisaye after a while, "will you tell these ladies and gentlemen here as clearly as you can what plan you can adopt in order to deliver the Maurel factories into our hands? Then we shall be able to see how best we can co-operate with you in the matter."

"I can manage things all right for you," said Leroux roughly. "I am chief overseer of the powder factory now—what?—so I have my quarters inside the precincts. I live in the Lodge—you know it—it stands in the centre of the group of work-sheds over against the powder magazine. What I can do is this: I can keep half a hundred of my mates—those that I know I can rely on—to work overtime one evening. They can easily slacken work during the day, and I should then have the right to keep them back for two or three hours in the sheds."

"They will form the main garrison inside the precincts," explained M. de Courson. "On their quick and efficient work will depend our success."

"Yes, I quite understand that," assented de Puisaye. "Now, how is that garrison going to work for us? I presume that there are night-watchmen about in the various sheds and throughout the works."

"There are," replied Leroux briefly, "two in every shed, and Mathurin, the chief overseer of the foundries, sleeps in one of the main buildings, too. At night—if it is necessary—the alarm is given by ringing the bell in one of the clock towers. There are two of these towers in the precincts of the works, one in the main building of the foundries, the other above the Lodge in the powder factory, where I sleep."

"Therefore," commented Prigent dryly, "the first thing that you and your garrison will have to do, my man, will be to hold the two clock towers, and then to surprise and overpower the various night-watchmen as simultaneously as possible ... as silently as may be."

"Exactly," rejoined Leroux curtly.

"Well," added de Puisaye eagerly, "having disposed of the night-watchmen, what would you do next?"

"Some of us will stay behind on guard in the different sheds, and

131

a score or so will march on the compound, where the rest of our mates are penned up as if they were savage beasts that must be kept in cages."

"Aha! That means another hundred and fifty of you?"

"Yes, another hundred and fifty. There are sentries at the gates of the compound, but we can easily overpower those. The watch will not be quite so strict now that the General has come home."

"Ah!" ejaculated de Puisaye, "matters slacken up at the works when the master is home—what?"

"Not exactly," replied Leroux. "But those military overseers have been absolute brutes. Things cannot be quite so bad now they have gone."

"M. de Maurel is more easy-going, or more indifferent—which?"

Leroux shrugged his shoulders, then said gruffly:

"The General has altered a good deal since he has been away."

"At any rate," here interposed Madame la Marquise impatiently, "Laurent and I can vouch for the fact that the watch round the compounds is not over strict just now. We went past there last night. There were only a couple of sentries at the gates."

"Even so you will have to be careful, my good Leroux," added M. de Courson, "so as not to raise the alarm."

"No, we won't do that," rejoined Leroux. "We can deal with the sentry easily enough."

"And do you think that a couple of hundred men can march from the compound back to the works without being seen or heard."

"Oh, yes! if they are determined not to make a noise. It is not far to the factories. Less than a kilomètre. The roads are soft under foot. We'll be careful not to be seen or heard, you may be sure of that."

"And once you are all back at the works?" queried M. d'Aché.

"We'll just wait there, ready to let you in when you come," replied the man simply.

"What about arms?"

"There are thousands in the stores and in the cellars below the buildings! Enough to equip an army!"

"Splendid! splendid!" exclaimed de Puisaye with enthusiasm. "This man is a jewel! what say you, gentlemen?—and well deserves the money which I have pledged mine honour to place into his hands. Ten thousand francs for the brain that devised the scheme, a hundred francs apiece for those who carry it through. That's it, is it not, my brave Leroux?"

"Yes, that's it," replied the ex-convict with a leer.

"Very well," concluded de Puisaye, "then we'll call that settled. All that we need do now is to decide on the night when we do our coup."

"The sooner the better," said Leroux; "it is dangerous to leave a thing like that hanging about. It may be blown upon at any time. I have had to warn some of my mates that there was something in the wind. Any one of them may be a blackleg, for aught I know."

"The man is right," said M. de Courson decisively; "delays are always dangerous. Moreover, there is no cause for procrastination. The next four-and-twenty hours ought to see us fully prepared."

"I shall have just to think things over," interposed de Puisaye who, throughout his adventurous career, never failed for want of caution, but rather from too much indecision. "In a couple of days I could name the day—or rather the night—when I shall be quite ready—but not before."

"Surely, my dear M. de Puisaye ..." hazarded Madame la Marquise.

"Madame, I entreat you," he rejoined, "to trust to me in this. I have to make my dispositions as carefully as may be. May I suggest that we dismiss this man for the moment, with orders to report here for duty the day after to-morrow?"

"I don't see why we should wait all that time," muttered Leroux.

"There are many things, no doubt, my man," said M. de Courson haughtily, "many things in the councils of your betters that escape your comprehension. As far as arguing goes, we none of us think of quarrelling with the decisions of our chief. We all work for the same cause, and you must learn obedience, the same as we have done, or," he added significantly, "you will have to forfeit the ten thousand francs and your own liberty, which are to be your reward if you serve us as we desire. Now is that clearly understood?"

"But what do you want me to do, enfin?" growled Leroux, on whom the magic mention of money at once acted as a sedative to his surly temper.

"We want you to go on quietly," said M. de Courson, "just as you have done hitherto—trying to win M. de Maurel's confidence just as you succeeded in winning that of the military overseers. It is only a matter of a couple of days at most. Do not let more of your mates into the secret for the present, above all, remember to report for duty here the day after to-morrow at three o'clock in the afternoon. Now you can go."

Leroux would have liked to stay and argue for a while longer. Though he had fully made up his mind to do exactly as he was told, both for the sake of the reward and for the sake of getting even with life, as he would put it, by striking a big blow at constituted authority, he was far too conscious of his own importance, far too puffed up with pride, to take such peremptory orders without a protest. But neither de Puisaye nor any of the others were in a mood to waste time by useless arguings.

While Leroux was busy drawing upon his stock of impudence with a view to letting these "aristos" know that he had them in his power, and would stand no domineering ways from them, they had already coolly turned their backs on him and were deep in whispered consultation together. This haughty ignoring of his personality had the

133

effect of damping the ex-convict's arrogance. He rose and gazed somewhat sheepishly on the array of backs turned so resolutely upon him. He twiddled his hat between his fingers, fidgeted first on one leg, then on the other. At last he was driven to acquiescence and said roughly:

"I'll be here at three o'clock the day after to-morrow. And if you are wise, all of you," he added significantly, "you'll arrange for matters to come to a head that same night or there'll be trouble. Foi de Paul Leroux!"

Then he turned on his heel and strode out of the room.

But just as he was about to bang the door behind him, he happened to turn back again, and he encountered Mademoiselle de Courson's blue eyes fixed upon him with such an expression of loathing, that much against his will, and quite understandably, a hot flush of anger—or was it of shame?—rose right up to his forehead and to the roots of his hair.

CHAPTER XV

A NOTE OF WARNING

I

"Now do you see how impossible it is that we can fail?" exclaimed Madame la Marquise triumphantly, as soon as the man had gone.

"I do not see how we can," assented de Puisaye.

The others all concurred. Leroux, despite his ill-favoured appearance, despite his criminal antecedents which none of them here could ignore, had made a favourable impression on them all.

"The man means to go straight, I think," said Prigent.

"He hates his present condition," commented M. de Courson dryly, "and would sell his soul, if he had one, to be freed from it. Bonaparte will find that it is a dangerous experiment," he added naïvely, "to try and use men like Leroux and his mates to help him prosecute his infamous wars."

"I suppose," continued M. d'Aché, "that the mates on whom this man reckons are ex-convicts like himself?"

"Oh, yes!" replied Madame la Marquise quite unabashed. "Most

134

of the men who are detailed to the powder factories in France now were serving life sentences for murder, rape, or arson before."

"I suppose that we can trust them," said Prigent, with a doleful sigh.

"We must," replied Madame decisively. "We must get hold of the factories, and there is no other way."

"One way is as good as another," concluded de Puisaye cheerfully. "When we have done with those brigands we must rid ourselves of them as quickly as we can. They will bring themselves soon enough once more under the ban of the law."

"In the meanwhile, my dear de Puisaye," said M. de Courson earnestly, "will you tell us exactly what our respective parts are to be in the great coup which those jail-birds will prepare for us? Laurent and I have four hundred men in hiding between Courson and Mortain; we have armed them as best as we could with a few weapons which we received from the English agency in Jersey—not nearly enough, and most of the men have only got sticks ... but, of course," he added hopefully, "there are magnificent stores at La Frontenay when once we hold the works."

"There really will be no need for arms," rejoined de Puisaye. "On the night that we decide for our coup we will assemble at our usual place, the Cerf-Volant woods to the south of Mortain. I propose that I take four hundred men, and with them march quietly up to the factories. Leroux will be waiting for me, and we will order him beforehand to have all the arms that are necessary for the men ready out of the stores. We will then have six hundred men inside the factories, all thoroughly armed and equipped with splendid guns placed in position. We will be able to hold out against any attack made upon the works by de Maurel's work-people, even if they are aided by the local peasantry. In the meanwhile, you, my dear de Courson, will march with two hundred men on Mortain, and Laurent with another two hundred on Domfront, and if you both are as clever and resourceful as I take you to be, you will each of you surprise the small garrison in those respective towns, seize the town-halls, collar the sous-préfets, and hold the forts until François Prigent, on the one hand, and our good d'Aché, on the other, arrive to reinforce you, which should be at about midday."

"Splendid!" ejaculated Laurent. "Monsieur Prigent and M. le Comte d'Aché will, of course, have marched all the way from Avranches?"

"Yes. We have another eight hundred men there; they are strong and eager, but, of course, there, as well as here, our trouble is the want of arms. With the armament stores of La Frontenay in our hands we shall be absolutely invincible. I propose, therefore, that Prigent and d'Aché march first on La Frontenay, equip themselves with arms and guns, and then divide into three companies, one to remain with us, one to march back on Mortain to reinforce M. de Courson, and the other to

135

push on to Domfront. This manœuvre will cause a little delay, but its advantages are, I think, so obvious that it needs no discussing. With Domfront and Tinchebrai in our hands, we can think of La Ferté-Macé. Our brilliant success—for it will be a very brilliant success—will rally a great many waverers around us, and, of course, holding the foundries and factories of La Frontenay will make us literally the masters of Normandy. Avranches will fall to us within a few days, and after that it will be Caen and Brest; then foreign support to any extent! Oh, my friends! my dear friends!" he added, his voice hoarse and choked with excitement, "what a day! what prospects! what a future! Madame la Marquise, by coming back to settle in these parts, by effecting a reconciliation with your eldest son and installing yourself in this château, you have reconquered France for our King!"

Madame's eyes were moist with pride and emotion. Laurent could no longer sit still; he was pacing up and down the narrow room, and for the moment he almost forgot to look at Fernande, who had remained sitting quite still beside the window, gazing—still gazing—out into the distance to the slope of the hill, where lay the woods of La Frontenay and the silent pool.

II

"I think that your plan is quite admirable, my dear de Puisaye," said M. de Courson after a while, "and I, for one, can only give it my very hearty approval. In fact, you have thought everything out so well, that all my nephew and I can do is to obey implicitly. Now when do you think that you can be ready with your men?"

"When can you be ready with yours?" retorted de Puisaye.

"Oh, we are ready now. Laurent and I can assemble our company together any day you may decide. We can easily pass the word round and muster up at the Cerf-Volant woods outside Mortain on any night you think most suitable. It would not be safe to muster at Courson, and though Mortain is a good deal farther, it is much more lonely and, as you say, it would be best for us all to start out at one and the same time—shall we say, at eleven o'clock in the evening. You would then reach La Frontenay and Laurent get to Domfront almost simultaneously, bar accidents. Laurent and I can surprise the garrisons at dead of night before either of them can get wind of the affair, and thus obviate the possibility of their falling on you ere you on your side can reach La Frontenay."

"That being so," rejoined de Puisaye, "why not decide on the day after to-morrow? I shall have my four hundred men assembled at Mortain too, by that time, and we have given the man Leroux orders to

136

present himself here on that day. We will—with her permission—entrust Madame la Marquise with the happy task of telling Leroux that he must arrange his coup for the same night, and be prepared for my arrival with my small contingent. Whilst he waits for me he must open up the stores and get out all the small arms that he can; then directly I arrive I can get what guns there are into position, and prepare for a regular siege if it is necessary. I cannot help wishing that the next morning may see us attacked in full force by de Maurel's work-people, for then, when Prigent and d'Aché come upon the scene, they would get the attacking party in the rear, and though insufficiently armed, they would, nevertheless, effect heavy slaughter, and gain an immediate and brilliant victory."

"How are we going to live until the day after to-morrow?" sighed Laurent.

"How, indeed?" was echoed by all the others in the room.

The very atmosphere seemed redolent of triumph, of exultation, of confidence in victory. The co-operation of the ex-convict and of two hundred of his kind had brought forth a situation which had endless possibilities in it. The general consensus of opinion was that failure was absolutely out of the question. Never, since the English agencies had withdrawn their active support, had the prospects of a successful Royalist rising been so rosy. De Puisaye was glowing with enthusiasm, Prigent had laid aside his solemnity, d'Aché ceased to ogle Fernande; even M. de Courson's pale cheeks were flushed. As for Madame—she was already present in thoughts at the first reception which Queen Marie-Joséphine-Louise would be holding at the Tuileries. As for Fernande, everyone was fortunately too much excited, too much engrossed in schemes and plans to pay much attention to her, or her silence and extraordinary aloofness from the all-absorbing topic of conversation could not have passed unperceived.

It was late in the afternoon before everything was said that had to be said, before every plan had been discussed, every argument worn threadbare. Then at last the council of war agreed to disperse, and Joseph de Puisaye and his two friends took final leave of Madame la Marquise and of Fernande, whilst M. de Courson went with them, in order to escort them as far as the boundary gates of the park.

III

It was only when the men had gone that Madame la Marquise bethought herself of her niece, and of the latter's strange attitude while the council of war had been going on; whereupon she frowned and then remarked testily:

"Of a truth, Fernande, I do not understand you. Here you have been sitting like a stuffed dummy, the while the destinies of France were being talked of by men who are sacrificing their lives for her. Where is your enthusiasm of a year ago, my child? Where is your patriotism? And what, in Heaven's name, hath come over you these past few days?"

"Nothing, ma tante," replied Fernande with a little sigh of impatience; "only a foreboding, I think."

"A foreboding?" queried Madame. "What about?"

"I don't know. But it seems to me that you are all so confident ... so sure of success...."

"Well, are not you?"

"I think that M. de Puisaye—that you all, in fact, are not taking one vastly important factor into your reckoning."

"What do you mean, Fernande? What factor are you alluding to?"

"To M. le Comte Ronnay de Maurel, of course," replied Fernande.

"Well," queried Madame tartly, "what about him?"

"Only, ma tante, that M. de Maurel is not the nonentity that you and M. de Puisaye seem to imagine. He has just come back from Poland, and at once dismissed the military overseers who had taken his place in his absence. Does that look as if he meant to let the reins of government slip through his fingers?"

"I don't know what you mean, child. Ronnay de Maurel may have every intention in the world of ruling over his work-people and being master in his own factories, but we are going to relieve him of that responsibility in a day or two's time."

"That is where you are wrong, ma tante," broke in Fernande firmly. "Ronnay de Maurel is not a man from whom you can wrest a responsibility or a right quite so easily. Think you he doth not already suspect Leroux' treachery and hath not taken the first steps to combat it?"

"No, I do not think it for a moment," replied Madame with her usual decisiveness. "Ronnay has only been home two days; he cannot yet have taken up the reins of government at his factories with any assurance. Moreover, Gaston de Maurel hath claimed all his nephew's attention. The old man is really dying at last, I do believe."

"M. le Comte de Maurel is quite capable of devoting his time to his sick kinsman and of keeping an eye on the administration of his factories at the same time."

"You seem to have a very high opinion of my son's capabilities, my dear," said Madame la Marquise snappishly.

"I have seen him with his workmen, remember," retorted Fernande. "I have seen him deal with men like Leroux."

"Well?... And?..."

"And as I told you just now, he is not a man whom the Leroux' or

138

the de Puisayes are going to hoodwink, or to make a fool of; he is not a man who can be caught napping, or from whose nerveless hands the sceptre of power can so easily be snatched. Ronnay de Maurel may to all outward appearances be a rustic—an unsophisticated boor—but he is a man, for all that—a man and not a puppet—he is very wide-awake—he is alive, oh! very much alive!—and, believe me, he will know how to guard what is not only his own, but is also of priceless value to the Emperor whom he worships."

"Hoity-toity, child!" exclaimed Madame with ill-concealed asperity. "Your indifference of a while ago seems to have given place to marvellous vehemence in the defence of our common enemy. 'Tis lucky your future husband is not here to see your flaming cheeks now and your glowing eyes. But perhaps," she added with a dry, forced laugh, "you will be good enough to explain the meaning of these Cassandra-like prophetic warnings, for, of a truth, I do confess that I do not understand them."

"An you will jeer, ma tante," said Fernande quietly; "'twere better I said no more."

"It is your duty to say more, child, now you have said so much," said Madame gravely. "What is it that in our council of war has struck you as rash or ill-advised? I will confess that you do know my son Ronnay better than any of us; you have seen him more often. He has made love to you, and, in so doing, he may have revealed some traits in his character which have remained hidden from us. Speak, therefore, child, openly and frankly. You wish to warn us all. Against what?"

"Against bribing a criminal—a jail-bird like Leroux, to betray his master," replied Fernande calmly.

Madame laughed and shrugged her shoulders.

"That," she said, "my dear, is childish. On Leroux' help rests the whole edifice of our plans and our entire hope of success."

"I know that well enough," rejoined Fernande. "I know that you are not like to heed anything I say. I only spoke because you forced me. Think you," she added more vehemently, "that if I had thought for a moment that you, or father, or M. de Puisaye, would have listened to me, I would not have dragged myself at your feet and kissed the ground and licked the dust and never risen until you heard, until you gave up all thought of joining issue with a miserable traitor, a criminal like Leroux. It is because I knew that my voice would count as less than nothing with you all that I remained silent."

"You speak with strange excitement, child...."

"I speak as I feel," she retorted hotly. "I speak because something in me tells me that some awful disaster will come to us and to our cause through trafficking with Leroux and his kind. Of this I am as convinced, ma tante, as I am of the fact that M. de Maurel already suspects our machinations, and on this," she concluded with marvellous forcefulness, "I would stake my life."

139

"You are mad, Fernande!"

"Mad?" retorted the girl hotly, "mad because I implore you not to sully our cause by joining issue with a handful of felons; mad because I foresee an abyss of misery and of remorse for us all in this monstrous treachery which we have planned. Ah! if it only meant a ruse of war, a clever intrigue to catch an unwary foe! But what M. de Puisaye has planned may mean murder, ma tante—the murder of a brave man—and that man your son ...!"

"Fernande! In Heaven's name, what does this mean?"

The cry came from the door, which had suddenly been thrown open, and Fernande, almost beside herself with the vehemence of her emotion, turned and found herself face to face with Laurent, who was standing under the lintel, his cheeks pale, his breath coming and going in rapid gasps through his parted lips, his dark eyes fixed gloweringly upon her.

"Mother, will you explain?" continued the young man peremptorily, as he turned to Madame la Marquise and, closing the door behind him, strode into the room.

"Nay, my good Laurent," replied Madame testily, "that I cannot do. The explanation of this extraordinary outburst on the part of your fiancée can only come from her. As for myself, I confess that I am utterly bewildered by this torrent of recrimination which Fernande has chosen to let loose upon us all. It seems that M. de Puisaye is a murderer and we his accomplices ... that we are bribing a felon to assassinate Ronnay de Maurel, for whose welfare my niece appears to evince an extraordinarily deep interest. You must forgive me, therefore, if I leave you to deal with the situation as best you can. When Fernande is in a more rational frame of mind, we can discuss the question of her leaving for Courson as soon as may be."

IV

Madame sailed out of the room and Laurent was left alone with Fernande. Already the strain seemed to have been lifted from her nerves; the hectic flush of a while ago had fled from her cheeks and left her face pale and her eyes calm and clear. Laurent approached her, quivering with excitement; the insensate jealousy which never ceased to torture him had him now under its evil sway. He tried to draw Fernande close to him, and almost uttered a cry of rage when she appeared unresponsive and turned quite coolly away from him.

"Fernande," he said, and tried in vain to subdue the harshness of his voice, which he felt must grate unpleasantly on the young girl's overstrung nerves, "I heard most of what you said to my mother. She is hurt—and justly so—at your attitude. Will you let me go to her with a message from you, telling her that you were overwrought and hardly conscious of what you said?"

"You may go, Laurent," replied Fernande coldly, "and tell ma tante that I am deeply grieved if what I said did really offend her. I did not mean to offend. I only meant to strike a note of warning. It hath proved jarring," she added dejectedly, "and of no avail. Therefore am I doubly sorry. But, even so, I would not have it unsaid."

"Not even if I were to tell you, Fernande, that your hot defence of that traitor went to my heart like a knife and caused me infinite pain."

"If what I said about your brother hurts you, Laurent, then you must be harbouring thoughts about me which are an insult to your future wife."

"If only I could believe that you loved me!" he cried, as with sudden and passionate impulse he once more tried to take her in his arms. His glowing eyes strove to meet her glance, but she seemed utterly unapproachable as she stood beside him like a slender white lily, with her small head averted and her blue eyes looking out into the distance as far away from him as was the heaven of which he dreamed. His arms dropped listlessly to his side.

"If I only could believe that you loved me, Fernande," he reiterated sadly.

"Poor Laurent," she murmured gently. Of her own free will now she placed her cool fingers upon his lips, and he seized upon them hungrily and covered them with kisses. "Poor Laurent! I told you, did I not, on the day nearly a year ago now, when I solemnly plighted my troth to you in response to my father's wish, that I had it not in me to love any man? Methinks that I shall never know really what love is.... I shall never know," she added, with a quaint, melancholy little sigh, "the kind of love which is for ever wounding and hurting the thing it loves."

"Forgive me, Fernande," he cried, already repentant, cursing himself for his perpetual folly, and knowing all the while that nothing would ever cure him of it. "I am a jealous brute, I know. I hate and despise myself every time that my temper offends you. But if you only knew, Fernande ..." he sighed, "if only you could understand...."

"I do know, Laurent, and I do understand ... am I not always ready to forgive?... But you must try, dear, to trust me a little better. A scene like the one we have just had is not an over good augury for our future, is it?"

"I hated to hear you speak so warmly about that man."

"I called him brave ... can you deny that he is?"

"No ... but...."

"There! there!" she said soothingly, dealing with him with infinite gentleness now that she had reduced him to a state of remorse. "Go and speak with ma tante, and make my excuses to her, if you think they are necessary."

She held out her cheek to him with one of her most captivating smiles, and poor Laurent was ready to sob with delight. She allowed him to take her in his arms and to kiss her sweet lips, her eyes, her hair, and if she did not respond to his caresses quite as ardently as he would have wished, he had, nevertheless, no cause to complain that she withdrew herself from them.

"My mother said that we were to discuss the question of your going to Courson," he said, before he finally took leave of her.

"Oh, as to that," she rejoined coolly, "you may tell ma tante that I have changed my mind. She did not approve of my going, did she? so I will, if I may," she added, with a sweet air of innocence, "remain at La Frontenay for a few days longer with her."

"Fernande, you are an angel!" he exclaimed. And he dropped on his knee and kissed her little hand with the same fervour as he would have kissed the robe of a Madonna. His head was bent and the tears of remorse still hung upon his lashes, or else, no doubt, he would have perceived the strange, elusive smile which lingered round his beloved one's lips.

V

Away from Fernande's bewitching presence Laurent de Mortain was conscious once more of the gnawing pangs of jealousy, nor did his mother contrive to soothe him in any way. Madame la Marquise was terribly angered against her niece. The girl's accusing words: "And that man your son!" rang unpleasantly and insistently upon her ear. Not that fanaticism allowed her for a moment to feel compunction—let alone remorse—at what she had done, nor did she delude herself for a moment as to the probable truth of Fernande's accusations. De Puisaye's plan of seizing the La Frontenay factories through the mediation of a set of unscrupulous blackguards would certainly entail bloodshed—murder, perhaps—if, indeed, the slaughter of a dangerous enemy could be called by such an ugly name when the cause was so holy and so just.

That the dangerous enemy happened to be her own son did not weigh for a moment with Madame la Marquise. Her heart and soul were wrapped up in the cause of King Louis, and if her beloved Laurent had at any time proved a traitor to it, she would have plucked him out of her heart and left him to die a traitor's death, with the stoicism of a Spartan mother sacrificing an unfit son to the general weal of her country. But though fanaticism did in so complete a manner rule her every thought and smother every one of her sensibilities, Madame did not like to hear her actions criticized, nor the callousness of her heart brought so crudely to the light of day. She was very angry with Fernande, and seeing that Laurent's jealousy had been very fully aroused by the scene which he had witnessed, she was willing to let her son be the avenger of her own offended dignity. She knew that Laurent could make his fiancée suffer acutely while he was a prey to one of his moods, and that he would find many a word wherewith to wound her as deeply as she had dared to wound his mother.

"It is strange," said Madame, with a good deal of acerbity, when she was discussing with Laurent, a quarter of an hour or so later on, Fernande's inexplicable conduct of a while ago. "It is strange that she should so suddenly desire to remain at La Frontenay when not more than a couple of hours ago she was so set on going away."

"What do you mean, mother?" he asked with a frown. "Do you think...?"

"I don't know what to think," broke in Madame testily. "Fernande has been very strange of late. Her attitude to-day has been absolutely incomprehensible."

"You don't think," murmured Laurent with some hesitation and not a little shamefacedness, "you don't think that she has met Ronnay again?"

"You never know what Fernande has done or what she may do," rejoined Madame evasively. "She has become so headstrong and so secretive, I really do not know what to make of her."

All of which did not tend to pour oil on the troubled waters of poor Laurent's jealousy; in fact, the more Madame talked, the more wretched he became, until his face became literally distorted with wrath and with misery. Then she felt sorry for him; compunction smote her, for she did not genuinely believe that Fernande had done anything to justify her lover's suspicions, and she also realized at the same time that she was doing considerable harm by irritating her son's nerves with her spiteful promptings, at a moment when he had need of all his coolness and courage to accomplish the important task which his chief had assigned to him. The campaign would begin now in earnest; Laurent would perforce be often separated from his fiancée, and the cause of King Louis would be ill served if his heart and his thoughts remained at La Frontenay while he was leading a surprise attack upon Domfront. This being, as always, Madame la Marquise de Mortain's primary consideration, she drew in her horns and did her best to undo the mischief which she had been at great pains to wreak.

"It is no use," she said soothingly, "to worry yourself unnecessarily about Fernande. She certainly is very headstrong—she is also self-willed and thoughtless; but she has loved you ever since you and she were children together. There is not a thought of guile in her, and the provoking little scene with which she regaled me just now may have been due to pique, that I did not at once accept her prophetic warnings."

143

"I wish I could think so," sighed Laurent.

"You must bring yourself to think so, my dear," retorted Madame dryly. "You have far more important things to dwell on at this moment than the vagaries of a young girl's moods. Not only will the success of M. de Puisaye's plans depend upon your coolness and your valour, but his life and the lives of the men whom he leads will hang upon the master-stroke which you will have to accomplish by surprising the garrison of Domfront ere wind of the affair hath reached the fort, and by holding a couple of hundred soldiers of Bonaparte in durance until reinforcements can reach you. It is a heavy task for such young shoulders, my son," she added earnestly. "May God give you strength to carry it through."

"I would give my life," murmured Laurent dully, "for the right to remain at La Frontenay for the next few days."

"A Marquis de Mortain," broke in Madame with rigid sternness, "cannot lag behind when those of his kindred are risking their lives for their King. Have no fear for Fernande, my dear boy," she added more gently. "It is as well that she stays here with me. I can keep an eye on her. You can trust me to keep your treasure in safety for you, against your speedy return."

Obviously Laurent was neither convinced nor pacified; but there was nothing more to be said. Within the next few moments M. de Courson returned, and uncle and nephew had to talk over their plans of the next forty-eight hours. It were best, so M. de Courson decided, that they should go immediately to Courson and make arrangements for mustering their men there before the general rally in the Cerf-Volant woods two days later. Laurent would have wished to take a final, impassioned farewell of his fiancée, but on this M. de Courson—as his senior and his leader—pronounced a decided veto. This was not the time for sentimental dalliance and indulgence in nerve-racking fits of jealousy. Laurent now was amenable to military discipline, which was all the more strict as subservience to it was purely voluntary.

Madame gave her unqualified approval to M. de Courson's decision. Fernande, she declared, would be well guarded and under her own eye. She—Madame—would see that the child's emotional nature did not lead her into some headstrong act of folly.

After a while Laurent had perforce to yield; disobedience was out of the question. At this juncture it would even bear an uglier name than that; and though the young man's heart was aching for a last sight of his beloved, though he longed to plunge his gaze into her blue eyes and to read within their limpid depths all that he would have longed to find, of love, of ardour and of fidelity, he braced himself up for a great effort, and with, at any rate, outward calm, he bade his mother an affectionate farewell and finally followed M. de Courson out of the château.

Madame la Marquise, from the window beside which she was standing, was able to watch the two slim figures—her son and her

144

brother—as they strode rapidly down the broad avenue of the park, until a clump of tall-growing conifers hid them from her view.

Then she fell on her knees, and resting her elbows on the window-ledge, she buried her face in her hands.

"God! My God!" she prayed, with all the ardour of a devotee, "give success to our arms! Bring those two back triumphant and victorious! Bring our beloved King back to his throne again!"

CHAPTER XVI

THE IRREPARABLE

I

Ronnay de Maurel had been absent nearly a year from his home. He had joined the Emperor in Poland, and despite his game leg, he had fought at Jena and Auerstadt, at Eylau and at Friedland.

When the two Emperors met upon the bridge at Tilsit and decided on the terms of peace, de Maurel, created Marshal of France on the field of Auerstadt, returned quietly to La Vieuville in time, he hoped, to close the eyes of old Gaston and to hear his last dying words. He had been home just three days. The day after his arrival he sent back the military representatives who had looked after his factories for him during his absence, and quietly took up once more the reins of government, which an unendurable heart-ache had caused to drop temporarily out of his hands. He laid aside his fine uniform and once more took up his blouse and his woollen cap. Old Gaston was too feeble to note the subtle change which had come over his nephew during twelve months of rough campaigning among the snows and the marshes of Poland; he did not perceive how passing seldom Ronnay ever spoke now, or how he sat late into the night staring straight out before him with a yearning gaze in his dark, deep-set eyes. He had passed through Paris on his way home and brought back a number of books with him—he who before this had never troubled about one in his life—and when his eyes ached from staring into vacancy, he would open one of these books, and drawing the lamp closer to him, he would rest his elbow on the table and shade his face with his hand and become so absorbed, that the grey dawn would oft find him still sitting

145

in the invalid's room, with the book open in front of him—unless he had pushed it aside and sat with his head buried in his hands.

On the day of his arrival he had, with the help of Madame Lapin, reorganized the La Vieuville household on a more comfortable basis. But little could be done in the way of comforts for the dying man; he was past noticing if his room was aired or his food brought to him at regular intervals. The village doctor visited him from time to time, but there was nothing to be done now. The machinery of life was worn out; for over a year now it had threatened to break down altogether—an iron constitution and an invincible will to live until the beloved nephew came home once more, had alone kept the enfeebled heart to its work.

To Ronnay de Maurel the aspect of La Vieuville seemed infinitely dreary; the thought of the factories and the foundries singularly uninspiring. What mattered it that he had come home—a great deal older, a little more crippled, more impatient and more indifferent? Old Gaston could not now last more than a few days, and the representatives of the War Office had seen to it that the output of guns and of munitions did not fall too far short of the Emperor's needs. Why should a man come home—a man who had courted death in an hundred desperate fights—a man who had nothing to live for, no one to care for, no one who would rejoice when he returned or who would weep if he fell ... when countless precious sons and brothers and lovers and husbands were left to rot unburied on the ice-covered plains of Poland, and countless mothers and widows mourned, broken-hearted, at their loss?

But it was not his way to let things drift. Peace had, of a truth, been signed at Tilsit, but it was not like to be a lasting peace. The European Powers had once and for all decided that France was not to remain in bondage to the Emperor whom she worshipped. He was in everybody else's way, he must be swept aside in order to make room for the effete and incompetent Bourbons, who were hanging on to the coattails of England and Austria and Russia, with a view to reaping the chestnuts which others had pulled out of the fire for them. De Maurel was one of those who would have preferred their idolized Emperor to sit at home after this last campaign, to enjoy the fruit of his victories and to prove to the world that France, when she divested herself of the old régime, had gained a benefactor, even though she had had to pass through fire and water, through crime and ignominy, ere she got him. But to know Napoleon intimately, as did the privileged few, was to realize that measureless ambition which was destined to hurl him, not only down from the giddy heights of triumph and of victory whereon his glorious achievements of the last two campaigns had established him, but also from his secure place within the heart of his people, a place which he would only reconquer when his mortal remains were brought back to France after the years of conflict and of misery which were to come.

146

II

That all was not well at the factories de Maurel did not fail to perceive within four-and-twenty hours of his return. The military overseers had done their duty—the output of munitions, if not lavish, had been adequate, and there had been no open rebellion among the workers. But in the first tour of inspection which the master made of his demesnes he realized how more than surly was the temper of former malcontents now and how sorely had the loyalty of the honest workmen been tried.

Complaints and grumblings had not been listened to now for over a year; the rough admonitions of a sympathetic taskmaster had given place to peremptory commands from military disciplinarians and to threats of condign punishment at the slightest sign of discontent. It would take many weeks of untiring patience and firmness to re-establish the happy concord which reigned in the foundries and armament works a year ago. As for the powder factories, de Maurel was compelled to reserve judgment as to where real grievances began and slackness and covert rebellion ended. Leroux, suave and obsequious, at once aroused his distrust, but the War Office representatives, when they left, had given the man an excellent character, both for trustworthiness and for industry, and de Maurel was not the man to act on mere intuition.

Intuition had played him such a damnable trick a while ago when he would have staked his soul on the loyalty of a pair of blue eyes!

Mathurin certainly struck a note of warning, but he found his master so unapproachable, that he dared not say much, and old Gaston had long since been too feeble to see anything that was going on.

Of Madame la Marquise up at La Frontenay he could glean but little information. M. le Marquis had been absent a great deal during the year with M. de Courson, and Mademoiselle Fernande had remained with her aunt during the absence of M. le Marquis; but neither she nor Madame had done more than pay the one visit to the foundries as the orders of the War Office authorities were very peremptory on that point. The ladies were seldom seen outside the limits of the château; they had dismissed all the servants whom Vardenne had engaged for them locally, and replaced them gradually by importations of their own.

It was generally understood in the district that Mademoiselle de Courson was now formally affianced to M. le Marquis de Mortain.

III

It was on the day following the council of war at La Frontenay that Ronnay de Maurel started out soon after dawn for one of his favourite tramps across the moors and through the woods. Before he went away last July he had left very strict orders that no one should henceforth be allowed to wander in the La Frontenay woods. The explanation was given that valuable game was being preserved there, and one of old Gaston's last efforts at administering his nephew's property was to establish in accordance with Ronnay's express instructions, a veritable army of keepers in the district, with discretionary powers to warn every trespasser off the forbidden grounds.

De Maurel, therefore, when he started off on that exquisite June morning to re-visit the place where he had suffered the most terrible mental torture which heart of man could endure, felt confident that he would remain secure from intrusion; that, above all, he need not fear a rencontre which would inevitably reopen the burning wound which time had not even begun to heal.

To him, now that a year of hard work and hard fighting had passed over that awful day of misery and of shame, it seemed as if time had stood still; as if it had been but a few hours ago that he had started out—just as he did now—on that walk beneath the early morning sunshine, which had ended in such an appalling disaster—in the total wreckage of his life, of his newly-awakened youth, of every newly-risen hope of home and of happiness. Then, as now, the dew still lay upon the carpet of moss, the mountain-ash and the elder were in full bloom, and the mating birds had finished building their nests. Then, as now, the swallows circled swiftly overhead, and a lark rose from the ground at his feet and sang its joyful song of thanksgiving to God.

But then the world held for him an exquisite being who was all tenderness and charm, who had lured him with her blue eyes, until he remembered that he, too, was young and he, too, had a right to love and happiness; the woods had held for him a nymph with feet like the petals of flowers, with sun-kissed hair which shone like living gold. A nymph! a creature of grace, of air, of light, whose fragrance was akin to a wilderness of roses, whose laugh was like the song of the lark, and whose arms were white and slender like the lilies! And when she stood before him or lay placid and drowsy in his arms, mysterious voices in the woods had murmured in his ear insidious promises of happiness to come.

He, poor fool, had listened to those voices—sirens' voices, which are wont to lure the unfortunate mariner on life's ocean to his own destruction—to his own misery and undoing; sirens' voices which whispered that the exquisite fairy-like form which lay like a nestling bird in his arms would one day be his for always—that she would always snuggle up, just like this, against his shoulder; that he would one day cull a kiss from those perfect lips, that he would one day have the right to hold her and keep her and to guard her for always against every ill.

Since then the voices of the sirens had turned to harsh and dismal screeching; the hopes of a year ago had turned to blank despair, and the savour of that triumphal aspiration turned to the dead sea fruit of unconquerable humiliation.

Prussian cannon had disdained the prey which Ronnay de Maurel had offered with crazy recklessness; he had come back laden with honours, a broken-hearted and lonely man; and the birds still sang, the woods were still fragrant, the world of sunshine and of springtide, of flowering trees and full-blown roses mocked at his irretrievable beggary.

IV

And when Fernande de Courson started out that same morning, soon after daybreak, in a random spirit of wandering, and her footsteps led her—unconsciously, perhaps—in the direction of the woods, she, too, had little thought of meeting Ronnay de Maurel again. The hour was so early that not another soul was abroad—so early that not a sound stirred the quietude of valley and of hills save the distant murmuring of the tiny stream which found its resting-place in the silent pool.

It was an hour, too, wherein even the keepers established by old Gaston to patrol the La Frontenay woods usually slackened their vigilance. It was too late for poachers, too early for tramps; Fernande, as she left the meadows behind her, turned into a woodland path unperceived.

For a time she walked on somewhat aimlessly. It was deliciously cool under the trees, and the smell of budding blossom, of wet moss and of pine, acted as a tonic on her overstrung nerves. She wandered on, not allowing herself to think. All through the past few days she had tried not to feel that Ronnay de Maurel had come back; she had tried to forget that he was near, that any day, any moment, if she took her walks abroad she might come face to face with him.

And, in a measure, she had succeeded. She was now Laurent de Mortain's future wife, the follies of a year ago must yield to a sober view of future events. Except for that one brief, if vehement outburst yesterday in the presence of Madame's monstrous callousness, she had succeeded in relegating the man to whom she had done an infinite wrong to the furthermost recesses of her mind. But here, in these woods where every murmur among the trees, every call of bird or fragrance of flower, reminded her of him—in the woods through which she had once passed nestling against his shoulder, secure in the embrace of his strong arms, thoughts of him went hammering through her brain. All the dangers which beset him through Joseph de Puisaye's plan of campaign and Leroux' treachery caused her heart to beat with a nameless horror and fear. At every moment she thought to hear his rugged voice calling her by name, and even now her heart almost stilled its beating as a woodland echo seemed to bring back to her ear that cry of triumph which had rent her very soul: "You love me, Fernande!"

And as she wandered on, she lost count of time, and soon she found that she had lost her way. She had never entered the La Frontenay woods from the direction of the château since first she came to stay there, and she had no idea now which way to turn in order to go back home again. Soon she felt tired and dispirited; she did not know how long she had been wandering, nor how far she had gone.

Then all at once she knew where she was. She had walked a few steps along a moss-covered path, which wound its way right through the thicket, and suddenly there came a break in the coppice, and there before her lay the silent pool, with its mossy banks and clumps of wild iris and of meadowsweet, and the fallen tree-trunk where she had sat that day—a whole year ago.

And as she made her way nearer to the water, she saw Ronnay de Maurel sitting there on the bank; he was leaning against the fallen tree-trunk, his elbow resting upon it and his head supported by his hand.

She would have fled if she could, for at sight of him she had at once realized that to meet him here and now was the last thing in the world that she had wished. She realized that rather than he should see her, rather than she should speak with him, she would have run for miles, fearful only lest he should follow her track. How could she meet him—even to speak the words of contrition which for the past year she had longed to utter one day—how could she meet him whilst up at La Frontenay her own kindred, her own friends, those whom she loved, were planning treachery and murder against him!

But unfortunately now there was no time to run away; already he had seen her, and before she could stir from the spot, he had struggled to his feet and was coming towards her. Even then she would have given worlds to be able to go, but she could not. For one thing, he walked more haltingly than he had ever done before—and then he looked older, less sure of himself, more forlorn and solitary. He dragged his wounded leg more markedly—more as he used to do in the olden days when he was overtired, and all her womanly tenderness and

150

pity went out to him, because of that indefinable air of helplessness which his lameness momentarily gave him. Not only did Fernande de Courson not beat a hasty retreat, but when he paused, irresolute and timid, it was she who came a step or two nearer to him.

"I am afraid that I am trespassing," she said tentatively, for, of a truth, she felt suddenly frightened—frightened at his look—a look of bitter resentment, she thought, of hate perhaps as absolute as she had felt for him in days gone by.

"Nay, it is I," he retorted dryly, "who have no right to be here, seeing that it is evidently Mademoiselle de Courson's favourite walk. By your leave, I will vacate the field. The keepers should have warned me. Had they done so, I would not have come."

He bowed in his usual awkward style and made as if to go, but with a word Fernande called him back. For a moment or two he hesitated. No doubt he, too, had as great a desire to run away as she had; but the girl now—with one of those contradictory impulses which are peculiar to sensitive temperaments—felt an unconquerable wish to speak with him ... if only for the purpose of challenging him to those words of reproach which he had spared her on that day when Laurent's cruel scorn and her own callousness had struck him as with a physical blow.

"M. de Maurel," she cried, moved by that sudden impulse.

"At your commands, Mademoiselle," he replied.

"I ... I ... believe me I had no thought of meeting you here ... or of intruding upon your privacy ... but now that we have met, I beg of you that you will let me tell you...."

She paused, feeling that a hot flush had risen to her cheeks and that her words sounded both halting and cold. And yet he had made no movement to stop her. It had never been his way to interrupt. For good or ill, he always listened to the end of whatever anyone chose to say. He had listened to the end, when Laurent, with a few harsh words, had shattered the shrine wherein he had set his fondest illusions; he stood quite still now, ready to listen to everything she might wish to say. But somehow it was just his attitude of quiet expectancy which stemmed the flow of her words. It was only when she had been silent for some few seconds and apparently was not going to speak again, that he interposed calmly:

"Is there any necessity for you, Mademoiselle, to tell me anything? Surely not, seeing that it distresses you. Will you, on the other hand, permit me to offer you my well-meant congratulations on your approaching marriage with my brother?"

Already Fernande had recovered some measure of self-control. Her dignity was on the qui vive. Apparently he meant to meet every advance on her part with frigid enmity. The look of resentment in his eyes had deepened, and to Fernande's keen senses it seemed as if they held no small measure of scorn as well.

"I thank you," she said coolly. "It was ma tante's intention to send you an announcement of our fiançailles, but we only heard yesterday with any certainty that you had returned."

"There is no occasion for my mother to trouble herself about such trifling conventions with me," he retorted. "I feel so sure that she hath no desire to claim the slightest kinship with a de Maurel that any formalities of the kind which she seems to contemplate would be a mere farce."

"You are very irreconcilable, M. de Maurel," said Fernande coldly, "and are making your mother and Laurent suffer for the thoughtlessness which I committed a year ago, and of which I would like you to believe that I have since bitterly repented."

"I have no recollection of any thoughtlessness on your part, Mademoiselle ... certainly of none which should cause you any regret."

"Your actions belie your words," she rejoined quietly. "If, as you say, you have not only forgiven but forgotten the foolishness of a year ago, then why have you kept aloof from your mother ... from us all? You were wont to be a constant visitor at Courson, your mother and Laurent have enjoyed your hospitality for the past twelve months. Yet you have not been nigh La Frontenay, and 'tis three days since your return."

"My uncle Gaston is dying," he said curtly; "he and the works have claimed my attention."

"Does that mean, then, that you will come?" she asked, "one day soon when you are not so engaged?"

Then, as he made no reply, she added more insistently: "Your mother and Laurent bore no part whatever in the wrong which I alone committed. M. de Maurel, why should you remain at enmity with them?"

"At enmity, Mademoiselle?—am I at enmity with my mother or with my brother? Surely not."

"Why not go to see them? Why not come to see us all as you used to do?"

"Chiefly, I think," he replied roughly, "because up at La Frontenay no one has any desire to see me. My brother and I have nothing in common—my mother and I still less. You, Mademoiselle Fernande, proved to me a year ago what an utterly ridiculous boor I was, fit only to be jeered at and made game of. Now a bear is not usually a good plaything for women; he is apt to snarl and render himself odious by his antics. He is far better out of the way, believe me."

"You are ungenerous, M. de Maurel. God knows how bitterly I have regretted my folly! I had no thought of seeing you here, 'tis true, but now, despite your harshness, I am glad that we have met. Words of sorrow and of repentance which refused me service a year ago have seared my heart ever since. I could not speak then, I was too much overcome by shame and by remorse. But I entreat you to believe that not a day has gone by during the past twelve months that I did not in my heart pray for your forgiveness. I was very young then, very thoughtless and very inexperienced. I knew nothing of men, nor was I vain enough to gauge the amount of mischief that thoughtless coquetry on my part would wreak. M. de Maurel, for the hurt I caused you that day I do sincerely beg your forgiveness. Before then ma tante and Laurent had reason to believe that in you they had found a friend. I entreat you, do not add to my remorse by venting on them your resentment which should be for me alone."

Her voice broke in a short sob. Her blue eyes were filled with tears. Overhead the sun had hidden its radiance behind a bank of clouds, and all around the woods appeared grey and desolate, and from the pool there came the melancholy croaking of frogs and the call of wood-pigeons was wafted through the trees.

"The bear must dance again, eh?" rejoined de Maurel harshly. "He may prove dangerous if he slips his chain. I wonder what it is that does go on inside La Frontenay that all this mise en scène should have been resorted to once more in order to hoodwink me?"

Fernande drew back as if she had been struck. A hot flush rose to the very roots of her hair; it seemed to her as if an unseen and aggressive hand had thrown a veil right over her head, and then dealt her a heavy blow between the eyes. Everything around her suddenly appeared blurred and a strange sense of cold crept into her limbs.

"I don't understand," she stammered.

"Ah! but I think you do, Mademoiselle Fernande," he retorted. "A year ago it was thought necessary to enchain the Maurel bear so that he might dance to Royalist pipings; for this he was lured and cajoled and fed with treacle and honeyed words. The foolish, awkward creature began to dance; he was ready to see nothing save a pair of blue eyes that looked as limpid as a mountain stream, to hear nothing save the piping of a voice as clear and guileless as that of a lark. Unfortunately the jealous ravings of a puppy wakened the clumsy brute from his trance ... wakened him too soon, it seems, but so roughly that, feeling dazed and shaken, he preferred to crawl away out of sight rather than remain a butt for mockery and ridicule. Now he has come back and may prove dangerous again—what? Bah! the same old methods can easily be tried again, the same honeyed words spoken, the same blue eyes raised tantalizingly to his. Too late, Mademoiselle Fernande!" he added, with a laugh which sounded strident and harsh as it echoed through the woods. "The bear has awakened from his winter sleep, he is not like to be caught napping again."

"M. de Maurel," protested Fernande, "you are not only ungenerous now, but wilfully cruel and unchivalrous; and, of a truth, your harshness now hath killed every feeling of remorse which I have felt. You have, of a truth, the right to hate me, the right to hate us all; but I spoke to you in all sincerity, and my humility and repentance should at least have saved me from insult."

"Sincerity!" he exclaimed, "sincerity from a Courson! Ah! Mademoiselle Fernande, you said just now that I was at enmity with my brother Laurent. By my faith, I will remain for ever his debtor. But for his interference on that memorable day meseems that Madame my mother would have succeeded in staging once again the tragedy which had already once been enacted at La Frontenay, when a de Maurel took a de Courson for bride, and the final curtain rang down upon his broken heart."

"A broken heart!" she retorted hotly, "you! Nay, every word that you utter hath proved to me the foolishness of my remorse. Your heart hath been full only of outraged vanity and of unreasoning resentment, the while I wept countless tears of sorrow and of regret."

"Regret for what, Mademoiselle?" he exclaimed roughly. "What, I pray you, had you to regret? You say that you wept countless tears—what for? Had you to mourn the only illusion of your life? Had you to mourn the loss of every hope which for days and nights had haunted you with its sweet, insistent call? Had you to weep because the one being in this mean and sordid world whom you thought pure and true—almost holy—suddenly appeared before you false and cruel—double-tongued and insidious, a commonplace siren set to lay a trap for men? Had you to weep because the being whom you had learned to worship had with wanton frolic and a mocking smile plucked out your heart-strings and left you forlorn and desolate, a prey to ignominy and to lifelong regret? And had you to weep tears of bitter humiliation in the knowledge that those who hated and despised you were laughing their fill at your folly? Oh! I, too, Mademoiselle Fernande, was young then ... I, too, was inexperienced ... I was a dolt and a fool—but what wrong, in God's name, had I done you that you should treat me so?"

Silently Fernande had listened, her hand grasping a clump of branches of young chestnut, else mayhap she would have fallen. That feeling of a veil enveloping her head was still with her; there was a buzzing in her ear through which his harsh voice came with a sound like hammering upon the portals of her brain. The agony and misery which rang out from his words found their echo in her own heart. Indeed, many a time in the past year had she felt pitifully sorry for the man whom she had wronged with such unpardonable thoughtlessness, but never before had she felt as she did now; never before had she realized the full extent of the misery which she had caused.

His voice broke into a heartrending sob. He covered his face with his hands with a gesture of such racking pain, that she would have given her very life at this moment for the right to comfort him.

"M. de Maurel," she said gently, and, indeed, now her voice was softer than that of a cooing dove, "God alone knows how deeply your words have hurt me; and I go away to-day feeling that you have made me atone for all that I made you suffer. Indeed, indeed, I had no thought a year ago that my senseless coquetry could arouse in a noble-hearted man like you, feelings which I so little deserved. Whatever you may think, however, I did not lie to you when I told you that for the past year, not one day has gone by without a thought of burning remorse in my mind for what I had done. I did not lie when I sued for your forgiveness. This I do swear to you by every memory that clusters round this glade, by every memory that speaks to you as well as to me in the rustle of the leaf-laden trees and in the murmurings of the woods; I swear it by the unforgettable hour when we both heard the gentle cooing of the wood-pigeons, and my hand rested in yours in complete amity. As for the future, 'tis not likely that we shall ever meet again. I hope to leave La Frontenay very soon—to-day if I can. May I therefore beg you in all earnestness to take up the threads of friendship with your mother—there where my own foolishness caused them to snap? Go to her, M. de Maurel ... go to-day if you can. Do not forget that she is your mother.... Do not let her forget that you are her son. God be with you and guard you! And whatever may happen in the future, will you at least try to bear in mind that Fernande de Courson would gladly give her life to heal the wound which she hath inflicted. Time will inevitably do that," she added with a choked little sigh, "and in the years to come you will mayhap think less bitterly of me."

Then she turned and, like a deer, she vanished in the thicket. Ronnay's hands fell from his face. For a long while he remained there gazing on the spot where she had stood. Through the murmurings of the wood he still could hear the echo of her silvery voice, and it seemed to him that her pale face, with the tear-filled eyes, still peeped at him from between the branches of the coppice, and that the perfume of her white gown and of her golden hair still filled the air with their intoxicating fragrance.

Then with a heavy sigh he, too, turned and went his way.

CHAPTER XVII

A LAST APPEAL

I

Fernande had said nothing to Madame la Marquise of her rencontre with Ronnay de Maurel. Of a truth, Madame, despite her many promises to Laurent, had not kept a very close eye on her niece's movements. Fernande had been away from the château during the best part of the morning; she came home with tear-stained eyes, and her gown had obviously trailed in the mud, but Madame apparently noticed nothing. All the day she wandered about the château in a perfect fever of excitement. In the afternoon a runner came over from Courson with news from all the chiefs. The next day was now irrevocably fixed upon for the attack on the foundries. Leroux was to be given his final instructions, and Madame herself be prepared to hold the château against any assault delivered against it by the local peasantry, who no doubt were well armed by de Maurel and had been drilled against any emergency.

M. de Courson had added a special note to the letter telling Madame, that the Comte de Puisaye had decided to send his friend Prigent with forty or fifty men to La Frontenay in case of attack.

"The château can very easily be held," M. de Courson's note went on, "and we have no fears for you, knowing your energy and resourcefulness. Give Leroux the fullest instructions possible, then do not send for him again during the day. I have an idea that he is being watched by spies of de Maurel's, and he will have to be very circumspect for the next thirty-six hours. As for us all, we are more full of hope than ever. We reviewed our men last night in the park. They are marvellously enthusiastic and firm in the belief that their prowess will rally thousands of waverers to the Fleur-de-Lis. De Puisaye has recruited a further two hundred, and hath now a force of over six on the further side of Mortain. Everything, therefore, is for the best, and nothing but some absolutely unforeseen accident can now rob us of success. Above all, I entreat you, my dear sister, be as silent and discreet as the grave. Remember that walls of French châteaux have oft had ears in the course of their history. Speak to no one of our plan for to-morrow ... not to Matthieu Renard, not to his wife. Do not discuss it with Fernande in the presence of those whom you think most loyal. To-morrow afternoon at three o'clock see Leroux in your private boudoir. Be sure that door and windows are closed and that no one lurks behind curtains or screens. Then tell the man to have everything ready for that night. De Puisaye will arrive at the foundries soon after midnight, and he will expect to find arms for six hundred men ready to his hand. After that he will see to everything himself. Command Leroux to speak to no one, to trust no one—but to select with the utmost care the fifty men whom he requires to remain at the factories with him, in order to surprise the watchmen and prevent the alarm being given. Keep Fernande out of your councils, my dear Denise, as far as you can. The child appears to me to be overwrought and might do some act of headstrongness which might ruin everything. Something seems to have occurred between her and Laurent just before we left La Frontenay. You will know, no doubt, what it was. Laurent is a prey to most acute jealousy. He has worried me considerably since yesterday. He hath need of all his courage and coolness to bear his share of our work to-morrow night. While I lead the attack on Mortain it will be his duty to hold up the garrison of Domfront, else they may fall on de Puisaye and his men, or else on me, when perhaps not one of us would come out of it alive. I would not wrong Laurent by suggesting that he is not up to the task, but it were well if Fernande sent him a loving message by this same runner, in order to reassure him and to brace him up for his task. Now, my dear sister, I can do nothing more save commend you and my child to the care of God."

The letter closed with many assurances of affection and a tone of seriousness, which showed that M. de Courson was not perhaps quite in such an optimistic frame of mind as were his chiefs.

II

Madame had frowned and uttered an exclamation of impatience when in her brother's letter she had read the passage about Laurent. The Fates which are wont to spin the threads of human destinies without heeding the best-laid plans of men, smiled, no doubt, in their lonely eyrie up on the summit of the Brocken, when Madame la Marquise de Mortain, disdaining her brother's advice, chose in her usual dictatorial, self-willed way to send a message to Laurent herself, rather than ask Fernande to do so.

She couched her message in loving and reassuring terms, but she said nothing to Fernande on the subject. Why, she could not herself have said. There was no reason why the girl should not be told that her fiancé was in the throes of a maddening attack of jealousy, and that a word from her might soothe his perturbed spirit and restore to him that courage of which he would presently be in such sore need. But Madame had a horror of anything that might present her beloved son in an unfavourable light. Any failing or weakness of his would, she felt,

157

redound in a measure to her discredit. That is the only reason why she said nothing to Fernande, and why she herself sent the message to Laurent which, as events unfortunately proved subsequently, had not the effect of reassuring him.

In other matters she acted entirely in accordance with her brother's orders. Obedience in that case meant military discipline, and rather flattered Madame's sense of her own importance and responsibility. She spent the best part of the day in her own room, and, entirely self-absorbed, she completely ignored Fernande's presence and Fernande's movements. From the château she could see or hear nothing of the bustle and movement of the distant factories, but it seemed to her as if their unheard throbbings found their echo against her heart. To-morrow, she thought, they would for the last time manufacture engines of war to help the King's enemies in their disloyalty and their treachery; for the last time to-morrow would the abominable Corsican upstart look to La Frontenay for the cementation of his throne. She could not spare a thought for the son against whom she was intriguing with such ruthless callousness. A year ago she had planned to win him over to her side. In this she had signally failed. She might have tried again now, only that there was no time for protracted diplomacy.

To bring Ronnay de Maurel back to heel was a doubtful proposition; if it did succeed, it would be months before good results could be hoped for. In the meanwhile the King could not wait. Ronnay de Maurel stood in his way: therefore must the loyal adherents of the King sweep the offending obstacle from his path.

III

Leroux arrived punctually at three o'clock the following afternoon. Madame la Marquise was in Fernande's room, talking platitudes to the young girl in a tardy fit of remorse at having neglected her so completely these past two days.

Fernande appeared more dejected than she had been before, and Madame had much ado to keep her temper from breaking away against so much pessimism, which almost amounted to disloyalty.

It was old Annette who announced Leroux, and Madame la Marquise sent a message down to say that she would see him immediately. As soon as Annette had gone, Fernande, with one of her sudden, impulsive gestures, threw her arms round Madame's shoulders.

"Before it is too late, ma tante," she cried, with a tone of desperate entreaty, "will you not think—just once more?"

"Too late for what, child?" retorted Madame impatiently, and she shook herself free from the young girl's arms which encircled her with a forceful and passionate grip.

"Too late to avert this appalling calamity," replied Fernande. "That man Leroux is a criminal, a murderer," she continued with ever-increasing vehemence. "His greed for the money which has been offered him will render him utterly unscrupulous. I could see it in his face the other day ... when he was here ... and M. de Puisaye was speaking to him. He will stick at nothing, ma tante, at nothing in order to gain his ten thousand francs."

"Well, my dear," rejoined Madame coldly, "we want a man who will stick at nothing. King Louis hath no use for velvet gloves, for mincing ways, or for half-hearted cowards these days. We have to fight an unscrupulous foe, remember. What is Bonaparte, what are these regicides, I'd like to know, but criminals and murderers! What is Mademoiselle de Courson at this moment," she added, as with flaming cheeks and glowing eyes she turned on Fernande and would have smitten her with a look—"what is Mademoiselle de Courson now save a half-hearted coward, unworthy to stand shoulder to shoulder with her father, her lover, her kinsfolk in their homeric struggle for justice and for right?"

But Fernande bore the withering looks and the insult unflinchingly. It seemed as if in the last two days she had stepped boldly across the dividing line which separates blind unquestioning childhood from understanding and reasoning womanhood. All the horror for past crimes and past excesses committed against her King and against her cause was still present in her mind; but now she refused to accept the complacent theory that crime must beget worse crime and that revenge and reprisals, murder and pillage, would ever help the righteousness of a cause or be justifiable in the sight of God.

"Bid me fight, ma tante," she retorted proudly, "side by side with my father; bid me meet the enemies of my King in loyal combat, and I'll warrant you'll not find me weak or cowardly. Fight! Yes, let us fight— fight as did George Cadoudal and Louis de Frotté and Henri de la Rochejaquelin—let us fight like men, but not like criminals. In God's name let us not stoop to murder."

"Murder, child!" exclaimed Madame, "who talked of murder, I should like to know?"

"Would you swear, ma tante," riposted Fernande slowly, "that whilst you traffic with a man like Leroux, the possibility of an awful, hideous, horrible murder has never presented itself to your mind? That you have never envisaged the likelihood of Ronnay de Maurel getting wind of this affair and of his taking Leroux to task for his proposed treachery? Have you never thought, ma tante, of what would happen if Leroux thought that his master suspected him, and if he then came face to face with him—somewhere alone...?"

Just for the space of one second Madame la Marquise de Mortain stood quite still—rigid almost as a statue—with eyes closed and lips tightly set. Just for the space of that one second it seemed as if something human, something womanly, stirred within that heart of stone. Then an impatient exclamation escaped her lips.

"Tush, child!" she said. "I'll not be taken to task by you. Who are you, pray, that you should strive to throw your childish sensibilities, your childish nonsense across the path of your King's destiny? Ronnay de Maurel must take his chance in this fight," she added, as she threw back her head with a movement of invincible determination. "He has chosen the traitor's path; while he and his kind have the power, they stick at nothing to bring us into subjection. We have the chance now ... one chance in a thousand—to gain the upper hand of all these regicides and these minions of Bonaparte. To neglect that chance for the sake of a craven scruple were now an act of criminal folly. Let that be my last word, child," continued Madame, as she made for the door; "do not let me hear any more of your warnings, your prophecies, or your sermons. What has been decided by our chiefs shall be done—understand?—and what must be, must be. And when your father returns, after having risked his life for the cause which you seem to hold so lightly, take care lest the first word he utters be one of condemnation of a recreant daughter."

IV

Madame la Marquise did not pause to see what effect her last stern words had upon Fernande. She sailed out of the room with no further thought in her mind of the passionate appeal which had left her utterly cold. To her now there existed only one thing in the entire world, and that was the project for the seizure of the La Frontenay foundries and its consequent immense effect upon the ultimate triumph of the Royalist cause. Everything else, every thought, every feeling, every duty she swept away from her heart and from her mind as petty, irrelevant, and not worthy to be weighed in the balance with the stupendous issue which was at stake.

Indeed, as she sped down to the hall for this final momentous interview with Leroux, she felt greatly thankful that yesterday she had not acted on her brother's advice, and that she had written to Laurent herself rather than allowed Fernande to do so. The girl, in writing to her lover, might have indulged in one of those dithyrambics which were so unexplainable, and which might still further have upset Laurent. As it was, everything was for the best, and Madame dismissed any latent fears from her mind just as readily as she had dismissed any slight

160

twinge of remorse which Fernande's words might have caused to arise in her heart.

Leroux, gruff and surly as usual, had been shown into a small library adjoining the great entrance-hall of the château, a room which M. de Courson had of late used as an office for transacting the correspondence of his party and receiving any messengers sent to him by one of his chiefs. Here the man had waited, while Madame was being detained upstairs by Fernande's last tender appeal.

He greeted Madame la Marquise with a rough and churlish word, and as soon as she had closed the door behind her he began abruptly:

"We'll have to be very careful," he said; "something of our project is known to de Maurel. I'd stake my life on it."

The flush of anger of a while ago fled from Madame's cheeks, but otherwise nothing in her attitude betrayed to this boor the slightest sign of fear on her part.

"What makes you think that?" she asked coolly, as she took a seat in a high-backed chair, and graciously waved her hand to Leroux in token that he, too, might sit down.

"Yesterday I wanted to come here and speak with you about one or two matters," replied the man, "when I met the Maréchal upon the high road."

"The Maréchal?" queried Madame, with a supercilious lift of the eyebrows.

"Why, yes! Our General is Marshal of France now," said Leroux with a sneer. "He gained his baton fighting against the Prussians, so I've been told."

"All of which is of no consequence, my man," broke in Madame impatiently. "We have no time to waste this morning, and you were telling me that you met M. le Comte de Maurel when you were on your way hither."

"I did," rejoined Leroux sullenly.

"And what did he say?"

"He asked me where I was going."

"And...?"

"I told him that I was free to come and go as I pleased, seeing that I was chief overseer of the factory now."

"It was very imprudent to give your present master such an impertinent answer," said Madame peremptorily. "You were expressly ordered to curb your temper and to gain M. de Maurel's confidence as far as lay in your power."

"I did curb my temper," rejoined the man. "And I did not give him an impertinent answer. I spoke as if I had honey in my mouth. I am merely telling you the drift of what I said. My actual words were cringing enough."

"Very well, then, what happened after that?"

"The Maréchal told me that though the military representatives

161

had appointed me chief overseer, he himself had not confirmed that appointment, nor would he confirm it, he said, till I showed myself really worthy of his confidence. He didn't say much, for he is never over talkative with any of us. But he looked me through and through in a way that I didn't like."

"Never mind how he looked. Did he say anything else?"

"Yes. He told me that he expressly forbade every one of his men to have any intercourse with the château, and that I was distinctly to understand that he forbade me most strictly to come to the château, or to hold converse with any of its inmates."

Madame bit her lip and her slender white fingers beat an impatient tattoo upon the desk beside her. But she said quite unconcernedly:

"Was that all?"

"Yes, that was all. But I thought it best not to come yesterday. To-day I had to come, because we absolutely must do the work to-night—even to-morrow might be too late. I am certain that I am being watched; every hour's delay means danger of discovery. You should have taken my advice and done the trick two days ago; it would all be over by now...."

"And it will be done to-night," broke in Madame firmly. "You were told two days ago that it would be for to-night, and you had no right to endanger your position at the works by being discovered coming here so often."

"I was told nothing definite two days ago, and I was on my way here for the express purpose of warning you."

"In any case, there's not much harm done," rejoined Madame coolly. "Even if M. de Maurel comes to mistrust you, no change can take place in the arrangements for to-night. He would not dismiss you at a moment's notice, would he?"

"He would not dare to do that," retorted Leroux roughly.

"From what I hear," said Madame la Marquise, "there is not much that M. de Maurel would not dare."

"Well, in any case, he could not turn me out neck and crop from the Lodge. I am there securely enough, at any rate, until the time when I hand over the works to your people in consideration of ten thousand francs for myself and a hundred apiece for my men."

"That is all understood, of course. And you are quite prepared for to-night?"

"Quite. Fifty of my mates are slackening off already. When I return to the works I shall give out that those fifty must work overtime to-night. Don't you be afraid; there's not going to be any hitch."

"Pray God there won't be," murmured Madame fervently.

V

She was about to recapitulate some further instructions to Leroux, when a timid knock at the door, repeated more insistently a moment or two later, caused her to order Leroux to stand aside for a moment while she herself went to the door. She had no premonition of any trouble just then; long afterwards, when in her mind she lived over again every hour of that memorable day, she always was quite certain that she went to open that door without any thought of an approaching calamity.

Old Matthieu Renard was at the door.

"It is M. le Maréchal," he said simply.

Strangely enough, although both he and his wife were firmly attached to M. de Courson and to Madame la Marquise, they had never thoroughly imbibed the contempt which all loyal Royalists were compelled to feel toward the honours and distinctions which were conferred on his adherents by the usurper Bonaparte.

Madame drew back at his words very suddenly, like someone who, wandering in a peaceful glade, comes unprepared upon some fearsome thing. She had certainly this time become white to the lips, and the hand wherewith she beckoned to Matthieu to enter trembled visibly.

"You mean M. de Maurel?" she queried huskily. "Where is he?"

"Just coming up the perron steps," replied Matthieu, who also appeared very agitated. "He took his horse round to the stables first. I was in the garden. I saw him. He called to me and sent me to announce his visit to Madame."

"I had best go," muttered Leroux hurriedly and shuffled up to the door.

Madame stopped him with a word.

"Impossible," she said. "If M. de Maurel is coming up the perron steps now, you cannot fail to meet him face to face in the hall."

"I don't want him to see me here."

"Stay where you are, man," commanded Madame imperiously, and Leroux, whose sallow cheeks were the colour of ashes, muttered something between his teeth and withdrew into a dark corner of the room. Then Madame turned once more to old Matthieu.

"You did not think," she said, "of saying to M. de Maurel that I was from home."

"Yes, I did," replied the man. "I told him you were away."

"And what did he say?"

"That he would wait until your return, and in the meanwhile would speak with his overseer, Paul Leroux, who he believed was within."

There came a violent oath from Leroux, and Madame put a handkerchief up to her lips which felt cracked and dry; and during the silence that ensued there came echoing through the silent house the sound of a footfall with a curious lilt in it—the unmistakable footsteps of a man who is lame.

"Stand aside, Matthieu," said Madame, with as much dignity as she could command, even though her voice sounded raucous and hoarse. "I will go speak with M. de Maurel. Do you follow me into the hall, and you, Leroux," she added, once more turning to the craven creature who made no attempt to disguise his fears, "stay here!"

CHAPTER XVIII

THE WORD OF THE MASTER

I

De Maurel stood waiting for her in the pillared hall. In accordance with the custom which he himself had established during his last visits to Courson, he was in uniform without his sword and mantle. Madame la Marquise had already fully recovered her self-possession; her short progress across the hall restored to her the full measure of her habitual sang-froid. With a well-schooled smile upon her lips she came forward eagerly to greet him.

"Ah! my dear Ronnay," she said, as she extended a gracious hand to him, "this is indeed a surprise—none the less joyous as it was so wholly unexpected. Indeed, we here at La Frontenay had come to believe that you had wholly forgotten us."

He bowed low over the gracious hand, and even touched the finger-tips with his lips.

"You look more bronzed than ever, M. le Maréchal," added Madame with an arch smile, "and your numerous new dignities and the added gorgeousness of your uniform will play sadder havoc than ever before in the hearts of our impressionable young girls. You have come to pay me a long visit, I hope. Come to my boudoir, my dear Ronnay, the room which your generosity hath furnished with such lavish care for your old mother. We can talk undisturbed there."

"Within a few moments, Madame," he said quietly, "I will be

entirely at your service. But, first of all, may I, with your gracious permission, speak a few words with my overseer Leroux?"

The abruptness of the attack nearly caused Madame to lose countenance then and there. Of a truth, the danger was more real and more immediate than she had foreseen. For the space of a few brief seconds she debated in her mind whether she would deny Leroux' presence in the house altogether—feign ignorance of it, and risk an exposure which might prove disastrous and certainly would be humiliating. It all depended on how much Ronnay really knew. If he had actually seen Leroux entering the château, denial would be positively fatal; if his attitude at this moment only rested on surmise, then it might prove a good card to play. Unfortunately time pressed, and she was forced to decide on a course of action in the space of a few seconds while de Maurel kept dark, inquiring eyes fixed composedly upon her face. In any case, a little procrastination was imperative, and Madame, with a certain vague fear gnawing at her heart-strings, at last contrived to say with a complacent smile and an affectation of great surprise:

"Your overseer, my son? I do not understand.... Why should you seek your overseer in this house?"

"Because I happen to have seen him enter it, half an hour ago," he replied curtly, "in spite of my strict prohibition which I enjoined upon him yesterday."

"He comes courting one of my maids, perhaps."

"Perhaps. But my prohibition is none the less binding on him. So with your leave, Madame ..." he added, as he made a movement in the direction of the door whence Madame la Marquise had just emerged in order to greet him.

"My dear Ronnay," rejoined Madame, with all the haughtiness which she could command, "I trust that you will not inflict a scene upon me here in this house, which would be extremely unpleasant for us all. If you wish to speak with your overseer, surely you can wait till he has returned to your works. A factory or a workshop, or even the high road, are fitter places for a wrangle with a refractory workman than in your mother's private room."

"It is neither my fault nor my wish," retorted de Maurel dryly, "that a refractory workman in my employ happens to be in my mother's private room. Nor would I care to wait until the man chooses to return to his duties in order to give him the trouncing which he deserves. I have no time to waste in waiting on his good pleasure, and I specially desire to speak with him here—in this house—and in your presence, Madame, an you will grant me leave."

"In my presence!" exclaimed Madame, with a forced laugh which was intended to hide an ever-increasing terror. "My dear Ronnay, meseems that you have taken leave of your senses. What in the world

165

have I got to do with your overseer and with your quarrels with your men?"

"That is just what I desire to ascertain, Madame," rejoined de Maurel quietly.

"Well, you cannot do it," said Madame testily, "either here or now. You will not, I presume, have the effrontery of forcing your way into my private apartments."

"Your presumption is correct, Madame. I would not for the world intrude upon your privacy. But let me not, on the other hand, detain you here. I can wait your gracious pleasure, until you deign to turn my overseer out of your private apartments, and send him hither to speak with me."

For a moment Madame looked round her in hopeless bewilderment. The situation had developed in a manner wherewith she was unable to cope. For the first time in her life she would have given much to have someone else's support or counsel in this crisis which she began seriously to fear would culminate in disaster. But there was no one near to help her out of her difficulty. Fernande had not left her room, M. de Courson and Laurent were far away, and even old Matthieu had very discreetly retired as soon as he saw Madame la Marquise in close conversation with "M. le Maréchal."

There was silence in the vast pillared hall for a second or two while these two equally firm wills stood up in bitter conflict one against the other. There was never a doubt for a moment as to who would be forced to yield. Madame even now felt like some bird whose strong wings were in the hands of a ruthless tamer, who already was busy in clipping them. She tried to brave that tamer or else to defy him; but he, armed with a determination no less firm than her own and with a tenacity that nothing could conquer, was waging a war of attrition, and was calmly biding his time while Madame, torn between genuine fear and outraged dignity, was seeking in vain for a means of extricating herself from this harrowing position.

Ronnay de Maurel, in fact, was leaning against one of the marble pillars of the hall with a smile round his firm lips which, had not the situation been quite so tense, might almost have been interpreted as one of keen, if somewhat grim, amusement, whilst Madame stood before him, hot and defiant, her small foot tapping the ground in order to ease the exacerbation of her nerves.

"Very well," she said abruptly, and she deliberately turned on her heel and made for the door of the library, where Leroux no doubt was still standing, quaking in his shoes like the miserable craven that he was. "Very well! An you are determined to put this insult on your mother in the presence of such an oaf, I can do naught to prevent you. Go and speak with your overseer an you have a mind."

"And will you deign to be present at the interview, Madame?" he asked.

"If you wish it," she replied curtly.

Of a truth, she would not have trusted Leroux to speak alone with de Maurel; the man was three parts a coward, and it was more than doubtful whether under stress of fear he would remain true to his bargain with de Puisaye; whilst the part of him that was base and criminal might lead him to an attack of violence, which, whatever its results might be, was certainly not within the scope of Madame's reckonings.

Therefore she chose to make a virtue of necessity and, walking rapidly across the hall, she called curtly to de Maurel to follow her into the library.

II

Leroux had assumed an air of jaunty defiance which the pallor of his cheeks and the shifty looks in his eyes did more than belie. He had recognized his employer's voice at the outset, and one or two words spoken in Madame's somewhat shrill voice had prepared him, in a measure, for the interview which he so frankly dreaded.

Like most cowards, Leroux himself would have been quite incapable of saying definitely what it was that he was afraid of. He had oft proclaimed it audibly that he would as soon be sent to Prussia or to New Caledonia as to continue the life of honest work and of monotony which his present conditional liberation entailed. He could not, therefore, be afraid of a mere dismissal, whilst he was quite keen and shrewd enough to know that de Maurel was not like to resort to physical violence against him, and punishments, even degradation from his present position, could not longer affect him, seeing that he was pledged to de Puisaye and the Royalists.

It must be presumed, therefore, that Leroux' access of terror when his employer suddenly appeared under the lintel of the door in the wake of Madame la Marquise, was just due to the unpleasant physical sensation which assails a dastard in the presence of a brave and loyal man. He was standing close beside the window, and with his back to the door, and as Madame and de Maurel entered, he turned round suddenly, with something of a snarl like a savage creature trapped.

"M. de Maurel desired to speak with you, Leroux," Madame said, whilst de Maurel closed the door behind him, "and I have allowed him to see you in this house...."

"Where you had no right to be, as you know well, Leroux," interposed de Maurel, speaking calmly and in measured tones. "I

167

warned you yesterday that I would look on any infraction of my commands as direct and wilful disobedience."

Leroux shifted uneasily from one foot to the other, but he looked his master squarely in the face.

"Orders such as those," he said, "are for the men in subsidiary positions. I am chief overseer now—what? I come and go as I please and where I please."

"I told M. de Maurel," broke in Madame hurriedly, "that I saw no objection to your visiting my maid Marie, seeing that she is betrothed to you. I have begged him to overlook your transgression this time, and urged that your anxiety might excuse you. Marie is very ill," she continued, turning to de Maurel, "and this unfortunate fellow forgot his duty, I fear me, in his solicitude for the girl."

"A solicitude all the more remarkable, Madame," rejoined de Maurel with a quaint laugh, partly of amusement and partly of impatience, "as Leroux has already a wife of his own, whose faithful heart his many crimes have oft wounded before now. I fear me that you must look upon me as a gaby to unfold so specious a tale for my delectation. Nor—an you will forgive me for saying it—are you serving the man's interests by trumping up such hollow excuses for his disobedience."

"I come and go as I please, and where I please," reiterated Leroux surlily.

"You are neither daft nor deaf," said de Maurel quietly. "You heard and understood my orders yesterday."

"I am chief overseer now," retorted the man obstinately. "Such orders do not apply to me."

"Every order which I give applies to every man in my employ. I told you when first I returned and found you installed in a position, which I knew you neither deserved nor were able to fill, that I would leave you in it on probation only. I am now convinced that you are quite unfit to rule over any of my men, seeing that you have no idea of discipline, of obedience, or of truth."

"I am ready to leave your service," said Leroux with a muttered oath; "'tis not a downy bed—what?—to sweat day after day over those accursed mortars, with your life hanging by a thread all the time."

"You are not in my service, Leroux. You are primarily in the service of the State, whose laws you have broken, and who has given you this means of working out your punishment, by honest toil and loyalty to your country, rather than as a convict in jail or New Caledonia. But for the time being I am your employer. You eat my bread and owe loyalty and obedience to me."

"Then send me packing," growled Leroux, "if you are not satisfied."

"That is exactly what I intend to do," rejoined de Maurel. "At the hour when you chose flagrantly to disobey my orders you ceased to be my overseer. Go back now at once to the factories and report yourself to Mathurin, who will take over your duties at the close of the day. After to-day you will take up your place once more, among the rank and file and with the other workmen—the same place, in fact, which you occupied before you proved yourself unworthy of the trust which M. Gaston de Maurel reposed in you. Now you may go."

Already while de Maurel spoke, Leroux had slowly advanced toward him, with a measured tread that in itself implied rebellion, and hands held tightly clenched. Now he came to a halt as close to his master as he dared; his eyes shot defiance and rage, his breath came with a hissing sound through his set teeth.

"I'll not go," he said hoarsely, "I'll not. Curse you for your arrogance and your blustering, dictatorial ways. I'll not go, do you hear?"

"Leroux!" exclaimed Madame firmly.

The man turned to look at her; his shifty eyes encountered the warning glance wherewith she strove with all her might to enjoin outward yielding and prudence to him.

"M. de Maurel is perhaps somewhat harsh, my good Leroux," she continued, trying to put as much significance into her words as she dared; "but I feel sure that on consideration you will decide that submission is really the best in your own interests. Let me advise you to return to the factory now and to think over quietly the events of the past hour. I feel confident that by to-morrow you will have convinced M. de Maurel that you are a man worthy of confidence and of trust."

The moment she began to speak, a change came over Leroux' attitude. He had, indeed, forgotten for the time being and in the paroxysm of his rage, that within a few hours he would hold the employer whom he hated completely at his mercy—in the hollow of his grimy hand. Obviously—as Madame said—it was in his interest to appear submissive now. He wanted the next few hours to himself, to prepare the treacherous coup which was to satisfy both his greed and his desire to be revenged upon the execrated taskmaster. Any overt rebellion now might render his position doubly difficult later in the day, while he still had the power to rally his confederates around him. The advent of de Maurel upon the scene had, of a truth, been more than unfortunate; but all was not yet lost. He—Leroux—was still in possession of the Lodge, and, as far as he knew, his degradation to the ranks was not to take effect until after the close of day—not in any event till after he had been able to concert with his mates. All these thoughts coursed swiftly through his tortuous brain, and he contrived, after a moment or two of hesitation, to throw a reassuring look to Madame la Marquise. Then he turned to de Maurel, and said with an air of contrition and of shamefacedness:

"I was forgetting myself just now, was I not, M. le Maréchal? But even Madame la Marquise has deigned to admit that you have been unduly harsh with me. I have worked in your factories for over two years now; you will not, I hope, degrade me before all my mates in any hurry."

"I will act as I think best, my man," rejoined de Maurel, unperturbed. "You have wilfully placed yourself outside the pale of my consideration. At the same time, you may rest assured that I did not condemn you behind your back. Until I actually found you out in flagrant disobedience and disloyalty I would not have made a change in the administration of the factory. But anon at close of day all your mates will know that you have once more become one of themselves. Now go," he added more harshly, "and do not waste my time with further parleyings. When I return to the works presently, let me hear from Mathurin that you are back at your work, and that you are not trying by words or acts to incite the others to discontent. Remember that I know how to punish, and that I mean to bring back order and discipline in my works, if necessary at the cost of utmost rigour."

He pointed to the door with an authoritative gesture, and Leroux, no longer hesitating—eager, perhaps, to get out of the presence of his master—shuffled across the room. Madame was able to throw him a last, warning look, to which he responded by a significant nod of the head. Whether de Maurel actually saw either of these two signs, or whether his suspicions had been aroused during the interview, it were difficult to say. Certain it is that Leroux had already opened the door and was stepping across the threshold, when a peremptory "Stay!" from de Maurel brought him to a halt. He remained standing under the lintel, his hand upon the door and glancing back over his shoulder at Ronnay.

"What is it now?" he queried sullenly.

"You will vacate the Lodge at close of day, of course," said de Maurel curtly.

"Vacate the Lodge?" muttered Leroux. "I cannot vacate the Lodge all in a moment like that. What should I do with my clothes? Where should I sleep to-night?"

"In the compound," replied de Maurel dryly, "and you can collect your effects in an hour."

"It is like turning a dog out of his kennel," retorted Leroux with a snarl. "And who is to sleep at the Lodge to-night? Mathurin cannot leave the foundries. There are fifty thousand barrels of powder stacked in the shed behind the Lodge ... and fifty men working overtime to-night. Who is going to look after them? Who is going to see that the fifty thousand barrels of gunpowder are not blown into kingdom come through the carelessness of one of them?"

"Surely not you," rejoined de Maurel quietly, "whose disobedience is only equalled by your criminal carelessness. Yesterday, after closing hours, I found the side gate open and unguarded."

"Carelessness is not a crime," riposted Leroux in a more conciliatory tone. "We are all worked to death at the factory like galley-slaves ... I more than the rest.... I forgot to see to the side gate—what? It is not a crime. If I am to be turned out of my bed like a cur," he reiterated sullenly, "who, I should like to know, is going to sleep in it to-night?"

"I am," replied de Maurel simply.

"You!"

The word came simultaneously from two pairs of lips. Madame had spoken it instinctively, just as—instinctively—she had risen to her feet, and Leroux had uttered it hoarsely and raucously, as he suddenly turned on his heel, and once more faced the master whom he hated and feared.

"You?" he reiterated in an indefinable tone of incredulity, of rage and of terror.

"I spoke plainly enough," rejoined de Maurel unmoved. "Did you perchance think that I was jesting?"

For a moment or two the man was silent. He stood immovable and quite close to de Maurel, the while his shifty gaze tried to probe in the other's dark eyes what lay hidden within their depths. And Ronnay, from his great height, looked down on the coarse and evil face which was turned up to his; he, too, was trying to fathom all that was going on behind that narrow, receding forehead and behind the pale, protruding eyes, with their flaccid lids and lines around them of recklessness and dissipation. For that brief moment there was deadly silence in the room, silence through which the crackling of Madame's silk dress could distinctly be heard, as she was quivering from head to foot.

Then Leroux, challenged by de Maurel's fixed gaze, replied slowly:

"No!"

"Then see that the Lodge is vacated by ten o'clock this evening. Overtime work must be finished by then, and you can hand me over all your keys ere you go back to the compound."

It seemed as if Leroux meant to say something; once or twice he even opened his mouth, as if the words were about to tumble out of it; but every time that he looked up, he encountered de Maurel's gaze fixed quite steadily upon him, and after a while no doubt he realized that for the moment, at any rate, he was sorely at a disadvantage. So he contented himself with muttering a curse and a threat, after which he turned rapidly on his heel, and with a few quick steps he stalked out of the room, slamming the door behind him.

Madame had not moved since the moment when de Maurel's announcement that he intended to sleep at the Lodge that night had so completely staggered her that she felt momentarily dazed and quite unable to think. For a second or two it seemed to her as if her heart had completely ceased to beat, as if her body alone had remained sitting in the room there, while her spirit had fled on the wings of a nameless terror.

Ronnay de Maurel at the Lodge that night! What did that mean? How much did he know? What did he suspect? These were questions which went hammering through her brain while Leroux was finally cowed and dismissed. Now that she was once more alone with her son, it was obviously of the most vital importance that nothing in her attitude should betray the agitation which she felt. She had to make an almost superhuman effort to recover herself, to rise from her chair, and to steady her knees which were shaking under her. But all this she did, and even succeeded in saying, with every appearance of unconcern:

"I do think, my dear Ronnay, that you were unnecessarily harsh with the man. He is not a sympathetic personality I own, and, of course, he did very wrong in disobeying you; but now that we are alone, let me assure you that it is indeed my maid Marie whom he has been visiting of late. He knew that he had done wrong; your allusion to his own wife roused his surly temper, and undoubtedly he forgot himself. And now," she added glibly, "shall we forget this unpleasant incident? Fernande is in the garden. Shall we join her?"

"I thank you, Madame," he replied coldly, "but I must return home as soon as possible. My uncle cannot bear me out of his sight for very long, and there are many matters I must attend to before nightfall. An you will allow me to pay you my respects another time...."

"'Tis not much respect you have paid me to-day, my good Ronnay," rejoined Madame, who, indeed, by now was once again completely mistress of herself. "Why you should have dragged me into your quarrel with that creature I cannot imagine, and I ought to deal very severely with you for this want of consideration for me."

"I am sorry to have offended you, Madame, and fear me that I must do so again ere I go."

"'Twere not wise to do that, Ronnay," she retorted haughtily; "even a mother's indulgence hath its limits."

"I trust that I shall not be overstepping them, Madame, when I request you in all earnestness to refrain in future from any intercourse with my workpeople."

"Are you afraid that I might succeed in imbuing them with a spirit of loyalty to their King?"

"Whatever my motive, Madame, I earnestly pray you to follow my behests."

"You mean, your commands?"

"We'll call them that an you wish," he replied slowly.

"You forbid me to speak to your workpeople?"

"Absolutely."

"You are not over confident of their loyalty," she said, with a sardonic little laugh.

He made no reply. Madame's searching gaze was fixed upon him; she would have given worlds to divine his thoughts. On the whole, she felt reassured that he knew nothing of the vital issues which centred round the powder factory to-night. She was pretty certain that Leroux would try to see her again to-day—he had probably not left the château, and was waiting his opportunity to have speech with her as soon as de Maurel had gone. Something would have to be devised, something thought of, to meet the unlooked-for eventuality of de Maurel's presence at the factory to-night. But for this Madame required solitude and a calm view of the new situation. For the moment she was supremely conscious of the desire to be alone. Ronnay's presence now jarred well nigh unbearably on her nerves; the calm way in which he regarded her and dictated his will to her, with a certainty that she would obey, irritated her past endurance.

She turned away from him, for she did not choose to let him see how maddened she was, how thoroughly shaken was her usual haughty placidity. She walked deliberately to the window and turned her back on him, her aristocratic fingers beating a devil's tattoo against the panes.

"I'd best go now," suggested de Maurel, after a while, in that same awkward manner of his which seemed only to have dropped from him when he was dealing with Leroux.

"You are in your own house, my good Ronnay," rejoined Madame coldly, and without turning to look at him; "you have a perfect right to come and go as you please."

"Then am I your obedient servant," he said placidly.

Madame, from where she stood, could feel that his whole attitude was one of complete detachment. Her wrath and her scorn had no more effect on him than Leroux' threats of a while ago. She knew instinctively that he bowed and took his leave in that clumsy manner which she abhorred. Then she heard him moving across the room, opening the door, and finally shutting it behind him.

Even then she did not turn round. She remained standing beside the window, gazing out into the distance—seeing nothing and yet still gazing—her mind fixed upon the one great, all-absorbing puzzle. What was to happen to-night? She never moved, while her ears caught the sound of that firm, dragging step as it slowly died away in the distance. Then, when even its echo had ceased to reverberate through the silent house, she caught at the heavy curtain beside her, for suddenly in her whole body there was a relaxing of the tension on her nerves, and for the first time in her life Madame de Mortain felt ready to swoon. But even when she was all alone she would have scorned an unnecessary exhibition of weakness. A few seconds sufficed her to regain her self-control. She turned away from the window at last and sat down beside the heavy desk whereat she had so often penned enthusiastic reports to the Royalist agents. She drew pen and ink closer to her and sat thinking for a while. She had a mind to send a letter to de Puisaye—a runner might be found quick and clever enough to deliver it into the hands of the Chouan leader in the Cerf-Volant woods and to bring back his answer before nightfall.

In any case, before she wrote Madame was bent on seeing Leroux again. Leroux alone, she thought, would be able to cope with the situation as it now presented itself. Leroux was a man of resource, as his correspondence with Madame over the wall of the exercising ground had proved. He was not greatly troubled with scruples, and though he was by nature a coward, his temper, when roused, was apt to be both defiant and ugly.

Moreover, he was wilful, and would know how to act without any very explicit instructions, which Madame, in the absence of the chiefs, was not prepared to give him.

She put down her pen again, and pushing her chair away from the table, she rose with an impatient, nervy little sigh. Despite the warmth of this June afternoon she shivered, almost as if she felt cold.

Somewhere in the château a distant clock struck six.

CHAPTER XIX

THE PARTING OF THE WAYS

I

Ten minutes later Matthieu once more knocked discreetly at the door of the library, and in response to Madame's call, he opened the door very softly and peeped in.

"Leroux has returned," he said, instinctively dropping his voice, even though he knew quite well that no eavesdroppers could be about.

"Where is he?" queried Madame.

"Just outside. Shall I show him in?"

"Yes. At once. Stay," she added, as Matthieu had already made haste to obey. "Where is Mademoiselle de Courson?"

"In the garden, I think, Madame la Marquise. But I will go to see."

"No. Never mind now. But if you see Mademoiselle coming in, ask her to go and wait for me in my room upstairs; then let me know immediately."

"Very good, Madame la Marquise."

Leroux was standing waiting in the hall, when Matthieu came to tell him that Madame la Marquise would see him in the library. He shuffled into the room, looking sulky and villainous, nor did he moderate his attitude or assume the slightest show of respect when he found himself alone in the presence of Madame. He did not remove his tricorne hat as he entered, but merely pushed it with a nervy gesture to the back of his head. The first word which he spoke was a curse, and he spat on the carpet as he uttered it.

"Well?" queried Madame haughtily.

"Well!" he retorted with a leer.

She would have given worlds for the power to flare up at his impertinence, but she and her friends were too deeply involved with the brutish creature to venture on rousing his resentment at this hour, when the very throne of the King of France rested on the insecure foundation of a recreant's loyalty to a bond. The sinister aspect of the ex-convict caused her to shudder; she longed for the presence of her brother or her son to help her deal with the arrogant ruffian, to turn him from her presence with the contumely which she felt, yet dared not express. At the same time, she was longing, with a desperate, passionate earnestness, to hear what he had come to say—she longed to hear him put into actual words those thoughts of evil and of darkness which had assailed her ever since Ronnay had gone and which she did not dare to face. She felt like a man who has been mysteriously and grievously wounded, who feels some awful pain which he has not yet had the chance to locate, and knows that somewhere on his body there is a hideous and gaping sore, unseen as yet by him, which is gnawing at his very life, torturing him insidiously and hitherto only felt—not yet seen—by him. And, like him, she felt that at all costs must she see that hidden wound and realize exactly how deeply she was hurt.

Leroux, with keen, shifty eyes, was watching the play of emotions on Madame's haughty face. His mouth was distorted by a hideous grin of scorn and of arrogance. He knew well enough how completely he now had all these scheming aristocrats at his mercy. One word from him and he could send the lot to moulder in jail or else to the guillotine. But strive how he might, he could not perceive one single trait of fear in the cold, pale eyes which Madame kept fixed upon him; her calmness irritated him, even though he knew well enough that it only lay on the surface. An insensate desire seized him to see that proud lady cringe with terror, to see her blanch when he made her understand plainly the bond which existed between her and him.

"Why have you come back?" queried Madame after a while. "Have you not realized that M. de Maurel might return, too, and that...?"

"Well," retorted Leroux fiercely, "and if he does ... you don't want him in the way, I presume."

She made no reply, but lifted her handkerchief up to her mouth in order to smother the cry which had so instinctively risen to her lips.

"I thought," resumed the man gruffly, "that you would wish to know that, as far as I am concerned, the Maréchal's interference will not affect our plans in any way. There's plenty of time between now and the close of day to talk things over with my mates. Do not be afraid, my fine lady, we are prepared for every eventuality."

"Prepared?" she asked, and her voice sounded choked and hoarse. "Prepared?" she reiterated. "In what way do you mean?"

"Well, we must assume that the Maréchal is not coming down in force to-night to turn me out of my Lodge, mustn't we?" he queried with a snarl.

"No ... I suppose not," she replied vaguely.

"Well, then," he rejoined slowly, "we can deal with him easily enough if he is alone—what?"

Once more Madame had to make a vigorous effort to repress a cry of horror. The combat which she was fighting with herself while the impudent wretch stood looking down on her, his hands buried in the pockets of his breeches, his feet planted wide apart, his whole attitude one of arrogance and of scorn—was, indeed, a bitter one. On one side were ranged her fanatical enthusiasm for a cause which she held to be as sacred as that of her faith, and her boundless belief in the efficacy of the coup which had been planned for this night. To jeopardize its success now at this eleventh hour, by allowing her sensibilities to overmaster her, would in her eyes have been akin to the blackest, the most dire treachery toward her King and her country.

Indeed, at this moment she was putting to pagan uses and misinterpreting the dictum of the Gospel: "If thy right eye offend thee, pluck it out." She was wilfully closing her heart against every dictate of sentiment or of motherhood. As she would have been ready—and more than ready—to risk her own life for the sake of her cause, so was she willing to throw into the balance of her King's cause the safety of a man who happened to be in the way, even if at the same time he happened to be her son.

And Leroux, the servile tool in the nefarious work, knew exactly what was passing in the proud lady's mind: he knew that she had understood the covert hint which he had thrown out, and that by her very silence she had acquiesced in his schemes.

He had no intention of relinquishing the ten thousand francs which had been offered him because of that obstacle which he was more than ready to sweep out of his path. Murderer, incendiary, thief, jail-bird and convict!—what was a crime more or less upon the conscience of such a man? Nor did he feel the slightest respect for these people who had bribed him to do a monstrous treachery. Brute as he was, he was shrewd enough to look upon them as his equals in villainy, and to realize that they had far more to gain by the iniquitous deed which he contemplated than he had himself.

And for a while there was silence in the room while this man and this woman—the jail-bird and the high-born lady—looked straight into one another's eyes and tacitly sealed a bond of fraternity between them. The measured ticking of a clock upon the mantelpiece marked the passage of time which separated this unspoken and monstrous compact from its fulfilment by and by. A bundle of papers beneath Madame's hand rustled with weird persistency, and suddenly Leroux gave a laugh, throwing back his head and showing his ugly yellow teeth, and he shrugged his shoulders and spat once more on the carpet ere he queried with contemptuous familiarity:

"Then our plans are as they were—eh?"

"As they were," replied Madame.

The man turned on his heel and started whistling the old "Ça ira" of Revolution times through his teeth.

"Ça ira! Ça ira! Les aristos à la lanterne!"

His hand was already on the handle of the door, when he looked once more over his shoulder and said roughly:

"Your people are not going to leave me in the lurch, I suppose?"

"That is out of the question," replied Madame coldly.

"Because you know, my good woman," he said, still over his shoulder, as he opened the door and stepped across the threshold, "if the Maréchal gives us trouble to-night and your people fail us afterwards, it will mean hanging for some of us."

He looked at Madame and nodded with studied insolence by way of farewell. But she seemed to have forgotten his presence already. She sat upright and stiff in the high-backed chair, the silk of her gown falling in rigid folds around her, the darkness of her attire relieved by a white scarf round her shoulders. Her face was set and pale beneath the hard line of her white hair dressed in the mode of the past generation, her eyes stared, unseeing, before her. Leroux laughed once more—it was the scornful laugh of a hardened criminal for what he termed a white-livered beginner. Once more he shrugged his shoulders, then with a final muttered imprecation he stalked out of the hall.

The moment he had gone Madame pulled herself together with an almost superhuman effort of will; she shook herself free from the torpor which had momentarily paralysed her limbs, and, rising to her feet, she went quickly to the door which Leroux had left ajar.

It had seemed to her that the moment when the man's shuffling footsteps began to resound against the marble floor of the hall, he had uttered an exclamation of surprise, and that exclamation from Leroux had at once been followed by another sound—one soft and mournful like a sigh.

Less than five seconds later Madame was in the hall—just in time to see Fernande walking rapidly across it toward the monumental glazed doors which gave on the outside stairway and on the terraces.

"Fernande," she called authoritatively, "where are you going?"

Instinctively the young girl had paused when she heard her name, but it was only for an instant; the next she had resumed her quick walk, and had just reached the first glazed door when Madame overtook her and, without warning, seized her peremptorily by the wrist.

"Where are you going, Fernande?" she reiterated harshly.

The girl looked round at her somewhat wildly, then she made a vigorous effort to disengage her wrist.

"I am going out, ma tante," she replied, with a quietude which in no way deceived Madame la Marquise.

"Out?" queried Madame. "Whither?"

"Into the garden, ma tante. The heat indoors is oppressive and...."

"You lie, Fernande," broke in Madame curtly.

"Ma tante...."

"You lie. Tell me where you are going."

Then, as the girl made no reply but drew up her slim, graceful figure to its full height and looked fearlessly into the austere face of Madame de Mortain, the latter continued sternly:

"Did you see Leroux just now?"

"Yes," replied Fernande quietly.

"And you heard what he said just as he was leaving?"

"Yes."

For a moment or two longer the two women stood looking keenly into one another's eyes. The vast château was solitary and still; not a sound came from within, and the heavy doors shut out effectually all the many sounds which fill the air on a warm, midsummer afternoon: the call of thrush and blackbird, the distant croaking of frogs and cooing of wood-pigeons, the flutter of parched leaves upon the tiny

178

boughs and tripping of unseen little beasts through thicket and shrubbery.

It was Madame whose eyes were the first to veil themselves behind their heavy lids, in order to conceal the thoughts within from the searching gaze of the younger woman. The next moment Fernande was free to go; Madame no longer held her wrist.

"I will not ask you again, my child, whither you are going," she said quietly. "Since first the rising nations were torn between conflicting parties of men who had divergent aims there have been traitors as well as heroes in the world."

"Ma tante...."

"Listen to me, my child, for at this supreme moment of your whole existence you are standing at the parting of the ways, at the cross-roads where many a woman has stood before you, hesitating at the two turnings which faced her on the tortuous path of life. Many a woman before you has taken the wrong turning, Fernande. Take care that you do not do the same and for ever after weep endless tears of remorse and of shame."

"I would indeed weep bitter tears, ma tante," retorted the girl firmly, "if I were to allow the monstrous outrage to be perpetrated which that dastardly wretch hath even now set out to do."

"You rave, Fernande," rejoined Madame quietly, "and 'tis not my purpose to probe into the thoughts which are leading you at this moment into the path of treachery."

"There is no treachery, ma tante, in warning an unsuspecting man that a murderer's hand is raised against him in the dark."

"You talk at random, child, and your ears deceived you if you attribute such intentions to Leroux."

"In any event, ma tante, will you send a runner over to M. de Puisaye and let him know what has occurred?"

"What has occurred?" queried Madame, with a slight lift of her eyebrow in token of contemptuous surprise. "What—in your estimation—has occurred, my dear Fernande, that would justify my upsetting M. de Puisaye at this hour?"

"Will you let M. de Puisaye know that M. de Maurel will be at the factory to-night?"

"Why should I? In what way do you suppose that M. de Maurel's comings and goings can possibly affect the business of His Majesty the King, or the plans which his faithful adherents have formed for the triumph of his cause?"

"Ma tante," protested Fernande, with all the fervour and all the strength at her command, "you know quite well what I mean. M. de Puisaye must be told that if M. de Maurel goes to the factory to-night, Leroux has it in him to commit a dastardly murder."

"M. de Puisaye cannot obviously prevent M. de Maurel from going to his own factory to-night."

"No. But he can prevent the dastardly deed from being accomplished."

"It is not for me to try and influence the actions of our chiefs."

"It is for every woman—every human being who has a spark of loyalty and Christianity in them—to try and prevent murder being done."

For the space of a second or two Madame made no retort; there was a cold glance of mockery in her eyes. Then she said slowly:

"Had you perchance thought of confronting M. de Puisaye yourself and trying to turn him from his purpose by your wild and incredible tales? Let me assure you, child, that our chief is not the man to allow one life—and that the life of our bitter enemy—to stand in the way of His Majesty's cause and of its success."

"Ma tante!" exclaimed Fernande in horror.

"Of a truth, child," rejoined Madame coldly, "I do but waste my time in arguing with you. You are self-willed and obstinate, and in your heart you have chosen to range yourself on the side of the enemy of your King and of your kindred. Therefore, I will not argue. 'Tis for you to probe your heart, and find out for yourself how much disloyalty doth lurk in it against Laurent, against your father, against all your friends. With that I have nothing to do. In the happy times which are so near to us now, when the King of France comes to his throne again through the self-sacrifice and the heroism of those whom in your heart you proclaim murderers and outcasts—when that happy time comes, I say, repentance will come with it for you. Until then nothing I may say now will turn you back to the path of loyalty. But let me tell you this, Fernande," continued Madame with desperate earnestness, "that whatever you may think, whatever you may suspect, whatever you may fear, if you speak one word of warning to Ronnay de Maurel you will not only be betraying the cause of your King and of your country, but you will also betray your father, your lover—every one of your kindred and your friends. Your father, M. de Puisaye and Laurent are in camp at this moment in the Cerf-Volant woods on the other side of Mortain; within the next few hours they will have started upon their march: Laurent for Domfront, M. de Puisaye for La Frontenay, your father to carry out the surprise attack against the garrison of Mortain. If the slightest alarm be given to the garrison of Domfront—and you may be sure that after your warning, that is one of the first things which Ronnay de Maurel will do—Laurent will be the first to fall into the guet-apens which you will have been the means of preparing for him; with Laurent's failure to surprise that garrison, your father's attack on Mortain is bound to fail. Domfront will warn Mortain; your father's small force will be cut up, he himself either killed or a prisoner in the hands of the Imperialist forces, with the prospect of the guillotine or, at best, deportation before him. Of myself I will not even speak, and will

180

leave you to imagine the fate which will await M. de Puisaye on his march hither, once de Maurel's five thousand works men are prepared against his coming. The catastrophe of 1800, when Cadoudal and all his followers perished for our cause, will be repeated once again; and this time the fate of your kindred, of your lover and of your father, will be laid at your door, their blood will sully your hands. To save the man whom in your treacherous heart you have come to set above your King and your caste, you will have sacrificed your father, the lives of your nearest kin and the honour of your name. And now, child," she concluded calmly, "thank God on your knees that I was here in time to save you from committing a crime, beside which in the years to come the foulest betrayal that hath ever blackened the pages of our country's history will seem like the thoughtless prank of a child. I'll say no more, Fernande. You are free to take the turning which your heart will indicate."

The harsh, strident voice resounded from end to end of the vast hall; it beat against Fernande's brain long after the marble walls had ceased to send back its echo. Madame gathered her heavy silk skirts around her and then, without another word, without another look for the unhappy girl on whose finest feelings she had so ruthlessly trampled, she sailed across the hall and up the monumental staircase, and her soft footfall alone went echoing now through the silent house.

For a few moments Fernande remained quite still ... white and rigid like the marble pillars around her; only her mouth twitched convulsively, and there was a look of mute agony in her face. The swish of Madame's skirts soon ceased to resound from above; after a while Fernande's straining senses heard the opening and shutting of a door ... then nothing more—silence absolute, and the utter solitude of a soul that is irrevocably parted from its mate.

A heartrending sob broke from the unfortunate girl's overburdened heart. She staggered forward and, pushing open the heavy glazed door, she ran like one pursued down the monumental stone steps which led to the garden beyond. She ran—looking neither to right or left—across the terrace to a distant shrubbery which screened her favourite walk and a seat whereon she liked to sit and dream. As soon as she felt that she was quite alone, and that no prying eyes could look upon her misery, she fell on her knees, and throwing her arms over the seat, she buried her head between them.

"Oh, my God!" she moaned. "Dear God! tell me what to do! Give me some sign—a word—a token! Oh, my God! have mercy! Tell me what to do! Tell me which road to take!"

CHAPTER XX

THE STRAW

I

The clock in the tower of the château struck nine when Fernande, wrapped in a dark cloak and with a hood thrown over her head, stole on tip-toe across the hall and slipped through the glazed doors and down the perron steps. She went along with utmost caution, peering all round her ere she ventured along.

Once past the terrace she felt freer, and without hesitation she dived into the path which, winding through the shrubberies, led both to the main entrance of the park and to a small postern gate in the boundary wall.

After the sultriness of the day the evening was oppressive and dark; heavy banks of clouds had gathered before the crescent moon, and there was a stillness in the air which presaged a storm. The splendid gardens of La Frontenay were wrapped in gloom; not a breath stirred the leaves of secular oaks and chestnuts; not a sound came from out the thicket, save now and then the crackling of tiny twigs under the feet of furtive little beasts that ran scurrying by.

From over the hills there came from time to time the roll of distant thunder, and ever and anon a flash of summer lightning threw for the merest fraction of a second a weird glow on the far-off woods, and the vague outline of the factory buildings some three kilomètres away.

Fernando, holding her cloak tightly around her, slipped through the postern gate, and found herself in the lane which after a few hundred mètres abuts on the high road; from this point the foundries could be reached in a little over half an hour. She walked as quickly as the darkness would allow. She had never been along this way before, but she knew that she could not miss it. Darkness was her friend and her ally in her nocturnal expedition, since it kept her hidden from the view of the occasional passer-by.

The road was lonely enough. It was long after working hours; the factory hands and foundry men had, for the most part, returned to their homes; here and there in the distance a tiny light from a cottage window glimmered feebly like a yellow winking eye out of the surrounding blackness; and up on the height the village of La Vieuville clustered around its church and its château.

After the excitement and the soul agony of the day, Fernande felt perfectly calm. The horrible alternative which Madame la Marquise had so ruthlessly placed before her had put all her sensibilities and every one of her nerves on the rack, until the very faculty for suffering had gone from her, and she felt numbed and bruised both physically and mentally. But during that terrible hour, when driven forth like a hunted creature to seek shelter and solitude from the cruel taunts of Madame, she had prayed to God to guide her in her terrible perplexity, a resolution had gradually taken form in her mind, a resolution which she firmly believed had been instilled into her in answer to her impassioned prayer.

Madame la Marquise was, no doubt, right when she said that the life or death of a bitter enemy was not like to turn Joseph de Puisaye from his present purpose. An appeal or a warning to him at this hour from anyone but Madame herself would obviously not only be futile, but would waste several precious, irreclaimable hours.

On the other hand, if she—Fernande—did go to La Vieuville—as her first instinct had prompted her to do—and warned de Maurel not to go alone to the factory this night, there was no doubt that the plans of de Puisaye would not only be gravely jeopardized, but they would be rendered impossible of execution, and her father's position, not to speak of Laurent's and of the other chiefs', would be irretrievably compromised—their lives probably in danger. De Maurel, scenting a conspiracy, would at once pass the word round to the garrisons close by, and until their arrival he would know how to protect his property with the help of his own loyal workmen.

This, Madame had undoubtedly put very clearly before Fernande; she could not save de Maurel from the guet-apens which had been prepared against him, except by sacrificing Laurent, her father and her friends—her King and his cause. Indeed, it was only God who could show a way through such an appalling perplexity, and Fernande was more than justified in her conviction that the thought which came to her whilst she knelt heart-broken and in prayer, was a direct manifestation of His will.

"I can at least save him from that assassin," she thought, when at nine o'clock she started on her way.

II

Fernande had only once been to the La Frontenay factories, and that was over a year ago in the company of de Maurel. Since then she had purposely avoided taking her walks in that direction, and her recollection of the place was, therefore, hazy and incomplete. She had now been walking a little over half an hour when a sudden bend in the road revealed the proximity of the huge pile of irregular buildings—

standing partly within iron fencings, partly inside the precincts of high boundary walls—which nestled at the foot of the hills and represented Ronnay de Maurel's priceless patrimony.

Up to now she had met an occasional passer-by on the highway—a belated workman going to his home, a young pair of lovers out for a stroll, a housewife with heavy basket returning from Domfront—but here silence and loneliness appeared to be absolute. A row of street-lanthorns fixed in the boundary walls of the group of buildings shed uneven circles of light at intervals, and inside the precincts a few of the windows showed a light, whilst higher up two clock-towers loomed out of the darkness like monster glow-worms.

Fernande walked a few hundred mètres further on and then she came to a standstill, trying to co-ordinate her recollections of the place. That time—a year ago—de Maurel had conducted her through the foundries first, and then he had led her through a gate in the iron fencing, across a clearing to another gate built in the high wall. This gave on a vast quadrangle, on every side of which lay the worksheds of the powder factory. Her thoughts on it all were still very chaotic, but she had a vague remembrance of the large storehouse standing in the centre of the quadrangle and surmounted by its clock-tower, of Mathurin escorting her after she had taken leave of de Maurel, back through the postern gate and along a footpath until she came once more to the main road, where the carriole and the high-stepper stood waiting to take her home again to Courson.

Now when she closed her eyes, shutting away the confusion of lights which flickered through the impenetrable shadows, she was able to visualize the locality more accurately. The foundries obviously lay to her right behind the iron fencing; the powder factory lay beyond, some two-thirds of a kilomètre away, isolated, and well away from the road inside its high encircling walls. With the various positions thus fixed upon her mind, Fernande advanced more boldly. Her heart was beating tumultuously in her bosom—not with fear, but with vague wonderment as to what was to come. The sight of the high walls had given her the first pang of doubt. If gates were closed against her, if sentries challenged, what would she do?

But she had no mind to draw back. On her actions, she felt, depended the life of a brave man and also the honour of her cause. She walked quickly past the foundries on the opposite side of the road; then, when she saw the factory walls, she crossed over, and keeping well within the shadows, she found herself presently outside the main gates. They were of forged iron, high, massive and forbidding; a metal lanthorn was fixed immediately above them, and at the moment when she passed into the circle of light projected by the lanthorn, a peremptory voice called out from within: "Who goes there?"

At once she beat a hasty retreat and a frown of deep perplexity settled upon her brow. If she could not get to the Lodge at all, how would she speak with Leroux? What would she do to save an unsuspecting man—a brave man—from assassination?

Vividly, as in a flash of awakened memory, there came back to her mind every word of that conversation which she had overheard this afternoon between Madame, Leroux and de Maurel, she heard once more—as distinctly as she had heard it then—Leroux' savage question: "Who is to sleep at the Lodge to-night?" She heard the simple answer: "I am!" She heard Leroux' snarls and his overt threats, she heard de Maurel's accusing words: "Your disobedience is only equalled by your criminal carelessness!"

Then her heart gave a leap. Memory did not play her false; it brought back also the very words which now gave her renewed hope and courage. "Last night, after closing hours," de Maurel had said, "I found the side gate open and unguarded." Leroux, most like, surly and obstinate, would not redeem the carelessness of the day before. It was more than probable that he would leave the gate unguarded again to-night.

Buoyed by this hope, excitement getting the better of her quietude of a while ago, Fernande now retraced her steps in order to find the footpath which, somewhere between the foundry fencing and the factory wall, must, she knew, lead to the side gate through which Mathurin had conducted her a year ago.

Her memory had not deceived her; after a minute or two she struck the path and at once turned to walk rapidly along it. Darkness here was absolute; there were no lanthorns fixed either in the wall or the fencing, only a couple of hundred mètres on ahead a tiny glimmer of light flickered feebly through the gloom. Fernande was walking more cautiously now, and she felt the wall as she went all along with her hand. She had fixed her eyes on that tiny glimmer which seemed to her like a beacon which would lead her to her goal. Soon it revealed itself as a small, well-screened light fixed just above a low iron gate.

No one challenged her this time as she approached, and by the dim light above she felt for the latch. It yielded. She pushed open the gate, and the next moment she found herself inside the precincts of the powder factory. Everything was dark around her, and through the darkness there loomed up dense and black the pile of irregular low buildings—the sheds, the offices, the workshops, with, in the centre, the somewhat taller edifice of the storehouse, which contained the vast reserves of explosives. It was surmounted by a clock-tower, from which the rays of an unseen lamp projected a large circle of light on the pavement below; close by was a small building, presumably the Lodge. At any rate, this was the only spot in the large quadrangle which showed signs of life inside its walls. Everything else was absolutely still as well as dark. Fernande ventured nearer, then she paused, breathless. She had come to the end of her journey, to the point where her powers of persuasion would be put to the test, where she would have to rely upon herself, upon her own eloquence, her own personality, in order to compel a few miscreants to abandon their dastardly purpose.

For the first time here, where only a few mètres separated her from that band of assassins, she realized the possibility of failure; and she realized that her plan, which had seemed so simple and so direct at home, was, indeed, like a mere straw at which a dying man might clutch.

There was a light in two of the windows of the Lodge; one of these was open; through it came the murmur of muffled voices. Fernande tip-toed up to it as closely as she dared. She would have given worlds to hear what was said in there—by Leroux and his mates, whose purpose it was to betray their master this night—God help them!—to murder him if he stood in their way.

Oh, for the power to avert that awful catastrophe without betraying her own father, her friends and her King!

But though thoughts, projects, wild hopes and wilder fears went on hammering at the portals of her brain, it seemed to her that they went round and round in a continuous circle, which never diverged from that one appalling centre: "If the alarm is given, the forces which have started from Mortain under de Puisaye, under Laurent and under her father, cannot fail to be surprised—cannot fail to be overwhelmed and possibly annihilated; at best, the whole project whereon now rests the hopes of the entire Royalist party is doomed to fail; and she—Fernande de Courson—would be the traitor who had betrayed her own kindred and the cause of her King."

After a while she felt more calm. Finality to a brave soul does not mean despair—it means a renewal of courage to face or fight even the inevitable. No longer hesitating now, Fernande walked boldly up the steps which led to the entrance door of the Lodge; then she rapped on the door with her knuckles.

The strain of muffled voices which had come from within died down at her loud rat-tat, and through the open window she heard a sound like the shuffling and scurrying of heavy, furtive feet; then nothing more.

The roll of distant thunder had become louder and more continuous, the flashes of summer lightning more frequent. From the wooded heights behind the factories there came the intermittent soughing of the wind through the trees, followed by an absolute stillness, a calm which was the direct forerunner of the coming storm.

The air was sultry and filled with the sickening odour of sulphur. From time to time a heavy raindrop descended, large as a thumbnail, and Fernande fell to wondering how her father and Laurent would fare on their march if the storm broke with its threatened violence, and how far de Puisaye and his four hundred men were at this hour from La Frontenay.

After a while she knocked again. This time she heard distinctly a heavy, shuffling footstep approaching the door. Though her heart was beating so violently that its throbbing felt nigh to choking her, she was not the least afraid, and when, after a moment or two, the door was thrown open and Leroux' ungainly figure appeared before her, silhouetted against the light beyond, she spoke quite calmly and without the slightest tremor in her voice.

"It is I, Leroux," she said—"Mademoiselle de Courson—you know me?"

The man came nearer to her. She was standing on a step below him and the light from a hanging lamp in the room behind him fell full upon her face. He looked at her keenly for a few seconds, then he replied curtly: "Yes. I know you! What do you want?"

"To speak with you, Leroux," she said. "I have a message for you from Madame la Marquise de Mortain. Let me in."

"Madame la Marquise chooses her messenger strangely," he retorted sullenly, "at this hour of the night."

"No one else was willing to affront the coming storm. Our servants are cowards. Let me in, Leroux."

Leroux made no immediate reply. He looked over his shoulder into the interior of the room, apparently with a view to taking counsel with his mates. Fernande, with her hood and cloak drawn closely round her, waited on the doorstep.

That moment a vivid flash of lightning rent the heavy bank of clouds in the east, and a clap of thunder rolled echoing above the hills. She suppressed an involuntary cry of terror, but she called out more insistently:

"Let me in, Leroux. 'Tis a matter of life and death."

But Leroux did not stand aside; instead of this, he stepped over the threshold, and as Fernande instinctively retreated, he came down the steps, and then he closed the door behind him.

"Let me in, Leroux," she said more peremptorily. "I cannot speak with you out here."

"Why not?" he retorted. "I have no secrets that the night birds may not hear."

Every time that he spoke Leroux came a step or two nearer to her, and every time she retreated as far away from him as she dared,

187

without arousing his resentment and causing him to turn sullenly from her and refuse to listen to what she had come to say. Thus he had forced her as far back as the circle of light which came from the clock-tower. Here he paused and looked her up and down with every mark of surliness and insolence imprinted upon his face.

"Now what is it?" he queried roughly. "And be quick about it. There's men's work to be done here to-night. 'Tis not a place for women."

"I know that," replied Fernande boldly; "the work that I am doing now is really men's work. It is nearly four kilomètres from La Frontenay, and I have walked all the way. The storm will be at its height ere I can get home again. Think you I would have come, had it not been a matter of life and death?"

She looked the man fearlessly in the eyes. For the first time since she left home more than an hour ago, she realized the enormity of what she had done. Through the partially opened window of the Lodge she could hear men moving and whispering. How many of them there were she could not say. She was here all alone, unknown to every one at home, at the mercy of men who already had every conceivable crime upon their conscience. Not that she feared any violence on their part; she was under the unseen ægis of their new employers, of those who were paying them for the abominable work which was to be done this night. She had no thought of her own personal safety. What she dreaded was the failure of her enterprise, a failure which would result, perhaps, in her being forced to witness that which she would give her life's blood to avert.

"Say what you want, then," said Leroux gruffly, "and get you gone. Madame la Marquise should have known better than to send a comely wench like you philandering at night upon the high roads."

"She had no choice," rejoined Fernande quietly. "She had no one else to send, and she desired me to tell you that you must not think of misinterpreting her words of this afternoon."

"What words?" he queried with a frown.

"Madame la Marquise feared that she had not put it plainly enough to you, that whatever else happened this night, she and all our leaders would hold you responsible for the life and safety of M. de Maurel."

Leroux was silent for a moment or two, but it had seemed to Fernande as if through the open window she had heard a low laugh—one that in the stillness of the night sounded weirdly mirthless and satanic.

"Oho! that's it, is it?" quoth Leroux after a while, with a leer. "Madame la Marquise is suddenly troubled with remorse. The precious son, whom a few hours ago she was ready enough to sacrifice to her own schemes, has suddenly become as the apple of her eye...."

"You must not say that, Leroux," broke in Fernande steadily.

188

"Madame la Marquise never dreamed of sacrificing any of her friends to her schemes—let alone her own son; and apparently she was justified in thinking that you had misinterpreted her thoughts...."

"And you think that she was justified in sending you to plead de Maurel's cause—what?" retorted the creature with a snarl. "But if you have come here, my wench, in order to stand between me and that man, then the sooner you go back home the better it will be for you. You can tell Madame la Marquise that I'll deal with the Maréchal as I choose ... and if he were twenty times her son and twenty times your lover."

"You forget yourself, Leroux," said Fernande with quiet dignity, choosing to ignore the hideous wretch's coarse insult. "You are being paid—and heavily paid, in order that you should do as you are told. When Madame la Marquise gave you the orders for to-night, she did not reckon on M. de Maurel standing in the way of M. de Puisaye's plans. No one can prevent his coming here anon, we know, but his presence here—alone—cannot possibly interfere with any of our plans; therefore, it rests with you to see that no harm comes to him."

Again that muffled laugh, coming from the Lodge, grated ominously on Fernande's ear.

"Well," said Leroux cynically, "if it rests with me to see that no harm comes to the man whom I hate most in all the world, we may as well reckon that Bonaparte will have one Marshal less by to-morrow wherewith to beat the Prussians."

"And you will find," retorted Fernande, who was determined not to allow a hideous sense of foreboding to paralyse her courage, "that if you disregard Madame de Mortain's orders ... if you touch but a hair of M. de Maurel's head, my father and all our chiefs will exact the fullest reprisals from you. And, in Heaven's name, Leroux," she added in more persuasive tones, "will you reflect for one moment? What is there to gain by an act of violence which will redound with unmitigated severity against you? Our chiefs will disclaim any participation in such an outrage, and you will be left to bear the utmost consequences of your own act."

He looked at her for a moment, and his attitude now became so insolent, that, much against her will, a burning flush overspread Fernande's cheeks. After a while he gave a low chuckle and shrugged his shoulders.

"You are, of a truth, in a sad quandary—eh, my girl?" he said. "You dare not go to your sweetheart and tell him to keep out of my way, for fear that he might smell a rat and interfere with your precious friends' plans. At the same time, I for one do not see what else there is left for you to do. Go to him by all means and see if you cannot persuade him to remain quietly at home with you—no harm would come to him then, I promise you that—and he wouldn't be wasting his time, either. But if he chooses to come here and try any of his arrogance upon me, then, by the name of Satan, there'll be trouble ... that is all!"

While the abominable wretch spat out his hideous insults, his ugly face, by the dim light from above, appeared distorted by a significant leer. Fernande now was almost overcome with horror—not at her own helplessness, for, of a truth, she was ready to brave the villain to the last—but at the utter failure of her appeal, and at the certainty that, strive how she might, nothing would move him from his fell purpose. The man meant murder—dastardly, cowardly murder—against a defenceless man; his whole attitude proclaimed it, his words, his awful sneers. And Fernande, feeling now like a poor captive beast on the leash, knew that she was bruising her pride, her heart, her hands against the bond of impotence which she was powerless to tear asunder. The sense of horror had gradually crept into her innermost being—it was paralysing her limbs and her will.

But suddenly the man paused; the impudent leer fled from his face, giving place to an expression of tense excitement. He put up his hand as if to enjoin silence, then placed a grimy finger to his lips.

"Hark!" he whispered.

And Fernande, straining her ears to listen, caught the clicking sound of an iron latch and the creaking of a gate upon its hinges.

"Here comes M. le Maréchal," said Leroux curtly.

At once and with sudden impulse Fernande had drawn back hastily out of the circle of light into the dense shadow cast by the tall storehouse.

"He must not see me here," she whispered hurriedly.

"I thought not," riposted Leroux dryly. "But 'tis too late, my wench, to run that way," he added, seeing that Fernande was ready to fly. "You would fall straight into his arms."

Then, without any warning and before she had time or desire to scream, he seized her wrist, and drawing quite close to her, he whispered in her ear:

"You have just two minutes in which to make up your mind, my girl. Go to the Lodge now, at once, and wait there; he'll go in after you. Talk to him, persuade him, do anything you like. We don't want to hurt him ... curse him!... unless he interferes with us. I'll let my mates out by the back door, then lock you both in together in the Lodge—eh? And you and he would be quite safe and snug," he added, with a chuckle which was far more offensive than any words he might utter, "while we do your party's work out here."

With an exclamation of loathing, Fernande managed to disengage her wrist, and a savage oath escaped the vile creature's lips.

"Well, which is it to be?" he queried fiercely. "Am I to speak with the Maréchal or are you?"

With an almost superhuman effort Fernande contrived to conquer the feeling of sheer physical nausea wherewith this

190

abominable wretch inspired her, and she even succeeded in saying almost calmly under her breath:

"You are to act on the message which I brought you from Madame la Marquise. She and my father, M. de Courson, will hold you responsible for the life of M. de Maurel."

"Tshaw!" he exclaimed contemptuously.

Then suddenly, as the imminence of the catastrophe appeared to come nearer and nearer the while that firm footstep, still a few mètres away, dragged along the flagstones of the yard, Fernande suddenly felt all her pride falling away from her.

"Leroux!" she cried, and she was nothing but an humble suppliant now. She would have gone down on her knees had she thought to mollify him by this act of self-abasement. "Leroux! you would not sully your hands and our cause by such an abominable crime...."

But the whispered words died upon her lips, a hot, evil-smelling hand was summarily pressed against them, and a raucous voice murmured in her ear:

"Silence! He'll hear you! Silence, I say, or I'll strangle you first and shoot him after. Now, then, if you don't want him to see you, slip away round the storehouse; while he argues with me, you can run as far as the gate—and you may thank your stars that I don't happen to have the time or the wish to deal more harshly with you."

He pushed her roughly away from him, and she, feeling faint and sick, was only just able to totter back against the protecting wall of the building. Leroux had already turned his back on her, and suddenly through the gloom she perceived de Maurel's tall figure coming at a quiet, moderate pace across the quadrangle, swinging as he walked a safety lanthorn which he carried.

There was no time now for further pleadings, protests, admonitions; there was no time even to think. Fernande's mind was in a whirl, out of which only one thought remained clear: that she would stay and save Ronnay de Maurel even now if she could.

"They will not dare ... while I stand by," was the one distinct impression which she retained in the midst of her chaotic emotions. She had just time to withdraw within the shelter of a projecting piece of masonry, from whence she could still see Leroux standing in the full light of the tower lamp, defiant and expectant, not twenty paces away from her, and de Maurel approaching slowly, swinging his safety lanthorn in his hand.

CHAPTER XXI

THE CRASH OF THE STORM

I

He wore his working blouse and a cap upon his head. In addition to the safety lanthorn he carried a bundle tied up in a handkerchief.

He hailed Leroux as soon as he came near.

"So now, my man," he said quietly, "'tis time you went."

Leroux did not move. He stood with legs wide apart, his hands buried in the pockets of his breeches. The light from the clock-tower above lit up the top of his shaggy head, his wide shoulders and the tip of his nose. De Maurel had approached, quite unconscious apparently of the glowering looks which Leroux cast upon him.

"You had best get to the compound," he added, "before the rain comes down."

And quite unconcernedly he walked past Leroux and continued to advance toward the Lodge. The man watched him from over his shoulder, and when de Maurel had reached the steps of the Lodge, he said sullenly:

"I am not going."

De Maurel calmly shrugged his shoulders.

"What is the use of all that obstinacy?" he said. "We argued everything out this afternoon. You had best go quietly now, my man ... or there'll be trouble."

"Trouble?" riposted Leroux with a sneer. "I doubt not but that there will be trouble this night, M. le Maréchal...."

His first instinctive terror at sight of the man whom he feared above all others was gradually falling away from him. He had turned on his heel and was now facing the open window of the Lodge, through which he could feel, even if he could not see, his mates, who were there ready to stand by him, if necessary, if it came to an open conflict between himself and the employer whom he was pledged to betray. The sense of their presence close by gave him a measure of defiance and of courage.

De Maurel stood quite still for a moment or two, then he retraced his steps and came back to within a mètre or so of where the man was standing.

"You are contemplating mischief, Leroux," he said with his accustomed calm. "Someone has been egging you on to one of your attacks of futile rebellion, which you must know by now, invariably lead to more severe measures being taken against you. You know how lenient I can be, but also how severe. This night's work can only end in disaster for you ... the gallows probably, unless you realize that submission even at this eleventh hour will be your best policy."

"Very well spoken, M. le Maréchal," retorted Leroux, with a sneer; "but let me tell you that the hour has gone by when your arrogance and your threats had the power to cow me. To-day I am a desperate man, and desperate men are not apt to count the costs of their actions. I will not vacate the Lodge to-night, and unless...."

He paused and shrugged his shoulders. De Maurel had thrown down his bundle and transferred the lanthorn to his left hand, whilst with his right he drew a pistol from beneath his blouse.

"Put away that weapon, M. le Maréchal," said Leroux, "it will avail you nothing. There are twenty of us inside the Lodge, all well armed. Twenty others overpowered your night-watchmen half an hour ago. We are expecting a fresh contingent of our mates from the compound at any moment. Resistance or bluster on your part were, indeed, worse than futile. You have run your head into a noose this time, my fine gentleman, and your threats are about as useful as the pistol which you have in your hand. And if it comes to that," he added with a savage oath, "I, too, of late have learned how to shoot."

With a rapid movement he drew a pistol from his belt; but before he had time to level it, de Maurel had fired. The man uttered a convulsive cry of rage; his left hand grabbed at his shoulder, while his weapon fell with a clatter to the ground.

"You have shot me, you devil!" he shouted hoarsely. "A moi, my mates!"

The pistol shot and Leroux' raucous cry had drowned a woman's call—a call of warning and of agonized terror: "Take care!" but not before de Maurel's keen ear had perceived it, and even while an evil-looking rabble came pouring out from the Lodge the call was repeated, and the next moment a woman's slender form was interposed between him and the foremost group among the crowd.

"In God's name, save yourself," came in a frenzied murmur in his ear, and a pair of hands clung to his arm with the strength of unspoken anguish. "Into the shadow ... quick ... they'll not touch me ... only save yourself!"

The voice, the touch, sent a tumultuous flood of passion seething through de Maurel's veins. Overhead the thunder crashed and a vivid streak of lightning showed him a brutish, menacing gang of miscreants advancing towards him, their faces misshapen and distorted with the fulsomeness of their own savagery and malignant anticipation of triumph. There was a score or so of them, and the light from the clock-tower glinted on the steel of muskets.

"A moi, my mates!" shouted Leroux once again at the top of his voice, and in response there came from left and right the sound of tramping of many feet; and within a few seconds the open space in

193

front of the great storehouse was filled with a moving, oscillating crowd, the numbers of which could only be vaguely guessed at in the gloom. The light from above caught the outline here of a face, there of a square shoulder, always of a musket, a pistol, or even a knife held tightly in a rough, grimy hand.

II

Instinctively de Maurel had stepped back into the shadow. Perfect calm had immediately followed that sudden hot wave of passion which had filled his heart and brain at the moment that he became conscious of Fernande's presence so close to him.

He had but a few seconds wherein to act, wherein to disengage himself with almost savage violence from her dear clinging arms, and to force her into the shadow behind him. A few seconds wherein to whisper to her in desperate tones of appeal and of command: "While I parley with them, run to the gate ... they'll not see you.... Fernande, in the name of God, go!..."

He placed himself in front of her, his back to the storehouse; he had her life and his own to guard or to sell as dearly as he could.

"Go, Fernande," he commanded once again. He would have picked her up in his arms and run with her into safety had he dared. But the brutes were armed with muskets, and a stray shot meant for him might easily have reached her. He covered her with his body, praying with all his might that she might obey and seek safety while there was yet time, yet knowing all the while, with an intuitive conviction born of his own tumultuous passion, that she was resolved to remain by his side.

"Go, Fernande," he implored.

"I'll not go," she replied quietly; and he, feeling her so near him, hearing her voice quivering with emotion, with anguish for him, counted life well lost for these few rapturous seconds.

"Can I do anything?" she asked with perfect calm.

"Nothing," he replied. "There are at least a hundred against us, and the alarm bell is above the Lodge, the chain-handle just by the door.... Those cowardly brutes have cut us off from any chance of help."

Indeed, the crowd was pressing closer round him now; wherever he looked he could see faces on which the lamp from above cast a lurid glow—faces rendered grotesque by the flickering light and the dense shadows which hid eyes and mouth and accentuated nose and chin—faces in which menace and hatred had been fanned into open revolt by bribery and greed, and execration of all discipline and authority. De Maurel knew them all individually. Even through the gloom he could

194

distinguish the ringleaders—the malcontents with whom last year he had had many a tussle—whom the more iron rule of the military representatives had goaded into this senseless and abominable treachery.

De Maurel's quick eye had soon enough measured the odds that were against him; of a truth, they were overwhelming. Nothing but a miracle could save him if these men did, indeed, contemplate murder, of which he had little doubt. The great question was how to save Fernande—his brave, beautiful, exquisite Fernande, who was standing so magnificently by him, whose heroism and courage filled him with as much wonder as her beauty and tenderness had filled his heart with love. Forgotten were the humiliation and the bitterness of a twelve-month ago; forgotten was her cruelty, the hurt she had done to him; she was standing by him now—shoulder to shoulder—his friend in this hour of difficulty, his comrade at the moment of peril.

Oh! if he only had the strength, the wits to keep those maddened wolves at bay, the whole world would not wrench the memory of this blissful night from out his heart again.

But there was no time even to think of happiness or of the future; the present lay there before him, grim and hand in hand with death. The few seconds' respite while he stood facing the murderous crowd— eye to eye and silently—were already gone; the men were gathering more menacingly around him. What their ultimate purpose was he had as yet only vaguely guessed. On this, before everything, he wanted to be quite clear—definite knowledge on the point would then help him how to act.

"So that's it, my men, is it?" he said coolly. "Open mutiny, eh?"

"You may call it that, an it please you," said one of the men.

"Hatched during my absence—ready against my home-coming ere I had time to realize the treachery that was brewing. I ought to have guessed, I suppose."

Leroux, with a wound in his shoulder that was bleeding profusely, was in the forefront of the pack, supported on either side by one of his mates.

"Yes," he said huskily, "you might have guessed that men would not put up indefinitely with tyranny and oppression. We are not dogs, nor yet savage brutes to be kept to our task with threats of punishment. Those men who were here, who went two days ago—curse them!—were ready to use the lash on us had they dared!"

"And you dared not rebel while they were here! Were you frightened of the lash?" retorted de Maurel contemptuously. "You waited for my return. Did you think I should be a weaker fool than they?"

"We were not ready then. We are ready now," came from one of the men.

"Ready for what?" queried de Maurel. "What do you hope to gain

195

by this senseless mutiny? To overpower the watchmen for one night and run riot through the factories? To-morrow must bring reprisals. Ye know that well enough."

"To-morrow you'll no longer be here, M. le Maréchal," sneered Leroux, who, though losing blood freely, had still sufficient strength left to maintain his position as ringleader of the gang. "To-morrow you'll not be here," he reiterated roughly, "to browbeat and threaten us."

"You mean to kill me, I know," rejoined de Maurel coolly. "But my death will avail you little. Reprisals will be all the more severe. Think you the law will let you escape? I am not a man who can be assassinated and then thrown into a ditch without causing some stir. Where will you hide when your Emperor himself will demand from you an account of what you have done with me?"

"Bah! when we have done with you, my fine Marshal of France," replied Leroux, with an insolent laugh, "there will be no Emperor. We are working for the King—not for Bonaparte ... and when we hold the factories and foundries in the name of the King ... why, there's little we'll have to fear from the Emperor; and, moreover...."

A terrific clash of thunder drowned the rest of his words, while the lightning literally tore the dark clouds asunder. Some of the men—more superstitious than the rest—instinctively crouched back, muttering blasphemies—pushing those behind them back, too, so that the entire human mass seemed suddenly to be heaving and then receding like the scum of sea-waves upon the ebbing tide; a gust of wind swept across the quadrangle, driving dust and dried leaves before it. Some of the men cursed, others hastily crossed themselves, with a vague remembrance of past devotions long buried beneath the dark mantle of crime.

The silence which ensued was absolute. It lasted less than ten seconds, perhaps, during which hardly a man dared to breathe—so absolute was it, that the click of every firearm striking against its neighbour was distinctly audible, as was the soughing of the wind in the silver birches on the wooded heights behind the factory. Something of a nameless terror had crept into the bones of these godless miscreants. By that vivid flash of lightning they had seen their master standing alone unflinching before them—against the background of the huge storehouse—his massive figure appearing preternaturally tall, his face pale and determined. His head was bare to the winds and the storm, and it was turned full upon them, and neither in the dark, deep-set eyes nor round the firm mouth was there the slightest sign of fear. And they had caught sight of the slim silhouette of Fernande de Courson standing behind him, her graceful form seeming ethereal, like that of a protecting angel.

And for the space of those ten seconds de Maurel had just time to look on the situation squarely and with a clearer understanding than before. With his clumsy words, Leroux had in an instant revealed to him something of the dark treachery which had brought this mutinous crowd together—something of the murky undercurrent of intrigue which was driving the torrent of discontent to the flood of open rebellion. So this was the history of Leroux' defiance? this was the key to the riddle which had puzzled de Maurel when first he realized that these senseless brutes were actually not only in organized rebellion against him, but intent on murder—a stupid, purposeless and useless murder, which in itself would carry immediate discovery in its train, and with it the absolute certainty of terrible reprisals and penalties.

But now the whole thing became clear. It was his mother and her party who had engineered this trickery, and Heaven alone knew how near they were to succeed in the abominable project!

And in a flash he seemed to see every phase of the intrigue: his factories and foundries in the hands of these dastards, whilst the Royalist bands marched on La Frontenay. There were other details, of course—plots and counterplots—at which it was impossible to guess. Only the facts remained—the facts which confronted him now, together with this murderous pack of hungry wolves and the muskets which were levelled against him.

For his own life he cared less than nothing; many a time had he faced Prussian muskets as he faced those of a set of mutinous ruffians now. A few minutes ago he had felt one thrill of exultant happiness when Fernande's arms clung around his shoulders, and her sweet body lay against his breast in her endeavour to shield him against his aggressors. He was more than content that that one supreme moment of delight should be the last which this world held for him—more than content to go to his eternal sleep with the sweet memory of her last caress to be his lullaby.

But his life had suddenly assumed an importance which he himself never granted it before. He alone, at this moment stood for the protection of these mighty engines of warfare around him, of the materials which his Emperor needed for overcoming the enemies of France. The very instant that he—Ronnay de Maurel—fell, they would become the prey of traitors, the prey of those who concerted with the foreigner against their country, who trafficked with Prussia, with Austria, with Russia, in order to force upon the people of France a government and a King whom they abhorred. At this very hour, perhaps, a band of Royalists was on its way to La Frontenay. It was all so simple—so absolutely, so perfectly, so hellishly simple! If he fell, they would reach the factories and the foundries, and these murderous traitors here would deliver his patrimony into their hands—the patrimony which he devoted to the service of France—the new guns, the small-arms, the explosives, the stores ... everything. If anon he lay with shattered head or breast on the threshold of this precious storehouse, which he had been powerless to protect, the cause of freedom, of the Emperor and of his armies, would receive a blow from which it could only recover after years more of fratricidal combat and more streams yet of bloodshed.

This he owed to his mother, to his brother, to his kindred, who had fanned the flame of hatred and rebellion against him, whose hands were raised against their country, whom they professed to love, and who had coolly and callously decreed his death because he stood in their way. With the very wealth which he had placed at his mother's disposal, she had paid these brutes to betray and to murder him.

And Fernande?

At Leroux' words he had felt her quivering behind him; he had heard the moan which escaped from her lips. Fernande knew of the treachery as she had known of his danger, and, knowing of his deadly peril, she had come here in order to share it with him. That thought, as it flashed before him, lent de Maurel's entire soul a courage and an exultation which was almost superhuman. As the thunder clashed above him, and the lightning tore the dark clouds asunder, it seemed to him as if God Himself, in His glory, had deigned to reveal Himself, to give him the strength and the power that he needed, the guidance which comes as a divine breath from Heaven in the supreme hour of a man's life, when Death and Duty and Love stand at the parting of the ways and beckon with unseen hands.

III

The silence that ensued had only lasted a moment. Already the men were recovering from their brief access of terror; some of them were shaking themselves like curs after a douche. They all drew nearer to one another, satisfied to feel one another's support and grasping their muskets more determinedly in their hands.

De Maurel had turned once more to Fernande.

"It means death, my beloved," he murmured.

"I know," she replied quietly.

"You are not afraid?"

"No."

Questions and answers came in rapid succession. His hand closed upon hers.

"In my heart," he said, "I kiss your exquisite hands, your feet, your hair, your lips. You forgive me?"

"Everything."

There was not a quiver in her voice; for one second her fingers rested in his, and they were firm and warm to his touch. They were made to understand one another, these two; their courage was equally undaunted; they both looked on death without a tremor. He would

198

have given his life bit by bit for her, but at this hour, when the needs of France demanded a sacrifice so sublime that none but an heroic heart could have conceived it, not even the thought of his beloved came between him and his determination.

La Frontenay must be saved for the Emperor and for France at all costs—even at the cost of that one life which was more precious to him than his own, more precious than all the world, save France. And with one pressure of her slender hand she yielded up her will—her life to him. For this one supreme moment—a moment which held in it an infinity of love and passion—they met one another soul to soul. Hand in hand, in the face of death, this second was for them an eternity of ecstasy.

"You love me, Fernande!" he murmured.

"Until death," she replied.

"Then pray to God, dear heart," he whispered. "He alone can save us now."

Then he faced the crowd of cut-throats once more.

"Listen, my men," he said, speaking coolly and quietly. "For the last time let me tell you how you stand. As far as I can see, there are about fivescore of you standing there before me, and you think that you hold my life in the hollow of your hands. And so you do, in a measure. Your muskets are levelled against me, and even if I were to sell my life very dearly and blow out the brains of a few amongst you, you would have small work to lay me low in the end. You have been lured to this treachery by promises, and bribery; you have listened to insidious suggestions of treason. But let me tell you this. Others before you have listened to promises which came from that same quarter, and their bones lie mouldering now in forgotten graves. You think that if you delivered these works into the hands of M. de Puisaye and his followers you would be rendering such a service to the Royalist cause, that that effete and obese creature who dares to call himself King of France will inevitably come to the throne which his forbears have forfeited, and that he will reward you handsomely for any service you may have rendered him. But, believe me, that even if this night a few bands of rebellious peasants took possession of La Frontenay and its works, their triumph and yours would be short-lived. No one in France at this hour wants a Bourbon king; the army worships the Emperor, the people adore him, and with the army and the people against you, what do you think that you can do? La Frontenay is not the only armament factory in France; think you that you will cripple the Emperor because you deliver our stores into the hands of his enemies? Take care, men, take care," he added more earnestly; "'tis you who have run your heads into a noose, and with every outrage which you commit this night that noose will become tighter round your necks, and you'll find that I—your master—will be more menacing and more fearsome to you dead—murdered foully by you—than ever I was in life."

199

His powerful, rugged voice rose above the murmur of the storm. Some of the men listened to him in sullen silence; the magnetic influence which "the General" had exercised over them in the past was not altogether gone; his powerful personality, his cool courage, the simplicity of his words, reacted upon their evil natures, and also upon their cowardice. There was a vast deal of common sense in what M. le Maréchal was saying, and they, after all, had only been promised a hundred francs apiece for an exceedingly risky piece of work. But there were some ringleaders among them who expected to get far more out of their treachery than a paltry hundred francs; they relied on de Puisaye's vague promises of freedom, on his assurance that unconditional pardon for past infractions against the law would be granted to them by a grateful King. They—and, above all, Leroux—felt also that they were committed too far now to dare to draw back, and even while de Maurel spoke they broke in on his words with sneers and taunts, and, above all, with threats.

"You seem to think, M. le Maréchal," said Leroux in husky tones—for he was getting feeble with loss of blood—"you seem to think that I and my mates are here to murder you."

"Why else are you here?" rejoined de Maurel coolly. "You do not suppose, I imagine, that I am like to vacate the place and leave you to work your evil will with my property?"

"'Twere the wisest thing to do," retorted one of the men. "Eh, mates?"

"Yes! yes!" came with a volley of savage oaths from every side.

"Throw up your hands, M. le Maréchal," added a voice from the crowd, "and we'll see that neither you nor your sweetheart come to any harm!"

"Silence, you blackguard," thundered de Maurel fiercely, "or, by God, I'll pick you out of the crowd and shoot you like the dog that you are."

"Throw up your hands, M. le Maréchal," broke in Leroux roughly; "the men have no quarrel with you. But cease to defy and threaten them, or by Satan there'll be trouble."

"The trouble will come, my men, if you persist in this insensate mutiny. Throw down your muskets now at once, and go back to your compounds while there's yet time, and before the consequences of your own folly descend upon your heads."

A shout of derision greeted these words.

"The consequences of your folly will descend on your head, M. le Maréchal," sneered Leroux. "Get out of our way. We have parleyed enough. Eh, my mates?"

"Yes! yes! enough talk," some of them cried, whilst others added fiercely: "Put a bullet through him and silence his accursed tongue at last."

"Pierre Deprez, I know you," said de Maurel loudly. "Now then, all of you, for the last time—throw down your muskets—hands up!"

There came another shout of derision, wilder than the first.

"Hark at him!" cried Paul Leroux scornfully. "Even now he thinks that he can order us about—just as if we were a lot of craven curs."

"You are a lot of craven curs! And since you choose to be deaf to the voice of persuasion you shall listen to that of power. Down with your muskets! Hands up!... 'Tis the second time I've spoken."

"You may speak an hundred times, we'll not obey," retorted one of the men. "The days of obedience are past; the place is ours...."

"For the third and last time ..." began de Maurel.

Before the word was out of his mouth a shot was fired at him out of the crowd. The sound appeared as the signal for the breaking down of the last barrier which held these men's murderous passions in check.

"'Tis our turn to command," shouted Leroux excitedly. "Throw up your hands, M. le Maréchal, or...."

"Down with the muskets!" cried de Maurel in thunderous accents, that reached to the furthermost ends of the vast quadrangle, "or by the living God whom you have outraged, I'll bury myself and you and your dastardly crime in one common grave."

With a movement as rapid as that of the lightning above he swung the safety lanthorn against the wall behind him, and the protecting glass flew shattered in every direction, leaving a light naked and flaring, on which the storm immediately seized and tossed about in every direction. Above him towered the huge edifice which contained fifty thousand barrels of explosives. Immediately on his right was a narrow entrance into the building, to which a couple of stone steps gave access. In the space of a second he had run up those steps, his shoulder was against the door. The flame danced around him and lit up his stern face, which was set in a grim resolve.

"If one shout is uttered," he continued in a sonorous and resounding voice, "if another shot is fired, if one of you but dares to move, I break open this door, and within ten seconds, long before any man can find safety in flight, the first barrel of gunpowder will be aflame."

Overhead the thunder crashed—the storm raged in all its fury, and in the great quadrangle there was a sudden silence as in the city of the dead. Fivescore men were held paralysed with the horror of what they saw, spellbound by the might and power of a man who knew not fear; inert by the near sight of a hideous death. And while the crowd stood there, meek and obedient, quivering with terror like a pack of wild beasts under the lash of the tamer, he added with withering scorn:

"And you thought that you could filch from me that which I hold in trust for the Empire of France! You fools! You wretched, slinking, cowardly fools!"

"In God's name, M. le Maréchal!" came in an awed whisper from one or two men in the forefront of the crowd—"in God's name throw away that light!"

"Not until you have thrown down your muskets!"

A hundred muskets fell with a dull clatter to the ground.

"The light, M. le Maréchal! the light...!"

"Now one of you ring the alarm bell!"

"The light...!"

"Silence!" he called aloud, so that the night air rang with his sonorous voice. "The alarm bell, I said. Pierre Deprez—you! The others stand at attention. Hands up!"

One man slunk away from the rest, and, shrinking, walked slowly in the direction of the Lodge.

The naked light of the lanthorn flickered in the storm; every moment it seemed as if it must catch the edge of de Maurel's blouse or the woodwork round the door. One hundred pairs of eyes were fixed in frenzied terror upon him, yet so potent was the feeling of horror which held the men in thrall, that not one of them dared to move if only to stretch out his hand toward that light which threatened them all with such an appalling death.

A moment or so later the first clang of the alarm bell reverberated through the manifold sounds of the storm. It was followed almost immediately by the multisonous hooting of sirens in the distance and the peal of the alarm bell from the foundry half a kilomètre away.

And as the measured sounds of the bells and the sirens swelled to one majestic resonance, drowning now the roll of thunder and the soughing of the stormy blast, it seemed—for the space of one supreme second—that the men would repent them of their terror; for one second it seemed as if they would gather up their weapons again, and, throwing all prudence to the winds, rush and overcome that man who—single-handed—held them so completely in his power.

De Maurel, standing beside the door a step or two above them, saw the first sign of this reaction—the unmistakable oscillation of a crowd when it is moved by one common impulse. He felt the one weak spot in his armour—the possibility of his being struck even now by a chance musket-shot, so that not even with a dying gesture could he accomplish that which he was so grimly resolved to do. And without an instant's hesitation, even as like a wave the crowd swayed towards him, he lifted one corner of his linen blouse and held it to the flame; another second and the woodwork would most inevitably be ablaze.

A cry of horror rose from a hundred lips; the crowd swayed back—the supreme second had gone by; and coolly, with his free hand, de Maurel extinguished the flame on his blouse. Then he threw back his head and a loud laugh broke from his lips.

"And 'tis to such cowards," he said loudly, "that French men and women would entrust the destinies of France!"

202

IV

Five minutes later the quadrangle was seething with men. Mathurin had been the first to reach the precincts of the factory with the armed watchmen from the foundries; he was the first to recognize his master still standing with his back against the wall of the powder-magazine, holding a naked, wind-tossed light in his hand. There was no time for puzzlement or surprise; something of what had actually happened rose as a swift yet vivid picture before the loyal overseer's mind. The crowd of mutineers was not difficult to overpower—surrounded by the watchmen, they gave in without a struggle. They were still dazed with the fright which they had had and made no attempt at resistance. At any rate, until they were well in hand, de Maurel did not move from his post. But he had put down the lanthorn and stamped out the light with his heel; after that, he stood quite still, only giving a few directions now and again in his resonant voice to Mathurin and his capable coadjutors. The watchmen of the factory, who had been surprised, overpowered and imprisoned in the Lodge before de Maurel's advent on the scene, were soon released, and their numbers added materially to the easiness of the task.

Soon the mutineers, in orderly array, were mustered up in the quadrangle preparatory to being marched back to their compound. Order reigned once more within the vast precincts of the factory. The excitement of a while ago, the shouts, the threats, the tumultuous cries of rage, of hatred and of fear, had given place to quick words of command, to brisk comings and goings, to measured tramps of feet and methodical click of arms. Overhead the thunder still rolled at intervals, and now and again the sky was rent by a flash of lightning; but the brunt of the storm had spent itself in the two terrific crashes which had proved de Maurel's most faithful allies in arousing the superstitious terror of those ignorant dastards. A warm, soft rain began to fall, further damping the ardour of the gang of rebels, as they filed past with hunched-up shoulders and shuffling footsteps—like whipped curs that feared more severe punishment yet to come.

203

CHAPTER XXII

HEAVEN AND EARTH

I

Then at last de Maurel was able to turn to Fernande.

He came down the steps of the storehouse, and his eyes, so long dazed by the flicker of the naked light, searched for her in the gloom.

She had not moved from the spot which he had originally assigned to her, and he found her there, leaning against the wall, within the shelter of the recess formed by the framework and the steps of the doorway.

"Now I can carry you home, my beloved," he said simply.

After the nerve-rending emotion of a while ago, Fernande felt a sudden slackening of all her muscles, a numbness which invaded heart and brain. While de Maurel had stood facing the murderous crowd, with her life and his and that of all these men in his hand, while he was there resolved to annihilate his entire patrimony rather than to surrender it to the enemies of his Emperor, she had felt only conscious of one desperate longing, which was to be held tightly in his arms and to meet death with her lips touching his.

That she loved him with her whole heart, with every fibre of her body, and all the fervour of her soul, she had known since that day in the woods, when he had almost wrenched an admission of her love from her, and only Laurent's intervention had frozen the avowal on her lips. When—silent and cold—she had then been forced to part from him, she had done so believing that he would never forgive her for the shame which she had put on him, and that his love for her, tumultuous and passionate as was his whole nature, had quickly enough turned to hate. During the year that ensued, when she felt that never in life perhaps would she ever see him again, she had realized that, unknowing, she had loved him from the hour when first he lifted her in his strong arms and carried her through the woods, the while the birds twittered overhead, and she could watch his face and the play of emotion and of passion in his deep-set eyes through the cool veil of a sheaf of bluebells. She had loved him then, even though in the weeks that followed she often thought that she hated him; by the time that true knowledge came to her it was too late.

Since then the irrevocable had happened: she had become Laurent de Mortain's promised wife, and a gulf now lay between her and the man whom she loved, which nothing but death could have

204

helped them to bridge over. In the hour of that deadly peril, the unspoken word of a year ago had come to her lips; it had come, now as then, in response to his own compelling will, to that triumphant possession of her which already a year ago had nearly thrown her in his arms. "You love me, Fernande?" he had asked, and, face to face with the actuality which she had thought lay buried deep down in her heart, she could not deny its truth without perjuring her soul. And when he whispered in her ear: "It means death, my beloved!" she had been ready to throw herself in his arms, to ask for that one last kiss which would have made death both welcome and sweet. She felt then as if she were being lifted up on a huge wave of light to a glorious empyrean above, where her body fell away from her, and soul and spirit swooned in the enchantment of a divine ecstasy. She felt then that she was no longer mortal, that she had reached a state which was akin to that of the angels. She felt that sublime rapture which alone makes of Man a true child of God.

But now the danger was past; the tumultuous excitement of a while ago, the wild ecstasy of love in the face of death, had yielded to the sober reality of everyday life. It seemed almost as if, when de Maurel finally stamped out with his heel the naked light which threatened annihilation, he had, at the same time, extinguished the flame of passion which was searing Fernande's soul. With the last dying flicker of that light, exultation which had carried her to the giddy heights of bliss folded its wings, and she came down to earth once more. It had been a steep and vertiginous descent, and she felt sore, bruised and dazed, groping blindly for the light which had so suddenly gone out of her life and left her lonely and cold. The mystic veil wherewith love had enveloped her vision of reality in this past hour, was being slowly torn from before her eyes; and the world appeared before her, not as she had seen it a while ago, through the blinding light of an overmastering passion, but as it was now in its dull and grim positiveness.

Gradually the thought of Laurent first, then of her father, then of de Puisaye, of her cause, and of her King, penetrated into her brain.

Duty, honour, loyalty, began to whisper in her ear, and soon their voices succeeded in drowning the still insistent murmur of love.

Laurent!

All this while she had forgotten him; nay, not only him, but her father and her King, her kindred and her cause. While she allowed swift passion to course through her veins, while she yielded to the delight of Ronnay's voice, of his nearness, of the love-light which gleamed in his eyes, her father and Laurent were on the high road between Mortain and Domfront and Tinchebrai, still secure in the thought that the projected coup had been successful, and that de Puisaye was even now on his way to take possession of La Frontenay and its accumulated wealth of arms. She pictured them both—her father and her betrothed—weary and footsore, risking their lives without a murmur, in order to accomplish the task which their chiefs had assigned to them to do; she pictured them defeated in their purpose—the garrisons of Domfront and Mortain on the qui vive—de Puisaye surprised with his force ... the rebel army surrounded ... scattered ... annihilated ... her father and Laurent fugitives or dead!... whilst she stood here oblivious of all save of the man whom she loved.

She dared not think of what would happen within the next few hours—she hardly dared to think of her father and of Laurent; but now that their loved image once more flitted across her mental vision, she endured the tortures of bitter self-abasement. God had manifested His will. He had stood by the brave man who, all alone and undaunted, had known how to defend his heritage and the cause of his Emperor and of France. And she—Fernande—seeing the pack of murdering wolves around him, had yielded to a moment of frenzied horror at a crime which was nigh to being committed before her eyes.

In her heart she had betrayed her people when that moment of madness wrung an avowal of love from her lips. She had betrayed her kindred when she interposed herself between their sworn enemy and the murderer's bullet which would have laid him low. And she still betrayed them now when, instead of flying back to them on the wings of loyalty and of love, she lingered here, if only for a few brief minutes, savouring the bitter-sweet delights of the inevitable farewell.

Was there ever blacker, more hideous treachery?

The light from the lamp above showed her Ronnay quite clearly, his brown hair taken back from the low, square forehead, the firm jaw and sensitive mouth, the toil-worn hands and linen blouse whereon the charred corner still bore mute and eloquent testimony to the unflinching heart that beat beneath its folds. And, above all, it revealed to her those eyes of his of a deep violet-blue, wherein passion and tenderness had kindled an all-compelling flame, and she knew that duty, loyalty, honour, compelled her to fly while there was yet time, and as far away as she could, lest the magnetism of his love drew her back to his arms once more.

Her place now was by the side of Laurent and of her father—in the midst of her friends at this hour, when black failure had dashed to naught all their dearest hopes. At La Frontenay, at Courson, at Mortain, there would be tears to quench and wounds to heal—God grant that a veil of mourning be not spread over all the land!—and she Fernande must be there to comfort and to soothe.

206

All these thoughts and emotions coursed so swiftly through heart and brain that they left her dazed, bewildered, with limbs icy cold and teeth chattering, the while her head felt as if it were on fire. Reaction had set in; the excitement had been so intense, when death and passion fought for mastery over her entire soul, that the sudden relaxation of her nerves nearly caused an utter collapse of every one of her faculties.

It required an almost superhuman effort to regain complete possession of herself, to collect her thoughts, to chase away the last shreds of the dream. It would require a greater effort still to wrench herself away from this spot where she felt that henceforward her heart would remain buried. For the moment it meant gaining power over her limbs, which seemed disinclined to render her service, and over her head wherein tumultuous thoughts still refused to be marshalled in orderly array it meant, in fact, waiting for an opportunity to slip away as soon as she could. She knew in which direction lay the postern gate, and she knew her way back to La Frontenay. If she only could reach the château within the next half-hour, some means might yet be found to acquaint de Puisaye of what had occurred. She wondered vaguely how much de Maurel knew at this hour of what was in preparation over by Mortain, or what he could do if he knew everything.

The sight of the crowd still moving or standing, compact and busy, all round the storehouse maddened her. These men were impeding her way to the postern gate; they stood in the way of her getting to La Frontenay in time to send a runner over, even at this hour, to de Puisaye. It was nearly two hours since she left home—an eternity!—over half an hour since the first hooting of the sirens must have roused the countryside; and she still was so shaken, so numbed, so bruised, that she hadn't it in her to make a dash through the crowd, to push her way through all these men who would intercept her and would draw de Maurel's attention to her movements.

If he captured her and brought her back, if he refused to let her go, would she have the physical strength to resist? Oh, for a moment's darkness, an instant of silence, which would cover her flight!

Then at last the opportunity came. The groups around the storehouse gradually dispersed; the way lay clear as far as the angle of the building beyond which was darkness and solitude. Mathurin was engaging de Maurel's attention, and he—Ronnay—was standing half turned away from her. She gave one last look round her—one last look at the man whom she loved, and whom mayhap she would never in life see again, and in her heart she spoke a last, fond farewell. But as surely as a magnet draws to itself a piece of steel, so did this look of love from her compel and draw his gaze. Before she had time to move, he was down the steps and standing in front of her, so that he barred the way.

"Now I can carry you home, my beloved," he said.

He put out his arms ready to take hold of her. The wild excitement of the past half-hour had left no impress upon his iron physique save in a certain pallor of the cheeks and a stiffening of the firm jaw.

"I would have given my life's blood, drop by drop," he said simply, "to have spared you all that. You do believe me, Fernande, do you not?"

She could not reply. The instinct to fly, to run away, to close her ears to his voice, her eyes to his gaze, was so insistent, that she could have screamed with longing and a maddened feeling of impotence. By an impulsive gesture of self-protection she put up her hands.

"Yes, yes!" she said, trying to speak coldly, indifferently, even though her voice sounded hoarse and choked, and she could not control the nervous chattering of her teeth and the trembling of her limbs. "Yes, yes! of course I'll believe you, mon cousin!... You did what was right ... and I.... But now I entreat you to let me go home.... My aunt will be so anxious and...."

"And you are cold and overwrought," he said ruefully. "Curse those brutes," he added, with a sudden access of primitive savagery, "curse them for the evil their treachery has wrought!"

Then as he saw that she suddenly shrank away from him and drew her cloak closer round her, he chided himself for his roughness. "I am a brute," he said gently, "and am for ever begging your forgiveness. My beloved, will you not trust yourself to me? You must be so tired ... and the rain is coming down. We could be at La Frontenay in half an hour."

The events of the past fateful hour seemed to have faded from his ken. It seemed as if he had never stood there—a few paces away—that naked light in his hand, threatening destruction to a crowd of mutineers, destruction to himself, to his patrimony and to his beloved. He was just the same as he had always been—half clumsy, wholly compelling—whenever Fernande met him in the woods, and there was nothing between them save a still unavowed passion. She looked round her helplessly in vain search for a means of escape. She could not—dared not—speak for the moment. If she did, she knew that she must break down. She had gone through too much to have full power over her nerves; she felt unutterably weary, even though she knew that so much still lay before her, and though she was firmly resolved to play a loyal part to the end. In her heart she called out to him: "Yes! take me in your arms, my beloved; let me nestle against your shoulder; care for me, comfort me! The world is too difficult for my weak hands to grapple with!" And she had to close her eyes and to hold her lips tightly pressed together, or the heartrending cry would certainly have escaped them.

How long she remained standing thus silent and with eyes

closed, she did not know—a minute perhaps—perhaps a cycle of ages. During that time she fought for mastery over her nerves and over her senses, and in the fight she felt herself growing strange and old, with every emotion in her dead, and only the determination subsisting that he, too, must be made to remember that she was tokened to his brother, and that never, never while all three of them lived must the past hour be recalled again.

And de Maurel, the while, remained beside her, waiting patiently.

That was his way! Vehement as were his passions, tumultuous when they broke through the barrier of self-restraint, he had with it all the supreme virtue of infinite patience; in wrath, as in love, he always knew how to bide his time. Perhaps he guessed something of what went on behind those blue-veined lids on which he was aching to imprint a kiss. He could not see her face clearly, only just the delicate outline of her against the dark background of the wall, and occasionally a glint of gold when the light from above caught the loose tendrils of her hair.

When at last her fight was won, and nerves and senses fell into line with her determination to be loyal to Laurent in the spirit as well as in the letter, she felt as if every emotion in her was dead—as if she never would again be able to laugh and make merry, to cry, to love, or to hate—as if she would henceforth be just a callous, heartless, unfeeling thing without even the capacity for sorrow.

She looked at Ronnay and endured his glance without a tremor, and at last she was able to speak, knowing that there would be no quiver in her voice now to betray the agony of what she suffered.

"Of a truth, mon cousin," she said, with an indifferent little laugh, "it is passing kind of you to offer to be my beast of burden once again, but I assure you that I would not care to become quite so ludicrous a spectacle as you suggest before good old Mathurin and all your work-people. Believe me, I would far sooner go back to La Frontenay on my own feet. It would not be very dignified—would it?— for the future Marquise de Mortain to be carried along the road like a bundle of goods."

He said nothing for a moment or two, nor could she, by the dim light, read very clearly in his eyes whether her words had conveyed to him the full meaning which she intended, until he said quite simply: "Ah! I had forgotten."

A curious ashen colour overspread his face like that of a man suffering great physical pain.

And Fernande—poor Fernande!—with a forced laugh plunged the knife still more deeply into the gaping wound.

"Forgotten, mon cousin?" she said. "How could you have forgotten that I am your brother's promised wife? Did you not tender me your congratulations yesterday?"

"Of course, of course; I understand," he murmured vaguely, and he passed his hand once or twice mechanically across his brow. Then suddenly, with that rough directness which was so characteristic of him, he added simply: "But as long as life lasts, my beloved, I shall thank God on my knees for the one glimpse of Heaven which He gave me this night."

"There is a great deal, mon cousin," she rejoined coldly and firmly, "that both you and I must forget after this."

"Yes," he retorted. "I, for one, shall have to forget that my mother and my brother armed the hands of assassins against me."

Instinctively she called out: "It is false!"

"It is true, Fernande," he rejoined quietly, "and you know it. Some of my men who have just arrived from Domfront say that the woods beyond Mortain are alive with rebels. That murderous dastard Leroux has already betrayed the various threads of de Puisaye's latest intrigues. In order to try and save his own skin, which he will not succeed in doing," he continued grimly, "he has chosen to tell us all he knew—that my brother Laurent is on the high road at this hour with a gang of armed Chouans at his heels; so is M. de Courson. Another gang is on its way to these works in order to reap the fruits of Leroux' treachery. But our alarm bells have set the garrison of Domfront afoot; couriers are on their way to warn the commandants of Mortain and Tinchebrai. This comes of bribing a coward to become a traitor," he concluded harshly; "the disasters of this night will lie at the door of those who trafficked with assassins."

But Fernande no longer listened to him. Her dream had, indeed, vanished—vanished beyond recall, and she was back in the midst of all the calamity, the sorrow which would follow on the mistakes of this night. Indeed, the pitiless cowardice which had sent a brave man to face a band of murderers, alone and unwarned, had already received its awful punishment. Everything had been foreseen in de Puisaye's plans, everything had been thought out and arranged ... save this: that one man, single-handed, would cow and dominate a crowd of murderous rebels!

Now there was nothing left but to stand shoulder to shoulder, and trust to God that the small armies under de Puisaye, de Courson and Laurent de Mortain, escaped with their lives. There was nothing left to do but to tend the wounded and bury the dead. Fernande's very soul ached now with the longing to be back at La Frontenay, and the magnitude of her desire gave her just the strength which she needed. Swift as a hare, she took advantage of a slight movement on his part and managed to slip by him out of her corner. And she had started to run towards the postern gate ere he succeeded in overtaking her at the angle of the storehouse and once more barring her way.

This time he seized her in his arms.

"Where are you going, Fernande?" he cried peremptorily.

"Home!" she retorted. "Let me go!"

"You cannot go alone. The roads are unsafe."

"Let me go!"

"Not without me."

"Let me go! My place is with those I love."

In a moment his arms dropped down to his side and she was free. But the violence with which he had seized hold of her had made her unsteady on her feet; she tottered back a little, and then had to stand still a moment while she recovered her balance. The spell of his arms round her was upon her still; the dream voices of a while ago called out to her from afar ... a last lingering farewell.

"Even so, an you will allow me," he said, after a moment or two, and his voice sounded cold and toneless; "even so I would like to escort you home. The sirens will by now have alarmed half the country-side—a vast number of men will be on their way hither—there will be a crowd upon the road—some of the men may be rough. Those who ... those whom you love," he added with a harsh laugh, "would not wish you to go to them alone."

Then he continued more gently, and his voice became full of tender yearning: "Think you, my dear, that I do not understand? Why, there is nothing that you might think, or feel, or say, to which my heart would not immediately respond. You want to be at this time with those ... with those whom you love; that is only natural, and in accordance with your sweetness and your kind and loyal soul. Your heart now is at La Frontenay. Let me take you thither. I swear to you that I will not come nigh you, that I will not speak to you unless you grant me leave. So I entreat you let me come with you.... I would not else know a moment's peace."

"You are very kind," she murmured, "but indeed, indeed, there is no cause for anxiety. Wrapped in my cloak I shall be quite safe, and the passers-by will be too busy to think of molesting me."

"Is my company, then, so distasteful to you, that you are so anxious to rid yourself of me?"

She felt her eyes filling with tears, but still she contrived to say firmly: "It were best that I went alone."

"As you will," he rejoined coldly.

He stood aside, and as she moved away from him, he called loudly: "Mathurin!"

"Here, M. le Maréchal," came from a distant corner of the quadrangle, and hurrying footsteps drew quickly near in answer to the master's call. Fernande, the while, busied herself with her cloak.

"Mathurin," said de Maurel curtly, as soon as the overseer was in sight. "Detail two of the men whom you can best trust—Henri Gresset and Michel Picart, if you can spare them—to escort Mademoiselle de Courson back to the château."

"Very good, M. le Maréchal," replied Mathurin.

"Tell them to await Mademoiselle at the postern gate."

"It shall be done, M. le Maréchal."

Then Mathurin saluted and turned on his heel. It was not his place to question or to show surprise. Even in the most remote cell of his brain there was not room for a rebellious or a disloyal thought. He had his orders and at once he set about to execute them, and a moment or two later his voice was heard calling to Gresset and to Picart.

"Will you at least allow me to walk with you as far as the gate?" asked de Maurel, after the man had gone.

"If you wish it," she replied. Then, with sudden unconquerable impulse, she added in a tone of agonized entreaty:

"My father ... and Laurent?"

"What can I do?" he said with an impatient sigh.

"You have influence," she pleaded; "you can save them if you have the will."

"From the consequences of their own treachery?" he retorted harshly.

"Treachery?" she protested hotly.

"Let us call it folly. If Leroux' coup had succeeded the heritage which I hold in trust for France would have been wrenched from me with the help of assassins and of traitors."

"My father ..." she pleaded.

"And my brother," he added grimly. "Both caught probably this night in arms against their country—condemned to be shot as traitors...."

"Oh!"

"As traitors," he reiterated firmly. "A year ago the Emperor granted an unconditional pardon and amnesty to M. le Comte de Courson and to M. le Marquis de Mortain ... and every day since then these loyal gentlemen have worked and plotted to hurl him from his throne."

"My father ..." she pleaded once again. And she added under her breath: "You said just now that you could understand ... everything. And M. de Courson is my father...."

"And M. de Mortain, your future husband," he broke in with a derisive laugh and a shrug of his broad shoulders. Then suddenly a swift wave of passion seemed to sweep right over him—a wave of rebellion against Fate, against his destiny, against all the misery, the sorrow, the endless desolation which that fact stood for. "Ah, Fernande!" he exclaimed hoarsely, "how can you trust me so completely, yet give your love to another man?"

She drew in her breath with a little moan of pain. He had hurt her by these words more surely than she had ever hurt him, for she, on her side, had never thought to doubt his love. She believed in it more than ever before, now that she knew that this parting must be for always. But she felt that she had his answer—his promise to help her father and Laurent if he could. Almost she was ashamed to have appeared before him in the end as a suppliant, yet proud in her heart that she had gained so much in the cause which she had pleaded; proud in the fact that Love held him so completely in its thrall, that no base thought, no mean desire for vengeance, had a place beside it in his heart.

Now there was nothing more to be said. The last word had been spoken between them, the last save the one which rose to their lips now ere they parted, but which must henceforth and for ever remain unsaid.

III

She pulled the hood of her cloak over her head, and then turned to go the way she had come just half an hour ago. The clock-tower was just striking eleven. At different points of the vast quadrangle small patrols of watchmen could be perceived making their rounds, seeing that everything now was well and safe. The last of the mutineers had been marched out through the main gates, the tramp of heavy feet was even now dying away in the distance.

The silence and quietude of a perfectly ordered organization was once more descending on Ronnay de Maurel's princely heritage, whilst in the heart of its owner there raged a tempest of sorrow and of longing which nothing on earth could ever still.

But he walked silently by her side, and though she was aching to get home as quickly as may be, she went along slowly, because she could hear him dragging his wounded leg more painfully than he had been wont to do.

It was a matter of two or three minutes only ere the postern gate, with its tiny light above, was in sight. Each side of it a man was standing at attention.

"Good-bye, dear cousin," she said, speaking as lightly as her aching heart would allow, "and thank you. I shall, indeed, feel quite safe under the protection of those stalwarts."

She paused, and for a moment it seemed as if she would hold her hand out to him. They were some twenty paces still from the gate— alone and with the darkness hiding them from every view.

"Fernande!" he called, in a voice which held a world of misery, of regret and of passion in its breaking tone.

"I must not tarry," she rejoined. "Laurent ... your brother ... will be anxious about me."

And with that she turned and ran quickly to the gate. The two men fell in behind her. Just for one brief second the tiny light from above glinted upon an aureole of gold. The hood had slipped down from her head, and she raised and slightly turned her face for one instant, just as she went through the gate.

And thus he saw her fair profile outlined by the flickering light, the line of nose and lips and the exquisite curve of her throat. A few drops of moisture clung to the loose tendrils of her hair and glistened like tiny diamonds in a setting of living gold.

Then she passed out of his sight into the darkness beyond.

CHAPTER XXIII

AN HOUR'S FOLLY

I

Madame la Marquise de Mortain had spent the evening shut up in her own room. At seven o'clock, and then again at nine, Annette had brought her some food on a tray. She ate it mechanically, feeling neither hunger nor fatigue. She did not know that Fernande had gone out, nor did she inquire after her. Of a truth, all thought of the young girl, of her own household, of everything, in fact, save the momentous events which were to occur this night had faded from her mind. After the solemn warning which she had given Fernande she felt no anxiety as to what the latter might do. The girl was undoubtedly under the spell of an unexplainable infatuation; but Madame la Marquise, self-absorbed and as callous of anyone else's feelings as she was of her own, put it all down to childish exaltation and somewhat unhealthy romanticism; marriage with Laurent would, she was sure, soon effect a cure. In the meanwhile Fernande would certainly do nothing to jeopardize de Puisaye's plan of campaign, now that Madame had put it so clearly before her, that M. de Courson's own life would be seriously imperilled if Ronnay de Maurel got wind of what was in the air.

Thus did Madame la Marquise dismiss from her mind all thoughts of her niece.

But she strove in vain to do likewise with those of her son. His face haunted her during those hours of lonely vigil in the privacy of her own room, while she waited for the first breath of news which would come wafted on the wings of the storm from the foundries to the Château of La Frontenay. She had steeled her heart against Ronnay— her eldest born—the son of the man whom she had hated beyond every

214

other human creature on this earth. She had hated Ronnay during all the years that he was kept away from her; she had hated him when first she saw him again—a stranger to herself and to her kindred, an enemy to her caste. And when something indefinable in his character compelled her admiration and respect, she shut her ears to the call of Nature, to the insistent call of child to mother—that sweet, imperative call, which was all the more potent in this case as it had remained unspoken.

Entirely against her will, she could not help but see herself—her own character—reflected in Ronnay far more truly than in Laurent; she saw in him her own unbendable will, her energy, her impatience of restraint: and, above all, she saw in him that same worship of a political ideal—even though the ideal differed from her own—and the same readiness to sacrifice everything at its shrine.

And because there was so much in him that was akin to her own temperament, she continued to hate Ronnay de Maurel even though she no longer could despise him. To-night she was able to envisage coldly the possibility of his falling a victim to political schemes in which she had a hand. There was no compunction in her heart, no pity. In Ronnay she saw only the enemy of her cause, the traitor to his King. She felt like the incorruptible justiciary of old, who condemned his own son to the gallows when that son had offended against the laws of God; and if at times in the silence and loneliness which encompassed her while she watched and prayed, a feeling of softness or a pang of remorse knocked at the portals of her heart, she dismissed them resolutely, and soon both softness and remorse were consumed in the fire of her indomitable enthusiasm and energy.

And the hours went by leaden-footed. Madame, in her mind, was able to trace every movement of the Royalist army on its march from Mortain to Tinchebrai, to Domfront, to Sourdeval, to La Frontenay; she reckoned the hours and counted the minutes, ere she could assume with any certainty that Laurent had reached Domfront, M. de Courson, Mortain, and that de Puisaye had arrived at the factories. By that time Leroux would have reckoned with de Maurel, if, indeed, the latter had put his threat into execution and attempted to interfere in the defence of his own property, at the very hour when the blow for the seizure of the factories would have to be struck. By midnight de Puisaye's men should be at La Frontenay and in undisputed possession of all the armament works; an hour later two contingents of them would be on their way to Domfront and back to Mortain, to relieve Laurent and M. de Courson and help them to complete the capture of the garrisons there.

After ten o'clock the lonely watcher began to strain every nerve in a wild endeavour to catch the first sound of distant firing, or see the first lurid glow that would illumine the sky. The storm then was at its height and vivid flashes of lightning, accompanied by terrific crashes of thunder, lit up for a second at intervals the park of La Frontenay and the heights far away in the distance, with the dusty main road winding its way like a pale-coloured riband through the woods and the villages scattered on the plain.

Madame stood by the open window in her boudoir, and to her overwrought fancy it seemed that the whole landscape was peopled with the armies of the King; that from Domfront and Mortain, from the valleys and the hills, there poured down toward the factories a victorious horde of Royalists who already held half the country-side in their power. Her heart was filled with a great joy—she felt like intoning a triumphant hymn of praise.

She could no longer stand still, but started pacing up and down the room like a caged panther. She had twisted her handkerchief into a tight, damp ball, and now and again she put it to her lips, else she would have screamed aloud in the agony of her suspense.

She carried the lamp into her bedroom, which opened out of the boudoir, leaving the latter in complete darkness, so that she might see more clearly out of the window.

"De Puisaye should be nearing the factories by now," she thought, "and Laurent should be well on his way to Domfront at this hour. Oh, God!" she added, in a fever of passionate excitement, "for one brief moment of second sight!"

II

Just then there came a knock at her bedroom door.

Madame thought it might be Fernande, or else Annette bringing her more food which she did not want, and impatiently she called: "Come in!"

The door was thrown open; she could see it from where she stood, and she turned, thinking that it must be Annette. The next moment she gave a cry:

"Laurent!"

She ran into the next room, her heart and mind suddenly assailed with a horrible foreboding. Laurent was standing on the threshold, pale, haggard, trembling visibly. His clothes were soiled, his boots muddy, his eyes looked dazed and feverish.

"Laurent, in the name of God, what has happened?" queried Denise de Mortain as calmly as she could, after she had dragged Laurent into the room and closed the door behind him.

He staggered to a chair and threw himself into it, in an obvious state of physical exhaustion.

"Where is Fernande?" were the first words which came to his lips.

"Fernande?" queried Madame with a frown. "I don't know. In her room, I think. But never mind about Fernande now. Tell me, in God's name, why you are here?"

"Fernande is not in her room," he retorted savagely, and, wearied though he so obviously was, he jumped up from his chair and stood facing his mother with hands clenched, eyes glowing and cheeks aflame. "Where is she?"

"I don't know," replied Madame as firmly and unconcernedly as she could. "She may be as impatient as I am and, unable to sit still, she may be wandering about somewhere in the house or round the gardens. I don't know, I tell you," she added fiercely. "Laurent, I insist upon knowing what your presence here means at this hour, when I thought you on the way to Domfront."

She tried to force him to look her squarely in the eyes. There was something so awful, so paralysing in the terror which was invading her whole being, that she dared not yet face the thoughts which at sight of Laurent had rushed wildly through her brain. She wanted to force an explanation from him, for she felt now that anything he said must be simpler, more intelligible than the horrible surmises which froze the very blood in her veins. But Laurent would not meet her searching gaze. Instead of this, he threw himself back into the chair, and, burying his head in his hands, he burst into a passionate flood of weeping.

He was weak, exhausted, footsore, his nerves were obviously strained to breaking point. Denise de Mortain's cold heart melted at the sight of his grief, but she made no movement to soothe him. The puzzled frown settled more deeply between her brows, and after a while, when Laurent's paroxysm had somewhat subsided, and he leaned his head in utter dejection and weariness against the back of the chair, she tapped her foot impatiently against the ground.

"Laurent," she said more quietly after a while, "you must tell me what all this means. You must try and collect yourself as quickly as you can and try to explain to me why you are here—and in this state—wildly calling for Fernande, when I, your mother, thought you at Domfront engaged in the execution of your duty."

"A man's first duty, Mother," he retorted fiercely, "is to watch over the treasure which God has placed in his hands. Something told me that a wolf was prowling round my fold, and I came to guard what was mine and to shoot the wolf ... if I could."

He spoke more coherently now. The violent paroxysm of weeping had eased the tension on his nerves. The look in his eyes was more full of anger, but less wild, and though heavy sobs still shook his frame from time to time, and a hot, feverish flush glowed on his cheeks and on his forehead, he was, on the whole, more master of himself.

"Will you explain more clearly what you mean?" queried Madame la Marquise coldly.

"I mean," he replied, "that ever since I parted from Fernande two days ago, torturing doubts have racked me till I thought my brain would burst. I have been on the threshold of frenzy, enduring torments of hell, the while de Puisaye and M. de Courson and all the others talked and manœuvred, and drilled and discussed plans, for the thousand thousandth time. Oh!" he continued vehemently, "I fought against my own thoughts, against my fears, against that lashing, flaying, maddening doubt. I fought against it till my head was in a whirl, and I began to marvel if, indeed, I was not insane."

"But why?" exclaimed Madame, in deeper perplexity than before. "In Heaven's name, why?"

"Will you deny, Mother," he riposted hotly, "that you, too, have felt doubts about Fernande?—that you, too, have watched the play of emotion on her face, the quiver of her mouth, the soft look in her eyes, the moment my brother Ronnay's name is mentioned?"

"Laurent!"

"Can you deny it?" he insisted.

Then, as she remained silent and merely shrugged her shoulders with well-affected indifference, he continued with the same vehemence: "Ah, you see, you cannot deny it! You cannot! You know that my doubts and fears are not the outcome of feverish hallucinations! Oh, my God!" he exclaimed, and put his hand up to his throat as if he were choking, "if only I could kill him with mine own hands...."

"I'll deny nothing, Laurent," interposed Madame calmly, and her harsh, stern voice acted like an icy douche on the young man's fierce passion. "I think that Fernande is foolish, childishly romantic. Something about de Maurel's personality has stirred her imagination. But there's nothing more in it than that, and...."

"Then why is she not here to-night?" he broke in savagely.

"You say that she is not here. But how do you know?"

"Because," he began, speaking slowly and measuredly, and Denise de Mortain had no cause to complain now that her son did not look her squarely in the face—"because two hours ago I saw Fernande stealing out of the château, wrapped in a dark cloak and alone, and making her way across the park. I did not want her to see me, so I stole to the gates and there watched for her coming. I wished to know whither she was going and I was determined to follow her. I watched and I waited, marvelling why she tarried. She did not come, and then I realized what a fool I had been. Whilst I had been standing on guard outside the great gates, she had slipped out by the side door in the wall, and I did not know whither she had gone. I was ready to dash my head against the iron gates; and there I stood, stupid, semi-imbecile, marvelling what I should do. Suddenly a passer-by came along and I hailed him. I asked him if he had seen a lady on the high road walking unattended and closely wrapped in a dark cloak. He answered me yes, and pointed the way she went. I thanked him, and as soon as his back was turned I started to run in the wake, as I thought, of Fernande. Then I came to a cross-road, where there was a sign-post, one arm of which bore the legend: 'La Frontenay,' and the other, 'La Vieuville.' La Vieuville, where my brother dwells! I spelt out every letter. I saw that it was distant five kilomètres. La Vieuville! Fernande had gone to La Vieuville to betray us all to Ronnay de Maurel!"

"That is false, I'll swear," exclaimed Madame, "and you, Laurent, are mad to imagine anything so monstrous against the girl whom you profess to love."

"Mad!" he riposted. "Of course I am mad! Did I not tell you that I had become mad?"

"What were you doing outside the gates of this château at nine o'clock to-night when...."

"When I should have been at Mortain," he broke in with a strident laugh, which seemed to go right through his mother's heart like a knife. "At Mortain, drilling a few oafs in the use of muskets which they haven't got. What was I doing here? Did I not say that I was watching over my property? I could not stay away, Mother," he cried wildly. "I could not! I suffered too much. I was going mad."

"So you—my son—Laurent Marquis de Mortain, preferred to turn deserter?" she asked coldly.

"Mother!"

"I have yet to learn how it comes that when my son is under orders from his chiefs, at the hour when the destinies of his King and his country are at stake, how it comes that he has deserted his post."

"I left my men in charge of young de Fleurot, my most able lieutenant. I only wanted to speak with Fernande—only to see her for five minutes. I was here—outside the gates at nine o'clock—I could have seen her and spoken with her and be back at my post long before now. Even so, there is no harm done. Our contingent was not due to start until midnight. I have arranged with de Fleurot—in case I was detained—that he shall start at the appointed hour, and I would pick up the company at the cross-roads less than a kilomètre from here and not more than three from Domfront. But I should have been back at Mortain long before now," he reiterated testily, "only when I saw Fernande stealing out of the park like a pert wench going to meet her gallant, I lost my head and I followed her."

"All the way to La Vieuville?"

"All the way."

"And you saw her?"

"No."

"Had she been to the château?"

"No one could tell me. The château was shut up and dark. I

219

hammered on the door. No one replied. I would have broken in the door, but it resisted my every onslaught."

"Then what did you do?"

"I lay in wait for some time—my pistol in my hand. If I had seen him, I would have shot him ... him and Fernande too."

"How long did you wait?"

"I don't know ... half an hour perhaps—perhaps more. No one came. The château was deserted. Somewhere in it, no doubt, Gaston de Maurel, that old reprobate, lay dying. But I realized that Fernande was not there, so I came away."

"Well? And then?"

"I came back here," he replied savagely. "I am here now to ask you where is Fernande?"

"Yes, you are here, my son," rejoined Denise de Mortain harshly, "at the post of dishonour, while your father and kindred are fighting for France."

"Mother!"

But now at last she turned on him with all the fury of a tigress roused to wrath. She had interrogated him coolly, firmly, smothering the horror and the indignation which she felt. But the floodgates of her emotion would no longer be kept back; they broke into a torrent of unbridled vituperation.

"Traitor! deserter!" she cried. "How dare you remain here another minute? How dare you whine and fret before me, while every moment of the night is fraught with danger for your King and his cause? How dare you run on the high roads after a wench, like a jealous, love-sick swain, while your King hath need of every ounce of energy, of courage which you possess. Out of my sight, craven deserter! and pray to God that He may grant you grace to atone for your treachery with your blood!"

"Mother ..." he protested firmly, as, stung by her words as with a lash, he had jumped to his feet and made a desperate effort to pull himself together.

"Not another word," she commanded. "When you have redeemed your cowardice by prodigies of valour, when you have held Domfront for your King in the face of overwhelming odds, you may come to me again ... but not before."

She turned her back on him without another look and swept out of the room, leaving him standing there miserable, dejected, a hot flush of shame on each cheek as if she had struck him there. Once in the darkened boudoir, she tottered as far as the open window. Her knees were giving way under her. She leaned against the window-frame and with her hand clung desperately to the heavy curtain. Not a breath of air came from outside; the storm was at its height—vivid flashes of lightning tore the heavens asunder and the thunder crashed continuously overhead. A great sob broke from Denise de Mortain's throat. She had suffered this night the keenest torture, the deadliest ignominy, which heart of woman can endure; she had seen her beloved son—the one cherished idol of her loveless heart—sunk to a level of degradation from which nothing could ever raise him again.

She had seen him the prey of a base and futile passion, tortured by insensate jealousy which caused him to forget the most elementary dictates of honour. Desertion at the hour preceding the battle was infamy so heinous, that in her heart Denise de Mortain would have been vastly happier if they had brought Laurent to her on a stretcher—dead.

III

She stared out into the night, and suddenly she perceived a sound which came to her straining ears above the roll of thunder, from the direction of La Frontenay—a sound which at first brought a frown of deep puzzlement to her brow and then an icy feeling like the grip of death to her heart.

At the same time a slight noise behind her caused her to turn sharply round, and she saw Laurent standing under the lintel of the communicating door. He stood with his back to the light, so she could not see his face, but only the silhouette of him, the graceful, well-proportioned figure, the straight and slender limbs.

"I am going now at once, Mother," he said coldly, though his voice sounded hoarse and choked, and as he spoke he passed his hand once or twice across his brow. "You are quite right, I deserve all you say. But my reason had fled from me—I was not fully conscious of mine actions. Thank God that it is not too late to redeem my folly. In any event, I can meet de Fleurot at the cross-roads, and we'll be at Domfront soon after midnight...."

"It is too late, my son," she broke in calmly—"too late for a de Mortain to do aught but die like a hero, even if he have lived his last hours like a coward."

"What do you mean, Mother?" he queried with a frown, for, indeed, for the moment he thought that it was his mother's turn to feel her brain unhinged. She had remained standing by the window, and now a flash of lightning showed her to him for one brief instant, a rigid, menacing figure, like that of a Sybil presiding over his destiny, her head thrown back, her hand grasping the curtain; her face was the colour of ashes, and her eyes, large and glowing, were fixed denouncingly upon him.

"'Tis futile to take on such tragic airs," he added irritably, "just because I chose to spend my time on the high roads rather than cool

221

my heels in the ditches of Mortain. I have told you that there's no harm done—that de Fleurot is in charge—that I shall pick him up on the way to Domfront—that I shall still lead our contingent just as it was arranged. I tell you that there's nothing lost...."

"Everything is lost, my son," she replied coldly; "even your honour."

Then as he made no reply, but with a shrug of the shoulders quietly turned to go, she called out peremptorily:

"Hark!"

Instinctively he paused on the threshold. From far away, in the direction where lay the factories of La Frontenay, there came through the intermittent hush of the storm the loud clang of a bell, followed immediately by the shrill hooting of a siren.

"The alarm bell and the sirens at the factories," said Denise de Mortain slowly.

"Good God!" exclaimed Laurent, as, rooted to the spot, he remained standing for one short second, straining his ears to listen. "What can it mean?"

"That the unforeseen has occurred," she rejoined harshly, "and that there are two traitors in our family, my son—you and Fernande."

"No! no!" he cried, horrified to hear his mother put into words that which he himself had dared to think.

"Fernande de Courson has betrayed her King in order to save her lover," continued the Marquise, as she pointed an accusing finger in the direction whence the hooting of sirens and the continuous clang of alarm bells rose above the confused sounds of the storm. "And whilst friends and kindred prepare to conquer or to die for their faith, Laurent de Mortain goes philandering after a petticoat!"

But the sting of her last words had not the time to reach him. Already he had run to the door, tearing it open as he ran; the next moment his scurrying footsteps were heard echoing all through the silent château—along the vast corridors, down the monumental staircase and across the marble hall, until the clang of the great glazed doors proclaimed that he was out of the house.

Then Madame leaned out of the window as far as she could. She could still hear Laurent running down the perron steps and at full speed along the gravelled drive. Once the lightning lit up the whole extent of the park, the trees, the paths, the flower-beds, and the tall iron gates in the distance; but she could not see Laurent. He was already far away.

The sound of sirens and alarms had not ceased. Over there around Mortain men were making ready to fight or die for their King. One of the last efforts for restoring an effete Bourbon to his throne was about to be drowned in a sea of bloodshed. The unforeseen had happened—what it was the lonely watcher could not conjecture, but she fell on her knees beside the open window, and, burying her head in her hands, she moaned and prayed: "God, my God! grant that he may die fighting; do not punish one moment's folly by a lifelong disgrace."

CHAPTER XXIV

AFTER THE STORM

I

It was close upon midnight when Fernande made her way to Madame la Marquise's boudoir. She found her there, on her knees still, her hands folded and stretched out over the window-sill, her head buried in her arms.

The rain was coming down in torrents. Fernande herself, on her way home, had been drenched to the skin. But this was not the time to think of wet and cold, of health or of prudence. She had thrown down her cloak in the hall and at once went up to her aunt's room.

The boudoir was dark, only from the next room there came the feeble rays of reflected light from the lamp. With a cry of burning anxiety Fernande ran to Madame. Denise de Mortain had knelt before the open window ever since her son's flying footsteps had ceased to resound through the château; she had knelt here absolutely prostrate with grief, her heart tortured with the desire to see her beloved son killed rather than openly disgraced. Fernande, as she bent over her, could feel that her arms and shoulders, her hands and her hair were soaked through. With gentle words and persuasive strength she tried to drag her away from the window.

"Ma tante," she said appealingly, "it is I—Fernande. Won't you speak to me?"

She felt a shiver going right through Denise's kneeling form; she racked her brain in wonderment as to what had caused this utter moral collapse in a woman who was always so full of indomitable energy.

"Ma tante!" she reiterated more firmly, "I pray you listen to me. There is something which I must tell you now—at once."

She managed gradually to raise Madame up in her own strong young arms, and to lead her to a chair close by. Denise was only half conscious. She sat in the chair, with her head rolling from left to right against its back, her eyes closed, her hands inert. Fernande ran into the bedroom. She brought in the lamp and a towel, and she dried

223

Madame's face and hands and wiped the moisture from her dress and hair. Then she took the cold, numb hands in hers and began chafing them, rubbing the fingers, trying to infuse life into them with her warm breath.

After a while consciousness began to return. The head ceased its weird rolling, and lay quite still against the back of the chair. A certain degree of warmth communicated itself to the fingers and an occasional tremor shook the pain-wearied frame.

Then Madame la Marquise opened her eyes. For a moment or two she looked round her dazed, and still held in the arms of semi-consciousness. She looked straight into the lamp, and the pupils of her eyes slowly contracted until they appeared like small pin-points, with the iris round them steely and pale.

Then her gaze fastened itself on Fernande—first on the hem of her gown, wet and muddy after the long tramp through the rain; then it wandered up by degrees to the girl's slender, white hands, with the delicate fingers interlaced and the diamond ring—Laurent's gift—gleaming in the lamplight.

Then she met the girl's blue eyes fixed compassionately, tenderly upon her. In a moment full consciousness returned to her. She drew herself up, and, leaning her hands against the arms of the chair, she was able to struggle to her feet.

"Ma tante ..." began Fernande gently.

"Who are you?" queried Madame la Marquise coldly, "and what do you want?"

Instinctively Fernande put out her arms: the strange query, the raucous timbre of the voice, struck with unexplainable terror into her heart—something, she thought, had happened during her absence—something awesome and terrific, which had unhinged this woman's cool and powerful brain.

"Who are you?" reiterated Denise de Mortain coldly.

"Why, ma tante," rejoined Fernande gently, "do you not know me? I am Fernande—I have just come home and found you here...."

"No, you are not Fernande," broke in Madame harshly—"not my niece, Fernande de Courson, the daughter of my dear, dear brother. You are a ghoul!" she cried excitedly, "a monster ... a hideous abortion ... a de Courson turned traitor.... I do not know you!"

Still Fernande did not realize the truth. She was convinced now that the excitement of the day and the weary watching throughout the evening had acted banefully on Denise de Mortain's brain. That she was unnerved there could be no doubt; there was an unnatural glow in her eyes, and the pallor of her cheeks was almost ghost-like. The young girl, genuinely alarmed, made a movement in the direction of the bell-pull. She and Annette could, at any rate, put Madame to bed ere a high fever brought on any further complications. But before she could reach the bell Madame had interposed calmly:

"I am neither ill nor insane," she said. "But this is my room, and I order you out of it. Go! Out of my sight—now—at once—do you hear?"

"Ma tante," protested Fernande, who, of a truth, felt so bewildered that she did not know what to think, what to say, what to make of this extraordinary, this appalling situation. "Something has unnerved you," she continued with calm dignity. "An you will not allow me to attend to you or to ring for Annette, I had best retire until you are in a fit condition to listen to what I have to say. But I warn you that it is urgent. Every second wasted in this unexplainable misunderstanding may mean danger ... if not worse ... to my father and to our friends."

"Your treachery," retorted Madame quietly, "has already wrought all the evil and brought untold danger to all our friends and death to a great many—to your father, perhaps, to Laurent, certainly. There is nothing that you can say to me now which can avert the awful catastrophe for which you and you alone are responsible."

"Treachery!" exclaimed Fernande. "I?"

"Yes, you! The surprise coup planned by de Puisaye has failed. The alarm was given at the armament works an hour and a half ago; since then there has been continuous firing in the direction of Mortain. The garrison there has been aroused, that of Domfront, too, no doubt. Some of our contingents have been surprised. They are selling their lives dearly at this hour. Your father is probably fighting over there. Who is it, then, who has betrayed us to Ronnay de Maurel and delivered our brave little army into the hands of our enemies?"

"Not I!" protested Fernande loudly.

Light had suddenly broken on the hideous mystery which had confronted her when she first entered this room. She understood everything now—her aunt's prostration, her despair, the semi-insanity which was overclouding her brain, making her see lurid phantoms of treachery. She—Fernande—was suspected of having betrayed her father, her lover, her friends; and Madame la Marquise, clinging to that abominable thought, was rapidly losing all sense of justice, of reasoning and of right. The girl's very soul was outraged at the monstrous accusation.

"How dared you harbour such abominable thoughts of me?" she cried indignantly.

A strident laugh broke from Denise de Mortain's throat.

"Would you prefer it if I thought that you had stolen out of the château to-night—and alone—in order to meet a swain behind the nearest hedge?"

"Oh!"

"That was Laurent's estimate of you; and I—like a fool—thought he must be mad."

"Laurent?"

"Laurent was here—to-night," continued Madame, as she came a step or two nearer to Fernande, and the words—hot, passionate, fierce—came tumbling through her lips. "For two days he was tortured with thoughts of your treachery. I tell you he seemed nearly mad. To-night he could hold out no longer. He deserted his post—he, who is the soul of honour! He came here, just in time to see you steal out of the château like a flirty wench. An hour and a half ago the alarm bell from the factories clanged through the night. Laurent was here then, pouring out his heart in bitterness and in misery. But the sound recalled him to his duty, which he had forgotten while thinking of you. He went back in order to redeem the hour of folly which led him to desert his post. He went back in order to die fighting beside my brother and his friends."

"Oh, my God!" moaned Fernande, as she covered her face with her hands.

Even while she allowed the torrent of Madame's unjust reproaches to break over her innocent head, she had already realized the hopelessness of her own situation, the hopelessness of it all. Guiltless as she knew herself to be, she almost understood, and was nigh to forgiving Madame's horrible suspicions of her. The awful seed of the dastardly murder projected against a defenceless man had, indeed, borne bitter fruits of disaster and of shame; and she, who had tried to avert one awful catastrophe, had unknowingly precipitated another. By her absence from home to-night she had left Laurent at the mercy of his mother; and he, with the guilt of desertion upon his conscience, was left to face her until, driven to desperation by the harshness and the cruelty which still glittered in Denise de Mortain's eyes, he had rushed off, blindly perhaps, to his death.

An overwhelming pity for this hard, callous woman suddenly filled Fernande's sensitive heart. All that she herself had suffered, all that she was yet destined to suffer, was as nothing compared to the bitterness of self-reproach which anon must assail the mother of Laurent—the mother of Ronnay de Maurel: and when, exhausted by the vehemence of her own eloquence, Madame la Marquise fell back into her chair, panting and overwrought, Fernande drew near to her, despite her vigorous protest, and knelt affectionately by her side.

"Ma tante," she said gently, while tears of sweet compassion gathered in her eyes, "you have been passing cruel and unjust to me, and just for a moment I felt nothing but anger against you. But since you have told me about Laurent, I feel that I can understand. Before the God who made me, I swear to you that I had no hand in warning our enemies of what was intended. How could I have, seeing that my own dear father's life was involved in the affair? I went to the factory to-night with the sole intention of staying Leroux' hand from committing a dastardly murder—a murder, ma tante," she continued with firm energy, "that despite victory, despite the utmost triumphs, would for ever have sullied our cause and weighed us all down with bitter self-reproach. Had Leroux listened to me, I still believe that M. de Maurel would never have suspected what was in the air; it was

Leroux' threats, Leroux' attitude, which put him on the scent. I was there; I saw it all. When Leroux, with his wild and menacing talk, had given away the best part of M. de Puisaye's plan, Ronnay de Maurel—your son, ma tante—stood with a naked light in his hand ready to blow up the entire factory rather than let it fall into our hands. Leroux and his mates were cowed; they were poltroons as well as fools, and M. de Maurel forced one of the men to ring the alarm bell. That is what happened at the La Frontenay works, ma tante. The hooting of the sirens roused the neighbouring villages and the garrison of Domfront. I escaped out of the factory as soon as I was able; since then I have been on the high road, tortured with fears as to what has happened to my father and what to Laurent. But by all that I hold most dear, ma tante, what I have told you is the truth."

Madame had listened in silence, at first with averted head and with a look of sullen obstinacy on her face. She would have given much to remain unconvinced. The burning indignation which she had felt at Laurent's conduct had to vent itself on the innocent cause of it. After a while she looked into Fernande's face with a piercing, searching gaze. She would have liked to hold the girl's soul naked before her eyes, and to search within its innermost recesses for a sign of guilt or even of weakness. But it was impossible to look for long into the sweet, earnest face and the limpid blue eyes which were the true mirrors of candour and of purity, and to affect doubt which no longer could exist. In her heart Madame knew that Fernande spoke the truth. Everything that she said bore the impress of actual facts witnessed and faithfully recorded. Madame was bound to admit it, but she was far too self-willed and obstinate to do so generously—and, above all, she knew that never as long as she lived would she forgive Fernande de Courson for having been the cause—however innocent—of Laurent's unpardonable conduct.

"It may be the truth," she said grudgingly—"it is the truth, no doubt, since you are prepared to swear it."

"Do you still doubt me, ma tante?"

"No. But one thing, my girl, is certain—and that is if Laurent had not seen you stealing out of the château—if he had spoken for five minutes with you—he would have gone straight back to his post, and would not now be under the suspicion of having deserted his men in the hour of danger."

To this senseless accusation Fernande made no reply. What would have been the use? She could not have convinced Madame that it was Laurent's insensate jealousy which had been the primary cause of his undoing. Except for those few brief seconds, when she boldly faced a horrible death beside the man whom she loved, she had not harboured one disloyal thought of Laurent, or spoken one disloyal word. Her love for Ronnay de Maurel she could not destroy; it had its roots in the innermost fibres of her heart. She was no more responsible

227

for that feeling than was Denise de Mortain for her callousness or Laurent for his vehement temper. All that she could do to wrench herself away from its influence she had done; and in the process she had plucked out her heart-strings and martyrized her very soul. In the lonely walk from the factories to the château she had fought against the veriest thought of rebellion; she had sacrificed her whole life, her every hope of happiness on the altar of unimpassioned loyalty. Whenever she met Laurent again she could look him fearlessly in the eyes, she could grasp his hand in all honour and friendship. The image of Ronnay de Maurel lay buried deep down in her heart, and to the memory of that one mad and rapturous moment she had bidden an eternal farewell.

Now when she felt Madame's cold enmity enveloping her as with an icy mantle, she felt how desperately far from her would happiness lie in the future. On the merest threshold of her life she saw the endless years that were in store for her, between a man who would for ever torture her with his turbulent passion and a woman who would paralyse her with relentless animosity. The catastrophe of this night—and God alone knew yet its full extent—would always be laid at her door. She saw this in Denise de Mortain's every look, in the scornful stiffening of her whole attitude, as she drew herself away from the slightest contact with her niece; and after a moment or two of silence, the involuntary appeal broke from the poor girl's lips: "Will you always hate me like this, ma tante?"

Madame la Marquise looked at her coldly.

"I do not know," she replied. "Always is a long time, and it is impossible for any human mind to know if it will ever forget. But this I do know, that never with my consent will you become my daughter. If Laurent is spared this night, I shall devote every hour, every moment of my life, to parting him from you."

"You will remain unjust to the last?"

"Unjust?"—and Denise de Mortain shrugged her shoulders calmly. "Love and hate are never just, and I could never dissociate you from the memories of this night."

She rose from her chair, her whole attitude now one of cool indifference. Ever since she had accepted Fernande's explanation she had made desperate efforts to regain the mastery over her nerves and to conceal every outward manifestation of the burning anxiety which she felt. At last she had succeeded, but the struggle had left her weary and wellnigh spent. Her face was pale, her eyes circled with purple, and there was a feeble quiver round her bloodless lips.

"It may be hours," she said coldly, "and it may be days, ere we get authentic news. What do you propose to do?"

"To start for Courson at daybreak," replied Fernande with equal calm. "I must be on the spot in case my father is able to return there."

"And I will remain here until I know that both he and Laurent are safe. But remember," she added, and something of the old

228

domineering, managing tone crept back into her voice, "that the peace and quietude of the past year are at an end; that once more we are on the branch, once more we stand with one foot on the way to exile. For the next few days there will be perquisitions, molestations, arrests. The infamous police of Bonaparte will not be slow to avenge the scare it has received this night."

"I shall be ready to follow my father whenever or wherever he may want me," rejoined Fernande coldly.

For a moment it was on the tip of her tongue to tell Madame that Ronnay de Maurel would look after the safety of her father and of Laurent. She had his promise, and he was not a man to leave a stone unturned ere he fulfilled that promise. Though her heart was aching with anxiety, she felt comforted in the thought that the one man who could help those she cared for, by standing by them at this hour, would do it whole-heartedly, and would throw into the scales of any pending reprisals the whole weight of his influence and of his wealth.

But it would have been worse than futile to mention de Maurel's name again now. Madame, in any case, would refuse to be comforted, and the floodgates of her resentment would certainly break out afresh. She—Fernande—was sorely in need of quietude; she felt that she could not endure another scene. She was desperately sorry for her aunt; Madame's anxiety for Laurent must be positively heartrending, but nothing could be gained by further recriminations, further reproaches, which only helped to embitter these hours of suspense and of dread.

Fernande felt confident that de Maurel would send her news as soon as he knew anything definite; until then many weary hours would go by, she knew, but at least let them go by in peace. Her hope rested in God and, next to Him, in the loyalty and the power of the man who loved her so selflessly.

So she bade her aunt a formal good night, and with a great sense of relief she went quickly to her room.

II

Denise de Mortain, too, was glad to find herself alone once more. She drew the chair to the open window and sat down, prepared to wait. Though she was so tired that she could hardly move, she felt that she could not rest. The house was very still now; all the servants had long since gone to bed. They were a set of faithful but utterly stupid peasants from the village, and had no notion of what went on outside the park gates. Matthieu Renard and Annette knew, and they remained on the watch. Old Matthieu would not go to bed until he could bring Madame la Marquise some news which would comfort her, and Annette waited where she could hear the bell, in case Madame wanted anything.

Madame, sitting by the open window, peered out into the night. The firing sounded more distant now and more intermittent; the rain had ceased and the darkness was less intense. Overhead large patches of star-studded indigo appeared between the fissures in the clouds. The weary watcher, gazing out into nothingness, her eyes aching with sleeplessness and many unshed tears, fell anon into a semi-wakeful languor, while the early hours of the morning sped leaden-footed by.

Suddenly something woke her to full consciousness. She sat up, shivering a little; the morning air struck fresh and cool against her face. Through her torpor-like sleep she had been conscious of the swift gallop of a horse on the hard road drawing rapidly nearer. Now she was fully awake, she could hear the clatter of the hoofs—someone was coming along at break-neck speed—bringing news probably. She jumped to her feet; the horse had been brought to a halt outside the gates; the next moment she heard a murmur of voices and then the sound of footsteps coming up the drive.

Madame, leaning out of the window, called out peremptorily: "Who goes there?"

But she received no reply. Whoever had arrived at this early hour had gone into the house. Through the dream-like recollections of what she had heard, it seemed to Denise that the voice of Fernande had mingled with that of two men, one of whom might have been old Matthieu.

She rang the bell violently. Then she looked at the clock. It was close on five.

After a few minutes there was a knock at the door, and in response to an impatient "Come in!" it was opened, and Fernande, pale, obviously tired to death, and with dark circles under her eyes, came into the room.

"What is it?" queried Madame, in a voice broken by fatigue and nerve-strain.

"One of the overseers from the armament works, ma tante," replied Fernande, "with a message from M. de Maurel."

"I desire no message from M. de Maurel," said Madame curtly; "let him tell you what he wants and go back the way he came."

"There is another man with him, ma tante," hazarded Fernande, after some hesitation—"one of our people—a prisoner with news of M. de Puisaye."

Madame waited a moment or two, frowning, debating between her pride which prompted her to refuse to see an emissary of de Maurel, and the agony of suspense which was near to killing her. Anxiety gained the victory.

"Very well," she said. "Let the men come up."

Fernande went, and a minute or two later she returned followed

230

by two men, one of whom was Mathurin, chief overseer of the de Maurel smelting works. Both men looked as if they had ridden hard. Mathurin's coat and hat were covered with dust; the other—a true type of the Chouans, of those who had fought under de Frotté and Cadoudal—was dressed in a tattered blouse and ragged linen breeches; the soles of his boots had parted from their uppers; he was unkempt and unwashed. Fernande closed the door behind them, then she slipped round behind Madame to the corner by the open window, where she could feel the fresh morning air and rest her aching head against the heavy curtain. Mathurin had already told her briefly what he had been sent to say: his orders were to see Mademoiselle de Courson first, and then Madame la Marquise if she asked for him. Fernande, ensconced beside the window, unseen by her aunt, could safely indulge in the luxury of tears and of silence.

When the men entered, Madame la Marquise had looked for a moment keenly and searchingly at the old Chouan. She was ready and eager to catch the slightest movement or flitting glance which might have been meant for a signal. She felt anxious and puzzled, marvelling why de Maurel had sent a messenger to her—at this hour—and what was the meaning of this prisoner brought hither to speak with her. Then she turned haughtily to Mathurin.

"Who has sent you?" she queried peremptorily.

"M. le Maréchal Comte de Maurel," replied Mathurin, after he had touched his forelock with every mark of respect.

"And who are you?" asked Madame again.

"Chief overseer at the smelting works."

"Why did M. de Maurel send you?"

"M. le Maréchal thought Madame la Marquise and Mademoiselle de Courson would be anxious to know what had happened last night."

"Well," she said coldly, "what did happen?"

"Our alarm bells and sirens went off at half-past ten, Madame la Marquise."

"I know that—I heard them."

"The mutineers, with Paul Leroux at their head, have been arrested by our watchmen. Leroux confessed that he had been bribed to murder M. le Maréchal, and to deliver the armament works into the hands of a band of Royalists under M. de Puisaye."

"Did M. de Maurel order you to say this?"

"He desired Madame la Marquise to know that Leroux was a coward as well as a traitor."

"Leroux' personality.... Who is Leroux, by the way?... does not interest me. Go on."

"Our sirens aroused the garrison of Domfront. The commandant sent over one of his officers with a small detachment of infantry to see what was amiss. He only thought of fire or of a mutiny among the convicts, and he was ready to send us help."

"Well? And then?"

"M. le Maréchal interrogated Leroux in the presence of the officer. Leroux made a clean breast of all he knew. M. de Maurel then sent his own couriers from the works to Domfront, to Tinchebrai, and to Mortain, warning the different commandants against possible attacks from roaming bands of Chouans. Within a couple of hours all the garrisons were afoot and in touch with one another."

"Then what happened?"

"This man here, Madame la Marquise," said Mathurin, indicating his companion, "will be able to tell you better than I can what happened in the ranks of the Chouans. He fell a prisoner in our hands early in the night. M. le Maréchal had ridden over to Mortain, and I was with him when this man was brought in a prisoner. M. le Maréchal questioned him, and then gave him over into my charge. 'Take the fellow over to La Frontenay, Mathurin,' he said to me. 'Madame la Marquise de Mortain and Mademoiselle de Courson will want to hear what he has to say.' So we both got to horse and rode hither as fast as we could."

"Very good," said Madame determinedly. "Leave the man here with me. I desire to speak with him alone."

Mathurin, at the peremptory command, appeared to hesitate. "Madame la Marquise ..." he stammered.

"Ah çà," she retorted haughtily, "has M. de Maurel sent you here perchance as my jailer?"

Mathurin, thus challenged, did not know what to say. Madame la Marquise had a way with her which imposed her will on every one around her. The worthy overseer was certainly not vested with powers to gainsay her wishes. He was a shrewd man, loyal to the depth of his simple heart and ready to be hacked to pieces for M. le Maréchal; he would have defied an army of haughty ladies if he thought any harm could come from a private interview with this ill-conditioned old rascal; but in this case prudence and conciliation was perhaps the wisest course. And somehow he felt that Mademoiselle de Courson's presence was, in any case, a safeguard against any further intrigues against his master. So after an imperceptible moment of hesitation he made a curt obeisance and backed out of the room, closing the door behind him.

Far be it from me to suggest that good old Mathurin listened at the keyhole, but I make bold to assert that very little of Madame la Marquise's private conversation with the old Chouan escaped him.

III

As soon as the door had closed on Mathurin, Denise de Mortain turned to the man and said, speaking curtly and rapidly:

"Your name is Jean Blanchet. I know you. Well, tell me quickly everything you know. When was the alarm given in your camp?"

"At about half-past eleven, Madame la Marquise," replied the man. "I and six of my mates were patrolling the approaches of the town, when we heard a rumour that the garrison inside the city was astir. News had arrived, so 'twas said, that bands of Chouans were preparing a surprise attack. M. de Puisaye had his headquarters in the Cerf-Volant woods south of the town; there was only just time to run and warn him of what was in the air."

"Well?"

"M. de Puisaye at once ordered the alarm to be sounded. Within ten minutes the whole camp was afoot and M. de Puisaye then commanded the retreat."

"What?" exclaimed Madame. "Without striking a blow?"

"What would have been the use?" retorted the man with a shrug of the shoulders. "We had next to no arms, and to make a stand would have meant fighting against at least two companies of infantry and a battery of artillery, which could easily have cut us to pieces even before reinforcements came from Tinchebrai and Domfront. There is a half-battery of artillery at both those places, and we knew by then that all the garrisons round were in touch with one another. To have made a stand," reiterated the man gruffly, "would have meant useless bloodshed. M. de Puisaye was alive to that. He chose the wiser course."

"Not the most heroic," murmured Madame, under her breath.

"He had a lot of undisciplined, ill-fed, ill-clothed men to look after. What could he do? Now if we could have equipped ourselves at the factories of La Frontenay ..." he added with a harsh laugh.

"I know, I know," said Madame impatiently. "And M. de Puisaye has retreated—whither?"

"I do not know. To Avranches, I should say. The way was open, and, in any case, his losses would be very slight."

"And...." A name was on Madame's lips; she checked herself. She did not dare to speak it—not before this man ... in case....

"And M. de Courson?" she asked.

"M. de Courson must be with M. de Puisaye, I think. I believe M. d'Aché is with him and M. Prigent."

Then at last anxiety could hold out no longer. Madame had made heroic efforts to appear calm, but now the hoarse query broke from her lips: "And M. le Marquis de Mortain?"

Was it her own fevered fancy? But it seemed to her as if the man hesitated for a second or two ere he replied; he twisted his cap between

233

his fingers, and a shock of unruly hair falling over his forehead hid the expression of his eyes.

"M. de Puisaye sent orders to M. de Mortain," he said at last, "to defend the rear in case the commandant of the garrison got wind of the retreat and sent a company in pursuit. But M. de Mortain was not at his post then. M. de Fleurot was in command."

Madame leaned her weight against the chair close by; she passed her tongue once or twice over her parched lips. The man was evidently determined not to meet her eye.

"What," she asked after a while, "was the firing which I heard in the direction of Mortain?"

"M. de Fleurot," replied Blanchet curtly, "fighting a rearguard action and covering the main retreat. I was in his company."

"And ... what was the result ... of the action, I mean?"

"I cannot say. I was taken prisoner quite early. I only heard rumours afterwards."

"What were they?"

"That our small contingent was entirely cut up ... there were some prisoners taken ... but it is generally believed that scarce a man escaped."

"And ... has anything been heard of M. de Puisaye?"

"No, Madame la Marquise, nothing."

"Or of M. de Courson, or any of the others?"

"No. But," added Blanchet significantly, as he nodded in the direction of the door, "I believe that Mathurin there knows something."

"You think ..." began Madame involuntarily. Then she paused; something in the man's look—furtive and compassionate—froze the words upon her lips.

"Can't you tell me?" she asked under her breath.

"I don't know for certain, Madame la Marquise," he replied.

IV

It meant another struggle against resentment and against pride. But, in any case, the present uncertainty was unendurable. Denise de Mortain felt that she would have gone on her knees to the devil himself if he brought her authentic news of Laurent. She went boldly to the door, and, opening it, she called:

"Mathurin! Are you there?"

"At your orders, Madame la Marquise," replied the man.

He came back into the room, reluctantly this time. He was a good fellow, with wife and children of his own. Temperamentally and traditionally he hated these Royalists—packs of rebels and intriguers, he called them—and he knew this haughty lady had plotted against her own son—M. le Maréchal—whom he adored; but there was something which he had yet to tell her, and in his own rough way he shrank from the task, feeling nothing but pity for her, because of what she was doomed to suffer.

"The prisoner tells me," began Madame la Marquise, as calmly as she could, "that you can give me news of M. le Marquis de Mortain, my son. Is that so?"

"Yes, Madame la Marquise," replied the man slowly.

"Well," she asked, "why did you not give me that news at once?"

Thus commanded, Mathurin could not help but obey as quickly as possible. He shifted from one foot to the other, and a look of real pity softened for a moment the rugged lines of his face.

"Well, Madame la Marquise," he began, "you must know that after the fight with M. de Puisaye's rearguard we had several prisoners in our hands. M. le Maréchal took the trouble to interrogate each one separately. When he had finished, he ordered me to accompany him, and together we went to the spot where the affray had taken place. It was on the edge of the wood. It was then about three o'clock in the morning and the dawn was breaking. The place was littered with dead. I counted over sixty myself, among them young M. de Fleurot, whom I knew."

"Yes?" said Madame la Marquise quietly, for the man had paused. She knew well enough what he was about to tell her. He looked her straight in the eyes. They expressed a query, and he nodded silently in reply. A low moan of pain broke from Madame's lips; she pressed her handkerchief to her lips to smother a louder cry.

"M. le Maréchal found M. le Marquis de Mortain lying amongst the dead," said Mathurin slowly after a while. "He told me to tell Madame la Marquise that M. Laurent must have died like a hero; he had a broken sword in his hand and three bullet wounds in his chest.... M. le Maréchal lifted him up in his arms and carried him to his horse. I helped to lift the body into the saddle, and M. le Maréchal ordered me to ride back to Mortain as fast as I could and to send out half a dozen men to him at once. 'When you have done that, Mathurin,' he said to me, 'go to La Frontenay as quickly as may be, take the prisoner Jean Blanchet with you, and see Madame la Marquise de Mortain and Mademoiselle de Courson. Tell them that I have conveyed M. le Marquis to the Château of Courson, and that there I will await their pleasure.' And that is all, Madame la Marquise," concluded Mathurin clumsily, for, indeed, he felt overawed by the look of hopeless grief which had spread over Madame's marble-like face. "M. le Maréchal ordered the carriole to be sent for Madame la Marquise. It should be here by now."

When he had finished speaking she gave him a stately nod.

"I thank you, good Mathurin," she said slowly. "I pray you go back to your master now and tell him that Mademoiselle Fernande and I will be at the Château of Courson within the hour."

She appeared like a statue, pale and unbending. One slender hand rested on the back of the chair to steady herself; the other closed tightly over her lace handkerchief. The kerchief round her shoulders looked less white than her cheeks: the golden light of a summer's morning crept in through the narrow window. A glorious sunshine followed on the storm of the night; the warm rays glinted on Madame's white hair, on her pale forehead and on the rings upon her fingers. Mathurin, who had been in Paris in the hot days of the Terror, remembered, as he looked on her, the martyred Queen going to her death.

He gave a sign to Jean Blanchet. He would not have dared to say another word; he felt the majesty of this overwhelming grief, and, having made a profound obeisance, he and the old Chouan went out of the room.

V

Fernande's arms were round the unfortunate woman who had sunk half-swooning into the chair.

So this was the end of it all: the sequel of so many intrigues, so many hopes, of the carefully-laid plans and the certainty of victory. Laurent, with his tempestuous, impulsive nature, had atoned with his life for his one hour of folly; the small band of Royalists was dispersed, its leaders fugitives; and a proud and self-willed woman would henceforth be destined to eat out her heart in vain remorse and regret. Callously she would have sacrificed one son, even whilst God decreed that He would take the other. Laurent de Mortain had fallen a victim to the dastardly attempt planned against his brother, just as much as to the unreasoning jealousy which had made him desert his post and forfeit his honour.

Madame la Marquise was a broken old woman now; even her hatred against Fernande was swallowed up in the immensity of her grief. She allowed the young girl to attend on her, to find her mantle and hood, and then gently to lead her downstairs. She could not bring herself to speak to her, however; in her heart, beside the bitterness of self-reproach, there lurked the dull resentment against the woman who had ruled over her son's heart until the hour of his death.

Half an hour later the two women, sitting side by side in the carriole, were driven rapidly to Courson.

236

CHAPTER XXV

THE WHITE PIGEON

I

Fernande waited in the hall below while Madame la Marquise went upstairs to see the last of her son. Half a dozen men from the La Frontenay works formed a guard of honour for the dead.

It was impossible even for Fernande, who knew her aunt so well, to guess at what Denise de Mortain felt. Her heart was so little capable of grief, that it was doubtful whether she really mourned Laurent, or whether pride, in that he died a hero's death, acted as a soothing balm upon her sorrow. When half an hour later she rejoined her niece in the small boudoir downstairs, she appeared outwardly quite calm, and talked of nothing but the new plans which already were seething in her brain, and which were destined to retrieve the mistakes of the night.

"De Puisaye was wise," she said, "not to jeopardize his forces. They are practically intact, ready for a coup which must in the near future be successful. We fell into many grave errors this time, and we shall now stand in the happy position of being forewarned."

Fernande thought it best to say nothing. What had been the use of arguing that Marshal de Maurel was also forewarned now?

"I have not given up the idea of a possible seizure of the La Frontenay works," Madame went on in her cold and placid way, just as if all her schemes of the past twelve months had not culminated in the death of the one being in the world whom she had professed to love; "but I still think that my own original idea when I first came to Courson last year, of being in open amity with my son Ronnay, was the wisest after all. I must speak with your father and with de Puisaye about that."

Fernande kept back, with difficulty, an exclamation of horror. More schemes! more intrigues! more tortuous by-paths! Was the whole of her young life to be linked indissolubly to this endless chain of treachery? Was she to be passively acquiescent—a tool, where need be—whenever plots were hatched that revolted her every sense of loyalty and of truth? Fortunately for her, Madame was too deeply engrossed in her own calculations to pay much attention to her, and after a while she—Fernande—was able to escape out of the boudoir where the atmosphere had already become stifling.

With aching heart she bade a final adieu to Laurent—the companion of her childhood, the man for whom she had such a tender affection and whom she had never loved, but also the man to whom she would have remained rigidly true, despite all that he would have made her suffer.

Then she went out into the park.

Yet another year of neglect had gone over the terraces and the walks. It looked perhaps a shade more tangled, a shade more forlorn. The heavy rain of the night before had broken down the slender, unpruned twigs of the roses, and the paths were littered with young branches torn from the parent trees. The scent of wet earth mingled with the fragrance of heliotrope and white acacia; there was a riot of bird-song in the old chestnuts and a hum of bees in the avenue of limes.

Fernande instinctively had wandered to the postern gate which gave on the apple-orchard. It was ajar, and she pushed it open and wandered out on the wet grass and under the apple-trees, already weighted down by the wealth of young fruit.

From the village distant a kilomètre or so from the park gates there came the sound of a clock striking seven. The air was redolent with the scent and savour of an early summer's morning. Fernande breathed it in with delight. The wet leaves of the apple-trees sent down an occasional shower of raindrops over her hair as she passed, and now and then she stooped to pick a sprig of brilliant-hued wild sorrel or a clump of snow-white marguerites.

How lovely was the world! Why should men and women plot and scheme to make it hideous with their own passions and their manifold treacheries?

As Fernande left the orchard behind her and struck a narrow path that wound its way through some ripening wheat-fields, a lark rose from the ground close by, and its gladsome song filled the lonely wanderer's heart with a sudden joy. She looked around her and recalled every phase of that journey, which she had taken a year ago in the strong arms of the man who knew so well how to love. From him there had never come reproach, mistrust, misunderstanding. Even at the hour when she had hurt him most deeply, he told her that he understood, and if—after the events of the past night—they were destined to be for ever parted from one another, she would still retain the certainty that in his great and simple heart he would never harbour one bitter thought against her. Her friends and kindred, her own father, her promised husband, had hatched a dastardly and murderous plot against him, and for her sake he had found it in his heart to gather his dead brother in his arms, and bring him in honour and loving gentleness to his last resting-place.

And Fernande, with a sudden gesture of heartfelt longing, stretched out her arms in the direction where the young birch and chestnut of La Frontenay woods gleamed through the golden haze of this midsummer morning.

"Take me, my beloved," she murmured under her breath; "let me

238

rest in your strong arms again. Let me forget the world and its intrigues and its treachery within the safe harbour of your sheltering love!"

II

She wandered on, almost like a sleep-walker in a happy dream; her feet and the hem of her gown were soaked through with the sweet-smelling raindrops that still clung to the grass; the wet branches of the young chestnuts beat against her face as she plunged into the coppice. Her lips were parted in a strange, elusive smile, and her eyes gazed into the distance, right through the thicket, as if a compelling voice was calling to her from afar.

A soft breeze stirred the branches of the mountain-ash overhead, the scent of elder and acacia went to her head like wine.

He was waiting for her beside the silent pool, and as soon as she saw him, she knew that he had called to her, and that the compelling power of his love had drawn her to him, through park and orchard and fields, in answer to his call.

She stood still on the other side of the pool, and for a moment they looked across at one another, with the banks of moss and meadowsweet between them and a whole world around of love and trust and promise of happiness. No words could be spoken between them, because there was so much still that must part them for a while. He understood that well enough, for he always understood; but she had come to him on this the first morning, when his every thought, every feeling, had called to her to come, and now he would be satisfied to wait—that was his way—to wait and bide his time, knowing by the look in her eyes, by the unspoken avowal on her sweet lips, that she would come again.

The breeze sighed among the branches of the trees, the birch whispered to the larch, the chestnut to the oak, and a gentle ripple stirred the twigs of the meadowsweet. And from somewhere within the bosom of the silent pool there came the soft and melancholy call of a number of wood-pigeons.

And to this man and this woman, who stood here in a world of their own, a world peopled with angels and fairies and sprites, and with everything that is most fair and most exquisite, it seemed as if from out the pool there rose something ethereal, luminous and white, something that was so sacred and pure, that it rose straightway heavenward, and was soon merged with the fleecy clouds overhead, whilst the call of the fairy pigeons was stilled.

The trance-like vision lasted only a moment. De Maurel slowly dropped on his knees, and above the murmurings of the wood Fernande heard the voice of the man she loved calling to her:

"You will come to me, my beloved?"

And she replied: "Very soon!"

THE END

www.ingramcontent.com/pod-product-compliance
Lightning Source LLC
Chambersburg PA
CBHW011521240626
47154CB00009B/2909